MEDICAL
Pulse-racing passion

**Neurosurgeon,
Single Dad...Husband?**
Charlotte Hawkes

**Highland Fling With
Her Best Friend**
Becky Wicks

MILLS & BOON

NEUROSURGEON, SINGLE DAD...HUSBAND?
© 2023 by Charlotte Hawkes
Philippine Copyright 2023
Australian Copyright 2023
New Zealand Copyright 2023

First Published 2023
First Australian Paperback Edition 2023
ISBN 978 1 867 27394 3

HIGHLAND FLING WITH HER BEST FRIEND
© 2023 by Becky Wicks
Philippine Copyright 2023
Australian Copyright 2023
New Zealand Copyright 2023

First Published 2023
First Australian Paperback Edition 2023
ISBN 978 1 867 27394 3

MIX
Paper | Supporting
responsible forestry
FSC® C001695

Published by
Harlequin Mills & Boon
An imprint of Harlequin Enterprises (Australia) Pty Limited
(ABN 47 001 180 918), a subsidiary of HarperCollins
Publishers Australia Pty Limited
(ABN 36 009 913 517)
Level 19, 201 Elizabeth Street
SYDNEY NSW 2000 AUSTRALIA

Cover art used by arrangement with Harlequin Books S.A.. All rights reserved.

Printed and bound in Australia by McPherson's Printing Group

Neurosurgeon, Single Dad...Husband?

Charlotte Hawkes

MILLS & BOON

Born and raised on the Wirral Peninsula in England, **Charlotte Hawkes** is mom to two intrepid boys who love her to play building block games with them and who object loudly to the amount of time she spends on the computer. When she isn't writing—or building with blocks—she is company director for a small Anglo/French construction firm. Charlotte loves to hear from readers, and you can contact her at her website: charlotte-hawkes.com.

Visit the Author Profile page at millsandboon.com.au.

Dear Reader,

The inspiration for this story began when a friend—who specialises in selective mutism in adults—and I were walking in the woods with our wonderfully rambunctious nine-year-old kids.

I found the subject fascinating and heartbreaking, and by the time I returned home with my blissfully happy child, I realised that I wanted to write a story that somehow featured the topic. And so *Noah*—my story's six-year-old, who is suffering from trauma-induced selective mutism—was born.

For neurosurgeon and confirmed bachelor Seth, it's terrifying finding himself guardian to his nephew. Seth is used to solving problems and helping people, but he can't seem to help his own nephew.

When his scrub nurse, Andrea, steps in, able to bond with Noah in a way Seth couldn't have even hoped to, he knows that he has no choice but to bend his own strict rules about keeping his distance from colleagues.

I really do hope that you enjoy reading Andrea and Seth's story in *Neurosurgeon, Single Dad...Husband?*, and I love to hear from readers, so feel free to drop by my website, www.charlotte-hawkes.com, or social media.

Charlotte x

DEDICATION

For Z

Forever with us

04/25/2021–07/02/2022

CHAPTER ONE

'THE DAMN THING is a beast. It's wrapped completely around these major vessels.'

'Perhaps,' Seth Mulder mused, peering through the co-observation surgical microscope at his patient's brain tumour to where his fellow surgeon, and friend, was indicating. 'Although, given how well-developed both the post-central and inter-parietal sulci are, they should make particularly good landmarks.'

The clearer those grooves were, the easier it would be for his team to identify the separate functional centres of their patient's brain and avoid cutting into the most essential areas of it.

'I reckon we might be able to take advantage of this in order to achieve a particularly anatomical resection—at least of the most superficial parts of the tumour.'

'And attempt preservation using microsurgical techniques,' his colleague agreed. 'Nice, yes, I like it.'

'Once arterial release is achieved, we should be able to remove the bulk of the tumour in order to create a little more working space in there.'

Seth lifted his head from the microscope and felt some of the tension of the last few weeks began to eek from his body. It felt good to be back in the operating room after the past few, hellish weeks away.

As complex as this surgery was—and as much as he would never wish such a beast of a tumour on anyone—he found he'd missed being in the OR more than he could have imagined.

Brain surgery was his world. It was what drove him on. It was what he was good at—brilliant at, in fact. Complex neurological procedures on patients who had not just paid handsomely to be treated at the state-of-the-art private wing of Baystone Medical Practice but to be treated by him personally.

Up until a month ago, these surgeries had been the sole focus of his highly driven life. They'd been all he lived for. All he wanted to live for. Which was just as well, since he clearly made a lousy excuse for a father. Or surrogate father. Or whatever the hell he was supposed to call himself now.

A wave of something cold and hard seeped into his chest—with an underlying current of something he couldn't quite identify.

The kid deserved better.

He wasn't designed to be a good parent, he thought guiltily. He wasn't designed to be a parent at all. His sister had always had the maternal instincts—generous and patient, just like their beloved grandmother had been. Meanwhile, he was the one who had inherited all the traits from their parents, who had all the parental instincts of cuckoos dumping their young on someone else to look after.

No, he was designed to be a bachelor: free to

play the field and love his life as a neurosurgeon. So how was he supposed to help a six-year-old kid who couldn't even stand to look at him, let alone speak a single word to him?

Not for the first time, Seth wondered if he really was the best choice for young, grieving Noah—no matter what his sister's will had instructed. If he was such a good uncle and brother, then he would never have left her to raise her son—his nephew—without any familial help at all.

Another wave of guilt seeped into him, and this time Seth recognised that underlying current for the self-loathing that it was. He was her brother, but he'd been too consumed with his own career, his own life, that he hadn't really acted like a good brother these past years. He'd never meant to let her down. He'd let work, life and Stacey's aggravating insistence that he needed to find a decent woman get in the way. Perhaps, deep down, he'd always thought he'd have time to make it up to her. But now she was gone, and he had Noah to consider.

The irony of it was that he'd begun to tire of that part of himself that played the field a while ago. The parties had started to make his skull pound, the city's most exclusive hotspots looked like tedious carbon copies of each other and the women he dated were certainly beautiful but left him feeling unstimulated. Outside the bedroom, at any rate.

He was only too aware of how shallow that made him sound. A couple of months ago his usually quiet scrub-nurse Andrea Perkins had asked directly, curiously but clearly with no agenda, if he ever wearied of being the 'Smoulder' half of the 'Smoulder and Heartstop' duo of fellow surgeon Jack Hart and him. But surely that was better than becoming the kind of deficient father that he'd had the misfortune to call his own?

Lifting his head, Seth steeled himself for that now-familiar punch as Andrea's striking eyes caught his, and in that instant everything stilled unexpectedly around him and he forgot where he was just for a moment.

What was it about this gentle, reserved woman that seemed to get under his skin? That made him feel as though, if he let his guard down even an inch, she would be able to see right through to his very soul? It was not merely because her eyes were the most stunning shade that they reminded him of the pale blue plumbago that his grandmother used to cultivate in her garden.

The memory jolted through Seth's head before coming to a juddering halt.

Where had that sprung from?

He shut the memory down barely a fraction of a second later. But even a fraction of a second was more than he had allowed himself in the past—with anyone, for that matter.

Which wasn't to say that he hadn't noticed Andrea Perkins the moment she'd walked into his very first surgery at Baystone over seven months ago, but he'd quashed the inconvenient attraction instantly.

For all his playboy reputation outside the hospital, Seth had rules—boundaries. He didn't date, or even flirt with, colleagues. It was a line he didn't cross. It was too messy, too complicated. Without his set of carefully constructed rules, he'd be no better than the man who had fathered him—but had never actually been any kind of father.

And perhaps, if that excuse of a man had exerted some similar measure of self-control, then his desperately unhappy wife might not have turned herself inside out trying to be someone she wasn't—so focussed on trying to please her perfidious husband that she didn't have the energy to be any kind of mother to Stacey or himself.

All of which, Seth believed, proved exactly why he wasn't designed to be a husband or father himself. And why he should never cross his own self-imposed line in the sand. Yet if there was one colleague who consistently intrigued him it was the enigmatic Andrea.

He was almost grateful when her soft, professional voice dragged him back to the present.

'So the brain mapping you conducted at the beginning of the craniotomy, when the patient was awake, will help you to avoid eloquent areas of the brain?'

Irked, Seth yanked his gaze away and put the unexpected moment of weakness down to just how upside down his usually ordered life now was. But he needed that line to be there—now more than ever, when everything else seemed to be spiralling so dangerously out of his control.

Besides, he hadn't asked for Andrea to be on this surgery because she had pretty eyes or a way of making him feel oddly more anchored—even though he'd never thought he'd felt *at sea* before; he'd asked for her because she was a damned good scrub nurse. And not because she was the only scrub nurse who'd learned within one single procedure how to set out the instruments exactly the way he preferred, which gloves he favoured for different operations or which sutures he was likely to want in any given circumstance.

Rather, what made her such a good scrub nurse—and, to be fair, Baystone Medical Practice had many good scrub nurses both in the private wing and in the main hospital itself—was how, from the first time that Andrea had been on his team, she'd impressed him with her intuitive approach and her eagerness to learn. Not least as now, when it was the first time she'd been part of a brain tumour resection like this one.

Not for the first time, he thought about the HCP-med course he'd been invited to mentor: a five-year course that would allow a nurse like Andrea to transition to become a doctor. The longer he worked with her, the more she struck him as the ideal candidate—not that he relished the idea of losing such an intuitive scrub nurse.

Little wonder that he found himself specifically selecting her to be part his team whenever he knew she was on duty, and not just today. She'd make up part of the crew he considered to be his dream team whether as a scrub nurse, or if she went on to become a doctor—and wasn't that precisely what each and every one of his patients deserved?

'Yes, the brain mapping will help during the first part of the tumour resection,' Seth confirmed, giving her his attention as he finally answered her question. 'But, once we start to remove more of it and get to sub-cortical levels, there may well be brain shift, so we'll have to stimulate the brain again and look out for abnormal responses.'

'You won't wake the patient up again?'

'Not this time.' Seth shook his head as he lowered his focus back to the patient. 'We'll need to monitor brainwave patterns. Can we irrigate the brain a little more…? Great.'

He'd barely finished the request when she efficiently moved in with the ice-cold saline solution that would help to keep his patient's brain cool and avoid any stroke to the exposed tissue.

He definitely ought to ask her if she'd ever considered retraining as a doctor, with him as her sponsor. At least he could actually do something to help her, which was more than he felt he was capable of doing for his nephew. He might as well be a hated stranger to that six-year-old, and he didn't have a clue what to do about it.

How was it possible for him to be a surgeon so renowned for pushing boundaries in operations, and to achieve results that were gaining him global recognition, yet at the same time be so utterly incapable when it came to being some kind of father to little Noah?

It had always been his darkest fear that he was every bit as heartless, as callous, as his own father had been—which was why he'd always sworn he'd never want marriage or kids. And, with every day that passed with his nephew, that fear was proving more and more astute.

What the hell had his sister been thinking, naming him as Noah's legal guardian? Especially in light of the fact the boy's paternal grandparents wanted to take custody of him.

Something punched Seth in the stomach, but he refused to succumb to it. This was neither the time nor the place to deal with the daunting prospect of becoming a surrogate father to his grief-stricken young nephew. He had a craniotomy to perform, which was something he had no doubt he was the capable of doing.

Setting his mind firmly back on the surgery, Seth began to feel the tension ease a little.

'Okay.' He peered down the microscope and carefully manoeuvred his way around the major vessel that was being swallowed up by the tumour. 'Let's start freeing this one, shall we?'

For the next few hours the team worked steadily, resecting the beast of a tumour using microsurgery where necessary and very anatomical resections where the brain's landmarks allowed it.

They tested the edges of it and stimulated the brain whenever they needed to in order to ensure they wouldn't cause a stroke in the surrounding heathy tissue. And, when they'd removed as much of the tumour as they could without risking damage to the eloquent sub-cortex deeper down, they finally closed up.

Finally he took the suture kit from Andrea, watching as she carefully kept track of the tail and lifted it clear of the sterile field as she passed it across. She had a good career as a specialist nurse and she'd never once mentioned wanting to change it. So why couldn't he shake the impression that beneath her guarded exterior something in her hankered for more?

Was it just her hunger for learning that struck a chord inside him?

A short while later, the surgery finally completed, Seth and Jack finally moved out of the OR to de-gown and scrub out, Andrea following as she noted final instructions for the handover to the ICU team and post-op care.

Seth stepped through the doors and activated the taps with his elbow.

'It's been a nice job,' he heard himself tell her. 'Well done.'

Did he imagine that brief flicker of surprise in her eyes before she carefully schooled her features?

'Thank you.'

Was it really that unusual for him to compliment his team? He really didn't think so. But perhaps he did take it as read that his team would perform well.

'I have another interesting surgery this afternoon, an ependymoma. Do you know anything about them?'

Andrea tilted her head.

'Ependymoma? They're relatively rare tumours. I think they account for less than two percent of all central-nervous-system tumours. I haven't actually seen one performed before.'

'I thought you might benefit from the learning experience.' Seth nodded. 'The scrub nurse who was dealing with this case has been pulled away to an emergency case and I need someone who can get up to speed quickly.'

He ignored the suspicion that he also preferred the idea of Andrea working alongside him.

'Right.'

'This surgery will be on a thirty-eight-year-old female who presented with a ten-week history of neck pain radiating down both arms and numbness in both hands. A neurological examination was relatively normal, but a cervical spinal MRI showed a well-demarcated inter-medullary lesion around the level of C6.'

'I would love to be a part of that surgery,' she admitted regretfully. 'But I don't think I'm scheduled to be on your team this afternoon.'

'Leave it with me, I'll sort it.'

'Thank you...' She hesitated, as though about to say more, but then stopped herself. 'Meanwhile I'll liaise with the ICU team in terms of the brain stimulation responses we had during the surgery.'

'Good.'

He liked how Andrea pulled the conversation neatly back to the patient.

'I'll also advise them of the particular abnormalities you said to look out for as he regains consciousness.'

'I have a few patients to see now, but I'll check in after that,' he confirmed, knocking off the taps as he finished scrubbing and drawing down a few sheets of paper towel to dry his hands.

It was only as Andrea left, the glass doors sliding smoothly closed behind her, that he noticed his friend's curious gaze on him.

'What?'

'I knew you had a soft spot for her.' Jack grinned, amused.

Something odd punched through Seth, but he managed a dismissive snort.

'Because I asked if she was interested in a surgery? Where are we—back in the playground?'

'You like her,' his friend insisted, unperturbed.

'You're the one who dates colleagues.' Seth shook his head. 'Not me.'

Jack laughed.

'Yeah, yeah, your infamous lines not to be crossed. But maybe, just once, you could break your own rules. You're not your old man.'

'I'm well aware,' Seth bit out stiffly. 'But that doesn't necessarily mean, just because I think a colleague might learn from a particular procedure, that I want to sleep with her.'

'It doesn't necessarily mean it, no,' his friend agreed. 'But in this case I believe it does. Either way, I thought you might like to know that Andrea might be leaving Baystone.'

Andrea was leaving?

Seth froze. Only for a moment, but it was enough. And he hated that the revelation upended him in a way it certainly shouldn't have had the power to do. Clearly, he wasn't himself at the moment.

'That's...a shame,' he managed at length when he could be sure his voice sounded vaguely casual. 'She's a good scrub nurse. Do you know why she's leaving?'

And then he kicked himself for sounding so interested.

'No idea. You know Andrea: she doesn't talk to many people.' Jack finished scrubbing his hands and began to dry them. 'But she might tell you. If you decide to ask, that is.'

A hundred different thoughts raced through Seth's head. He pushed them aside.

'Why would I do that?' he demanded crisply. 'If she's leaving, then that's her business and no one else's.'

And then, before he could analyse himself any further, Seth shot the spent paper towel into the bins and left the room.

CHAPTER TWO

'HEY, ANDREA, WHAT did you do to win the OR lottery?'

Lifting her head from the notes on her latest patient she was making, Andrea offered her colleague a bright, if curious, smile.

'Lottery?'

The other nurse, Kate, eyed her with amusement.

'Your surgeries today,' Kate prompted. 'Not least this morning's surgery with a certain Seth.'

Before she knew what was happening, Andrea found herself trying to rein in uncharacteristically errant thoughts about that morning. Not least the inappropriate, wayward things that were still fizzing wildly through her body at...*what*, precisely?

The fact that it had been inexplicably good to be back in a surgery where he was the lead surgeon now that he'd returned from his mysterious, unplanned month-long sabbatical? Or perhaps the fact that she'd thought Seth's gaze had lingered a fraction longer—more intensely—than usual?

Fool.

Most likely she was imagining it. For all his reputation as a playboy outside of the hospital, the sinfully sexy Seth was well-known for maintaining a clear professional distance between himself and his female Baystone colleagues. Why would he suddenly show a personal interest in her?

Even if he had, it shouldn't make any difference to her. Hadn't she always prided herself on her absolute professionalism, never flirting with any of the male surgeons even when other colleagues did?

But, still, she couldn't explain the way her skin prickled deliciously at the memory of Seth's golden-brown eyes holding hers.

As if she hadn't already learned her lesson where men too charming for their own good were concerned. Shouldn't she—of all people—know better than to fall for a handsome face? Not to mention the utterly masculine body accompanying it. His broad shoulders and muscles seemed more fitting for some scorching, sporty, outdoorsy, designer-aftershave model than a neurosurgeon who spent most of his time indoors, in an OR with no natural light.

So much for her valiant attempts to stay professional whenever she was around the man. No matter how fiercely she tried to school her traitorous body, her stomach still twisted itself in knots whenever he was near—as much as she tried to pretend otherwise.

Hating herself for her weakness, Andrea doused the unwanted feelings and pasted a bright smile on her face.

'It was a fascinating surgery, though I'd hardly call it a lottery.'

She hated that she sounded awkward, vaguely stilted, as she always did when the subject veered anywhere near dating male colleagues, so she was hardly surprised when the other nurse waggled her eyebrows and laughed.

'*Pfft!* The procedure isn't the lottery I meant.'

Andrea opened her mouth to deflect, but before she could speak another younger nurse glanced up curiously from her own work station.

'What's going on? Did I hear someone won the lottery?'

'The *OR* lottery,' Kate emphasised. 'Andrea only went and bagged herself a place on this morning's surgery with Smoulder and Heartstop.'

Andrea wrinkled her nose, thinking how much Seth hated the nickname. Shame for him that his disdain didn't stop it from being electrifyingly apt. Seth 'Smoulder' Mulder and Jack 'Heartstop' Hart: it could hardly have been more perfect.

Strangely, though, she found it so much easier to talk to Jack despite his incessant flirting. Probably because he didn't make her blood heat and her veins pump anything like the way that Seth did. Ironic, really, since both men were notorious for burning the proverbial candle at both ends: boundary-pushing surgeons as well as notorious playboys.

Perhaps it was because, whilst Seth maintained his distance with colleagues, Jack's harem included almost half of Baystone. Maybe her subconscious was allowing her a foolish crush on Seth simply because she knew, deep down, nothing would ever come of it. Even if she hadn't been a colleague, she wasn't the type of beautiful, glamorous woman Seth reportedly dated.

Nothing that described her.

Not for the first time, she cursed herself for her gaucheness. And she condemned herself for allowing her ex to make her feel so insecure. It had taken less than a few months after the end of their lacklustre marriage before she'd wondered how she'd allowed Josh to cow her for all those years.

Why she was letting him influence her decision to leave Baystone, even now? Spotting him walking into the main hospital a few days earlier with his very fresh-faced young wife had hurt, of course. And not just walking into the hospital but the prenatal department. How much more of a scalpel to the heart could he have wielded? How much more of a reminder could there have been of her own horrible, tragic loss?

Andrea had only just made it back into the hospital and to a staff bathroom before she'd been violently sick. She'd barely made it back to her flat to cloister herself in her room and spend the night weeping and grieving into her pillow so that her flatmate didn't hear.

But the shock almost-encounter had also confirmed to her that it wasn't *Josh* who had left a black, aching hole in the middle of her chest when he'd walked out on her. Every single bit of her bereavement was about the precious baby she had lost. The idea of motherhood that was never to be hers.

Even now, a wave of nausea came out of no-where, threatening to engulf Andrea. But she couldn't let it show. Not here. Not now. Battling to steel herself, she was almost relieved when Dina's swoon rescued her and dragged back to the present.

'Oh, my days!' The young woman sighed. 'You're so lucky. What I wouldn't give for a surgery with even one of the two hottest surgeons in this place. Smoulder, I think. No...wait... Heart-stop. No... Smoulder.'

Andrea fought to steel herself a little more.

'Either way, I didn't *bag* anything.' She cut Dina off as lightly as she could manage before the younger woman imploded with her dilemma. 'I didn't even know I'd been assigned to that surgery until I saw it on the board yesterday.'

'Yeah?' Dina grinned eagerly. 'Well, I'd have done all your observations if you'd have traded with me.'

'She can't trade with you,' Kate noted with a wicked grin. 'I've just seen the board and she's on their surgery this afternoon too. Which means one of them is specifically asking for her as their scrub nurse.'

To her astonishment, it was all Andrea could do to quell another rabble of butterflies in her lower belly. But at least that was better than the hollow grief and gnawing regret.

'I don't think so.'

'Well, I do,' Kate retorted. 'We all know that it

isn't unusual for a surgeon to favour certain colleagues for their teams, whether it's nurses, anaes-
thetists or co-surgeons. And didn't I say a month
ago that I thought you were on Smoulder's surgeries more than any other scrub nurse?'

Andrea hesitated.

The other nurse had indeed suggested that,
but Andrea hadn't believed her. And then Seth
had mysteriously gone on sabbatical for several
weeks and the topic had been forgotten. Something
lurched in Andrea's chest... Now she couldn't help
but wonder. Especially after that morning.

And then she hated herself for caring either way.

Andrea measured her tone carefully.

'Well, if it's true, then I admit that I'm delighted
to be on the team. Today's brain glioma is one of
the most interesting surgeries I've seen.'

And at least that much was true. The surgery had
been incredible, as had the teaching opportunity
Seth and Jack had created. Both men were more
generous with their knowledge and skill than any
other surgeons she'd ever known, not just in her
time at Baystone but probably in her career.

'And of course it's the surgeries you're interested in!' Kate threw her hands up in mock-despair.
'Rather than either of the surgeons performing
them.'

'Of course,' she declared.

She was proud of the way she sounded as though
she'd never actually noticed Seth was not only a

brilliant surgeon but also a ridiculously hot male. As though she'd never once had the slightest entirely inappropriate and less-than-professional thought about the man.

God help her, she wished she hadn't.

'Maybe I sound old-fashioned, or out of date, but Seth Mulder is a great surgeon and a good teacher: it's good for my career to learn surgeries with him. But, as far as dating goes, I really am not in the slightest bit interested.'

'Good to know.'

As all three nurses spun round, Andrea fought back a sickening sensation as time ground to slow motion. Of all people to overhear her, did it really have to be him?

This was so far from the sharp, professional image she usually took such care to project. And how arrogant was he going to think she was to sound as though she even thought he was interested in her?

'I'm so...' She could feel the heat staining her cheeks as she grappled for words. 'I can only apologise—'

'No need,' Seth cut her off briskly. 'A word about this afternoon's surgery, Andrea.'

And then he was already turning to stride off in the direction of his office, leaving her to hastily save the last of her patient notes and hurry down the sleek, polished corridors of Baystone's luxury private wing. By the time she caught up with him, he was already holding open his office door for her.

'About before...' Andrea muttered, before he held up a hand to stop her.

'There really is no need,' he clipped out. 'Hospital gossip doesn't interest me. I would prefer to discuss this afternoon's patient.'

'Right.' She bobbed her head even as she swallowed uncomfortably.

'But, before that, I would like you to answer a question. Are you planning on leaving?'

Andrea blinked.

'Where did you hear that?'

He at least had the grace to look slightly sheepish.

'Hospital grapevine.'

Something tugged unexpectedly at the corners of her mouth.

'Right.'

'So?' he prompted after a moment. 'Are you?'

'I don't know,' she admitted after another moment. 'It's a consideration.'

'Why?'

No beating around the proverbial bush; no softening of the question: typically straight-to-the-point Seth.

Andrea paused, an image of Josh and his soon-to-be new family in her head. Then she gave an imperceptible shake of her head. That wasn't what had first precipitated the idea of leaving—only what had made it feel as though fate was giving her another nudge.

But Seth didn't need to know any of that. It wasn't his business.

'Personal reasons,' she hedged.

Seth frowned. She might have known he wouldn't be impressed.

'"Personal reasons" don't sound like much of a reason,' he noted sharply. 'I understood your career was important to you.'

'It is,' she bit out quickly.

'Glad to hear it.' He didn't look glad. He looked... irritated...so unlike his usually unemotional self. 'Then you must have a very good reason for leaving Baystone. Our private wing is state-of-the-art, and we work much closer with our main hospital than many other places do, performing procedures some of them can only dream about. You're unlikely to learn as much elsewhere.'

His words unexpectedly scored a direct hit.

Other hospitals might claim that everything in this place screamed money and privilege—a medical clinic to the wealthy and powerful—but Baystone was so much more than that.

True, the place was a symphony of polished limestone, sparkling glass and sleek metal. Staff might speak of Smoulder and Heartstop as though they were akin to medical soap opera stars, but the truth was that both of them were talented, innovative surgeons, who were constantly taking the opportunity that working at a place like Baystone provided. Both, Seth especially, were constantly pushing the surgical envelope and achieving results that their predecessors hadn't even dreamed possible.

Baystone was undoubtedly one of the best places in the country for her to constantly learn and improve. But what choice did she have?

'I'm aware of that.' This time, the regret in her voice was evident. 'But I might not have a choice.'

'Oh?'

She opened her mouth then closed it again.

His irritation seemed to ramp up a notch.

'If I understand what your reasons are then maybe I would know whether Baystone should be fighting a little harder to keep a scrub nurse who makes such a good addition to any team.'

It sounded reasonable enough. So why did she feel almost disappointed—as if she'd hoped he would want her to stay for *his* benefit, not just the hospital's?

Sucking in a breath, Andrea told herself not to be so silly.

'It's complicated. There are several reasons.'

'Such as?' he demanded, unrelenting.

She wrinkled her nose.

'My flatmate is getting married.'

He looked distinctly unmoved and Andrea tried again.

'In truth, she just got engaged, and she'd prefer

to live with her new fiancé than a work colleague. I can't really blame her. And it's her name on the lease.'

'And you can't find anywhere else?' Seth frowned. 'There are always flat shares being posted on the hospital employees' bulletin board. It seems non-sense that we should be losing such a good scrub nurse simply because of logistical difficulties.'

'Not where this one was.' She lifted one shoulder in what she hoped was an eloquent gesture. 'It was close enough to hospital to walk, but it also came with an allocated parking spot.'

'If it's close enough to walk to work, does that matter?'

'Yes, I need a car.'

'What about somewhere a little further out, then?'

'Unlike surgeons, most of us don't get parking spaces at the hospital. The parking charges for staff are ridiculous. I'd be using a significant chunk of my monthly pay just paying them.'

He offered a vexed grunt.

'And there are no private parking garages in town near to your accommodation?'

'Not close enough.' She pulled a face, then hedged again. What could it do any harm to tell him the truth? 'No one else knows this, but my mother...isn't well.'

'Isn't well?'

His instant concern was touching, but that didn't

mean she was about tell him all her secrets. No one else at Baystone even knew that much. It was no one else's business.

'It's a long-term illness.' She waved her hand, not prepared to tell him about the unsympathetic disease that was MS that had blighted Maureen Perkins' life for decades. 'It isn't something new—and we've long since learned to deal with it. The point is that I need to be able to get home to her easily and that means a car. It's no good living wonderfully close to work but then not being able to park my car anywhere when I need to get out of the city.'

'I see,' he ground out.

She liked that he was respecting her privacy even if he wasn't entirely satisfied with her answer.

'Thank you,' she heard herself say. 'For saying I'm a good scrub nurse.'

She hadn't realised how much her ex-husband had gradually sapped her self-confidence until she'd found herself so closely guarding compliments from people like Seth. But then, she'd never been the most outgoing of kids. Not since she'd turned ten, anyway.

No wonder her naïve, nineteen-year-old self had let herself get taken in by someone paying her a little attention. She shook her head to empty it of the less than palatable realisation, then caught Seth peering at her curiously.

'You don't think you're a good nurse?'

'Yes, of course,' she lied hastily. 'That is, I work

hard, and I'd like to think I am. Still, sometimes it's nice to hear one is doing a good job.'

Or maybe Seth didn't need to hear that. Maybe he was wholly secure and confident in his own skills and abilities. She couldn't imagine him allowing anything or anyone ever to knock his confidence.

She envied him that.

The silence hung around them for a little too long.

'Well, for the record, you *are* a good scrub nurse,' he rasped eventually. 'You're invariably engaged, switched on and able to anticipate the lead surgeon's needs intuitively during surgeries. If there are unexpected bleeds, you're swift to request additional sutures and ties from the circulating staff; if there's a particularly heavy bleed, you're quick to solicit bigger swabs; and you instinctively know when to set up additional diathermy and bipolar.'

She could feel another flush staining her cheeks, but apparently he wasn't finished.

'On top of that, I've always found you quick to remedy any pre- or post-op issues as you liaise between surgical and ward teams, as well as always seeming keen to learn more about the procedures.'

'The more I learn, the more I can anticipate more efficiently,' she confirmed quietly.

'Right.' He dipped his head. 'Hence why you're one of the head scrub-nurses. But have you ever considered retraining?'

'Retraining?' she echoed, taken by surprise.

'As a doctor, say?' he continued, standing up suddenly and moving around the desk, his unexpected proximity sending her body haywire without warning.

'A doctor?' she echoed weakly.

This time she couldn't be sure whether it was his proximity, or the fact that he was actually suggesting her long-abandoned dream was possible. The childhood dream she'd had of being a doctor had faded when her beloved father had died. Josh had scorned it, and she'd given it up as never being within her reach.

'I'm sure you know about the Healthcare Professionals Medical Degree programme?'

'I…' She faltered, still not sure she could believe the turn of conversation.

She wasn't entirely surprised when Seth looked disappointed and took it to be a lack of awareness.

'The HCP-med is a five-year degree that would allow a nurse like you to train to become a doctor whilst still working. It isn't for everyone, but I do think you'd make a good candidate.'

'Yes,' she managed, fighting to gather her thoughts and sound calm and collected. 'I have heard of it. My hesitation was more about the fact that you need good references and money behind you.'

She tried not to blanch at the sharp look Seth cast her.

'Perhaps you are unaware, but there are Nursing Council- and Midwifery-approved programmes now to help with the retraining whilst still allowing you to work.'

Andrea nodded slightly. She almost told him that she avidly read any articles that discussed such programmes, but that the tuition costs had always deterred her. She was aware that Baystone sometimes sponsored conversion courses, especially for staff from its sister hospital in town, but you'd have to sacrifice vestal virgins to give you the power to complete their application forms.

So she stopped herself from speaking. It would reveal too much to Seth, and he already seemed to be able to read her too easily.

'As for the references, I would be more than happy to provide them for you, Andrea. As I said, I think you're a very good scrub nurse, and you're always keen to learn something more. I believe you could be a very good doctor.'

All at once, heat prickled behind Andrea's eyes. Apart from her incredible, warrior mother—who had always wanted more for her than cruel circumstances had ever allowed them—the last person ever to sound as though they believed in her had been her father. Right before his death, a week after her eighth birthday.

Right before she'd become carer for her mother and her life had changed beyond recognition.

Dr Perkins. She hadn't allowed herself to dream

of that in two decades. And now Seth Mulder was the person dusting off that dream and making her feel it could be possible. Making her feel believed-in.

It felt good. And bad.

It made her feel vulnerable in a way she'd sworn she would never let herself be again.

Somehow—Andrea had no idea how—she managed to grab hold of that familiar suit of armour Seth had somehow managed to prise open and clamp it tightly back around herself.

She took a discreet breath. And then another.

'Thank you for the offer,' she managed at last, proud of the crisp note to her voice. 'I shall certainly consider it. Now, I've been going over the notes, but is there anything in particular I need to know about this afternoon's surgery?'

CHAPTER THREE

'BYE, NOAH...' SETH scoured his brain for something else to say as he watched the six-year-old boy being led into Pine Bay's primary school, head down but without a backward glance.

'Have a good day,' he added, no doubt lamely, though he was fairly certain the child wasn't even listening to him. A desperate part of him hoped that the new nanny he'd hired to pick up Noah from school would have more luck, though he feared she wouldn't.

His nephew stepped in through the school entrance to be swallowed up by the efficient slide of the electric doors. Seth stared at the slick metal and glass for a moment before taking half a step towards the building. Then he stopped. The child didn't want him—that much was clear.

How was he ever supposed to do this?

It was incredibly frustrating to realise that they hadn't just failed to make progress but had actually regressed. Today was worse than the day before. Little wonder that now, for the hundredth, thousandth, time, he wondered what had possessed his late sister to designate him as the boy's guardian in her will.

How had she even been able to trust him with her precious son, after the way he'd effectively walked away from her? Sure, he'd seen her, on his own terms and when he could fit it in—and had then made up for it with expensive Christmas and birth-day gifts—but that had been no substitute for being there for his sister, offering her real help—even a shoulder to cry on.

Perhaps it really would be better for him to agree to the boy's paternal grandparents having custody after all. The child's father might be a waste of space who had never had anything to do with his son, but it was clear that the little boy's grandpar-ents wanted to be a part of his life.

It was certainly more than could be said for his own parents.

How many times had he pulled up his lawyer's number on his phone to advise them as much—only to terminate the call before it could connect? If Stacey had wanted her ex-boyfriend's parents to have her son then she would have written them into her will rather than him.

He had to honour her wishes no matter how badly he believed she'd handled the entire situa-tion. The child deserved that much at least—hadn't he already been through enough in his short life?

Seth glowered harder at the doors.

Now what?

It took his typically sharp, gifted brain a few mo-ments too long to remember that he still needed to get to work. Another day of surgeries lay ahead of him, surgeries which, up until last month, had been all he lived for. Now he had no idea how to handle it. Since the previous evening, following Seth's first day back at Baystone after a month off trying to bond with Noah, the little boy had refused to communicate with him altogether.

Logically, Seth knew it was to do with the child feeling abandoned again so soon after his mother's death, but that didn't make him feel any less of a failure as his nephew's guardian.

It wasn't a feeling he relished, but what choice was there? He was a surgeon; it was what he did, who he was.

Which brought him right back to why Stacey had given him custody of Noah. What the hell was he supposed to do with a six-year-old kid he didn't even know how to talk to, let alone care for?

Had his own grandmother still been alive, she would certainly have known the right thing to say. And do. She had been the kindest, most caring grandparent that he or his sister could ever have wanted. She'd been there for the pair of them throughout their childhood, taking them on nature walks, teaching them to bake and playing the silliest of games with them whilst their own parents had always been far too wrapped up in their twisted relationship and warped games.

Then again, if his grandmother had still been alive, then Seth had no doubt that Stacey would have made her Noah's legal guardian and the kid would have wanted for nothing. But the old lady was long gone, and resurrecting old memories wasn't going to help anyone. He had to find a way to reach the six-year-old himself.

Jamming one fist into the pocket of his heavily tailored jacket, despite the relatively mild weather, he somehow propelled energy back into his reticent muscles. He should concentrate on things he *could* control—such as the patients who were waiting for him at the private clinic, anxious to be reassured after his absence these past few weeks.

He stalked back to his car, a sleek, muscled beast that had boasted a waiting list of two years but which he'd bought as soon as he could afford to. The kind of car that had been well suited to Seth Mulder, neurosurgeon and bachelor, but was less than ideal for life as a little Noah's replacement father.

Another part of his life that would have to change. Not that he resented it when he tried to imagine what kind of hell this had to be for his young nephew, but how had his sister ever thought that he would make a good legal guardian when he could have been so much more supportive of her? Stacey had never made a fuss about not seeing enough of him, understanding how pressurised his career was. It was only now that she was gone that he was beginning to see that he could have been there for them, even if only a little more.

He might be well on his way to becoming one of the country's most respected neurosurgeons, achieving surgical outcomes that were little short of miraculous, but that certainly didn't make him a potentially good stand-in father figure.

Damn it.

Seth felt wholly out of his depth. It wasn't a sensation he was accustomed to feeling, and he most certainly didn't appreciate it.

With a flick of his key fob, the doors to the supercar unlocked and Seth took a moment to admire the smooth action of the butterfly doors as they moved elegantly up and out via hinges on the A pillar. He realised he was actually looking forward to starting the engine, and hearing it leap into life with its muscular, guttural roar, without having Noah in the seat next to him, shoving his tiny hands over his ears just to muffle the sound.

A last vestige of Seth's former life, but he'd get rid of it today. He could well imagine that his ultra-efficient, no-nonsense PA would be only too happy to pick up the phone and have what she called his *brutish* car spirited away within the hour. Perhaps he could confide in her about the difficulty he was having helping Noah adjust. He imagined she'd only be too willing to help.

No, he couldn't do that. This was his problem to solve—no one else's—for his late sister's sake.

His mind occupied with such thoughts, Seth swung round, only to mow down some innocent bystander.

'Oof.'

He summoned a practised smile and suppressed

his irritation as he reached out a hand to catch the woman mid-stumble.

'My apologies,' he said smoothly. 'Entirely my fault; wasn't looking where I was going. Are you all right?'

'I'm fine.'

The voice was all too familiar and Seth was wholly unprepared for the frisson of awareness that jolted through him even before his hand made contact with her elbow.

'Andrea?' He breathed in shock as he helped to right her.

She frowned at him, those expressive eyes heading towards a more violet hue that instantly clenched in his belly—and lower, if he were honest. He pushed it back, but it was too late—the damage, it seemed, was already done.

He felt caught off-guard and, no matter how much he tried to scrabble for his customary shield of professional distance, it seemed to be eluding him.

'What are you doing here at a school?' He barely recognised the rasp in his voice let alone the thoughts that were flowing, unchecked, from his brain to his mouth. 'You don't have children, do you?'

He regretted the question the instant it was out. Firstly, it was none of his business. Secondly, he found he loathed the way her eyes darkened without warning, the plumbago replaced by Rich Blue Sun, as if he'd somehow wounded her.

Then the fleeting expression was gone, leaving Seth thinking he had imagined it. He heard her breath catch in her chest when she glanced down at the sight of his hand at her elbow, still steadying her.

She shifted awkwardly, not quite pulling her arm from his hand, yet somehow ending up stumbling against him. Another shot of pure electricity tore through him, enough to make his heart stop—if only for a split second.

And, when it managed to pump itself back to life, it thumped inside his ribcage hard enough to bruise, an echoing drumbeat like nothing he'd ever experienced before. The strangest sensation, though not unwelcome. It was impossible not to appreciate the body-tingling contact, or to relinquish his hold on her.

Ridiculous!

Somehow—he wasn't sure how—Seth loosened his hold on her elbow and withdrew his hand.

'I apologise. That isn't really any of my business.'

Yet he couldn't bring himself to turn away.

For a moment, she continued simply to stare at him. Then she startled, as though pulling herself back together. Finally, she made a point of brushing herself down and, as his eyes were drawn magnetically to follow the smooth movement of her hands, he found it threw up a whole new set of problems.

Gone were the shapeless scrubs of her hospital attire, replaced instead by a pretty, soft wool jumper that moulded to her feminine curves. It made his palms itch just looking at her. Surprised by his reaction, Seth struggled to pull his gaze away, but when his eyes dropped lower it seemed that was no less of a minefield. Inky-blue jeans clung lovingly to long, lean legs that looked as though they'd been hand-crafted to wrap around a man. Around him.

A low growl escaped Seth's throat as the image threatened to topple his brain into all manner of sinful thoughts. It was almost a relief when she finally replied to his initial, arguably brazen, enquiry.

'I'm not in until this afternoon. Sometimes I help out my sister-in-law by bringing her brood to school.'

'I see.'

'Might I wonder what you're doing here?'

This was why he shouldn't have asked about her personal life.

Seth opened his mouth to shut her down.

'I was bringing my nephew to school.'

'Your nephew?' Her eyes widened a fraction before she shook her head. 'Sorry, I didn't even realise you had siblings.'

It was on the tip of Seth's tongue to tell her about Stacey before he bit the words back. He couldn't have said why. Years of being cautious, maybe. Yet it wasn't as though he thought that it would end up on the hospital grapevine if he told this particular woman anything.

'A sister,' he hedged. 'And I was bringing her son to school.'

Her eyes slid curiously to the supercar over his shoulder and then to the building behind her.

'You brought him to school in that?'

A host of different responses jostled in his head. Not least that this was precisely why he feared he was an impostor in Noah's life, a presence that was causing the six-year-old more harm than good.

But why would he want to share that with Andrea—his colleague, his scrub nurse? He hadn't even shared that with Jack—the closest thing he had to a best mate.

'Is there a problem?' he clipped out at length, even as he cursed himself for not simply shutting her down completely. As if the same reservations that he told himself he could read in her expression hadn't just been winding through his own brain.

And then things in his head seemed to upend again as she flashed a smile that was bright yet taut all at the same time. How was that even possible?

'My apologies,' she murmured. 'I guess I never really thought of you as a family-orientated guy. More just as a surgeon and as...'

'As *Smoulder*?' he suggested when she tailed off hesitantly.

'Sorry.'

She tipped her head at him and a pretty blush stole over her cheeks. Seth found he had to fight back the strangest impulse to reach out and cup her cheek. Or perhaps to lean into her quiet self-assurance and tell her what he was really doing here.

He balled his fist tighter in his pocket whilst cranking his voice to stay breezy.

'Don't worry about it.'

Spilling his guts was the last thing he ought to do, even with Andrea. Especially with Andrea; she was his scrub nurse, not Noah's grief counsellor. Seth was beginning to suspect his atypical need to talk was simply down to the absurdity of him—*him*—suddenly having to step into the role of a father figure. Could anyone be less suited to it?

Suddenly, all he wanted to do was get away—from this place, from this woman and from all the things that had turned his carefully ordered life on its head—and get back into his OR.

Just for the next twelve hours.

He needed just that time to shove the complications of the past few weeks out of his head. Just twelve hours to return to being the dedicated, driven neurosurgeon whose only focus was the next surgery. Back in the OR there would be order, purpose and the work that he loved.

It would be the time he needed to clear his head.

After that, he would throw himself into becoming the kind of uncle, and surrogate father, that the child deserved.

Either way, breaking down in front of his scrub nurse outside his nephew's new school was not part of the plan.

With a muttered grumble, Seth excused himself and threw himself into his car, flicking the button to hear that longed-for engine roar as the doors slid back into place. Then, spinning the steering wheel, he pulled away from the kerb and out of the school grounds...before the all-too-arresting Andrea could say anything more to him.

And before this strange, slithering thing in his chest could take root.

'More suction,' Seth requested quietly as Andrea leaned in to the patient.

Another day, another procedure. But for once her mind was too busy whirring to appreciate the way she usually would. She couldn't decide whether her thoughts were thrown more from his suggestion the day before that he believed she would make a good doctor, or from their unexpected encounter outside Pine Bay Primary that morning.

There was something about the encounter that had felt...odd. As though she'd been missing a salient detail.

Mentally berating herself, Andrea re-focussed on the procedure—an aneurysmal subarachnoid haemorrhage, or bleeding to the brain, which generally had heterogenous outcomes, but was always interesting to observe with Seth at the lead.

He'd been right the previous day when he'd pointed out that she could learn things at Baystone she was unlikely to learn elsewhere. With a procedure like this, outside of the setting of their private medical unit, around forty percent of patients generally suffered neurological or cognitive defects. However, with surgeons like Seth and Jack always top of their game, Baystone boasted much lower rates. This remained the case whether the procedure being used was open aneurysm clipping—in which Seth would use a metal clip to obstruct blood flow to the weakened area of a blood vessel in the brain—or whether it was endovascular coiling, inserting platinum coils through a microcatheter to induce clotting and prevent blood from getting to the aneurysm.

Even with extensive follow-up, complications such as delayed cerebral ischaemia, where a brain injury occurred due to insufficient blood flow, weren't unusual outside of Baystone. So was she really going to walk away from her dream job without at least trying to find somewhere else nearby to live? As much as she might need Andrea's help, her mother would be devastated to think that her MS had thrown up yet another career obstacle for her daughter.

Andrea hated that she had allowed her shock at seeing her ex entering the prenatal department, with his new wife and her perfect womb, to influence her decision. It was strange how talking to Seth had somehow eased the torment and had made her realise that seeing them had been like scraping a scab off an old wound—it would soon heal again.

It had been fourteen months since her devastating miscarriage. Fourteen months since her marriage had ended. But whilst Josh had been able to walk away to start a new life with someone else—sprint, actually!—she was still left behind, trying to come to terms with everything the doctors had told her. Trying to reimagine her life now that she knew that family, children, weren't going to be a part of it.

And she had reimagined it. Perhaps she wouldn't be a mother, but she could be the best aunt her nieces and nephews could ever hope for. She could be the best scrub nurse. And knowing that someone like Seth believed she could make a great doctor was an unexpected ego boost.

None of which took away the initial shock of seeing Josh walk into that prenatal department. But she'd be fine now that she was beginning to get her head around it.

Perhaps she ought to take a leaf out of Seth's book. Not from the part of the wild and untameable reputation, but from the way he was married to his career.

'I was thinking about your suggestion yesterday,' she heard herself say before she could bottle it and change her mind. 'Career-wise.'

No need for the entire OR to know the ins and outs—they'd likely assume she simply meant a specialist course or something similar.

'You've given it some thought?' Seth asked approvingly, dropping his eyes back to the surgery.

'I have. Actually, it's an idea I've already con-templated before,' she admitted, though she wasn't about to tell him of her foolish childhood dreams. 'But I've given it more careful consideration since our last conversation and I realise that it isn't pos-sible for me at this time.'

Quiet, assured, final…as if it wasn't like a fist twisting in her chest.

Seth, however, wasn't buying it.

'I believe it's entirely possible, though it will take hard work and dedication. I didn't think you were afraid of that.'

'Of course not.' She scrunched up her face crossly beneath her mask. 'But I'm not in a po-sition to afford the associated costs, not least the part-time element. All the same, I'm grateful for the vote of confidence.'

He was right about the fact she could work for the first three years, but it would only be part-time work to allow for part-time study. The final two years would require her to join a main medical de-gree course, which meant it simply wasn't feasible.

Seth lifted his head again, frowning.

'It would be an investment in your future,' he pointed out. 'Given you have no family, save for nieces and nephews, what better time to do it?'

She thought about her mother and the money they had been saving to try to move into a new home—one that would be more wheelchair-friendly

for the periods when the unpredictable disease that
was MS took its toll.

For two decades after the initial diagnosis, her
mother hadn't needed a wheelchair. In fact, she'd
abhorred the idea of ever becoming the one in three
MS suffers who ended up needing one. But the past
six years had been harder, with the bad days having more impact, and Andrea knew her mother now
needed a home that was more suited to those periods. A place that had lower light switches, wider
doorways, a shower that could take a specialised
wheelchair when necessary and maybe a kitchen
that had a lower worktop, as well as a regular-height
one, for days when her mum couldn't cook standing up,.

Dropping back to part-time work, with a corresponding reduction in pay, simply wasn't possible.

But neither Seth nor anyone else needed to know
her private business.

'I have...other demands on my time.'

She fought not to squirm as he lifted his eyes to
fix her with a dark, unreadable expression.

'We'll continue this discussion this afternoon,'
he asserted in a tone that brooked no argument. 'I
have a clinic after this surgery, but I should be finished by four. I'll see you in my consultation room
after that.'

Andrea didn't care to analyse what it said about
her that she didn't object. She simply nodded once
and returned to the surgery.

CHAPTER FOUR

ANDREA SHIFTED UNCOMFORTABLY in the unusually deserted reception area for Seth's clinic, trying to tell herself that she didn't still feel odd, jittery, at speaking to him about her future.

It was as though she'd be letting herself down in his eyes by not being more ambitious. By not grasping with tight fists the opportunity he was offering. She hated the idea that he might begin to think less of her for turning down the chance to become a doctor.

But what could she do, short of telling him about her mum's situation? And that wasn't a secret she was prepared to share—even with Seth. *Especially* with Seth. What was it that was making him get under her skin so much at the moment?

She'd always been aware of him, of course—attracted to him. But lusting after a man—however scorching-hot he might be—was definitely not her style. So why was she sitting here, waiting for him to finish his last consultation in the next room, her hand on her chest, as though that could somehow slow her wildly racing heart?

Andrea was so caught up in her thoughts that she leapt like a scalded cat when the door behind her swished open.

'Joyce.' She greeted Seth's long-time secretary

with a bright smile then stopped at the sight of a little boy being ushered in front of the older woman.

In all the time she'd worked at Baystone, no one had ever even known that Seth had a sister let alone a nephew. Yet today she'd not only bumped into Seth outside the primary school, but the child was here now. The only rational explanation was that Seth's sister was unwell and he was stepping in.

As if the man could get any more noble.

Habit from being with her own extended family made her smile brightly at the boy, who she estimated to be about five or six years old.

'And you must be Noah. Hello.'

The child didn't even look at her, but instead edged around Joyce and made his way to the furthest corner of the room, sitting down and taking a book from his backpack that Andrea recognised as her own nephew's favourite *Space Kids* easy-reading series.

'He's shy,' Joyce informed her quietly with her usual aplomb. 'But I'm afraid Mr Mulder is in with a patient.'

Was it her imagination, or did the secretary look uncharacteristically uncomfortable beneath the practised veneer?

'I know.' Andrea shook off the notion. 'He asked me to stop by after his clinic. It's work-related.'

Of course it was work-related. Why had she felt the need to explain? Joyce, however, didn't appear to notice. Her gaze momentarily slid back to the child.

'Perhaps…today isn't the best day after all.'

She didn't say anything more. She didn't have to. Clearly something was going on with Seth's sister or else Noah wouldn't be here. There was no way Seth would otherwise have allowed his personal life to cross over into his work.

'No problem.' Andrea nodded. 'I'll speak to him tomorrow. You'll tell him I was here, though?'

'Of course.' Joyce offered a half-smile that looked suspiciously like relief.

Bending down to sort out her belongings, Andrea was just packing her bag when the door to Seth's consultation room opened and both he and his last patient emerged. As the patient hurried out of the opposite door into the main reception area, Andrea watched Seth's glance sweep from her to his nephew, then to his secretary.

'I was just leaving,' she managed—somewhat lamely, in her own opinion.

But Seth wasn't listening.

'Did you find out what happened?' he demanded quietly, his voice too low for his apparently absorbed nephew to hear.

'I managed to get through to the agency,' Joyce told him. 'Apparently the new nanny who was to start today and collect him from school had a family emergency.'

'A family emergency?' There was no missing

Seth's fury even if he was valiantly restrained. 'You made it clear that he's suffering from trauma-induced selective mutism brought on by the death of his mother? He needs stability, not family emergencies.'

Trauma-induced selective mutism?

Even as she tried desperately not to listen, Andrea couldn't help but pick up the little titbit. It seemed to slam into her head, bringing with it a host of dusty memories. She lowered her bag on the chair and straightened up.

'I made that perfectly clear,' Joyce confirmed, her tone making it clear exactly what she thought about the nanny's behaviour. 'Noah's head teacher was good enough to bring him, given the circumstances, and knowing you would likely be in surgery. I took it upon myself to take us both to the canteen to buy a snack.'

Andrea watched as Joyce laid out a variety of choices on the table, from an apple and a banana to kids' crisps, little cartons of sugar-free juice and a small bottle of water.

'He couldn't tell me what he wanted so I got a selection,' she continued lightly, though Andrea knew her well enough to hear the hint of concern in her tone.

'Thank you,' Seth murmured before lifting his voice and injecting it with a cheerier note. 'Noah, do you want to choose a snack?'

The two of them smiled kindly at the young boy

who raised his head, stared at them for moment then returned his gaze to his book.

Andrea couldn't help noticing the teddy bear practically held in a death grip in his tiny hands.

It was all there—from that shuttered expression to the stance, to the clutched toy. And something else that she couldn't have articulated but which was so familiar to her all the same. To all intents and purposes, he might as well have been her own brother, Daniel, when he had been about the same age.

'Noah, you need to choose now, please.'

Seth picked up the selection and crossed the room to kneel down directly in front of his nephew, his voice gruff but slightly softer than usual, as though he wasn't entirely sure of himself.

It took Andrea by surprise. She'd never thought of Seth Mulder that way before. He was a neuro-surgeon, but that didn't mean he had any experi-ence of what it was like to manage a young child who refused to talk.

Then again, just because she'd dealt with her brother two decades ago didn't mean she knew how to do so either. So why did she feel the need to at least try?

Instead, she held her counsel as the boy stared helplessly at the snacks for several paralysed mo-ments. His hand twitched, as though part of him was desperate to reach out for something but he just couldn't bring himself to do so. Then, he looked as his teddy bear, as if for support. Finally, he shifted to the next chair, clutching the soft toy to him and staring at his knees. It was all heartbreakingly familiar to Andrea.

With a deep inhalation of breath, Seth let the boy go and slowly returned to the reception desk.

'Did he ask for anything at all?' he murmured, turning his back to the room so that his nephew wouldn't hear.

Joyce followed suit.

'Not a word,' the older woman confirmed regretfully. 'Just as you said.'

He nodded slowly, though his tight shoulders suggested to Andrea that he felt a lot more frustrated than he was prepared to let on—his infamous control at play, it seemed.

'I'd be grateful if you'd contact the nanny agency and advise them that their services will no longer be required,' he said through gritted teeth. 'I understand there were family circumstances, but Noah is six, his mother has just died and I was in surgery.'

'I already took the liberty of doing so. They couldn't apologise enough and asked me to pass on my assurance that a similar incidence will never occur again.'

'It will not,' Seth bit out. 'As they will not be given the chance to do so. I shall make other arrangements.'

'I assumed as much,'

Another curt dip of the head.

'I can look into after-school care if you like?' offered Joyce.

'Yes,' he answered after a moment. 'Thank you.'

Feeling as though she was eavesdropping, Andrea moved away, not realising she was instinctively travelling in the direction of the little boy until she found herself on the row of chairs next to him. She stayed a couple of seats away, not too close, certainly not crowding him.

She looked around for something that she hoped might help her to communicate with the little boy— something that would allow for non-verbal communication, which had always been the first step with Daniel. Her gaze settled on a wooden alphabet abacus that sat nestled amongst the small offering of children's toys. It was almost the perfect prop. A final glance across the room assured her that neither Seth nor Joyce was paying attention to her.

Andrea picked up a doll, the perfect toy to mirror Noah's teddy bear, and pretended to stand the toy in front of the abacus, the plastic hand spinning the blocks.

'Hmm,' she murmured, as if to herself or the doll. 'A is for apple, B is for banana, C is for car... but I'd prefer it to be for crisps, wouldn't you, Dolly? And we could pretend that R is for raisins rather than rabbits.'

She spun the B block around a few times until stopping it on the letter rather than the picture.

'I guess you like bananas, huh, Dolly? I wonder what Teddy Bear likes.'

And then Andrea found herself actually holding her breath, just praying that it could work.

For the longest time—which was probably only a minute, but it felt like a century—Noah didn't move. But then, suddenly, a tiny hand gripping the teddy's furry paw reached forward and spun the R block. Her insides flip-flopped and it was all she could do to keep her voice even.

'Raisins, huh, Teddy? That's a great choice.' She deliberately didn't address the little boy but kept her focus on the toys. 'Okay, what do you say, Dolly? J for juice, and W for water?'

The hesitation was shorter this time, and then the furry paw spun the letter J.

'Oh, yes. Another great choice.'

Slowly, carefully, she reached her hand down to push herself back into a standing position to head for the desk. But, before she could do so, Seth stepped forward and silently passed her the snacks.

For a moment, his eyes locked with hers and her stomach flip-flopped all over again and then he stepped back to the desk. But this time she could feel two pairs of eyes on her. She straightened her shoulders, as if to shake off the additional pressure.

'Raisins and juice for you, Teddy,' she said airily, carefully sliding the snacks to Noah's side. 'And banana and water for you, Dolly.'

The little boy lifted his hand, paused then carefully reached for his snacks. A few moments later he tilted his head so that, whilst he was not exactly looking at her, he could see her. He paused with apparent uncertainty and the cogs in Andrea's brain began to spin. She was all too aware of Seth's gaze still on her, watching her with Noah. Was the little boy hesitating because she wasn't eating her snacks? It certainly seemed like it. Sitting the doll in front of her, she crossed her legs and began to peel a banana.

'Shall we eat, Dolly?' she murmured before taking a bite.

A moment later, Noah took the bag of raisins, opened it, proceeded to take a raisin and offered it to Teddy before putting it in his own mouth. Then another. Then another. Then he took the carton of juice, pulled off the straw and slid them nervously across the floor to her.

Without missing a beat, Andrea unwrapped the straw and pushed it gently through the hole in the carton before gently pushing it back to the little boy.

'Thank you,' he whispered, in a voice so painfully quiet that she had no idea whether Seth had heard.

If he had, would he be pleased or not? She had no way of knowing that. So long as Noah was happier, she would stand up to anything his uncle might have to say to her.

For the next few minutes, Andrea sat in companionable silence with the little boy as they each enjoyed their snacks. Briefly she considered trying to get him to talk again but quickly decided against it. Patience was the key. It had taken months with her brother. For every five steps forward, they had seemed to take two back, and pushing him too far too fast had never seemed to work. Better to stop now whilst Noah was experiencing a confidence boost without feeling under pressure.

A fluttering movement by the desk caught her attention and she looked up to see Seth beckoning her, a grim expression on his face. It was hardly engaging, and she was almost tempted to ignore him. But at the last moment she thought better of it.

'That was lovely, Dolly,' she announced, picking up a banana peel. 'I've really enjoyed spending this time with you, Teddy and Noah but I have to go now. I trust you to look after my new friends.'

With that, she carefully got to her feet and moved across the room, not surprised when Seth inclined his head to summon her to follow him into his consultation room.

She was barely into the room before Seth spoke, closing the door behind them.

'How the hell did you do that?' he demanded, his tone a careful balance of both relief and frustration.

Andrea bit her lip, wondering how little she could get away with telling.

'Luck,' she offered awkwardly. 'And perhaps a little experience.'

'Well, it's experience I don't have,' he ground out

angrily. But there was no question that his anger was directed at himself rather than her. 'I've spent the past month trying.'

'It can take months,' she reassured him. 'Sometimes it can take years.'

He shook his head.

'It took you minutes,' he pointed out.

'I got lucky,' she repeated. 'It could easily not have worked at all.'

'But it did. I need you to teach me how you did it.'

Something kicked low in her gut. Seth wanted *her* to teach *him*?

He, who was usually the one teaching everyone else, the one pushing the proverbial envelope, now wanted her help? Suddenly, he was looking to her for guidance?

The tiny hairs on the back of her neck pricked up. What if she couldn't help him? No two children were precisely the same so there was no guarantee that what had worked for her brother would work for Noah. What if she made things worse?

Except that she hadn't made it worse just now, had she? She'd actually managed to help the little boy and that felt ridiculously good—especially when she remembered all the fear and frustration she and her mother had felt when they'd spent months trying to feel their way to helping Daniel.

But it didn't necessarily follow that just because she'd managed to connect with Seth's nephew today she would be able to do so tomorrow. Or the day after. If he suddenly decided he didn't want to communicate through his teddy any longer, then what?

Still, at least she had some kind of idea how this all felt. What she would have given, almost twenty years ago now, to be able to talk things over with someone who had even a little experience with selective mutism. Perhaps she could be that person for Seth, even just acting as his sounding board. The idea made it feel as though the balance was subtly shifting between them.

And Andrea wasn't entirely sure how she felt about that at all.

CHAPTER FIVE

THERE WAS AN incommodious buzzing inside Seth's head that he simply could not get rid of—worse than any bothersome mosquito—and it was stopping him from thinking straight.

Or thinking at all, quite frankly.

How had Andrea achieved in ten minutes what he had been wholly unable to achieve in ten days? More to the point, how had she made it look so damned easy?

He ought to feel more grateful to Andrea, and he did. But he wasn't sure that this thing that sloshed inside him was solely comprised of gratitude. He was supposed to be a neurosurgeon who understood the mechanics of the brain, yet he'd been entirely incapable of making some kind of connection with his own nephew, wheareas his quiet colleague had come along, sat down next to the kid and managed just that.

It was incomprehensible, galling, and humbling. It also felt as though a burden, as heavy as the weight of Atlas carrying the heavens themselves, had just been lifted from his shoulders.

Noah had communicated which, to Seth, meant that his own ineptitude this past month hadn't damaged the little boy the way he'd feared he might have. His gruff ways clearly hadn't encouraged his nephew to want to connect with him. Ironic, since he had often managed to connect with a paediatric patient who had been distancing them self from their own parents.

But now—thanks to Andrea—he knew that Noah was ready to communicate. He just had to learn how. He *would* learn. For his late sister's sake, as well as the boy's.

Yet Seth couldn't help wishing that he could learn from someone less...damned appealing than Andrea Perkins. He'd spent the past few months convincing himself he didn't feel some inexplicable pull of attraction to the scrub nurse.

He would have kicked himself for such misplaced pride, yet even now he could still vividly recall the fizz of chemistry that had arced between them that morning during their unexpected encounter outside the primary school. It was as though being away from the usual environs of the hospital had blurred all his usual lines.

And now, alone in his office, he could practically feel it vibrating around him, inside him. Getting louder and more insistent the longer he remained in such proximity to Andrea. He couldn't even remember having rounded the desk to stand right in front of her, but here he was, blood roaring through him, pooling where it certainly shouldn't be.

With more effort than it rightfully should have required, Seth forced his brain to focus on reminding himself why he had brought her here to his office—or how she had managed to forge that connection with his nephew so quickly.

She'd looked horrified when he'd demanded that she teach him whatever it was she'd just managed to do with his nephew. He wasn't sure he could blame her—he was hardly being gracious about the whole incident. But she still hadn't answered his last question, so Seth gritted his teeth, forced his voice to something less commanding and repeated it.

'Will you teach me how you did that?'

Andrea wrinkled her nose in that awkward yet appealing way of hers.

'I want to help,' she told him. 'I do. But I'm not a speech therapist. They're properly trained allied health and medical care professionals.'

'I know what they are,' he ground out. 'But I've just watched you coax the child into communicating with you, even speaking to you within minutes of meeting him—which is more than the speech and language therapist he's been seeing has managed. I want to understand how.'

Andrea chewed her lip and stared at him. He got the impression she was trying to decide what to say.

'It was just an old trick I once knew,' she hedged. 'I thought it was worth giving it a go, so I tried it. It could have just as easily not worked.'

'But it did work,' he countered, not about to be

put off so easily. 'You clearly have some experience in this field, whilst I have none. I need your help.'

Did she have any idea what it cost him to admit that?

Not that in his professional life he'd ever had any problem calling in fellow surgeons to assist in surgeries that included elements from other specialist fields. But Noah was his nephew—not a patient.

'I do want to help.' Andrea dipped her head at last, even as she folded her arms across her chest in a tell-tale defensive response. 'But, like I said, I'm not a speech therapist so I'm not qualified to teach you anything. If I end up making things worse...'

The sheer futility of it all suddenly tumbled through him. Taking a step back, Seth raked his hand through his hair.

'I don't know that it can be any worse; you saw how it is with the child. I shouldn't be putting you under pressure, and I apologise for that, but it has been like that ever since...'

'Ever since his mother died,' she finished when he stopped abruptly. 'I overheard you talking to Joyce. I'm so sorry for your loss.'

He didn't miss the micro expression that touched her expressive eyes and instantly found himself hungry to understand it.

'You lost someone too?' he asked abruptly. 'That's how you knew what to say and do with my nephew.'

Her expressive violet-blue eyes glinted, but this

time he couldn't afford to be distracted by them. He lifted one shoulder.

'I make no apology for wanting to do whatever I can to help that child out there.'

Her expression flickered again.

'Perhaps you should stop calling him "that child" for a start,' she suggested pointedly.

He probably should... Seth dipped his head in acknowledgement.

'You're right,' he acknowledged. *Noah.*

'And his mum...?'

'My sister died last month,' he finished for her as something punched deep in his chest. Seth ignored it.

He'd spent his entire career dealing with patients whose lives hung in the balance. But it had taken Stacey's death for him to begin to realise that life might be shorter than he'd ever appreciated.

The irony didn't go over his head.

'Right,' Andrea managed carefully. 'And, given your unexpected sabbatical the past few weeks, I'm guessing you're now Noah's legal guardian?'

Seth thought about the brutal custody hearing he'd attended only a few days before. The next one was due in less than a week. A part of him argued that it wasn't Andrea's business—aside from Jack and his secretary, no one else knew—but instead he heard himself answering.

'Stacey named me as her son's legal guardian in her will. His father hasn't had anything to do with him since the pregnancy.' He paused again as something new flashed through Andrea's eyes, but the tight expression which swiftly followed deterred him from asking. Seth chose to concentrate on his nephew's story instead.

'However, his paternal grandparents are fighting me for custody.'

'Will they get it, given the history?' Andrea asked.

Seth balled a fist at his side.

'The fact that Noah refuses to talk to anyone— or had been refusing, up until five minutes ago— isn't particularly helping my case.'

Nor was the fact that, save for the obligatory visits at Christmas and birthdays, and the occasional weekends, he hadn't seen as much of his sister or nephew as he should have since Stacey had moved out of his penthouse and into her own modest apartment four-and-a-half years earlier.

Andrea looked unconvinced.

'Surely, if Noah hasn't been talking to anyone, then that would help or hinder both parties in exactly the same way?' she asked, though her tone was gentler now.

'They're claiming that they've never had the opportunity to build a relationship with Noah, whilst I have. And that if the boy trusted me then he wouldn't now be choosing not to communicate.'

Though he tried to keep his tone even and remain factual, it was impossible to keep the regret from threading around his words.

Andrea shook her head.

'It doesn't necessarily work that way. Trauma-related selective mutism is more complex than that. That's assuming that Noah's mutism began as a consequence of his mother's death?'

'Noah is the one who found her. She'd died in her sleep.' Seth clenched his teeth, every word tasting acrid in his mouth. 'An undiagnosed heart condition, of all things. I don't know how, but he had the presence of mind to call 999.'

Andrea made a soft, sympathetic sound.

'That would have certainly been traumatic,' Andrea acknowledged sympathetically, her hand reaching out automatically, as if to touch his arm, before catching herself and dropping it again.

He'd never before realised it was possible to lament the loss of something one had never had. But he shook it off.

'And there hadn't been any problems before that?'

Seth shook his head.

'Noah was a brilliant baby, and my sister was wonderful with him. He was her world. Even the teachers at his former primary school report that he was a bright, friendly, talkative little boy right up until...'

'I understand.' She nodded softly when he didn't

finish, though he wondered how it was so hard for him to say words he had to say every day.

It was as though telling Andrea would somehow make him *feel* his sister's death more intensely. As if Andrea somehow made his guard drop a little. *Absurd.*

'And I appreciate that bringing Noah here, an hour away from his old home, may not be ideal. But I've been staying in my sister's home for the past few weeks, and Noah didn't communicate there either. Ultimately I'm a surgeon here at Baystone Medical, and I have patients and responsibilities that I can't simply drop.'

'I understand that too,' Andrea said quietly. 'I was eight when my father died in a car crash. My younger brother was seven. Dad had gone out to retrieve Daniel's wooden toy sword and shield that had been left out in the rain. A drugged driver crashed into him. Despite the fact that we were a loving, close family who had always hugged, talked and laughed a lot, Daniel developed selective mutism. We didn't move house, he didn't have to change school and I know he still loved us—but it was just his way of coping.'

'I see.' Her unexpected confession had caught him off-guard, and he was both grateful and surprised that she trusted him enough to tell him. 'Can I ask how long it lasted—the lack of communication?'

'The lack of verbal communication lasted five

months but we did manage non-verbal communication. Plus, our situation had additional…complications.'

'Complications?' he echoed, but she was already shaking her hand dismissively.

'My mother wasn't well, but that isn't relevant to your and Noah's situation. The point is, from what I've seen today, and in my limited experience, I think Noah wants to talk. He's just trying to make sense of whatever it is he saw, and I think it's likely he needs you to help him.'

'I have no idea how to do that.' Seth exhaled harshly, angry with himself for his apparent inability to help his nephew.

'You'll learn.' She shrugged. 'You'll feel your way. Though, for what it's worth—and I appreciate you have responsibilities as a surgeon—long days of surgeries aren't going to help Noah right now.'

'I realise that.'

'So can you cut them back?'

Seth eyed her for a moment.

'I don't think I've ever seen you be quite so blunt, Andrea.'

She had the grace to flush a little—a pretty colour that tiptoed over her smooth cheeks and down the elegant line of her neck. Not that he should be noticing.

Even so, she clearly wasn't about to relent.

'So,' she prompted. 'Can you?'

'I've already instructed Joyce to reduce my case

load and try to keep it to more of a seven-to-seven, Monday to Friday. Fortunately, the board are supportive and are bringing in a new surgeon to take up the slack.'

It felt odd, of course. For over a decade, he'd put his career first—ahead of anything or anyone else. But right now his nephew needed him and Seth was prepared to do whatever it took to give Noah what he needed.

Including, he decided in that moment, convincing Andrea to help him reach the little boy.

Whatever it took.

Something had changed. Andrea couldn't be sure what it was, but she felt it. A shift in the room and Seth's shrewd, assessing stare on her, rooting her to the spot. It was so penetrating that she feared he might see through all her bravado—the carefully constructed veil of confidence that she had spent years piecing together, even before her ex's betrayal—to the imperfect individual she'd always felt herself to be, complete with all her shortcomings.

It was the craziest sensation. And beneath it all that current of awareness still lapped around her.

Somehow, *somehow*, she managed to speak.

'So the nanny I heard you mention to Joyce was supposed to cover either side of the day, before and after school?'

The look of disdain was unmistakable.

'Indeed. But after today's shambles I wouldn't

ever trust them again,' he bit out, his expression grim. 'Either way, it's being dealt with.'

His protectiveness of his nephew caused a delicious shiver to ripple through Andrea—one she wasn't remotely prepared for. She'd never thought of Seth Mulder as a family man—she doubted many people ever had—but the image was a dangerously seductive one.

She shoved it from her mind.

'You seem to be doing all the right things, although I don't believe there's any one single solution. You just sort of have to feel your way. Like your surgeries, I guess.'

'Except that in my surgeries I at least have an idea of what I'm doing.' Seth blew out.

'Only because you've learned.' She offered a half-smile. 'And you'll learn with your nephew.'

'And with your help.'

Andrea halted briefly.

'I told you, I'm not qualified in this. And no two individuals are the same. What worked for my brother won't necessarily work for Noah.'

She wished Seth's gaze didn't skewer her quite so much.

'I don't care how unqualified you declare yourself to be,' he answered simply. 'I want you to teach me. Because whatever you did just now worked. Noah talked.'

Andrea wrinkled her nose, hating herself for that swell of pride at Seth's words. She reined herself in.

'I'd hardly say *talk*,' she cautioned. 'And if I'd pushed him to say more then I think he would have clammed up again. But the first thing I tried was talking to him without putting him on the spot. So I didn't ask him anything directly, instead I started up a conversation with a prop—the doll—in order to let him know that I was happy with a one-sided conversation and he didn't have to answer me.'

'Yes, but how did you know that would work?'

'I didn't know for sure.' She shrugged. 'I just saw the way he clutched his teddy bear in front of him, as though he was using it to protect himself. And it was so like what my brother used to do that I took a chance.'

'Okay, but then you still asked him what snack he wanted,' Seth pressed. 'Just like I did.'

She squinted, thinking back to what she'd done. It had all been so instinctive, so organic, that it was hard to remember things precisely. Plus, it was strange, being the one teaching Seth for a change.

But strange in a good way, not a bad one. Or was that her pride again?

'I took a chance using the wooden alphabet aba-cus as another prop,' she explained. 'Noah might not have liked letters, or he might not have been good at phonics, but I was just showing him that I was happy to accept non-verbal communication. Joyce tried it too, when she laid out the snacks and invited Noah to choose one, or just point at what he liked.'

'He didn't choose anything with her,' Seth pointed out, his frustration evident.

'But he might have. Instead, in this instance, Noah became overwhelmed and took himself off to the corner. I just thought that playing a game by spinning the blocks might introduce a little more fun, or at least enough of a distraction.'

'And you kept talking to the doll, instead of him, so that he didn't feel under pressure.' Seth realised this abruptly. 'But when we put the snacks on the counter all three of us were watching him.'

'Right.'

Seth was beginning to understand already. She really shouldn't be surprised. His ability to learn and adapt was what made him such a good surgeon.

'So what else would you suggest I do to help him feel less overwhelmed?'

'I don't know, I'm not…' she began, catching herself when she saw his expression. 'With Daniel, we tried to give him something fun to focus on whilst we tried to reconnect—taking him to the playground, going on a nature walk. The primary school has a new jungle gym that my nieces and nephew are going crazy over; do you know if Noah likes it?'

'I don't know,' Seth admitted, his jaw locking tightly. 'Why?'

He was so accustomed to having all the answers; this had to be galling for him.

'There's a soft play centre and climbing wall

about twenty minutes away,' she told him. 'I thought maybe you could take Noah.'

'I guess.' He looked thoughtful. 'I seem to recall my sister saying he used to love climbing this huge, ten-foot-high sandstone rock in their local park. She used to say her heart was always in her mouth even as she encouraged him to be bold and confident.'

'Well, there you go.' Relief pulsed through Andrea. 'Just like my nieces and my nephew. And they all love going to the local play centre. I could ask my sister-in-law if she wants me to give her a few hours' break tonight.'

'Tonight?' Seth hardly looked eager.

She thought about the little boy in the room down the hall and steeled herself.

'No time like the present, surely?' she pressed, reminding herself that this wasn't about her inconvenient attraction to this man. It was about helping a young boy who was going through the same thing her brother had once gone through. 'I was heading to their house tonight anyway for a couple of hours; I'm fairly confident she'll say yes. Though, if it's too far out of your comfort zone...?'

'It isn't exactly appealing,' he admitted wryly.

All at once, unwanted images of Seth on hot dates assailed her.

'No, I imagine it's nothing like your usual nights of glamorous dates at exclusive restaurants.'

She could tell he didn't like that, though he didn't deny it. Still, why she was deliberately goading him was anybody's guess. Apparently she'd developed some kind of death wish.

'I just don't want them to think Noah is too much hard work and ignore him,' Seth ground out at length. 'Won't that isolate him all the more?'

Laughter instantly bubbled up inside her as she thought of Daniel's and Julia's wonderfully crazy brood.

'That lot play with everyone!' She chuckled. 'They couldn't ignore someone if they tried. They're full of confidence—*swagger,* my brother and his wife call it. And I'll make a point of telling them that Noah needs them to look out for him.'

Seth still looked dubious.

'You're sure that will help Noah?'

'No, I'm not sure.' She shook her head, determined to be honest. 'It's just an idea. It might work, it might not. So it's up to you.'

'Right.'

Andrea waited a moment as he seemed to weigh things up; she couldn't have said why she was holding her breath. This was about a six-year-old boy, not about Seth choosing to spend an evening with her instead of on a date with some model.

'Have you ever been to anything like it before?' she asked curiously, though she was fairly sure that she already knew the answer.

But, a moment later, he surprised her.

'Once,' he said. 'Three or four years ago, with Noah and my sister. It was full of screaming kids.'

She couldn't stop herself from laughing at his unimpressed expression.

'Yes, well, that's sort of the point.'

At least he had the grace to look abashed.

'I suppose that's true.'

She didn't know why this chagrined, uncertain Uncle Seth was just as damned sexy as the self-assured surgeon Seth who had caught her from stumbling outside the school that morning.

'So you know where it is?'

'I think I can remember.'

She couldn't work out if he was being genuine or if there'd been a little bit of sarcasm in his voice. She erred on the side of genuine, though she suspected the latter.

'If you give me your mobile, I'll input my number, just in case you get lost.'

'You're too kind.'

This time there was definite dryness. She resolutely ignored it.

'Do you want to ask Noah if he wants to go?'

'Ask Noah?' His brows knitted and once again Andrea found herself trying to ignore her body's sudden reaction as his gaze washed over her, just like before.

'Tell him where you're thinking of going and give him the choice of whether he wants to do that or not.'

Seth blew out another breath.

'I don't know how to give him the choice. If I ask

him what he wants to do, he doesn't answer me. But if I tell him where we're going, he just obeys.'

'Right.' She nodded slowly.

'I'd ask him if he would answer.'

There was a hint of uncharacteristic defensiveness in his tone, which was perhaps understandable, but Andrea decided the best way to deal with that was simply to ignore it.

'Well, you could just tell him where we're going and bring him along, then allow him to join in or not when he's there. Or we could try asking him.'

She stopped abruptly. There was an idea in the back of her head but it wasn't fully formed.

Seth eyed her curiously.

'What would you have done had it been your brother?' he demanded, as though reading her thoughts.

She pursed her lips, wondering at the wisdom of treating Noah exactly as she might have treated her brother.

'It's worth a try, you said,' Seth reminded her quietly, and she nodded slowly.

'Sometimes Mum and I would come up with a plan together and then we'd deliberately discuss it in front of Daniel. He'd usually find a way of conveying to us whether he wanted to go or not.'

'How?'

She offered an apologetic shrug.

'It varied. But he'd find a way if it mattered to him.'

Seth bobbed his head, his brain clearly working overtime. For several long moments they stood in silence, the only sounds coming from the sprawling park beyond his office window.

'Okay, let's give it a try,' he decided at last. 'I'll follow your lead.'

She was reminded again how somehow they seemed to have switched roles, with her the teacher and Seth the student. And Andrea wondered what she was to make of the fact that his quiet vote of confidence had done more to boost her self-esteem than anything else in a long time.

CHAPTER SIX

RELAX, SETH TOLD himself less than forty minutes later as he watched the play area from his chipped, once-glossy table—his back ramrod-straight in the uncomfortable, plastic bucket-chair.

Relaxing was easy to say, not nearly as easy to do.

He gripped the off-white mug, more for something to hold than actually wanting the drink. A glance around the other parents, all happy and at ease, should have helped, but it didn't. He wasn't exactly a *parent*, and he just felt tense and out of his depth. Certainly not sensations he was accustomed to.

He ought to be able to take comfort from the fact that Andrea had been right about Noah communicating his desire to come. They'd been talking to Joyce—Andrea had done most of the talking, of course, casually but deliberately discussing her nieces and nephews and how much they loved this place. Then she'd appeared to speculate as to whether Noah might want to join and the little boy had stood up and walked over. Without a word, he'd handed the doll to Andrea then slipped his hand into hers—his teddy bear clutched tightly in his other hand.

It was all Seth had needed to convince himself

that Andrea was one person he needed—no, his young nephew needed—right now.

So here they were at the local kids' soft play centre, his muscular supercar surprisingly not incongruous, parked amongst some expensive saloon cars and four-by-fours out in the car park. Noah, Andrea, her five-year-old twin nieces and her seven-year-old nephew were all somewhere in the mayhem of climbing frames, rope ladders and clear plastic tunnels, with a four-metre-wide and two-storey-high bumpy slide running through the middle.

The smell of cooking chips and freeze-dried coffee assailed his olfactory senses, whilst his ears were ringing from the ceaseless shouts and screams. It should have felt like hell to him.

It *did* feel like hell.

'Wishing you were somewhere else?' Andrea's amused voice cut into his thoughts. 'Like on some dazzling date?'

He turned his head to deny it, then caught her eye and felt a wry smile tug at his mouth.

'A date? No,' he heard himself admit. 'Though maybe a surgery.'

'I should have known!' She laughed and rolled her eyes, and something startling tiptoed warmly through him. 'I told you that you should have had a go on the long slide. It's quite good fun.'

'I'm not sure the equipment could take my

weight,' he replied evenly, as if that was the only thing that would stop him.

Andrea glanced around the vast space.

'You're probably right, this place is built for kids. Or for adults like me who have never grown up.'

But, though she tried to hide it, there was an edge to her tone that he thought was revealing. It made him think back over things she'd already told him, his brain trying to piece it together, wanting to understand her better.

He was no longer able to squash his curiosity the way he'd been able to when they'd been merely colleagues. Though did that mean that they were more than colleagues now? Could one evening of her helping him with his nephew constitute a friendship?

More to the point, why did he want it to do so?

And still his mind whirred. Now he knew about her father's death when she'd been eight, and her brother's time suffering from selective mutism, Seth couldn't help but wonder if that had made her grow up too soon. It would explain that deeply serious side to Andrea which didn't quite match most of her Baystone colleagues.

Yet tonight he realised she had a surprisingly fun side too, which the women he dated usually didn't. At least, not in this pure, uncorrupted way. Their kind of fun was usually had in bed.

Too late, Seth realised his mistake. Putting together images of Andrea and thoughts of sex was a huge blunder. It set off a chain reaction in his body that he felt was wholly inappropriate. Yet, even as he castigated himself for his lack of self-control—reminding himself that she was his *scrub nurse*, for pity's sake—he found his gaze being drawn back across the table. Drawn to those expressive eyes and that all-too-inviting mouth; to the long, blonde curl of ponytail that danced on her shoulder, and the hint of a swell of flesh that disappeared beneath her simple tee.

A far cry from the bland tunic uniform she wore for work. Even now, her legs, encased in plain blue jeans, she seemed to speak to him in a way that was far more primitive than the women he'd known who dressed in the shortest skirts or poured themselves into the most plunging, figure-hugging evening gowns.

He needed to regain control. Damn it but this wasn't about him or the greed that this woman awakened in him, licking at his sex.

'Seth?'

Snapping back to the present, he realised the object of his unseemly thoughts had been speaking to him and was now eyeing him strangely.

'Sorry?' he rasped.

'I was saying that there is a climbing wall for adults over that barrier behind you, if that's more your speed. It's designed for older children, or for parents and guardians to have something to do whilst their kids are playing.'

Blinking, he turned his chair to look.

'I do enjoy climbing,' he managed.

'I know. Jack has often mentioned the two of you going in the past. I've tried a little wall, but not roped up, and not one that high.'

'It's good fun,' he admitted, not mentioning that, at about twenty metres, the wall didn't look that high to him—not compared to the rock faces he usually scaled. 'It's rewarding, reaching the top after a challenging climb. I've missed it this past month.'

'Come on, then.' She stood abruptly. 'Let's have a go instead of sitting around here being ignored by our lot. We'll tell them where we are and we'll go right there, just over the barrier, so no more than four metres from where we are now. They can easily get our attention if they need us. I know that's what my brother does when he comes, hence why they picked this table.'

Her grin was infectious and Seth was almost tempted. When had any date of his ever wanted to do something more exciting than be taken to the latest hotspot in the city?

Not that this was a *date*, of course.

'And it's safe?'

She waggled her wrist in front of him, complete with electronic tag.

'That's what these are for. The gate is manually operated and no kid is allowed to leave the area without the adult with the corresponding tag.'

It was incredibly tempting, though Seth told himself it was more about the climb—however tame—than the woman who was currently jiggling her hand in front of him like a big kid herself.

A lot like his sister had been, he realised with a jolt.

Stacey would have liked Andrea.

Seth pulled up short. Not for the first time during these last few weeks, he wished he and his sister hadn't drifted so far apart in the last four years.

Dimly, in the back of his mind, he could recall a conversation he'd with his sister where Stacey had teased him for not knowing much about his date, and he'd shrugged and told her that he knew all he needed to—namely that she'd liked red wine, didn't eat anything apart from salad and was hot in bed.

An unexpected stab of grief pierced him as he recalled the way his sister had rolled her eyes, told him that he was shallow and declared that she couldn't wait for the day when some woman finally cut him off at the knees—or some other, more apt, part of his anatomy.

He'd dismissed her, of course, since that would never have happened. Still, he could imagine Stacey's amusement now if she could see the knack that Andrea Perkins had for getting under his skin.

It was bizarre. Andrea was pretty enough, but nowhere near as glamorous as any of the women he dated. Yet she seemed to get to him in a way that no one ever had before.

Had it always been that way, back in his OR, where he'd smothered the inconvenient attraction beneath all those professional lines he'd always maintained he never crossed?

Now he allowed himself to consider it, it occurred to him that she'd always had a way of making those perfectly groomed, expensively dressed, socially rich women seem plastic and superficial. He'd begun to wonder how he hadn't seen it for himself before.

Thrusting the image aside, Seth strode across to where Andrea had tracked down the quartet, watching Noah's unconcerned response as she suggested what they were thinking of doing.

It struck him that the little boy actually looked at ease. The closest to happy that Seth had seen ever since that awful moment when Seth had collected him from the solicitor's office.

Another thing that was all down to the ever-surprising Andrea.

This had been a terrible idea.

The realisation crashed through Andrea as she stood stiffly, acutely aware of Seth kneeling down in front of her. Her entirely body felt hot, crackling, *needy.* And all the man was doing was untying the harness around her body and preparing to slide it down her legs and off.

It all felt ludicrously intimate.

He'd been wearing his usual bespoke waistcoat

when he'd arrived, which always clung so lovingly
to him over his crisp white shirt. It should have
made him look ridiculous and out of place, given
the location. But of course it didn't. Andrea had
even noticed more than a handful of women sending flirtatious looks their way.

The attention had only increased when Seth had
decided to give her an impromptu climbing lesson
and the waistcoat had come off. He'd even untucked
the shirt and rolled up the sleeves to reveal perfect
tanned, muscular forearms which had the oddest
effect on the butterflies in Andrea's stomach.

'Relax.' His low voice slid through her. 'You did
fine. I told you I wouldn't let you fall.'

Except that she feared she had. Not from the
wall, but into lust, with a man who was as good as
her boss, for pity's sake.

His hand brushed her hip and it was all she could
do not to react visibly. Her humiliation would reach
new depths if he realised her reaction was more
about him than her nervousness about climbing
the wall.

She could feel his hand on her ankle and his
touch at her waist, guiding her from hand-holds
to foot-holds, catching her so easily when she lost
her grip and swung from the vertical face, making
sure she never dropped on the rope.

And then the harness was off and he was standing back up, right in front of her. So close that it

stole the very breath from her lungs as she lifted her head to look up at him.

'You did really well,' he murmured, his eyes meeting hers and holding them.

Something roared through her, even as she pretended not to be aware of it.

'Thanks. Though not as well as you did when you had to give staff a demonstration that we could climb under our own supervision—suit trousers included. I think they were about to offer you a job here.'

He laughed. But even that sounded like a low, intimate sound.

'I usually climb in jeans,' he rasped. 'And I can't say this would be a bad place to work.'

'You'd miss your surgeries.' She laughed shakily.

'That's true.'

'And your galas and super-yacht parties,' she heard herself tease. 'Your glamorous dates.'

His face grew sombre...more intense...and a sensual shiver rippled through her.

'I've had more fun with you today than I have with anyone in a long time,' he answered suddenly, and she wondered which of them was more shocked at the revelation.

Yet should she really be so taken aback? Hadn't there been brief moments when they'd both seemed to forget where they were and why they were there? And, in those moments, hadn't he'd looked at her in a way that made her feel eaten alive?

A hot flame licked over her at the idea as a deliciously wicked part of her wished that he would do just that. And, once the image was in her brain, she couldn't quite get it to leave. So she stood scant millimetres from him, with her breath lodged somewhere in her chest, feeling utterly hollowed out.

'I'm not sure I can believe that,' she answered at length, in a voice that sounded so husky, so raw, that it took her moments to realise it was her own.

The black, hungry look in Seth's gaze only made the flame burn that little hotter.

'Andrea...' he croaked, his hands lifting to cup her shoulders.

'Andrea... Aunt Andrea.'

With a jolt, Andrea registered the chorus of little voices calling her name. Later, she would wonder how she'd managed to break the delicious contact of Seth's hands on her, but she found herself hurrying to the barrier.

'What is it, is anything wrong?'

'We've lost Bear,' her twin nieces chorused with a level of excitement that only a child could manage.

Automatically, her eyes slid to Seth's, the question in those blue-grey depths mirroring her own.

'Bear?' she asked calmly. 'Do you mean Noah's teddy bear?'

Then, to her shock, a white-faced Noah nodded his head faintly, before speaking quietly but firmly.

'Bearosaurus,'

'You know…like Tyrannosaurus or Stegosaurus?' her nephew piped up enthusiastically. 'It's such a cool name. And it's Bear for short.'

'Bearosaurus…' Seth echoed neutrally, and Andrea knew only she could read the myriad emotions that tumbled beneath his controlled exterior.

No doubt he was processing the fact that his verbally non-communicative nephew had apparently spoken to her nieces and nephew. Even if only a single name.

But then, her nephew spoke again.

'Noah said that Bear looks after him, so we have to find him. *Now.*'

Andrea didn't think Seth could have looked any more stunned if the ground had shifted sideways and tipped up. But there was no time to dwell on and absorb the revelation, as the two of them shed the rest of their climbing equipment and hurried to the gate into the play area.

A grim expression had pulled Seth's features taut and she didn't need him to tell her he was worried about how it would affect Noah if they couldn't find the teddy bear, the thing that had become the little boy's security blanket since his mother's death.

For the next ten minutes, the group checked every inch of the soft play area, Seth's expression growing ever more ominous as they remained empty-handed. And then, just as it seemed hopeless, Andrea spotted a member of staff walking to the reception desk with the teddy—with *Bear*—in hand.

Ten minutes later, as she gathered up her nieces' coats, Andrea watched as Billy dodged around her to walk next to Noah and proceeded to talk about his own polar bear teddy which he'd made himself at a Build a Bear party a year or so ago.

'Are you okay?' she whispered quietly to Seth as they followed behind.

The disconcerted look he shot her made her wonder if anyone had asked him that in some time. Her stomach flip-flopped for no apparent reason.

'I'm fine,' he replied automatically, before pausing. 'Actually, averted disaster aside, I feel good. Better than good. Today feels like completing a successful, complex surgery—you know the patient might have months of recovery and rehab ahead of them, but the surgery has gone well, and that's the best start you can hope for.'

Her stomach flip-flopped again, but this time for a less agreeable reason.

'I don't want to rain on your parade,' she murmured as he stepped forward to open the door to outside, the early evening-air hitting them. 'But don't be surprised if Noah regresses.'

'He only said a few words.' Seth frowned. 'How can he regress?'

'Daniel did.' Andrea remembered as they stopped beside his unmistakeable car. 'Many times. Mum and I used to feel that, for every two steps forward that we took, he always took one step back.'

'I see.'

If it had been anyone else, Andrea thought they would have looked almost defeated. But this was Seth, the surgeon who carried out extraordinary operations on a weekly basis. If anyone had the patience and determination to succeed, it was Seth.

She only hoped he knew that being a surrogate dad to his six-year-old nephew was going to be a heck of a lot harder than any of the impossible neurosurgeries.

CHAPTER SEVEN

THIS WAS WHERE Seth lived?

Stepping into lift, Andrea managed a weak smile at the concierge and tried not to grip the side rail too tightly. The last thing she'd expected when she'd dropped her nieces and nephew back with her sister-in-law was to receive a text from Seth summoning her to his home and sending her the address.

Already nervous, it was now proving even harder to stop her nerves from jangling riotously. Not least because it transpired that Seth lived in one of the most sought-after buildings in the city, in a sprawling penthouse which occupied the top two floors. And one which required the elderly concierge to accompany her up in the private lift as if she were some kind of impostor who he didn't really trust to be there.

Or perhaps that was just her overactive imagination. The older gentleman had been nothing but courteous from the moment she'd walked through the pristine glass doors, advising her that Mr Mulder was expecting her.

Now, the higher the lift rose to the penthouse, the more elevated her sense of disquiet became.

'Here we are, Miss Perkins.' The concierge smiled warmly as the lift glided to a stop and the doors slid smoothly open.

And of course Seth had to be waiting by his open

door, watching her step out stiffly as she thanked the older man.

'Thank you, Stan, I'll take it from here,' Seth murmured pleasantly before turning to her with an arch expression. 'Are you coming in, Andrea? Or do you intend to ride the lift back down like a fairground attraction?'

She wasn't prepared for the way his words rippled deliciously over her. She told herself to move away, but couldn't. Not when he was pinning her in place with that killer gaze.

'I was just making a coffee.' He stepped back into the apartment, breaking the spell. Or perhaps that was just fanciful.

'I don't...' She began to step forward before faltering. 'Why am I here, Seth?'

'For what it's worth, you were right to warn me about regression with Noah.'

If she'd been looking for an excuse, then this was it. Straightening her shoulders, Andrea took a breath and forced herself to follow.

'Is that why you sent the text SOS?'

'I wouldn't call it an SOS.' He pulled a grim smile. 'But I did hope you might have some advice for me.'

'What happened?'

Seth busied himself making coffee from a machine that wouldn't have looked out of place in a coffee house. His sleek, neat kitchen area was tastefully decked in burnished steel appliances, white granite surfaces and sleek dark-chocolate-coloured wall tiles.

She didn't dare turn round to look at the space behind her, but that meant concentrating on Seth.

'Did he stop communicating with you entirely?' she asked.

He'd still been wearing a suit jacket at the play centre—not that it had stopped a decent number of women from staring at him. Not that she'd cared, of course. Not one bit.

'Actually, not entirely,' Seth replied. 'I was able to ask him direct questions without him retreating into his room, and he indicated he wanted a bath with bubbles.'

'Well, that's good.'

'It is,' he agreed. 'I just...suppose I was hoping he might actually say something to me. Even just one word.'

'Give him a chance; he's doing well.' She looked around the room suddenly. 'I take it he's in bed now?'

'He's in bed, yes. In fact, he was pretty much asleep the moment his head hit the pillow.'

'Apparently, the twins do that.' Andrea grinned. 'Or so I'm told. That's the beauty of being the aunt—I get to take them out and have fun and if that tires them out, then, great. But, if it over-tires them, it's Daniel and Julia's problem, not mine.'

'You're particularly good with them.'

'Thanks.'

'Do you want any of your own?'

She blinked, momentarily thrown off-balance, despite the fact it wasn't an uncommon topic of conversation between colleagues. Nonetheless, it took her a moment to regroup.

How was Seth to know that it was a subject she always avoided as carefully as she could? The last thing she wanted to start talking about with her Baystone colleagues was her past. Not about her husband, nor her miscarriage and certainly not her septate uterus—the anomaly which meant a membrane ran through her uterus, dividing it into two parts. And even though she knew she'd done nothing to cause it, that it was something she'd been born with, it had still been the reason for her miscarriage, and it was what made her feel less than a woman every time the subject of children came up.

That cruel twist of fate meant her chances of getting pregnant were low—her chances of actually carrying a baby to term, even lower.

It was impossible to describe to anyone quite how…defective that made her feel. Especially when she'd once dreamed of becoming a mother and giving her children the kind of childhood she wished she'd been able to enjoy.

Little wonder that she doted on her brother's brood, even if neither Daniel nor Julia knew her secret. She'd decided long ago not to burden her family with her problems, though whether because she thought her family had dealt with enough, or because she didn't want to say the words out loud, she couldn't be sure.

'I haven't really considered kids,' she lied stiffly.

She might have known Seth wouldn't be fooled. He lifted his hands instantly.

'My apologies, I was merely curious. You seem so natural.'

Handing her what had to be a designer coffee-mug, he made his way round the kitchen island and indicated for her to follow, the subject apparently dropped. And finally she had a chance to see Seth's incredible penthouse.

The sheer dizzying scale of the place was all too evident. The stunning, two-storey area, with the vaulted ceiling of the main area painted a sharp, clean white to give the place a spacious, light feel, walloped her with its soaring height. All further helped by the wide expanse of sparkling glass that ran the entire length of the building.

On one side, the side she was on now, an oval glass dining table with designer, metal-framed chairs sat boldly in front of the view.

The other side of the main space boasted the living area. It contained a dark, plaid couch sitting opposite two dark leather easy chairs, the coffee table in between looking like another expensive de-signer piece in crystal-clear glass. A staircase just off to the side and rear appeared to float out of the side of the main wall, with its glass railing almost invisible from this angle.

Finally, her eyes were pulled from one expensive piece of artwork or sculpture to another, and then another, each more stunning than the last.

The place screamed out that it was the residence of a successful, wealthy, confirmed bachelor. The kind of aspirational apartment that looked as though it had come straight out of the pages of a slick architectural magazine, pristine and minimalist. She could barely have afforded a square foot in a place like this. Seth's life was so far removed from her own that, for the first time in a very long time, Andrea actually felt intimidated enough to make her wonder what on earth she'd been thinking in coming here at all tonight.

'You don't like it?' He sounded amused as he unfolded himself onto the couch with all the grace of a predatory hunter.

'Actually, I do like it,' she told him sincerely.

'The frown lines on your face seem to say otherwise.'

She wrinkled her nose, considering.

'It's spectacular,' she told him at last. 'But—and this is just my opinion—it isn't homely. There's nothing soft in here; nothing that suggests it would be home to a six-year-old child.'

'That's pretty much what Stacey would have said,' he murmured softly.

'Your sister? You mentioned that she and Noah lived with you for the first eighteen months of his life. She didn't try to...?'

She stopped, not wanting to offend, but Seth's smile held a tint of regret rather than affront.

'Make it more *homely*?' he finished for her. 'She did.'

She should leave it there; she knew that. But she found herself still speaking.

'But *you* didn't like that?'

He didn't exactly shrug—he was too *male* for that.

'It looked quite nice, as it happened. But after she left I got rid of some things. The cushions, the pictures...things like that.'

Another shadow passed over him; a sadness which she could do nothing about. Suddenly all she wanted to do was lighten the mood and see that striking smile of his again.

'Hence the dark wood, the glass and the sleek metal.' She forced a grin. 'Remarkably unblemished by sticky fingers—though, give it time. This place is masculine and bachelor to a tee.'

'I suspect that isn't the compliment that it sounds.' His voice rumbled over her—*doing* things to her—but he still didn't sound offended.

'That bookcase, by contrast, tells a different story about its owner.'

He followed the direction of her gaze.

'Is that so?' He arched one eyebrow. 'And what, I might wonder, does it tell you about me, Andrea?'

The sound of her voice on his tongue sent a lick of pure lust straight through her, and it didn't matter if she tried to remember why she was here. Or who she was with. She might as well be drowning in the deepest, darkest well with no way to get out.

So instead Andrea focussed her attention on the shelves. She regarded the battered, leather-bound books, the antique globe with tiny holes here and there and the unusual pieces of art which she couldn't categorise but looked original.

It was almost thrilling, trying to piece together this man from his personal belongings that she suspected not every woman got to see. Or, perhaps, not every woman who'd come to this penthouse had bothered to look.

'I'd say you travel a fair amount.'

'A fair assumption.' He lifted one shoulder. 'You'll have to do better that that.'

'Okay,' she mused. 'How about the fact that the tiny pinpricks in that old globe tell me that you don't spend months, or even weeks, deliberating on your trips? You close your eyes and stick something in at random. Then you just pack a bag and leave, like some kind of adventurer.'

He looked discernibly more impressed.

'Observant.'

'I take it that *is* a compliment?'

'Do you want it to be?' he asked heavily.

Another lick moved though her.

'I don't suppose it matters,' she lied.

Why did she care what he thought?

'What *does* matter?' Seth murmured quietly, taking a very deliberate step towards her.

Heat rolled between them. She ought to move away, but she was powerless to. Least of all when he lifted his hand and grazed the tips of his fingers down one side of her jaw, his expression so intensely hot that it licked through her chest.

She silenced the voice inside screaming at her that, for all intents and purposes, this was her boss. That he didn't date colleagues. That she certainly didn't.

But then suddenly he was kissing her. A kiss like nothing she'd ever known before. A kiss that breathed life into something deep inside her that had been dormant for so long.

Had it ever existed like this before?

Without even realising what she was doing, her hands splayed themselves out on Seth's chest, resting on the angular muscles beneath and letting the heat seep from his body to hers as his mouth moved, unhurried, over hers. As though he had all the time in the world.

It was a heady experience and it made her melt. Everywhere.

'And this?' he muttered dryly against her mouth. 'Does this matter?'

Andrea had no idea how she broke the contact long enough to reply, let alone to murmur to him.

'Should it?'

It was as though she wasn't the inexperienced,

frigid woman that her ex-husband had always accused her of being. As if she was versed in seductive ways, the way so many of her acquaintances and colleagues seemed to be. As if her previous experience, as limited as it was, had been hurried, perfunctory and almost always unsatisfactory.

Any minute, she thought to herself, *he's going to see me for the fraud that I am.*

But Seth didn't appear to see anything of the sort. Instead, he simply angled his mouth against hers to deepen the kiss, sending her further and further away from anything she considered to be sane, with every deliciously wicked slide of his tongue.

Again and again he kissed her, stoking up that fire inside until it was so high that the heat was practically scorching her from the inside out.

She wasn't aware of moving, yet Andrea became aware of the fact that her back was against the same bookcase that she'd been avidly studying what felt like a lifetime ago. Worse—or maybe *better*—that her legs had parted and Seth was settled between them, steel against molten softness.

Shifting her hips, she revelled in the low, primal sound that slid from him. The way his hands seemed to glide down her back with such restrained leisure only made her feel all the more desirable. All the more precious.

The way her body was responding to Seth's

skilled touch, in a way she'd never known it was capable of doing, was a revelation.

With your boss, a muffled voice tried to remind her.

But she wasn't listening She wanted more. So much more.

As if reading her thoughts, Seth lifted his mouth from hers, moving to trail hot, sensual kisses right along the jawline that he'd caressed minutes before. When he dipped further to kiss down the long column of her neck, she couldn't stop her gasp of pleasure as she tipped her head back to grant him better access.

She felt raw, exposed, and she was loving every moment of it.

When he hooked one finger on the buttons at the front of her top, pausing as if to give her a chance to stop him, she merely met his gaze. The dark hunger mirrored her own.

'Do you have a particular attachment to these buttons?' he growled, and the sheer desire in his voice made her tremble.

'Attachment?' she echoed dully.

'Too late.' He grinned wickedly, snagging his finger so the buttons popped off.

One.

The sound was deliciously rude.

Two.

It echoed sinfully around the space.

Three.

Four.

Had there ever been such a decadent sound?

Five.

Then she didn't have time to think anything, because his hand was hooking the lace of her bra, exposing the taut, dark nipple and taking it into his mouth.

Like fireworks.

Andrea gasped as his tongue, his teeth, grazed over her. Without realising what she was doing, she found herself arching into him, wanting more. *Aching* for more.

And Seth gave it. He lavished attention on her breast, sending sensation rushing through her that had her crying out. And, when he'd finished on one side, he turned his attention to the other. Andrea couldn't think straight. All she could do was let him.

Let him lead her wherever he wanted to go.

When he removed first his top, then hers, she took the opportunity to lower her head and trace the taut lines of his chest with her hands, then her mouth, in much the same way that he'd done for her.

Almost as though he was giving her a kind of power over him, lower and lower as she followed the sharp contours, until her hands were on the belt buckle of his trousers. She almost protested when he uttered a low curse and caught her wrists in his hand.

But the next thing she was on her back on the deep rug and her trousers were discarded, thrown somewhere—she didn't care where—his almost-black eyes snaring hers and daring her to look away as his hand grazed up the inside of her thigh.

Higher.

And higher still.

Until her pulse was leaping around erratically and her breath was sawing in and out of her.

And then as he reached the apex of her legs—the part of her that ached for him the most—he skimmed the back of his hand over her heat and trailed his fingers down the inside of her other leg.

Andrea heard a primal groan, but it took a moment to realise that the low sound came from her.

'Patience,' he commanded, his mouth crooked up into an indecorous smile.

Then he lowered his head and allowed his mouth to take over from his hand, working back the other way now, his warm breath making her skin shiver with anticipation.

'Seth,' she managed, her voice glutted with lust.

His eyes burned blacker, as though the sound of his name on her voice was almost too much for him to stand.

And then, just as she expected him to tease her once again, he lowered his head between her legs and pressed his mouth to the very heart of her need.

Andrea fractured.

There was nothing but the feel of Seth between

her legs, licking her, tasting her, *feasting* on her as though he'd been waiting to do for centuries. But it wasn't just his tongue that he wielded against her so expertly, but his fingers too, sliding inside her, in and out, until she was writhing against his touch, seeking out more. Then more again.

With every slide he was sending her higher and higher, spiralling upwards until her body didn't even feel like her own. It had never, *never,* been like this.

And then he did something—a twist, perhaps, or an added bit of pressure—and Andrea was gone, splintering apart in the inky night sky.

Andrea had no idea how much longer she stayed there, soaring in the nothingness, but by the time she came back to herself Seth was stretched out languorously next to her. But he was betrayed by the hungry expression on his face, and the unyielding lines of his hard, ready body.

'I… I didn't know,' she faltered. 'That is, I've never…'

But, whatever it was she was struggling to say, it didn't matter. A muffled cry came from upstairs— the unmistakeable sound of Noah caught in a bad dream.

She'd barely moved before Seth was already up, pulling his clothes back on without missing a beat.

'I have to go,' he muttered.

She was eminently grateful that they were out

of sight on the other side of the bookcase from the stairs and gallery.

'He won't tumble on the stairs, will he?' she asked hazily. Her brain, it seemed, was still trying to process what had just happened between Seth and her.

'I doubt he's even out of bed. He'll still be asleep; it happens most nights,' Seth assured her before rounding the bookcase away from her. 'He just needs someone to sit with him and talk softly. Wait here.'

The worst of it was that there was a part of her that desperately, desperately wanted to obey. As if she hadn't already learned the worst lesson of all when it came to men who wanted something from her.

Pushing herself shakily up onto her surprising wobbly legs, Andrea pulled her clothes back on as quickly as she could.

What kind of an idiot was she, anyway?

Because it was one thing to decide that maybe this was her time to let loose a little and have some fun. But it was another thing entirely to be foolish enough to think that having fun meant rushing headlong into heartbreak with a man like Seth.

CHAPTER EIGHT

'DRILL, PLEASE.'

Seth checked the vitals on the monitors that were connected up to his patient—an eighteen-year-old girl who had been hit by a truck when she'd stepped out from behind a waiting bus. She'd been flown straight in by helicopter, having been found to be deeply unconscious with a blown pupil at the scene, and scans had confirmed an acute subdural haematoma.

Now it was a race against time for Seth to evacuate via a craniotomy, and he'd already made his first incisions and removed the temporal muscle to gain access to his patient's skull. Taking the medical tool, Seth concentrated on drilling the burr holes that would allow him to remove the necessary area of bone to access the leathery, tough dura. Once he could get to the bleed beneath that, he could finally start to remove the blood which was compressing his patient's brain.

It was a process he'd successfully carried out hundreds of times in the past and, whilst he never allowed himself to become complacent, he was nonetheless grateful for the distraction. As well as for the fact that Andrea Perkins wasn't his scrub nurse for this procedure today. Fortunate, really, considering what had happened between them the last time they'd met.

What had he been thinking? He didn't date work colleagues. He sure as hell didn't have feverish sex with them. He had rules, and no other woman had ever come close to making him break them the way that Andrea had.

'Hold that a little more to the right, please,' he instructed. 'And a little more irrigation. Better.'

He suppressed his irritation as the scrub nurse, whilst solid, didn't act quite as intuitively as he felt Andrea would have. He tried to eject the thought from his head but it refused to go.

Last night had thrown him. Heck, the woman herself had thrown him. He'd acted instinctively, and he never did that. Not where women were concerned, and definitely not since his nephew had entered his life.

But with Andrea he'd thrown out the damned rule book. Seth couldn't understand what it was that was so different about her compared to any of the women that he had dated—not that he was dating her, he reminded himself hastily. Yet nonetheless she seemed to have sneaked under his skin. He had no idea what he was supposed to do about that.

If it hadn't been for Noah calling out, then Seth was fairly sure that Andrea would have ended up in his bed. And, despite all his professional lines and boundaries, he couldn't say he'd been remotely unhappy at the prospect. Despite the *very* cold shower that he'd taken last night, he'd lain awake for a long time, staring at the ceiling as he'd tried to work out exactly what it was about this one woman that had him so easily casting aside all his previous rules— and since when had he ever lost sleep over a woman before?

Invisible lines and rubric set him apart from the man whom he had called a father, but who had never actually *been* any kind of father. He'd been a man who had spent his entire life taking what he wanted, and doing as he pleased, with no heed for the consequences for anybody else. Especially not for his and Stacey's desperate mother.

With deep distaste, Seth thrust any memory of his so-called father out of his head. He refused to compare himself to that man. He might be the son, cut from the same damaged cloth, but he would not live the same life.

He might have the same playboy reputation that his father had, but the difference was that Seth wasn't married. He wasn't cheating, flaunting all his indiscretions in his frantic wife's face.

By contrast, Seth had always prided himself on never so much as flirting even in the direction of one of his colleagues.

Those were his rules—whatever they might be worth.

Was it the disconcerting experience of having had his life turned upside down that had caused this unusual state of affairs? It would be easy enough to use his sister's death and his nephew's presence to explain away this inexplicable attraction to Andrea Perkins—his damned scrub nurse.

Besides, he tried to argue to himself, it didn't even make sense to be so ridiculously drawn to her. The woman was certainly pretty, but by no means displayed the kind of glamour and glitz of the women he was accustomed to dating. Part of him had been growing weary of that kind of woman for some time, anyway.

It would be easier still to tell himself that the attraction was borne out of gratitude for her help around the situation with Noah. He recalled his relief at seeing his nephew begin to come alive—if only for an hour or so—at that play centre the day before.

But an *easy* excuse didn't mean an accurate one. And Seth suspected that the reasons for his attraction to Andrea Perkins went beyond any excuses he could conjure up by way of explanation.

'A little suction here,' he instructed as the small incision he was making in the scalp began to provide the excess blood with an escape, somewhat obscuring the field.

He worked quickly and meticulously, making a series of incisions to ensure as much of the bleed as possible had a route out.

'Yep, that's looking good,' he declared at length.

'Ready to put the dura back in place?' his resident asked, peering at the site.

'Yeah, I think so,' Seth confirmed.

Though he wouldn't close up one of the layers of connective tissue that completely covered and protected the brain and spinal cord in case his patient's brain began to swell and needed room to expand.

'Scalp on or off?'

'I would say it's safe to put the scalp back in place—we've left enough room. Now it's down to the intensive care team.'

And Baystone had a great ICU unit; his patient would be in good hands.

Efficiently but flawlessly, Seth completed the surgical procedure, scrubbing out and heading through the doors back to his office—where Joyce was waiting for him.

'Noah's school called.'

His stomach lurched instantly.

'Is he okay?'

'He isn't injured,' Joyce assured him straight away. 'Though he was apparently involved in an altercation with another boy.'

Seth frowned.

'Noah was? What happened?'

'They wouldn't give me all the details,' Joyce apologised. 'But, since they understand you're in and out of surgeries all day, they asked me to pass on that another boy was teasing Noah about not being able to talk and was threatening him with some old football net that he'd found. It seems Noah decided that wasn't happening, and did something with the net and the boy first.'

'I see,' Seth remarked grimly.

'If you ask me, Noah did well to stand up for himself if he was being bullied. But the school would like you to call in for a conversation as soon as you are able.'

Seth grunted. Joyce's allegiances were clear, and heartening. He tried to not wonder what Andrea's opinion on the matter might be. In many ways, it was moot—she was only an aunt, the way that he was an uncle. Yet he couldn't shake the feeling that, in the same situation, she would be handling all this so much better than he currently was.

What would her advice be if she knew all the circumstances? The school was only too aware of the custody dispute involving Noah's paternal grandparents and their own views might come into play. Anything that suggested Noah was struggling emotionally could be used down the line to prove that, as Noah's uncle, Seth was less suited to being the boy's new caregiver than the grandparents.

No doubt Andrea would know the right way to react.

'Is there anything I can do to help?' Joyce asked kindly.

He imagined she made a wonderful grandmother to her five young grandchildren—just as wonderful as his own beloved grandmother had been to Stacey and him—and would be only too happy to offer sage advice.

'Thank you, Joyce. I shall deal with it,' he declared, striding back up the hallway and to his office.

But saying he could deal with it and actually having a plan were, it turned out, two very different things. Stumped, he moved to the window and stared out at the park beyond.

An image of Andrea slid, unbidden, into his brain. He tried to eject but it just squatted down lower, reminding him that he still had her phone number. He could still call her outside the hospital—if that allowed him to keep some semblance of maintaining his lines in the sand.

Glowering at the freshly mown lawn, he strode back to his desk and sat down again. He was a neurosurgeon, top of his field. People came to him from across the country—across the world. He didn't need a stranger to help him resolve an issue concerning his own nephew.

Determinedly, he flipped up his Internet browser and typed in a search. A few moments later, he shut the page down, picked up his phone and swung his chair back to the window.

This, he told himself resolutely, was not about his own ego but about what was the best solution for Noah.

Nothing more.

Andrea circled the large play area in the country park for the third time and wondered if inviting

Seth and Noah to her family's picnic had been her best idea.

She wasn't sure why she had. Obviously she wanted to help Noah, especially when Seth had told her about the altercation in school, but there was still the issue of what had happened between her and Seth the other night.

Self-consciously, she lifted her fingers to touch her lips. They still felt as though they were tingling, just as her body still seemed to be fizzing with something inexplicable.

Fool.

That was why she'd suggested the huge public park. Not only was it a public space, but her family would be around. She couldn't make a fool of herself here, surely?

Striding down the path, her eyes still alert for Seth, Andrea rounded the little bend to take in the beauty of the miniature lake and felt her chest ease a little. It didn't matter how many times she saw it, the pretty sight always seemed to make her smile, complete as it usually was with ducks and their ducklings. Today, a handful of couples also dotted the view, out on the water in little punts, cocooned in their romantic bubbles, and she felt a strangely unexpected pang of envy. She struggled to catch herself.

Hadn't she got over the idea of false romance a long time ago?

Even her mother had noticed her odd frame of

mind when they'd been doing the daily physio that
Maureen Perkins needed to help her MS. Today had
been a harder day—the last few months things had
been getting progressively harder, if she was honest—and it was clear that her mum really needed
more help.

Perhaps being evicted by her current flatmate,
however nicely, was the push she needed to find
somewhere a little bigger which she could share
with her mother. A place that would allow her to
be on hand more for her, even if that meant being
further away from Baystone and work.

Maybe fate would smile on them and she would
find a new place that would make it easier for her
mum to manoeuvre herself, instead of the tight corners she was trying to negotiate now. Somewhere
with wider hallways and doors, lower light fittings
and an accessible shower.

But all that took money, and they didn't have
enough. Love might always have been plentiful
in the Perkins household, before and after her father's death, but after his death money had become
an issue.

Her mother had always worked—she still
worked now—because she was a fighter and
because she'd always insisted on it, despite her
illness. But, with only one income and two growing kids to feed, one income hadn't stretched far.
When her brother had grown up and moved out, it
had eased the strain; and when Andrea had grown

up, and begun her nursing career, her second income had been a life saver.

If she decided to leave her job, and didn't simply walk into a new one, they might have to survive on her mother's income alone. At least her brother's work meant that he was now back in Baystone full-time, with his family. It was all additional help that made Andrea feel like the responsibility wasn't hers alone.

'Andrea.'

Seth's rich voice halted her in her path as she jerked her head up to see him heading towards her, looking as sinfully handsome as ever—and she felt instantly wrecked. Though, she derived a modicum of satisfaction that he faltered when he saw her, just for a split second.

So much for her idea about coming here to remind herself of the easy, professional relationship they'd once had. Rather, all she could think about was the other night. The way he'd felt and tasted. The way he'd tasted her.

'Hello, Seth,' she managed.

Seeing him at work had been one thing, but meeting him here was something altogether more nerve-racking. He affected her far too much.

Instead, she concentrated on the little boy walking next to him.

'Hi, Noah, I'm really happy you're here. Billy and the twins can't wait to see you again.'

She smiled, relieved when Noah glanced up at her and offered a shy smile.

'Come on, I'll introduce you to my family.'

'That sounds great, right, buddy?' Seth encouraged cheerfully, falling into step as she made her way back to where they'd set up their picnic.

For the next half hour or so, Andrea watched as Seth easily charmed her sister-in-law, before launching into a game of quasi-football with all four children, as well as her delighted brother.

She wasn't sure what she'd expected but it hadn't been for Seth to fit into her extended family's dynamics so seamlessly. Andrea had to school herself not to feel that punch of delight that he'd achieved in thirty minutes what Josh had never managed during multiple family events.

And then, at last, Seth excused himself from the game and made his way over to her.

'I was thinking that we could maybe take a walk?' He lowered his voice, though no one was around. 'Talk about Noah?'

'Sure.' She nodded, trying valiantly to ignore her sister-in-law's conspicuous thumbs-up.

'Perhaps we could walk around the lake I saw on the way in, if the path continues all the way?'

'You've never been here before!' she exclaimed before she could help herself.

'I haven't.'

'It's literally between your penthouse and the hospital, which is why I suggested it.'

He offered her a grim look.

'Which no doubt makes it all the more pitiable that I haven't been here, but no less true, I'm afraid.'

'Right. Sorry. I just thought maybe you'd been here in the early days, with Stacey and Noah?'

The muscles in his face pulled taut.

'Not even then,' he confessed uncomfortably. 'Clearly I was a pretty lousy uncle and brother.'

'That wasn't what I was implying.' Andrea felt instantly guilty. 'It doesn't matter. I was just…surprised, that's all. It's a popular place.'

'So I can see,' he agreed. 'Although, I can't say I can imagine you being one of those people to take a romantic row out on some lake.'

She never had been, as it happened. Yet for some reason she found herself bristling uncharacteristically at the dryness in his tone.

'You're saying you don't think anyone would want to do something romantic with me?'

She could have kicked herself, especially when Seth emitted a less than amused laugh.

'That isn't what I'm saying, no,' he clarified. 'I'm just not a fan of romance, personally. I find it gets in the way of practicality. You always gave the impression you felt the same.'

She probably had, Andrea realised, thinking about the few romantic gestures Josh had ever made, and how hollow they seemed when she thought about the way he had treated her the rest of the time.

'I guess,' she answered flatly. 'I used to think I would love to be romanced. Now I realise it can just be a way of getting away with treating the other person like dirt. Like doing something wonderful for them on their birthday yet treating them badly for the rest of the year.'

She regretted her words the instant she felt his piercing gaze on her. She had no intention of revealing her pitiful past to anyone, least of all Seth.

'Personal experience?'

'No, of course not.' It was all she could do to feign nonchalance as they fell into step alongside each other and began an easy walk around the shimmering water. She reached around for something more positive to say. 'I was four when we moved to the area. My parents were always doing fun, romantic things.'

'Like rowing out on that lake?'

'Actually, that was one thing they missed. My father promised my mother they would on their tenth anniversary, but then he died and…' She tailed off, shaking her head.

Seth was watching her very carefully and she was scared he could read too much.

'So she hasn't ever been?'

'My brother has been trying to take her out ever since—I know he'll try again today—but she always politely declines. She says it's a lovely idea but that it isn't the same.'

'Your mum isn't here yet, though?'

'No.' Andrea bit her lip as though to keep in the truth that she had never told anyone at Baystone before. She hesitated. 'Mum was meant to be here earlier, but today's...a bad day. Hopefully she'll make it later.'

His gaze raked over her again.

'Bad days from what? Is that why you think you have to walk away from the conversion degree?'

Whether it was the fact that she knew so many of Seth's secrets, or whether it was the simple fact that it was Seth himself, she found the words slipping out anyway.

'My mum has MS. I've been helping to care for her ever since I was eight years old.'

CHAPTER NINE

'YOUR MUM HAS MS?'

Andrea nodded stiffly, wondering what on earth had possessed her to utter the words. It wasn't something she told that many people. She certainly couldn't believe she'd told Seth.

Turning awkwardly, she moved jerkily along the path, resuming their lake walk as though it was no big deal. But everything was still tumbling around her head.

'So you're still her carer.'

'We pay someone to come in a couple of times a week, when she needs it. She's a warrior, and you'll never hear her complain, but we both know that MS is an unsympathetic disease.'

He nodded, but his too-shrewd gaze bored into her all the same, locking her in place. She was suddenly afraid that he was able to read a whole raft of secrets that she'd always hugged so close to herself.

'When you were telling me about your brother's selective mutism, you said it happened after your father had died in a car crash,' he continued when she didn't answer, and she realised that he was racing back through all those tiny snippets of personal information she'd reluctantly dropped in the past week.

'Yes,' she muttered, because what else could she do but confirm what he already knew?

She could practically see him piecing a jigsaw together, slotting all the scraps together with his super-speedy brain.

It was impressive and terrifying all at once. Not least because the last time he'd looked at her so intensely had been that night in his penthouse. And look what that had led to...

At the memory, her body gave a delicious, involuntary shiver, as if it had simply been waiting for the chance to relive the experience.

God help her, was that why she'd so readily invited him to her family picnic—just for the excuse to spend more time with him outside the hospital, lines and boundaries be damned?

'You also mentioned that the reason it lasted six months in your brother's case was because there were additional complications.' Seth dragged her back to the less than thrilling conversation. And, despite everything, she couldn't help feeling surprised he remembered. 'By which you meant your mother's MS?'

Did she answer, or did she shut the conversation down?

'Yes,' she admitted a beat later.

'So her MS has always been quite severe?'

Andrea opened her mouth then closed it again. She needed to weigh up exactly what she was going to say next.

'Not always.' She inhaled deeply. 'Before Daniel's birth, she didn't even know.'

'Daniel's older than you?'

'Younger. When she was pregnant with me, she suffered a little with fatigue and discomfort, but nothing that really threw up red flags, and no one was looking for MS. After I was born, apart from a difficult couple of months, the symptoms subsided again.'

'Ah. So it went back to some semblance of normal until the second pregnancy?'

'Pretty much. With Daniel, her symptoms were more pronounced. The pain was more intense, and she suffered a lot with weakness of limbs and dizziness.' She only had vague memories of this time. 'By the time Daniel was born, she was showing more signs of muscle spasticity.'

'And this time they made the MS diagnosis?'

She nodded.

'Yes, there was more to go on by then. Mum has always been very strong and determined. She refused to let it control her life and she kept her job going. She still had flare-ups, but Dad was her main carer, and they worked together to try to ensure it didn't affect Daniel or I.' She closed her eyes for a split second. 'Then Dad died in the crash.'

'I'm sorry.' Seth's low voice rumbled through the air. She couldn't have said why, but she felt that he would have given anything to spare her that memory.

It was enough to steel her again.

'After he died, everything changed,' she contin-

ued. 'More for me than for Daniel. I was eight, but
I had to become Mum's carer whenever she was
having a relapse. I started being late for school, or
missing days altogether when Mum needed help
to get up and showered. Or I had to take care of
my younger brother, either because he'd stopped
talking and the school wanted Mum to go in and
explain what was happening, or simply because
someone needed to cook the family meal. Mum
hated that she had to rely on me, but what else
could she do?'

'I'm sorry you had to go through that.'

He sounded touchingly sincere.

'Thank you.'

'It certainly explains some things,' he murmured.

She wasn't sure whether it was more for himself
than her, but it piqued her curiosity all the same.

'Things like what?'

He eyed her for a moment.

'Like why someone as bright, as ambitious and
as keen as you never tried to become a surgeon
yourself, or even a doctor.'

'That's how you see me?'

The question was out before she could stop herself. Being a doctor had always been her secret
dream, but she'd never, ever voiced it to anyone.
The idea that someone like Seth could imagine her
achieving it was ridiculously gratifying.

'That isn't how you see yourself?' he challenged
quietly.

She couldn't bring herself to tell him about her marriage. About how she'd allowed her egotistical ex to slowly squeeze every ounce of self-confidence she'd ever had.

It was too shameful.

'As a young kid, I used to want to be a doctor,' she admitted. 'I thought I could be the kind who fixed people like my mum. Dad always encouraged me and I got good grades. But when I became Mum's sole carer it was enough to look after my younger brother and the house. Homework fell by the wayside and my grades suffered. After that, it was never an option.'

'You still did well for yourself. I can't think of many people who could carve out a career as a head scrub nurse, having had to sacrifice so much of their childhood and education to be a child-carer,' he pointed out, as though it was obvious.

But it wasn't obvious. She'd spent most of her life feeling as though she'd fallen short. And Josh's disdain for her job had only further damaged her self-confidence. As though he'd had any kind of measure of success. What a fool she'd been for allowing him that power over her.

'And, as you grew older, your brother couldn't help? Allow you to go back to school and get the grades you needed?'

'Daniel got a job on an oil refinery. He was away for months at a time, but his job paid very well, and he sent much of it back home to help with Mum.'

'Even when he got married?'

'Yes.'

She didn't add that her own ill-conceived marriage had cost her money, bailing Josh out from his many gambling debts as she had over the years they'd been together.

Nor did she allow a voice to that tiny part of her that had always wondered if part of her brother's monthly offerings had been guilt money to salve his conscience over leaving her alone to help their mother all these years.

Not that she didn't love her fierce, determined mum with all of her heart. But, even though she didn't say any of this to Seth, she couldn't shake the suspicion that when he looked at her he could read all too much of it for himself.

'I did try once. Along with my wages and Mum's, Daniel's money gave us enough to get someone in once every week or two and let me go back to an adult learning college when I was about twenty.' Andrea forced a smile. 'But after the first month Mum woke up one morning to find she was having a relapse, and that was it; I couldn't go. I couldn't leave her.'

'And that's also why you can't do the conversion degree now.'

Regret washed through her.

'Exactly. It would demand so much time and money. I simply can't guarantee either. But you didn't come here to talk about my mum.' She gave herself a mental shake. 'You came to talk about Noah.'

She thought that Seth might have grunted a little but at least they were off difficult conversations and onto the point of why he'd asked to meet her.

'I'm asking if there's anything else you know of to help speed things up with getting Noah back to talking. After what happened in school this week, it's clear that his refusal to communicate is causing issues and stopping him from making friends.'

Andrea raked her hand through her hair. Her heart went out to both the little boy and the man walking alongside her.

'I wish I could help speed things up, but I can't. Noah just needs to go at his own pace and you're going to have to find a way to make him feel comfortable communicating with you.'

'He doesn't want to talk to me. Yet he talked to you within minutes of meeting you,' Seth pointed out, his frustration palpable. 'He talked to your nieces and nephews, too. He even told them the name of his bear.'

'Because he felt comfortable and happy. As ironic as it may be, since he doesn't talk to you, he probably felt more secure talking to us simply because he knew you were there.'

'I'm afraid that *secure* is the last thing I seem to make him feel.'

'Not necessarily.' She shook her head. 'You're the one person who has been stable in his life since his mother's death, but at the same time maybe you're the one he has come to associate with her loss. Even so, it's still possible that he feels safer simply by you being there.'

'I wish I knew that.'

'It is possible. You just have to give it time.'

'I don't have time,' Seth bit out before shaking his head in apology. 'I told you about his paternal grandparents fighting me for custody.'

Andrea nodded as it began to slip into place.

'You said that he doesn't talk to them either.' She nodded. 'And that they're arguing that's only due to them not having had any contact before now, hence why Noah would ultimately be better with them.'

She couldn't put her finger on why, but she was certain that, if Noah had connected easily with his paternal grandparents, and if he was happy to be with them, then Seth would have agreed to them having care of Noah after all. She'd never known Seth to have a false ego.

'I worry that they're right,' he confided. 'Yet, though I feel compelled to honour my sister's will, it concerns me that Noah hasn't spoken to anyone in almost a month—until your family.' A shadow skittered through his golden-brown eyes but otherwise Seth kept his voice even, low, like a surgeon delivering the worst kind of news to a patient's family. 'When my sister was alive, I remember him being a bright, confident kid; he always seemed to do well in school and he had plenty of friends.'

'This was when they lived with you?'

'No, afterwards. He was always a happy baby, though they left my apartment when Noah was eighteen months. Even so, Stacey brought him for a week at Christmas and a week or two in the summer.' Seth lifted his shoulder in self-censure. 'I was often working, but we did spend some time together, and they always looked to be having a good time. Noah adored his mother, and she adored him.'

Andrea's heart twisted. She had been so close to her own father before his death, so it was only too easy to imagine what was going on in Noah's head right now. But at least she'd had her mother. And her brother—however badly he'd taken it. They'd still been a unit. A family.

Noah had lost the only parent he'd known, shipped off to an uncle he'd not seen very much and might not even really remember well. No wonder he wasn't talking.

'I really think you need a proper medical professional, and qualified speech and language therapist.' She felt oddly helpless.

'He has one. He saw her again yesterday and he didn't say a word to her,' Seth told her. 'For whatever reason, he trusts you. And your family. I could hand-pick the best professionals in the country, but it's you who he wants. Who *I* want.'

She told herself it was the gravelly timbre of his voice that was causing all that strange sloshing inside her—and not the fact that those words could be interpreted so differently.

'The other night…' she began, but Seth cut her off.

'We crossed a line the other night—*I* crossed a line—and for that I can only apologise. And assure you that it won't happen again. I just want you to help Noah.'

'All right,' she answered softly, automatically; not at all sure what she was agreeing to. 'I'll try to help, but I can't guarantee anything.'

'I'm not asking for guarantees. I just want you to try.'

'Right.'

She thought of the little boy in question. Seth was right—this was about Noah, not about them. No matter that her thoughts—and her body—seemed to go haywire whenever Seth was around.

She simply couldn't fail to connect with him. Seth might have assured her that he wasn't looking for a guarantee, but she knew so much riding on it that the prospect was almost daunting.

'And when you say you don't have much time, how much time are we talking?'

Seth's expression pulled tight.

'We're due for another court assessment next week. If I could just show them we've made some progress, even the tiniest bit, then it would buy me another week or two. I just want to see my nephew somewhere like back to his old self. He'll still process his mum's death in his own way, but at least he'll be able to talk to people. And at least he won't have the additional weight of being bullied because other kids can't understand why he won't speak.'

She understood that—more than Seth could know.

The question was, how could she best connect with Noah?

'We could try more places like the other day.'

At least they would be public places and not back at his penthouse. Anything to keep her mind from what had happened the other night. More to the point, how much more she'd *wanted* to happen, had they not been interrupted.

'Like the play centre?' He grimaced.

'I thought you half-enjoyed that in the end!' She hadn't meant to laugh. It just bubbled out of her at the memory.

He offered a half-sheepish look.

'I did. In the end.'

But the look he sent—however fleeting—made her breath catch in her chest.

Then he blinked and it was gone.

'Public places, then,' he agreed tightly.

For the little boy's sake, she had to set aside her private feelings for Seth, and complications with this particular man was something that she didn't have the time or energy for. Especially not now.

Yet, every time she thought about what had happened between them the other night, she worried that she couldn't trust herself around him at all. Since when had she ever acted so impulsively?

This was why, whatever else happened, she was determined that she wasn't going to set foot in Seth Mulder's penthouse ever again.

She is astonishing.

That was the only thing Seth could think as he watched Andrea move elegantly down the stairs in his penthouse from where she'd been wishing Noah goodnight.

As if she belonged.

Irritably, he chased the errant thought from his brain and wondered what was wrong with him.

Of course she didn't *belong* here; she shouldn't even be here. She was a work colleague, not a date. Aside from fellow surgeon and friend, Jack, no other colleague had ever been invited into his home.

True, his life had been completely turned on its head with Noah's arrival. Also true, the lines between professional and personal were a little blurred at the moment as he attempted to navigate this new situation, but he really shouldn't keep losing sight of the fact that Andrea wasn't even here for him.

Rather, she was here for that little boy upstairs who she'd clearly been tucking into bed. And he was grateful for her presence—not least after his fear back at the park that she had no intention of visiting his apartment again after the other night. But somehow, after offering to drop her mum home, it was where she'd ended up.

'Did he go to sleep okay?'

'Seth, I didn't hear you come in.' What did it say about him that he got a kick out of the way she startled? Then her urvilleana eyes momentarily darkened before she pulled down those shutters. 'Yes, I think he was asleep before his head even hit the pillow.'

Seth nodded, relieved. Though he shouldn't be surprised; he got the impression Noah would happily take Andrea over him any time.

He watched as she descended the rest of the stairs and crossed the room, stopping a safe distance from him. It was as though she was afraid to get too close for fear of a repeat of the last time she'd been in his penthouse.

He couldn't say he blamed her. Not when the very air seemed to crackle in the room around them.

'Thank you for driving my mum home this evening,' she managed, her voice cracking slightly with the tension. 'You didn't have to.'

He didn't point out that, with Daniel's car full with his family, and Andrea's mother clearly unable to fold herself easily into her daughter's little car, it had seemed like the only sensible solution. He certainly hadn't liked the idea of her waiting for a wheelchair-friendly taxi, as she'd arrived in.

'I wanted the excuse to test out my new car anyway.' He tried to play it down. 'It's a different feel, being in a four-by-four to my previous car.'

'I can imagine.' A wry smile tugged at her soft mouth and his eyes followed the movement. 'But you still didn't have do it, just like you didn't have to row her across the lake.'

'It was nothing.' This time he dismissed Andrea's gratitude, feeling oddly embarrassed.

'Actually, it wasn't,' she continued softly. 'You made her laugh more than I've seen her laugh in a long time. Consequently, I think my sister-in-law is about ready to divorce my brother to marry you, and my brother is more than happy to let her. You made my whole family happy.'

'I'm glad they're happy,' Seth replied. 'Though I have to say that I didn't do it for them. I didn't even think about them, really. I did it for you.'

Her mouth opened into a perfect O, but she didn't speak. Instead, that now-familiar, pretty blush started in her cheeks and stole down over her neck...and lower.

He wondered how much lower before he was hastily forced to shut down the deliciously naughty image that had instantly invaded his brain.

It was ridiculous how easily she made him feel like some hormone-fuelled teen.

Boundaries.

He shouldn't have to keep reminding himself that Andrea Perkins was his colleague just to keep those sinfully sexy images from assailing his brain. What was it about her that kept making him forget his rules, his code? Did he really have to keep reminding himself that perhaps if his father had believed in that same code then his childhood, and Stacey's, would have been so very different?

They would have felt wanted, loved and safe— the way that his sister had been determined her son should always feel. The way he now owed it to Stacey to ensure Noah always would. The way that Andrea made the little boy feel…. He was beginning to understand that.

The reason Noah talked when Andrea was around because he felt safe with her there. Therefore, the more Andrea was around, the more secure the little boy would be.

Which meant…what?

'Did he say anything?' Seth couldn't keep the gruffness out of his voice as his brain whirred with only half-formed ideas.

Hardly a state of mind he was accustomed to.

'He whispered that he had a good time and asked me to tell you goodnight,' she murmured softly, crossing the room to where he stood in the kitchen area, only to hover there, as though uncertain whether to sit or leave.

He ought to encourage her to do the latter.

'Coffee?' He found himself reaching for his eye-wateringly expensive machine before she shook her head.

'Thanks, but I try to avoid it after seven p.m.'

Which they both knew was an excuse—if a sensible one.

'Probably wise,' he acknowledged, and then poured himself a mug anyway—possibly more for something to occupy his hands than anything else.

Because, despite his own private self-admonishment earlier, whenever he looked into those incredible eyes, each time he was drawn to that sensuous mouth—or, worse, every time he let his gaze slip to the lushness of her mouth-watering body—it belied every word he managed to utter.

It was getting harder and harder to keep all his boundaries straight in his head. Especially today, when he hadn't seemed to be able to take his eyes off her. It could have been the carefree, fun way she'd played and interacted with her family, or it could have been those endless legs that lay beneath the summery dress.

He suspected it was a little of both—and he should probably be more ashamed of his apparent inability to control his lust. But every time he saw Andrea a tautness wrapped itself around him and began to tug, slowly but surely, until he believed he might fracture and shatter if he moved to be with her.

It was nonsensical, really. Since when had he ever lusted after any woman like this? She wasn't even his usual type.

She wasn't lithe-like, as were most of the women

he'd dated recently. Yet, despite the fact she was clearly toned, she boasted soft, subtle curves in all the best places. Curves that made his hands itch with the desire to reach out and touch her. To trace every glorious contour.

Every time she'd laughed with her nieces, he'd had to pretend that he didn't feel the sound winding right through him, curling sensually around his insides.

It was nonsensical the way she had him reacting like some kind of untrained schoolboy. His body was hard and ready before he could even turn round. He'd never felt so out of control before. *Never.*

And then, as if to prove his point, Andrea slid elegantly onto the stool at the breakfast bar and his mouth instantly went dry. He couldn't have said what it was about the movement that affected him, but he couldn't seem to drag his eyes from her long, lean legs. A far cry from her in the shapeless scrubs that she usually wore in his company.

He fought valiantly to regroup but his tightening body apparently had other ideas. And maybe he would have acted on it under other circumstances. The worst of it was that he knew the attraction certainly wasn't one-sided.

She might have her own set of lines that she didn't cross, but Seth could read her desire for him in every hot glance she cast his way when she caught herself off-guard. Could read it in the

way her pulse beat that little bit too wildly when
he stood close to her, and the way each time she
swayed instinctively into him before reining herself back.

As it was, he kept reminding himself that she
was here because he'd asked her to help him with
Noah. And he couldn't do anything to jeopardise
that.

Noah, he reminded himself quickly. The reason
she was even here.

She splayed her hands on the granite countertop
as though she was also trying to pull herself back
in check. 'I think the most significant part, though,
is that he is now talking to you again.'

'It is.' Seth bowed his head in acknowledgement.

That had come like a punch to the chest, knocking all the air out and leaving him paralysed for
what had felt like a lifetime. His nephew had finally
talked to him at the picnic. Right *to* him, looking
him straight in the eye and speaking a full sentence.

It was almost too good to be true. And he had
this woman to thank for it.

But what would happen if she left Baystone
the way she'd said she might have to? Would his
nephew regress again, like yesterday?

So don't let her go.

The thought slammed into his brain, harder than
a racquetball and just as impactful—a wild idea
that perhaps there was a way they could help each

other. He slid his hands into his pockets as if that could somehow silence himself.

The force of the attraction was crazy. And thrilling. And entirely inappropriate. Which was precisely why it would be a good thing for his haywire libido if she were to leave Baystone Medical. The thoughts flip-flopped in his head.

What was best for him versus what was best for Noah.

He might value his standards and rules, but Andrea was the first person to whom Noah had opened up. It was clear that the lad was beginning to blossom due to her presence, like a sapling reaching for the sun.

Would his little nephew wilt again if she suddenly disappeared?

He couldn't risk it, Seth told himself.

'How's the flat hunt going?' His mouth seemed to formulate the words all on their own.

She scrunched her nose.

'It isn't,' she admitted.

Reluctantly, he thought.

Because she didn't want to leave? Or because she thought this was none of his business?

'Now I know that you declined my suggestion of your HCP-med degree more out of familial obligation than out of *time and money,* as you suggested, I believe I have a workable solution.'

What did it say that he liked the flash of fire in

her eyes that reminded him that Andrea wasn't at all intimidated by him. Far from it.

'You don't understand the situation,' she bit out.

'Having seen where your mum is currently living, I can see that it might have been okay at one time, but that her needs have changed since her MS has progressed.'

'Then you'll understand that I can't afford to drop back to part-time work to allow for all the studying that the degree requires.' Evidently she was trying to appear logical rather than frustrated, but she didn't quite succeed, and it was clear how much she secretly wanted that degree. 'I need to work full-time and use that income—as well as anything Daniel can spare—to get my mum into a better place. Somewhere that has a wheelchair-accessible shower and lower kitchen counter-tops, for starters.'

'Which is why I propose your mum moves into my late sister's apartment on the other side of town,' he suggested calmly—though with a surprising undercurrent of triumph. 'My name was on the lease, so it has come to me now, and I was going to keep it as an investment for Noah. It a spacious ground-floor apartment with dedicated parking.'

'Well, yes, that's great. But I don't think…'

'It has a pretty, low-maintenance garden.' He deliberately ignored her interruption. 'And it would easily lend itself to being modified for your mum with the accessible shower and countertops that you mentioned. Whatever she needs.'

'I don't have the money for that!' Andrea exclaimed.

'You don't need to. I'll cover the costs. Plus, it's three-bed, so enough room for your mum, for a carer whenever they need to stay and for you when you eventually move back in.'

'When I *eventually* move back in?' Andrea peered at him. 'Where will I be until then?'

It shouldn't have felt like trump card—but somehow it did.

'Until then,' he told her calmly, confidently, 'You could move in here.'

CHAPTER TEN

'OKAY, LET'S START the cortical stimulation, starting at two-point-zero milli-amps, please.'

Andrea observed, fascinated as always, as Seth worked on a low-grade glioma in their patient's right parietal lobe. Her own mind was grateful for something tangible to concentrate on, if only to stop her from dwelling on Seth's shocking offer.

Had it really only been twelve hours ago? It felt like a lifetime.

He wanted her to move in with him.

Well, not *with him* per se, more with Noah. But the entire notion was preposterous.

Wasn't it?

Every time she replayed it in her mind, the sheer shock of it walloped into her. For the longest time, she hadn't answered. She'd waited for him to make a joke. To take it back. He'd almost looked appalled. But he'd looked something else, too. Something that she couldn't name, but that had set off detonations inside her chest. No matter that Seth had made it all sound so rational, so logical—a quid pro quo, with her helping him with Noah, and him giving her a temporary accommodation reprieve.

It all made perfect sense despite the part of her brain still attempting to rationalise what he was suggesting. And, even though she wasn't sure she'd quite processed it, there was a strange, reckless part of her that wanted to agree.

That wanted to leap at the offer.

Though not, she suspected, for the right reasons.

'Andrea.' Seth's voice pulled her up from her thoughts. 'Want to tell us why we're doing this?'

Her face hot, Andrea snapped back to attention.

They'd already been operating for some time, working meticulously from their first incision in the man's front temporal lobe and removing the section of scalp and the dura, to localising all the significant structures inside the brain.

And, as much as she knew they were fighting to save a patient's life, there was an undeniable beauty in what Seth was doing that was almost mesmerising to watch. It made learning from him something like a joy.

So far, she'd already seen how he'd used neural navigation to identify the tumour limits, and now he was mapping the motor cortex and sub-cortex to try to reduce the risk of post-operative neuro-logical deficits.

Guilt weaved through her at allowing herself to be distracted, as well as something else she pre-tended not to understand.

Steeling herself, Andrea stepped forward and answered his question. 'The location of this par-ticular tumour is near the eloquent tissue, so neu-rological deficits could include loss of sensory or motor functions in the patient's face, arms, legs or even cause speech deficits. You've already established the limits of the tumour, as we saw before, and now you're going to map motor functions over multiple assessments using the asleep-awake-asleep method of anaesthesia.'

Whilst they were mapping the involuntary motor functions, the patient would remain under light anaesthesia, but once Seth was ready to map the language centre he would need voluntary functions, so they would wake up the patient.

She already felt more a part of it than she'd ever felt before, so how would it actually feel if she were on a nurse-to-doctor conversion course? Not that she fooled herself that she would ever become a neurosurgeon like Seth, but that had never been her dream. And it was Seth who had given her this new lease of life.

Was she really going to turn down his offer just because she was afraid she was too attracted to him?

Seth wasn't her ex, saying one thing but doing another—he'd been more than clear about the terms of the proposed agreement. It would be somewhere convenient for her to live whilst she found a new flat share, at the same time as helping him to bond with his nephew.

It was that simple. A win-win.

He'd made it abundantly clear that sponsoring her for the HCP-med degree wasn't at all contingent on her decision, assuring her that both Jack and him would provide the references and sponsors. It was like an answer to the prayers she hadn't even dared to say. Like a lottery win…only better.

Because it meant that Seth was so confident in her ability to achieve her long-abandoned dreams that he was actually prepared to put himself out there for her. And just knowing that fact somehow revived a sense of worth in herself that she had thought had been killed off years ago.

If only her insides weren't rioting or aching for something even remotely non-practical about everything he was suggesting… The tiniest hint that a traitorous part of him wanted her there because he still sensed that pull of attraction that had walloped them both that first night.

But of course he didn't want her around for his own personal reasons—something about which she should be pleased.

Something about which she *was* pleased, she silently berated herself.

Seth had been clear on what he wanted from her, and what he was prepared to offer in return. He had set out clear terms. He had end dates. As long as she went into it with her eyes wide open, then how could he ever have the power to make her feel as small, as inconsequential, as Josh had made her feel?

What a time to be learning such hard truths about herself. What a time to realise that she'd let her ex-husband steal more than the money out of

her purse. She'd let him steal her trust in anyone—
but especially in herself.

Shaking her head to empty it of the wayward
thoughts, Andrea dragged her focus back to the patient on the table. She watched Seth meticulously
map his patient's brain, increasing the milliamps
until the cortical stimulation could be recorded, and
keeping the exposed stimulated cortex constantly
irrigated with ice-cold saline solution to minimise
the risk of stimulation-induced seizures. Once he
had localised the motor and sensory areas of the
cortex, he turned his focus on the spatial awareness mapping.

'Okay, Andrea, you're up.'

Her heart pounded with adrenalin as she picked
up the clipboard she'd prepared with a series of
vertical lines drawn on an A4 sheet.

She handed the pen to the patient and waited
whilst Seth's team explained to the man that he
would carry out a line bisection test whilst they
stimulated the inferior parietal lobule cortex. She
felt almost proud when no disturbances were de-
tected and the man's strike-throughs remained
smooth and steady.

And then he began the tumour resection itself.

'We're using microsurgical technique in an attempt to preserve all major vessels, since it's the
best way to avoid stroke in the normal brain tissue
surrounding the tumour,' he advised the room before turning his attention to his resident. 'You can

use the sulci as landmarks to ensure a more precise resection of the more superficial areas of the tumour. Just be aware that the tumour can distort these landmarks at a deeper level, hence the importance of through mapping.'

For several hours, they continued to work on their patient, stopping where normal tissue was encountered or where the neural deficits would have been too significant. This, Seth had warned her in advance, would be the difference between a gross total resection, where he would be able to remove the tumour in its entirety, and a subtotal resection where he would concentrate on removing only the necessary parts of the tumour to alleviate his patient's motor symptoms without creating even greater deficits.

He'd described it as the most delicate balancing act and, being in the OR with him now, she could clearly see why.

But his passion and dedication were inspiring to watch. When she thought about the sheer complexity of the neurosurgery that he did, and coupled it with the way he was more than happy to set his own ego aside and ask her for help with his nephew, it only made her admire him all the more.

And, more treacherously, it would have made her fall for him all the harder—had she been falling for him at all, of course.

Which she wasn't.

She would control that.

She just needed to remember the parameters of their agreement, in the same way that he'd established the parameters of this awful tumour, and not allow herself to get too comfortable, too complacent, living with Seth.

How hard could that be? It wasn't neurosurgery, after all.

Perhaps not, a voice murmured insidiously inside her head.

Because, no matter how piously she tried to claim otherwise, the fact remained that she was ridiculously, undeniably attracted to the man. Consequently, she was horribly afraid that she was letting her heart influence her decision. And surely that made agreeing to his terms—however generous they may be—all the more dangerous?

On the other hand, unless she wanted to leave Baystone and start afresh all over again—which she definitely didn't—then how could she possibly afford to turn him down?

Andrea rode the private lift up to Seth's penthouse two days later. But this time it felt different, and it wasn't just the fact that neither Seth nor his efficient concierge were accompanying her.

She patted the key card in her pocket, as though for reassurance, and clutched her small bag to her. She still wasn't sure that moving into Seth's home was a good idea. Aside from the financial and career aspects, or the fact that she wanted to do everything she could to help little Noah, it was the tell-tale, thrilling tingle that excited her the most. As if, despite all her brain's logical and practical arguments, her heart was entertaining illicit fantasies all of its own.

Well, that stops now, she commanded herself silently, and lifted her chin pugnaciously.

It felt like perfect timing when the lift chose that moment to come to a smooth halt and its doors slid quietly open to face the penthouse's main door.

Throwing her shoulders back and swinging her bag up, Andrea stepped across the floor before swiping her card at the door. The lock turned with an obliging sound, allowing her to push the door open. Even so, it took her another two or three steadying breaths before she could galvanise her legs into action and walk inside.

It felt...different.

The place felt should have felt less intimate in Seth's absence, less intimidating. And perhaps it did indeed feel the former, but it certainly didn't feel less intimidating.

Seth had suggested she take the time to take a proper tour and orientate herself without the pressure of anyone else being there. She realised now that it was probably a good idea.

She knew the way to Noah's room upstairs, and understood that her guest room was the door opposite his. Seth's master suite was apparently at the other end of the apartment, so that was good—there would be no need to venture down his way.

Ever.

The kitchen, dining area and living space downstairs were all as she remembered but, now that she looked around, she noticed a set of double doors on the other side of the front door. Seth's study, as it turned out. And, though he hadn't said that it was off-limits, she resolutely turned her back and refused to give in to some uncharacteristically curious part of herself that seemed to be itching to take a peek. As though the private space might reveal something about its often enigmatic owner... A treacherous part of her was desperate to learn more about Seth.

Determinedly, she turned her back on the doors and took a step back towards the kitchen area, her eyes honing in on two laundry bags behind the front door that she'd missed when she'd first entered, one marked with Seth's name, the other with Noah's.

Was he having the laundry sent out?

Andrea almost laughed aloud. It was so fitting. She couldn't imagine Seth even owning a washing machine, and she certainly couldn't imagine him using it. Then again, why would he need to, when he lived in a place like this? No doubt it was a complimentary service that was all taken care of by the infinitely capable Stan.

A far cry from her own life.

The closest her family had ever got to having

their laundry done for them was when she'd been nine and her mum had been going through a particularly difficult period with her MS. The lady at the local laundrette had told her that, if Andrea put the clothes in the dryer before she left for school, then she would fold them into a bag to collect on her way home again that afternoon.

Andrea crossed the room and picked up the bag containing the little boy's clothes, her hand hovering momentarily over Seth's bag before deciding against touching it. Then she headed upstairs, her low heels echoing loudly in a way she hadn't noticed before, making her feel all the more self-conscious.

On the landing, to the left of the stairs, was a kind of open mini-gallery, and on the right was a chess table which she hadn't noticed the other evening in the low light. Now, she couldn't help but imagine Seth sitting up here and playing a game— perhaps even teaching his nephew. It was surprisingly easy to picture him in this space. It was so *Seth*.

Andrea turned into the short hallway heading straight for Noah's room, but she couldn't prevent her gaze from sneaking to the set of double heavy doors that she knew to be Seth's master suite.

She didn't know why the sight of it now sent a little something rolling along her spine. Or, rather, she didn't want to admit why that happened.

Stuffing the unwelcome emotions back down,

she placed her hand on the handle to the little boy's room and stepped inside. The room was more spacious than it had seemed the other night—arguably bigger than both her bedroom and her mother's put together—and spotlessly clean, with what was clearly a red, blue and white designer nautical theme.

It looked straight out of a catalogue but lacked anything that made it seem personal. Sure, there was a small toy box in one corner, and a few books on a bookshelf, but there were no personal items such as drawings or crafts. And there were no photos—not even of Noah's mother.

Andrea thought of the little home where she'd grown up. It had invariably been full of pictures that she and her brother had drawn, or crafts that they'd made for Mum. Everything had gone proudly onto the fridge, or the walls, or had been propped on dressers.

Her mother's pride in her children had been so unwavering that the rest of it—their father's death, the fact that she needed them to help care for her—hadn't seemed so bad.

Irritation rolled through her. Seth was clearly neat and tidy, with very few knick-knacks and no clutter around his home. But that didn't mean Noah ought to live according to those standards. It was a conversation she intended to have with Seth as soon as possible, she decided as she busied herself with putting the fresh laundry away.

A few minutes later, quietly closing the doors behind her, Andrea made her way back out to the hallway, deliberately not looking towards Seth's master
suite. It was as though she was frightened of the
fantasises that would assail her if she did. Such as
the memories of what had happened between them
both only a few nights before: the image that filled
her head every night, right before she fell asleep.

But, in those fantasies, it never stopped at just
that.

So instead she headed for a wide single door
back down the hall, which Seth had mentioned to
her, and edged tentatively inside.

It was like a mirror image of Seth's room, except white sheets covered this queen-sized bed,
and there were paintings on the wall. The modern
splashes of colour brightened the space and made
it feel a little more welcoming, even if they weren't
precisely her taste.

Moving across her new room, Andrea peered
through another door to reveal a generous *en suite*,
complete with gorgeous roll-top bath which begged
to be filled with hot, bubble-laden water.

Yet another door led her into a walk-in closet
that had to be bigger than the bedroom she'd had
in her last flat share.

She defiantly ignored the snide voice in her head
warning her not to get used to it; reminding her that
in less than two months she would be out of Seth's
apartment and into her new flat share.

Back to real life.

But, for now, she was here. The first thing she would do would be to cook her new charge something from scratch—if Seth was sending his laundry out, she imagined he was feeding his nephew on the most expensive takeout in the city—and then she would tackle Seth about the bedroom décor.

Andrea hurried down to the kitchen, already mentally preparing a shopping list as she opened the fridge to check its presumably scant contents.

She stopped abruptly, staring in surprise, just as Seth came through the penthouse door with Noah in tow.

'Andrea!'

The little boy's cry of delight had her closing the fridge door and swinging round quickly, hoping that Seth wouldn't see her guilty expression as she levelled a bright smile at the little boy.

'Hey Noah, I hope you had a great day in school.'

Nodding vigorously, the six-year-old held up a poster for her to admire.

'Wow, "the life cycle of penguins",' she read aloud. 'This is excellent; did you do this?'

Another enthusiastic nod.

'Well, I think it's brilliant, Noah. I wonder if we should perhaps hang it on the fridge? Or on the wall in your bedroom? Show it off a little?'

'Yes,' Seth agreed loudly, making them both jump.

Was it her imagination or was this a chink in

his usually calm, unflappable demeanour? Did she see relief chasing through those impossibly handsome features?

'Yes?' she echoed before she could stop herself.

'I think hanging it is a great idea. I think I might have some tacks in my office. Noah, why don't you get changed out of your school uniform whilst I go and find them?'

And then, before she could say anything, Noah gambolled off up to his room whilst Seth turned quickly for his study. For a split second, Andrea hesitated, and then she followed Seth across the hallway.

'Was that eagerness because you want to see him hang the work in his room?' she asked as soon as she was sure Noah was out of hearing. 'Or because you didn't want to see him hang the work on the fridge?'

Seth looked up at her.

'I thought it would be good to begin to make his bedroom his own,' he answered simply.

'Right.'

She thought of the empty room and the questions only pushed harder against her brain. She couldn't have said why she bit them back.

'If you want to know why there are no pictures on the walls, you can just ask,' Seth suggested mildly.

Perhaps a little too mildly.

She couldn't help feeling wrong-footed. It was a

strange feeling when she was normally so careful never to say anything that could offend.

'Right.' She licked her lips. 'Why is Noah's room relatively empty?'

Carefully, he indicated a couple of large crates in the corner of the office behind the door.

'Both are full of the personal belongings I had packed up from my sister's apartment. They contain Noah's toys, artwork, anything Stacey had which I thought he might like.'

'Oh.'

'I hung up pictures from his old bedroom and I set up photos of him with Stacey that had been around her apartment. But when I went in the next morning he'd taken them all down and put them into the bottom of his toy box.'

'And you couldn't ask him why because he wasn't talking to you,' she realised with a thud.

He twisted his wrist upwards in acknowledgement.

'My best guess was that the pictures I chose reminded him too much of his life with Stacey. I figured he wasn't quite ready, and I didn't want to upset him further by pushing the subject.'

'You've been allowing him space to adjust to his new life in his own time.' She exhaled heavily. 'And you didn't put those crates into storage because you want them on hand the moment Noah might decide he wants something from them.'

'I might be a confirmed bachelor with a certain reputation...' He eyed her with something approaching tight-lipped amusement. 'But I'm not quite as inept with my nephew as you seem to think I am.'

'I didn't...' She could feel the heat rush into her cheeks.

Seth continued as though she hadn't spoken.

'I also enjoy cooking. My grandmother taught me when I was a kid, before she died, and I find it relaxing after long days in surgery. So, contrary to whatever you might have been thinking when you opened my fridge earlier, I have not been feeding my young nephew take-out morning, noon and evening.'

Andrea didn't answer. She didn't think she needed to; she felt her guilt was all too evident in her blooming cheeks. So, instead, she watched as Seth moved around the desk in the middle of the room, searching for the tacks he'd said he had, and took a moment to gaze around the space.

Like the rest of the penthouse, it was every inch what a confirmed bachelor might have—all dark wood and angular lines. The desk itself was a solidly built piece, fit for a man who looked stronger and more solid every time she saw him. The groaning bookcases boasted works that were clearly well-thumbed and there because they were wanted, rather than simply being there to impress anyone who cared to enter the space.

Her eyes slid to the worn leather chair in one corner of the space. It was a soft, yet utterly masculine affair which made it only too easy to imagine Seth sitting in this room, reading, learning.

As if he wasn't already the most educated man in almost any room he walked into. She could well believe that he would do everything he could to ensure that he learned all he required to do the best for his young nephew. So much for the notorious playboy.

Yes, Seth Mulder was definitely everything that she'd expected him to be.

Yet nothing like she'd expected.

'You do know that you're doing a great job, don't you?' She blew out a low breath.

A fresh jolt of awareness sliced through her at the expression that momentarily crossed his features. And then it was gone, replaced by one that was far harsher.

'I think my nephew might beg to differ,' he bit out.

'Kids are more resilient than parents often give them credit for.' Even to her own ears it sounded trite.

Seth's disdainful expression confirmed it.

'I'm well aware of that fact; I see it every day with my patients. But this is my nephew I'm talking about. I need to be there for him. Like I should have been there for my sister. If I had been...'

The sheer pain in his expression sharply cut into her, sucking the air from her lungs.

She knew that pain, that sense of loss, only too well.

'You can't go down that path.' She waved her hand, as though she could magic all that hurt away for him. 'Those arguments aren't relevant. The point is, you're here for Noah now.'

He looked as if he wanted to argue, but instead he dipped his head curtly.

'I am,' he ground out. 'But I still need your help.'

The bleak expression on his face had turned his usually animated eyes to a dull grey, as though the life and light had dimmed. It wasn't, Andrea realised abruptly, a look that she wanted to see on this usually dynamic man.

He was more complex, more wounded, than she had ever known.

All these years she'd thought she was seeing the real Seth, but she hadn't known him at all. And now she realised she would give almost anything so be the one to heal him.

'Come on,' she called out with deliberate cheerfulness. 'Let's get Noah and get out of here for a few hours.'

'Where are we going?'

Seth sounded dubious but she was gratified to note that he was obeying her.

'I've no idea.' She grinned at him suddenly. 'But somewhere fun.'

CHAPTER ELEVEN

THE FOLLOWING DAYS bled into weeks as Seth—still adjusting to living with his nephew—also began to adjust to having Andrea there.

He'd been prepared for the transition to be difficult, expecting to stay at the hospital more often than not, if only to give the two of them space. It was more than clear to him that Noah found Andrea's presence far easier to deal with than his own.

But, in the end, that didn't happen.

Andrea dragged them out on an almost a nightly basis, making it clear that she thought they would bond better on neutral ground rather than in Seth's apartment. And she was right: Noah was beginning to communicate more and more easily with every passing day. From swimming lessons to football in the park, and from racing remote-control boats on the lake to visiting the local petting farm, Andrea constantly engineered ways to help Noah and him get to know each other better.

To help the three of them get to know each other better.

Because, the more time they spent together, the more Seth found himself actually looking forward to getting home and seeing what exciting ideas Andrea had in mind for them that day. Though he was beginning to wish he could talk to her in work as freely as he talked to her back at the apartment.

He didn't care to examine what it might mean that the secretive nature of their situation was beginning to grate on him.

Perhaps that was why, tonight, he was taking advantage of Noah's much-demanded first sleepover with the twins and Billy in order to take Andrea out on a child-free date.

No, not *date*, he corrected himself hastily. Just two friends enjoying a meal out a restaurant together. Michelin-starred, of course, since Andrea had once told him she'd never eaten anywhere like that before.

He conveniently ignored the fact that he'd deliberately selected a restaurant that he'd never taken any woman to before—even if that meant having to drive an hour or so out of the city. And the fact that he'd been to his preferred barber for a cut-throat shave and a hair trim two weeks ahead of schedule.

Seth waited until the waiter had left with their orders, then turned to the Andrea. Her eyes were almost violet in the light of the restaurant.

'How is your mum doing?'

As though staying close to neutral topics could stop this dark, hungry thing that had been stalking through him ever since she'd emerged from her room looking like some kind of Hollywood star, in a deceptively simple little black dress that skimmed lightly over her body yet moved with her deliciously.

'Good.' Andrea nodded. 'Excited. The alterations you had carried out will be completed by the end of the week and she'll be moving in after that. So, thank you.'

He lifted his hand dismissively. He didn't want her thanks; he just wanted her to enjoy her degree course, secure in the knowledge that her mum was okay.

'Have you received your HCP-med schedule yet?'

'Not yet,' she answered, the happiness in her soft voice dancing over his skin. 'Next week, I'm told.'

One more week and then he'd lose her from his OR for many of his surgeries. He wasn't relishing it, though he wasn't sure since when he'd come to look forward to working alongside her as often as possible.

'Then we'll call this a pre-emptive, celebratory dinner,' he told her gravely.

She tilted her head, her gaze direct—and the blood quickened within his veins.

'Is that really why we're here?'

He wanted to brush off the question. Instead he heard himself answering, 'We're here because I think you deserve an outing that isn't geared towards a six-year-old for once.'

He was satisfied that 'outing' was a more appropriate term than 'date'. If only he could make his wandering mind remember that. 'And I wanted to thank you for everything you've done and continue to do. Without you, I fear that I would have already lost Noah to his grandparents.'

He didn't add he feared that he still could lose his nephew. That they were still waiting for final decisions with regard to custody.

'No thanks are necessary,' Andrea answered quietly. 'I told you a month ago that you were doing a great job, and I still think that's the case.'

You're doing a great job.

The uncomplicated declaration echoed around Seth's brain, bouncing off the inflexible walls of his skull. Andrea's words meant more to him than they had any right to—if only he could even half-believe them.

'A month ago I felt as though I was drowning in the responsibility of playing father—and mother—to my worryingly stoic little nephew,' he confessed. 'I told myself it was nonsense, since I'd never shied away from my responsibilities to any of my patients as a neurosurgeon. Not even once, no matter how hopeless the operation threatened to be. Yet the role of being a parent was terrifying me in a way that I would never have believed possible.'

'I can't help but wonder if part of being terrified was because you hated the idea of something you weren't good at,' she suggested softly. 'You're so used to being the best in your class—in Baystone, in your field—that the idea of not knowing what you were doing must have been an anathema to you.'

A few weeks ago he would have instantly denied it. Now, he couldn't help wondering if there wasn't at least a grain of truth to it.

'It's possible.' He dipped his head, taking a sip of his wine. It had a delicate flavour that seemed to complement the food and cleanse the palate, just as the sommelier had claimed. 'It has certainly given me a newfound appreciation for everything my sister achieved, all those years as a single parent.'

And it made him feel guiltier than ever that he hadn't helped her out more.

'If Noah gets through this—mind and soul intact,' he managed gruffly, 'It will be despite me, not because of me.'

It was an admission that he would never have expected to hear himself make—not even to his best mate, Jack. But there was a quality about Andrea that had a way of reaching into his very being and drawing the truth out of him.

Even if—right now—she was shaking her head.

'I think we both know that isn't true.'

'Do we?' His voice sounded harsh even to his own ears. 'Because all I know is that, without you around, he wouldn't even be communicating with me right now. The courts may well have already decided that he would be better off with his paternal grandparents, I would have failed Stacey.'

'His reaction to his mother's tragic death isn't a reflection on you. My brother stopped communicating with me—with my mother—and we were in his life every single day. It was simply his way of coping, just as it was Noah's way of coping. I suspect that, if he had been given to grandparents he didn't even know, then the problem would have only manifested even more severely—not less.'

Seth couldn't answer that. But he wanted so much to think that she was right. The more time she spent living at the apartment with them, the more evident it became that she made everything feel…not *lighter* or *brighter*, exactly, but less… dark? Less *heavy*.

Her outlook was more like Stacey's than his.

'You're still doing a great job,' she repeated firmly as his mouth tugged into a rueful smile.

'I think we have different definitions of *great*.'

'Whilst I think you have unrealistically high expectations of yourself,' Andrea countered gently. 'I suspect your sister left Noah in your custody, not because she knew you would instantly be the perfect parent to the person who was clearly the most precious thing in her life, but because she knew she could trust you to do everything you could to learn to be the best version that you could be.'

'Is that why, that first night you'd moved in, you wondered if my fridge contained anything other than beer? And if my nephew's bedroom was supposed to look like some kind of bare prison cell?'

'And I apologise again for that. They were my prejudices rather than yours.' Andrea grinned. 'Consider me re-educated now.'

He still wanted too much to believe her.

'Don't be so quick to vindicate me. There wouldn't even have been photos of Stacey around the place if not for you.'

Even now, he could still remember with vivid clarity how she had challenged him over that, looking incredulous when he'd told her he didn't have any.

'Not even from your childhood together?' she'd pressed several times, until he'd replied darkly how neither he nor Stacey had wanted to remember a lot from that time.

But Andrea hadn't let it go, and ultimately she'd reminded him of several happy memories he'd hidden away, of times he and his sister had spent with their grandmother. And then Andrea and Noah had found a way to access Stacey's old digital photo albums to uncover a pile of childhood pictures of the silvery-haired woman he remembered.

Now his nephew had photos of his mother and great-grandmother to look at whenever he wanted to.

Yet, as grateful as Seth was, it wasn't that which affected him the most. Instead, it was how unperturbed she appeared by everything. As if it wasn't so shocking. As if he wasn't the heartless monster he had felt himself to be since Stacey had died; the one who hadn't done more for his sister when she'd been alive.

Even when she and Noah had lived with him,

he'd managed five minutes or so of listening to her during the evenings he'd bothered to return to the apartment, before sequestering himself in his study in order to watch video after video of surgeries in order to perfect his own techniques. Why had it taken her death for him to regret just how much he'd allowed his work to keep himself too busy for either of them?

How had he ever thought that his career was more important than family? And why had it taken someone like Andrea to make him realise how much of a mistake that had been?

Not someone like Andrea, a whisper floated through him. *Only Andrea.*

Shame punched through him.

'Stop it.'

Her soft voice had him jerking his head up.

'Pardon?'

'Whatever that was.' She circled her hand in the vicinity of his face. 'Whatever you were just thinking. Stop. It won't help you, and it certainly won't help Noah.'

It unsettled him that she seemed to read him so easily—though he suspected not quite for the reasons it ought to. He was accustomed to people deferring to him, both in the hospital and out of it. Patients revered him, staff obeyed him, even dates conceded to him. But Andrea—though always respectful—had never been intimidated by him.

And, since she'd moved into his apartment,

there had never been any veneration or genuflection. She was refreshingly honest—to the point of disapproval.

'Anyway, I have something I want to talk to you about.' She swallowed, looking unexpectedly uncomfortable.

Sliding his hand across the table, he lifted his wine glass and took another sip, wishing it were a crystal brandy balloon containing a couple of fingers of his favourite cognac.

'If you have something to say, Andrea, then say it,' he prompted.

'I was considering brightening the place. Maybe. If you don't object. Perhaps reintroduce a few of those homely touches that your sister used to have?'

'Fine.'

She opened her mouth, as though to further her argument, then stopped.

'Fine?' she echoed. 'It isn't an issue at all for you?'

'I don't know that I'd say *at all*.' He supressed a grin. 'I mean, Stacey had taste. You might not.'

'I have taste!' she exclaimed, reaching across the table to bat her hand against his forearm before she realised what she was doing. 'As for the consequences, I believe your bark is far worse than your bite, you know.'

The electricity crackled straight through him. And, by the way Andrea's muscles froze, her fingers still against the skin of his arm, it crackled through her too.

Move, he commanded himself silently. *Move*.

But he didn't. He couldn't. And it felt as if they both stayed in place for an eternity, their eyes locked, neither of them speaking. Playing the gentleman with this woman was exhausting. He'd far rather play the big, bad wolf that she was pretending she didn't think he was.

He'd far rather show her that his bite could definitely be worse than his bark… With teeth…preferably all over her delectable body.

It was getting harder and harder to remember his rules about not blurring lines. Breaking rules—even his own—was something he'd never done. He'd seen how destructive that could be—watching his mother waste her entire adult life trying to make a selfish, egocentric man into something he could never become. Watching her ignore his sister and him because she hadn't had energy enough for them as well as the man who had fathered them—though had never been any kind of father to them.

That man had been too busy trying to nail anything in a skirt. He certainly wasn't the man that Seth had ever aspired to be. It wasn't part of the deal he'd made with Andrea.

He'd promised not to lay a finger on her. And he didn't break his promises.

Finally, *finally,* he broke the moment and slid his arm back.

'Ah, here comes our waiter...' His voice was more of a rasp than before.

'Oh. Good.' She pulled her own arm back, sounding as dazed as he felt.

For a moment, they both launched into thanking the waiter, as though desperate for something to break the sudden tension. And then the man was gone and they were plunged back into a taut silence.

Seth scrabbled for more prosaic conversation.

'You remember that you're shadowing me on an awake craniotomy the day after tomorrow? It's a surgery I think you'll really enjoy.'

And, when she lifted her cutlery and turned her attention to the exquisite food on her plate, he told himself that he welcomed it.

Andrea wasn't entirely certain how she got through the meal, though it was heavenly.

But somehow the evening seemed to have blurred into two halves—before that white-hot, blindingly bright flame had flared up between her and Seth, and after.

No matter how they'd tried to direct the conversation back to more banal topics, they somehow kept finding their way back to gentle teasing. And if she wasn't mistaken, given her pitted history in the art, flirting.

She suspected it had been happening more and more over the past few weeks, but she'd told herself she was imagining it. Tonight, whether it was the wine or the fact that they were out without Noah as a buffer, Andrea couldn't tell herself again that it was only in her head. No matter how much she tried to pretend otherwise, she was terribly afraid that she was coming to enjoy living with Noah and him that little bit too much.

How many times had she caught herself thinking that the three of them were like a ready-made family? How many times had she berated herself for imagining they could ever be the family she'd thought she would never have?

Without warning, when they rose to go, his hand slid to the small of her back as he escorted her from their table and to the cloakroom. And in a heartbeat her mouth ran dry, though she pretended not to notice.

It was harder to pretend when he ushered her into the buttery leather back seat of the luxurious car that he had ordered to collect them, then moved in alongside her, so deliciously close that his solid, muscular thigh pressed so tightly to her.

The action sent all sorts of dangerously illicit images hurtling through her brain. It felt as though he were the deepest, richest well of every single temptation she'd never before experienced in her life and she was teetering precariously on the edge.

And, if she toppled over it, then she was terribly afraid that she would fall for an eternity.

'I hope you aren't going to go so quiet at the gala this weekend.'

His rich, amused voice snapped her back to the present as she twisted her head to stare at him, her brain still processing the words.

'The gala?' She shook her head, as if that would get it to work faster.

'The medical ball,' Seth clarified. 'The fund-raiser for the main hospital.'

'Oh. Right.' It began to click into place. Then she shook her head. 'No, I'm not attending.'

Seth frowned at her.

'No choice—it's a three-line whip. We might be the private wing but we're expected to support all the same. Don't tell me you haven't attended before? You've been at Baystone for years.'

'I must have always been on shift,' she lied easily.

No reason for him to know that had been because she'd been only too happy to swap her shifts. The idea of attending a gala like that had always been a daunting one. Not least when it came to trying to find a dress that she could afford but that wouldn't make her stand out when she had to rub shoulders with some obscenely wealthy patrons.

She didn't imagine any of them would buy a cocktail dress from a charity shop, like the one she was wearing tonight. She was only grateful that Seth had been so complimentary.

'Besides, three-line whip or not, no one really cares whether a scrub nurse attends.'

'Well, this year I care.' He growled abruptly, sending her into freefall, spiralling downward.

'Don't be silly,' she managed, barely recognising her own voice.

'Whatever traits I may have,' he rasped, 'I don't believe *silly* is one of them.'

She felt flummoxed.

'No. But… I imagine you'll be far too in demand to care who is there,' she hedged.

'So, you imagine me?' His all-male voice wove around her, heating her blood from the inside.

'Sorry? No-no…' she sputtered, horrified, as he seemed closer to her without even moving. 'No, that isn't at all what I said.'

That was *horror, wasn't it?*

His quirky smile fizzled though her, making her feel all the more feverish.

'On the contrary, it's precisely what you said.'

He was definitely closer. Only she couldn't be sure whether Seth had moved, or her. Possibly both.

'I—'

'Perhaps it might interest you to know what I think when I imagine you?' He cut her with a gravelly sound that was like a feather-light stroke in all the places where she was beginning to ache most.

She stared at him for what felt like a lifetime.

'You imagine *me*?'

Was that really her own voice? It was difficult to tell. Difficult even to recognise herself when she felt as though she was being overwhelmed by the raw, unadulterated masculinity that emanated from this man.

Heady and gloriously decadent.

Not least when he reached out and twirled a lock of her hair around his finger, almost lazily, making her breath hitch right there in her chest.

'All too often,' he muttered as she twisted in her seat to face him.

But, no matter how loudly that voice inside her tried to shout that this was a conversation more dangerous than any stunt an adrenalin-junkie could undertake, there was no way to stop all those... emotions within herself from skittering off.

She lifted her hands without even being aware of the movement, compelled by something she didn't fully understand—or want to understand. By the feel of that powerfully built chest beneath her palms, and the faintest hint of his warm breath on her cheek.

So much for telling herself that she could handle tonight and a meal at a Michelin-starred restaurant with Seth Mulder. She'd warned herself against treating it like a date, and yet here she was, practically throwing herself at him in the hope that the evening might turn into something more.

Why?

It was almost a relief when the shrill sound of her phone broke the consuming silence in the car.

Fumbling in her clutch bag, she snatched up her mobile and checked the screen.

The moment between Seth and her disappeared in a flash.

'It's my mother.' Andrea bit her lip.

Her mum knew their restaurant plans, so she wouldn't have called unless there was a problem.

It was ridiculously gratifying when, without needing any further explanation, Seth instantly hit the intercom between the driver and them.

'Change of plan.' He spoke efficiently, before giving her mother's address.

And she tried not to read too much into the fact that he knew it by heart.

CHAPTER TWELVE

'THE MAN WASHED his wife's car,' Andrea read out.

'The man washed his wife's car,' echoed Seth's craniotomy patient, as Andrea noted the results whilst Seth mapped the speech centre of his patient's brain. She worked in harmony with him, as she had always done, without giving any of their hawk-eyed colleagues any reason to know about their new living arrangements.

Or the fact that he'd been the one to take charge the other night when her mum had taken a fall, offering support and a shoulder to cry on.

When was the last time she'd had someone do that for her?

It felt bizarre, and illicit, and unexpectedly thrilling—especially for someone who had spent her life trying to do the right thing.

'Okay.' On Seth's signal, Andrea turned back to her patient. 'Let's try another sentence: "the cat slept in front of the fire".'

'The cat slept in front of the fire.'

'Good, that's great,' she encouraged, pausing for the next signal.

'The rooster crowed at dawn every day.'

'The rooster crowed…day.'

'Great, you're doing well.' Andrea kept her smile bright, even as she knew Seth would be responding on the other side of the curtain.

It was the warning they needed that he was now entering the dangerous, eloquent areas of the brain. If the tumour was here, then he would need to leave it.

'The boy slid down the long, blue slide.'

'The boy…slide.'

'Good,' Andrea repeated, because it wasn't about the patient getting it right. It was about allowing Seth to understand where all the major structures of his patient's brain were located, particularly all the eloquent tissue. She watched as Seth marked out the areas of his patient's brain with a sterile marker.

The amount she'd learned already from Seth was incredible. She'd always found him to be generous with his time as well as with his expertise but, since his promise to sponsor her to undertake the nurse-to-doctor conversion course, he wasn't stinting on the time he afforded her.

'Shall we begin the comprehension section of the test?' she murmured quietly over the curtain.

'Go ahead.' Seth dipped his head as she selected the next set of sheets for the patient.

'All right, you're doing very well.' She smiled another bright smile. 'Could you now try to answer these questions for me?

'Do fish swim?'

The patient hesitated, and Andrea found herself almost willing the woman on.

'Yes.'

With a smile, Andrea noted it on her paper, then waited for her signal.

'Do cars have wheels?'

Another pause, and then the patient uttered a nonsense word. Clearly, Seth was back to a treacherous area of the patient's brain.

For the next half-hour, Andrea continued the tests, meticulously noting the results the way she'd been taught, knowing that, the more complete the map of the patient's brain, the more chance Seth could have of staying out of the danger zones when he went in to resect the tumour.

So far, she'd seen Seth perform these awake craniotomies on musicians as they'd played an instrument, on an opera singer as they'd sang arias and on a radio presenter who'd given them an almost impromptu radio show.

She knew that he had another operation scheduled to help an epilepsy sufferer to try to reduce the number of episodes he was having, once he completed this surgery. Whilst she, for her sins, would be heading off for the gala ball after all.

For no apparent reason, something zapped through her at the prospect of the evening to come, and she couldn't work out if it was fear or apprehension.

At least she'd finally found a dress. Dragged out by her sister-in-law, they'd traipsed into the city to the charity shops that so often offered a stunning find of vintage designer-style dresses which could hardly have been worn more than once, if at all.

Even now, she smiled beneath her surgical mask as she remembered how, she and her sister-in-law had both been drawn to the same rack of striking gowns the moment they'd walked into a particular shop. Clearly a collection donated by someone who had an eye for beautiful designs.

Andrea had gone straight for a stunning burgundy dress with an intricate gold-leaf overlay, whilst Julia had gone for a rose-gold one.

'I might not have a posh gala evening to wear it to,' she'd laughed as she'd swirled it round. 'But I have a feeling Daniel would like to see me in it all the same.'

Andrea had scrunched up her face and feigned an objection.

'That's my brother you're talking about. Too much information.'

But, even as she and her sister-in-law had laughed, Andrea had found it impossible not to wonder what Seth might make of her in such a striking-looking gown. If he would like it. If it would make him forget all his rules and see her the way he had that first night at his penthouse. Not that she wanted a repeat performance, of course, but it would be nice to think he still felt that attraction, the way that she did.

And Andrea might even have managed to convince herself that she really meant that—if only it hadn't been for her perfidious heart tattooing out its very own agitated beat.

Seth knew Andrea had arrived even before he turned to see her at the top of the sweeping stone staircase that led down to the triple-height, vaulting ballroom. He couldn't explain how he felt this growing awareness of her—even before that thorny night—save for the fact it was something about the way his skin suddenly prickled and he felt compelled to turn and look at the double-door entrance on the mezzanine level.

And in that one moment all the air seemed to get sucked out of his lungs. So much for all his stern lectures to himself about maintaining those carefully erected barriers.

Andrea stood at the top of the wide balcony looking more polished, more beautiful, than in any of the dreams he hadn't realised he'd been having.

Her hair was piled on her head and pinned with some intricate gold hair clip, whilst long, glamorous curls tumbled down from one side and tumbled over one semi-bare shoulder, given the way the straps were positioned to fall deliberately half-on, half-off.

He'd spent the past few weeks keeping his distance from her, throwing all his focus into Noah and his patients, and wresting his mind from thoughts of Andrea every time it had threatened to wander. But right now he couldn't seem to drag his eyes or focus away from the vision above him.

He'd had weeks of schooling himself whenever she was around, of finding a way to maintain distance between them even though she was living in his home, yet right now he couldn't find a solitary grain of self-restraint.

Excusing himself from the small group he'd been chatting with, he moved on dazed autopilot to the bottom of the staircase. And then, as she turned her head and bestowed the most dazzling smile to someone he couldn't see, something detonated in Seth's chest.

Something that felt ridiculously like jealousy.

Crazy.

He tried to move away but found himself rooted to the spot. It was surely going to take a damned sight longer for him to compose himself than the time it was going to take her to descend the stairs? If he could have turned, gone back up to the main doors and taken her home so that they could be alone, he would have done.

He wanted nothing more than to wrap her around him and swim in her until he drowned. No matter that he could never be capable of offering a woman like Andrea the kind of family life that he knew she wanted deep down.

Yet, still, he stood there waiting for her to descend the garland-festooned stone stairs.

'Seth.'

His name slid out of her mouth on a whisper, which in turn threaded itself right through him. It weaved through his ribs and spiralled perfectly through his core. And the way her eyes widened only put deliciously wicked ideas in his head of other ways he could make those violet-blue eyes darken in surprise and delight.

'I didn't think you'd manage to get away tonight,' she murmured quietly as she finally reached him.

He liked it too much that her thoughts about the evening had included his presence.

'I'm here,' he replied redundantly. His tongue didn't quite feel as if it was his own at that moment. 'You look...incredible.'

He hadn't thought her face could light up any more until that moment, even as her breath hitched. Something he could only describe as...a hint of possessiveness punched through him.

Mine.

'You think?' she began, then caught herself. 'Thank you.'

It was true enough, of course. Her dress looked like something from the most exclusive designer houses. It was a stunning affair that clung lovingly to her mouth-watering curves before fanning slightly at the knees. It made his arms—and, frankly, other more primitive parts of him—ache with the urge to reach out and test those glorious contours for himself.

'People are staring,' Andrea muttered to him after a moment. 'Are you sure the dress is okay?'

'The dress is stunning.' He lowered his head to her ear as they moved seamlessly together. 'But it isn't the dress they're staring at. It's you. You look radiant.'

And that was what was truly mesmerising about this incredible woman tonight—light seemed to sparkle around her, catching on the gold embellishments of the gown. Yet it was the light that seemed to be pouring out from her very core that was really drawing him in.

But he was already aware that he wasn't the only one who had noticed the vision standing with him. He found he was clenching his teeth so hard that he was shocked his jaw didn't shatter.

'This place is amazing!' Andrea breathed as her eyes darted left and right, up and down, from the sixteenth-century chequered tile floor at their feet, up the sixteen-feet-high columns which stood to attention around the space and to the barrel-vaulted ceiling above their heads.

'It was inspired by the Baths of Caracalla in Rome, though the history is a little potted. Architecture aside, however, let me introduce you to the people you should get to know.'

For the next hour or so, he threw himself into guiding her around the room. He told himself that he was playing the good sponsor, introducing her to those who could help her career as she studied to go from nurse to doctor.

The reality, he suspected, was far less altruistic. He simply wanted to spend time with her, to be close to her. But it wasn't enough and, the more he had of her, the more he wanted.

'Would you care to dance?'

Her eyes instantly snapped to his, but Seth didn't wait for a reply. Instead, he tucked her arm through his and led her through the throng, and her body pressed so close to his that it was all the answer he needed.

The heat of it seemed to sear into his own.

One dance. It wasn't part of their agreement, but he couldn't bring himself to care. One dance. Then he'd walk away.

He had to.

Because, if he'd found it hard to resist her at the penthouse these past few weeks, how in hell was he ever supposed to resist her tonight? It felt like an impossible task.

Or maybe it was just that he didn't want it to be possible. Maybe he'd had enough of denying the fire that had been smouldering between them ever since that first night.

Stepping out onto the ballroom floor, Seth swept her around and straight into his arms. She fitted against him as if they'd been hand-crafted for each other.

'I should probably have warned you,' Andrea

muttered belatedly. 'I'm not the best dancer. I'm not sure I'll know what to do.'

'You don't need to.' He lowered his head again, so close that this time he could feel her delicious shiver as he spoke softly in her ear. 'I'll lead; you just have to follow.'

And then, before she could voice any more objections, he gathered her closer and swirled them around the dance floor, up one side, then back down the other, holding her so very close the entire time.

It was possibly the most thrilling, intimate thing he could remember doing. He could feel Andrea's body pressed to his, hear the sound of her shallow, choppy breaths in his ear and feel the rhythm as it moved through him like some slow, sensuous drumbeat. He'd dreamed of her night after night after night, yet his wildest fantasies seemed to pale against the reality of having her in his arms.

Her delicate perfume seemed to fill his nostrils, the graze of her cheek against his doing such things to his body, whilst that searing heat scorched every part of him that she touched.

'Today's surgery was good,' she managed after a few silent, loaded moments.

It was true, but he hadn't asked her to dance in order to talk about the surgery.

'It was.' He was aware that his voice sounded thicker than usual. 'But that isn't what I'm interested in right now.'

'No?'

He liked the way her breath caught against his neck.

'No,' he confirmed.

And he didn't imagine the way her body moulded itself to his that fraction closer, or the electricity that arced between the two of them. Surely he could allow himself a turn around the floor...just that much?

As the band played, they danced and swirled. That first song led into another, then another and another. Seth didn't care that he was supposed to mingle, or network, or whatever else it was that he'd been instructed to do. He only knew that he wanted to stay here with Andrea.

Or be somewhere else with her.

Spinning her to an abrupt halt, Seth lifted a finger and slid it into the curl of her hair, unable to help himself.

'I think there's something we need to discuss.'

Her face pulled taut, that familiar red flush creeping instantly over her cheeks.

'If it's about the last time we—'

'Or we can keep pretending.' He cut her off, unable to bear seeing that embarrassment spread further. As though what coursed between them was something to feel ashamed about. 'We can continue tiptoeing around each other at my apartment.'

When she gave an almost imperceptible shake of her head as she breathed his name again, he took her hand tightly in his and led them both off the dance floor, weaving through the throng.

He was dimly aware of her asking him where they were going, but he didn't answer. To do so would mean stopping, and he was fiercely aware that if he stopped he might start kissing her. Right there, in front of the wealthiest in the country. Not that he cared who saw them—but he had a feeling Andrea might. Even if she did, she left her hand in his and was keeping satisfyingly close to him.

Moving this way and that, he dodged any number of patients or potential donors who were keen to catch his attention, with a cleverly dropped word here and there to ensure that they didn't feel snubbed, but the reality of the situation was that all he wanted was to be alone with Andrea. To bury himself in her molten heat. And to hell with whatever agreement they'd made weeks ago because he knew, without a shadow of doubt, that it was what she wanted too.

They'd spent over a month trying to pretend otherwise, trying to hold to the agreement they'd made, but neither of them had been particularly convincing.

They needed a new agreement.

For the first time in his career, Seth found himself cursing his rule against blurring the lines. Yet still he didn't stop. He didn't turn round.

A glut of...*feelings* he couldn't quite fathom swirled around him.

'You can walk away any time,' he ground out. 'Right now, if you want to.'

'And...if I don't want to?' she asked in a voice so unlike her own. 'If I want to stay? Right here?'

A fresh punch of desire slammed though him.

'Then I guarantee I won't be able to keep my hands off you, as per our agreement, any longer.'

She watched him, unblinking.

Slowly, painstakingly, he lifted his liquid-heavy limbs to pull her to him. And as she splayed her hands over the front of his chest his muscles beneath bunched and tightened under her touch.

'Then,' she muttered thickly, 'I'd ask what you were waiting for.'

Seth didn't try to fight it a moment longer.

His mouth was on hers, the way it had been aching to do for what felt like a thousand years, and every graze of their lips and slide of their tongues felt like a benediction.

Seth poured everything into it and she went straight to his head.

All the nights he'd spend hot, restless and alone in his bed, fantasising about being with her even as he'd chastised himself for such inappropriate thoughts, as if he was some kind of monk... And, before he'd even thought about the wisdom— or not—of all the self-imposed rules they were breaking, he had her with her back up against the stone pillar, covering all her glorious heat with his own body.

No fantasy could possibly have lived up to the reality of kissing this one woman. Or of being kissed by her. His mouth assaulted her with all the skill he'd ever honed, because she deserved nothing less.

And still he kissed her, his palms cupped around her face as if she was something infinitely precious. It was a heady sensation.

When the phone went off, slicing through the silent air with its demanding tone, it took Seth far too long to register where the wholly unwanted cacophony was coming from.

Half-dazed, he lifted his mouth from her soft, warm lips and tried to work out what he was supposed to be doing.

Not, he realised with a start, *kissing Andrea.*

Seth stared in dismay at the woman whose silken skin he was still caressing.

So much for his promises to maintain that distance between them. His assurances that he wouldn't lay his hands on her again. One sight of her in that flowing ball gown and he'd lost his head. Again.

To his chagrin, Seth realised that his damned phone was still ringing. No doubt the hospital—yet here he was, barely registering it over this rushing thing that crashed over him and made him ache simply to shut the world out for once and give himself up to this moment with Andrea.

But that was the last thing he could do.

'I have to take this,' he clipped out, ignoring the

thing which roared within him. 'I asked them to contact me if anything happened with my patient overnight.'

And it shouldn't have taken him even that second's hesitation to remind himself that his career was his priority. It always had been.

'Of course,' Andrea managed. But she sounded thrown. Bewildered.

'This...now...' Seth halted and wrenched his stare up to meet hers. 'It was a mistake. It shouldn't have happened.'

Except that it didn't feel like a mistake. It felt like the best thing he'd done in a long time.

'A mistake,' Andrea echoed weakly, making him feel even more of a heel.

He opened his mouth to apologise. Or, at the very least, qualify what he'd said. But the phone seemed to sense his vacillation and rang all the louder.

Or could that have been his own guilt?

In that instant, Seth decided he would have liked nothing more than to throw the phone into the fountains outside and erase everything else from her brain. Instead, he slid the phone out of his pocket and moved his finger over the 'accept call' button.

But it wasn't Baystone Medical calling. It was his lawyer.

For the second time in ten minutes, his entire world receded from view. His finger pressed 'accept call' even as his mind was racing through the ramifications.

'I apologise again,' he bit out to Andrea. 'You should get back to the gala before anyone sees you're missing.'

And then, before he could second-guess himself, he instructed the caller to wait a moment before pacing further down the chequerboard-patterned floor, heading for the library he knew was down the hall, and grasping the phone tightly in his palms.

'Go ahead,' he commanded, hitting the mute button and thrusting open the library door.

It took all he had to get himself inside and stride over to one of the gargantuan windows, glaring into the black beyond as though his entire future depended on this singularly important call.

Perhaps the truth was that it did. He already knew that if it hadn't been for that timely interruption then he would surely have crossed the invisible line and given into the temptation that was uniquely Andrea Perkins.

He would have been no better than the man he'd always sworn he wouldn't be—a man who couldn't abide by the rules he'd chosen to life his life by.

Admittedly, he wasn't married, as his father had been, overtly cheating with every woman who had taken his fancy whilst his wife had driven herself literally insane back at home with two small children. But staying away from colleagues had been Seth's own private rubric nonetheless.

Andrea Perkins was the only one who had ever made him forget all of that. And he had to put an end to it tonight. Now. Whatever this phone call was about, he had to cut Andrea from his life—free her. If he didn't, he was afraid that he'd never, ever be able to let her go—which was certainly against all his rules.

And, without those self-imposed guidelines that he had spent so many years pulling around himself like some kind of permanent shroud—then what would he even have left?

CHAPTER THIRTEEN

ANDREA DIDN'T KNOW why she was waiting outside the small library. Perhaps because she'd been jittery and electrified ever since Seth had met her so unexpectedly at the bottom of the staircase, never leaving her side as he'd walked her round that room, introducing her to prominent guests to whom she alone would never have had the courage to speak. It was as if he thought she was that important.

She'd been swept up in the magic of the evening, right up until that phone call had brought him crashing back to reality. She ought to return to the gala, as he'd rather harshly instructed. Instead, she dwelt on the expression that had crossed Seth's face the moment he'd seen the caller's ID.

An expression that had sent a tight band of tension winding around her chest. Though she couldn't put her finger on how she'd known, a sixth sense had warned her that the phone call wasn't about a patient.

She suspected it was about Noah. Her heart lurched. They'd decided that the best place for him to spend the night would be with her brother's family, especially since his friendship with Billy had only become stronger and stronger over the past month. But Andrea didn't think it had been her brother calling. If it had been, she was pretty sure that Julia would have called her at the same time.

And her phone had remained defiantly silent, no matter how many times she'd checked it.

Which meant it surely had to be the lawyers?

Forcing herself to lean back casually—the coolness of the stone pillar offering her a strange sort of comfort—Andrea tried to keep her breathing even, heart steady and her eyes locked onto the bookcase that she could just about see through the sliver where Seth had left open the door.

He hadn't wanted her to follow but how could she have done anything less, given the circumstances? Still, that didn't mean she felt confident enough to follow him into the room. Instead, she'd just have to content herself with waiting for Seth to emerge— her stomach feeling as though it was now lodged somewhere in the vicinity of her throat.

It didn't help that she'd spent the entire evening feeling as though her belly was full of nerves, knotted tighter than a tangle of coiled ropes. Only up until now her jumpiness had been squarely down to Seth's proximity, and the way he'd been looking at her, touching her, making her feel.

Love.

The word snuck inside her brain before she could shut it out. But she refused to accept it, telling herself instead that it was mere *lust*.

Lust from several hours of glorious tiny touches—a guiding hand on the small of her back, an encouraging squeeze of her palm, or a lingering moment as their eyes had caught—but thrilling enough to keep her senses jolting deliciously.

And then the dancing. Oh, how she'd loved that dancing. She, who almost never danced.

The way he'd held her. It had felt as though he had threaded a ribbon of intimacy around them, and somehow she felt more exposed and aware of him here than she had in all the nights they'd been alone just with Noah at his penthouse.

And, just like that, she knew what she wanted. What she was ready for.

It felt inconceivable that the judge would award custody of Noah to the little boy's grandparents. He had already carved such a space for himself in their lives—in Seth's life. And now Andrea knew that she wanted to be in their lives—permanently.

She pushed herself off the pillar, desperate to go inside and find out what was going on, but not quite sure enough of herself to take that step. She had no idea how long she stood, paralysed, as she stared at the space between where she was standing and the library door.

'Andrea?'

She practically cracked her neck spinning round.

'What did they say?' The question was out before she'd even had time to think.

He strode out of the room and, for a split second, she thought he was heading towards her to scoop her in his arms to swirl her around.

He stopped abruptly.

'The judge awarded custody of Noah to me. The decision came in late, and my lawyer was on another case so just picked it up, but she wanted me to know as soon as possible.'

Heat instantly pricked the back of her eyes. She was sure she could practically feel all the fears and worries seeping right out of her body and puddling on the chequered floor beneath them.

'That's fantastic.'

'Yes.'

Somewhere, in the back of her head, alarm bells were going off. Andrea ignored them.

'What did the judge say?'

She told herself she was imagining the beat of hesitation before Seth answered.

'Apparently Noah was very talkative with her and told her that he misses his mummy but that he loves his new life in Baystone. That he...loves me.'

Seth's voice actually cracked at this last part and Andrea took a half-step forward to reach out to him. But something stopped her. That unfamiliar, brooding expression almost warned her off without him even saying a word.

'That's good news.'

'Yes,' he agreed, unsmiling. Then, 'Thank you for all you did with Noah.'

And there it was again—that strange edge to his voice that shuddered through her.

'All I did?' She echoed the use of his past tense.

'You helped my nephew and I find a way to communicate with each other. Without you, I wouldn't be celebrating this news now.'

Except he didn't look as though he was celebrating. He looked relieved, admittedly, but he also looked tense in a way she hadn't seen before.

'You don't have thank me,' she managed hoarsely, because his proximity was sending her entire body haywire. 'It was a pleasure to do.'

All she could think of—all she could *feel*—was the heat of his body near her. But no longer pouring into her the way it had been when they'd been dancing. No longer making her feel as though she was being burned alive—only far more intense and far more pleasant.

Now it was different. Peculiar.

'Seth...' She breathed his name, not at all certain what else she even intended to say.

'You are officially released from your agreement with me,' he rasped, as though it was taking him far more effort than it should to say the words.

'Released?' She felt numb.

He continued as if she hadn't spoken. His voice sounded so intensely raw and harsh.

'You can walk away any time,' he ground out. 'Now, if you want to.'

The moment swirled around her. She felt as though she was in freefall, hurtling to the ground.

'And...if I don't want to?' She wasn't sure how she managed to speak. 'If I want to stay? Right here?'

He stared at her wordlessly for a moment.

'That wasn't the agreement.'

A hundred thoughts seemed to crowd into Andrea's mind at once. No, that wasn't the agreement. The agreement was that she would use her experience with her brother in order to help Seth communicate with Noah. But now Noah was speaking again. He was happy—in so far as a child who had lost their beloved mother could be—and she was surplus to requirements.

No longer useful, so easily discarded.

Just as she'd been to Josh.

The pain burst through her so brightly that she wasn't sure how she managed to stay standing.

What a fool she'd been.

Miraculously, she heard herself talking in a voice that actually sounded remarkably composed.

'I understand completely.' She dipped her head. 'I'm pleased that it all worked out as planned. Now you and Noah can get on with becoming a family and I can get back to my own life.'

Whatever hope she might have had about what he would say was dashed when he stared at her for a beat before nodding.

'Yes,' he agreed steadily. 'I believe that's for the best.'

Seth stared up at the ceiling, unable to sleep.

Andrea was planning to leave and it should be everything he wanted to hear.

It was for the best.

She'd helped Noah and him to communicate. She'd helped them to bond and the court had determined that he should be one to take care of his nephew, as per Stacey's will.

He should have been the one initiating Andrea's departure. She had fulfilled her end of their bargain and he had secured her place on the nurse-to-doctor conversion course.

Yet, despite all the earlier reminders about his rules and about keeping his distance, he realised that he was wholly unprepared for her to leave. No matter what he tried to pretend, or how logical he tried to be, there was logic in his body. It burned for her and ached for her in equal measure. Her delicate scent still haunted him as much as the way she'd felt in his arms all evening.

And there was no way that he was going to be able to sleep like this.

He threw the sheet off his body and swung himself out of bed; he couldn't stay in bed stewing about it. Better to do some work, or watch a surgical video. Throwing on a pair of low-rise joggers, he padded softly through the penthouse.

Someone had left the floor lamp on, so he used the soft glow to navigate to the kitchen without bothering to turn on the other lights. Flicking the tap, he poured himself a glass of water, as if that could douse the fire roiling inside him.

'You can't sleep either?'

Seth jerked up his head to see Andrea peering round the side of an easy chair.

He tried not to think about what it meant that neither of them was feeling settled tonight.

'I didn't realise you were down here,' he forced himself to answer. 'Do you want some water?'

'No.' She shook her head. 'Thank you.'

But she didn't retreat behind the chair either—her gaze held his. He picked up his glass and wandered past her to the chair opposite, where he sank down and eyed the book she was holding. Little wonder he hadn't noticed her, nestled as she was in the over-sized chair, her legs tucked beneath her, reading silently beneath the lamp. She wore soft yoga pants with a camisole vest-top, and he couldn't seem to drag his eyes from the thin ribbon straps that dropped over her silken tanned shoulders.

It revealed nothing, yet he found his mouth watering at the hidden promise. Irritated—and feeling something rather more carnal—he fought to drag his wayward glance away.

'Something on your mind?' he rasped, barely recognising his own voice.

It sounded different in the dark, somehow—raw.

'I was thinking when the best time to leave would be.'

He hated that an invisible fist tightened in his chest. It took far more than it should have done to keep his voice even.

'Are you in a particular hurry?'

'No,' she answered quickly. Perhaps too quickly...?

'Then...?'

'I just don't want to out-stay my welcome.'

A hundred responses crowded Seth's mouth at that moment. He swallowed back every one of them then took a mouthful of water, as though to wash them down.

The longer he was around her, the less sense all his objections and his rules seemed to make. He needed a moment to regroup.

'When you leave is up to you. I'd simply ask that you give Noah some warning. I appreciate he already knows the basic idea, but I don't want him to wake up one day and you're gone, like—'

'Of course not!' she cut in, looking horrified. 'I understand exactly what he went through with his mother. I would never do that to him.'

Good; at least he wouldn't come home from work one night to find that she'd packed her bags. Though Seth felt ashamed that the relief he felt wasn't merely on behalf of his young nephew.

'I'm not sure I know what we would have done these past weeks without you,' he admitted after a moment. 'I really do want to thank you.'

She watched him for a moment, clearly choosing her words.

'No problem,' she settled on in the end. 'I've enjoyed it. A lot.'

'Then perhaps there's no rush to leave after all?' he couldn't help asking.

And all of a sudden the flush in her cheeks revealed everything she was trying so desperately hard not to let him see.

She wanted him. Every bit as much as he wanted her.

His breath caught as surely as if she'd punched him in the chest—hard. No, not a punch, so much as a caress. And it was moving decidedly lower.

He clenched his teeth. It was enough of a challenge to ignore his attraction to her during the bright hours of day time. But here, in the quiet dead of night, everything felt softer. More out of focus. As though anything that happened between them could be theirs. A secret they could lock away as soon as morning came.

But he suspected it wouldn't be that easy.

'So, where will you go once you leave here?' He forced a light note into his voice, even if he didn't really feel it.

She blinked at him.

'I don't know, actually.'

As far as confessions went, it was an unexpected one.

'What about getting the apartment on your own that you talked about?' he asked, pressing on when she frowned at him. 'You mentioned it that day back at the play centre.'

'I remember the conversation.' Andrea seemed to catch herself at last. 'I was just surprised that you do.'

He couldn't blame her. No doubt it revealed a little too much about how arresting he'd found her, even from that first day. He could probably bluff it, but why bother?

The air in the room seemed to thicken and grow heavier.

'So…our agreement is officially over.'

Not a question, but a statement. This time he knew he didn't imagine how loaded it was.

'It is.'

And, if that prospect made his heart actually stop for a beat or two, then no one else needed to know it but him.

'I'm free to walk out that door any time I like?' she clarified. 'Barring what we've said about Noah, of course.'

'You are.' Seth barely recognised his own voice. It held a hoarse quality that he wasn't accustomed to. 'The latter being a request rather than a demand,' Seth confirmed.

Although, would he have made it a demand if he hadn't already known that this woman would never deliberately hurt the young boy? Possibly. But, if that had been the kind of person she was, then he wouldn't still have been here, beginning to lose the battle with his self-control.

The atmosphere shifted again this time, the kind of suffocating heat that was growing more overwhelming, and at the same time intoxicating, by the second. Had he ever wanted any woman the way he wanted Andrea?

He knew the answer, of course—it was why he needed her to leave. If he stayed here any longer he wasn't entire certain what he might say next, what he might do. Four strides and he could be in his study.

Standing abruptly and taking a step, he realised too late that Andrea had had the same idea. They each jerked to a standstill, scant inches from the other.

'Sorry... I...'

'No,' he growled, more to himself than to her.

The shallow, rapid rise and fall of her chest definitely wasn't helping matters. He knew the woman well enough to read the desire in her body language, the lust. Hell, it matched his own. But they shouldn't. They couldn't.

His arms lifted instinctively, his hands reaching for her shoulders of their own volition.

It was fatal.

Rather than moving her gently to one side, as he was sure he intended to do, he found his fingers curling around the bare skin that had snared his gaze only minutes before.

It was every bit as silken as he'd imagined.

Her mouth trembled.

'Seth... I...'

'You should go back to bed,' he rasped. 'Before...'

He didn't finish. Nor did he move.

'Before...what?' she whispered, her voice almost wickedly thick, wanton.

'Our deal is done,' he muttered. 'Which includes the part about me not kissing you.'

But he wanted to. And he wanted so much more than just a kiss.

'It does.' She dipped her head a fraction in agreement.

She still did not move even an inch.

She didn't add that it left them free of obligation. She didn't need to; it was in every line of her sinfully sexy body.

'Last chance to leave,' he ground out.

She exhaled, a shaky, choppy sound.

'Do stop being so chivalrous.'

Then, before he even had time to process her words, she rose up on tiptoe and pressed her mouth to his.

And any last vestiges of his resolve crumbled to dust.

He was kissing her.

Finally.

Thrillingly.

Andrea didn't think she'd ever felt quite so deliciously light-headed.

His mouth was on hers, and every graze of his lips and slide of his tongue felt like a benediction. It was over a month since he'd last kissed her, but it might as well have been a lifetime. And she poured everything into it. All the nights she'd spent hot, restless and alone in her bed, fantasising about being with him even as she'd chastised herself for such inappropriate thoughts, as if she was some kind of nun.

Besides, no fantasy could possibly have lived up to the reality of kissing Seth. Or of being kissed by him. Not when his mouth assaulted her with devastating skill, even whilst his hands were cupped around her face, as though she was something infinitely precious.

It was a heady sensation and one she might have said was every bit as glorious as she remembered from that last time, only it turned out that her gloriously irreligious fantasies about this man hadn't even come close to the real thing.

Slowly, painstakingly, she found the strength to lift her own liquid-heavy limbs and splay her hands over the front of his chest. The muscles beneath bunched and tightened under her touch, causing delicious heat to lick down the length of her spine.

His kisses were soft, intense, careful and demanding. It was as if he'd been waiting for ever to taste her again, and now he couldn't stop himself drinking her in. It was perfect. *He* was perfect.

She revelled in the feel of his palms against her cheeks, holding her there for what felt like an eternity as he deepened the kiss, angling her head for a better, deeper, marvellous fit. It could have lasted a lifetime, maybe two, and all the while myriad sensations cascaded through her. And, when he slid his hands down the long line of her neck, or gently into her hair, she revelled in all those sensations too.

This was what she'd been waiting for, *yearning for,* these past few weeks. This was what had kept her heart ticking up a beat whenever he'd walked through the door. Or first thing in the morning when she'd woken up and remembered where she was.

'Animal attraction', her brother used to call it. But she'd never experienced it—not even with Josh—so she'd never understood it.

Not until now.

How could she have missed feeling this incredibly *alive*?

Over, over and over again, Seth kissed her. And each time felt more magical than the last. He tasted her this way, and angled his head that way, and each slide of his tongue sent bolts of white-hot need straight through her. Straight to *there*—where she ached for him most.

Still, she wasn't prepared when he dropped his hands to her hips and used the contact to pull her against him to where he was hardest for her. A low sound escaped her lips and she found herself moving against him before she could help it.

'Careful.' He growled against her mouth, the sound rumbling over her lips.

It was meant to be a warning, but instead it fired up a devilish part of Andrea that she had long since forgotten existed.

'Or what?' she pulled her head back long enough to mutter. And then repeated the movement.

His groan of response only made her that much more needy, that much more molten.

'Or, so help me, I'll take you on that couch.'

'Is that supposed to offend me?' she whispered, pressing herself to him all the more and shivering with the unmistakeable promise. 'Only, as deterrents go, I have to tell you that it isn't really that effective.'

'Is that so?' he ground out, pulling back his head.

'We were on that couch the last time we…'

'I recall the event with perfect clarity, thank you,' he shot back, pulling his head from hers. His eyes glittered with heat, and something else she wasn't sure she could identify but liked the look of all the same. 'This time, I have no intention of it ending so abruptly. This time I want more—for both of us.'

And then, before she could offer any kind of response, he swung her up high against the solid wall of his chest and gave her little time to throw her arms around his neck before carrying her off. He crossed the living area within a couple of easy strides, taking the stairs two at a time before shouldering open the door to his room and depositing her with infinite care on his bed.

Seth took his time moving over her, lowering his head to hers and kissing her: her lips, her jaw, her neck. He took his time—though it damned near killed him—sampling her, claiming her, revelling in her.

And with every touch she wove some kind of glorious magic around them both. Again and again and again.

He couldn't possibly get enough.

The thought should have terrified him, but it didn't. Instead, it thrilled him. Slowly, almost reverently, he divested her of each layer of clothing—his gaze more possessive the flimsier and lacier they got—until, at last, she lay before him. Sprawled out on his bed like the most delectable feast laid out just for him.

Insatiable hunger and greed roared inside him.

Mine.

With a guttural sound he didn't think he'd made before, Seth lowered his head and took one proud, straining nipple into his mouth.

Andrea's response was instant, and he thought he could have lost himself for days in her low cry of desire, in the way she arched her body in blissful response, as though she was his for the taking.

And so he took.

He feasted on her. First one breast, then the other. He traced whorls on her breasts with his tongue, toying with her fingers with his teeth. Never hard, just enough to elicit those low moans which cascaded through him and into his very sex.

But he wouldn't indulge himself.

Not yet. Not when there was so much more he wanted to do to his captivating Andrea.

Instead, Seth contented himself with trailing kisses over the soft swell of her breasts, inching his way down over every delicious curve and contour until he reached her navel. He licked it before meandering down over her lower abdomen as if they had all the time in the world.

As if his body wasn't hard and aching with the need that had been thundering through him ever since that first night when he'd tasted her. As if he'd been hiding it from himself all these years, pretending he'd never dreamed of crossing that invisible line he'd always maintained for himself in work.

But he wasn't pretending any longer.

No. Right now he was taking, claiming everything she wanted to give him. Not least when he curved his tongue down to the inside of her thigh, his hands curling around her hips to hold her still as her sensitive body anticipated what was to come next.

'Seth... I don't...'

'I do.' He growled, lowering his head and pressing his lips to where she was hottest for him.

She tasted of cream and honey, of all things rich and smoky. It was a heady, intoxicating taste that he thought would make him drunk for days—delirious, perhaps. And as for those low cries of need she was making...

All for him.

It was incredible how possessive it made him feel. How savage.

Gripping her hips a little tighter in his palms, Seth licked, teased and sucked, triumphing in that carnal dance his tongue could make her perform. A dance that was as old as time. Over and over, until her shivers grew lighter and her shudders more intense.

And when she called out his name and raised her hips to meet him, he took the greatest of delight in sucking harder on the very core of her need and catapulting her right over the edge.

And then he kept going.

By the time Andrea had come back to herself, Seth was lying on the bed next to her, propped on one elbow and watching her breathing return to something more approaching normal. Her eyes blinked back into focus slowly, and the expression in them was little short of wondrous as she turned her head to look at him.

That aching need gripped his body once again, reminding him how very badly he wanted her—as if he'd been likely to forget.

As she reached for him, he barely had enough time to reach for protection from the bedside drawer before sliding his body over hers, liking too much the way he fitted perfectly between her legs, his hard length sliding sensually against her wet heat. He thought perhaps that he'd forgotten to breathe as he held himself above her when she grazed her fingertips over his chest, apparently delighting in acquainting herself with the angular ridges that she encountered.

And then he couldn't restrain himself any longer. The need to bury himself inside her was too over-whelming. With a shift of his hips, Seth nudged against her entrance, a surge of victory racing through him as she instinctively wrapped her legs around him. Another guttural groan and he was thrusting inside her, in and out, so gloriously deep that he had no idea where he ended and she began.

He'd planned to take his time, but there was something about Andrea that had him losing his usual control. She drove him wild in a way that he couldn't quite fathom. He slammed into her with all the need and desire he'd been quashing for all this time. And, with every thrust, she lifted her hips to meet him as if they were hand-crafted for each other.

Finally, when he didn't think he could take it any longer, Seth reached down between them and pressed his fingers to her core, hearing her cry out his name just as she shattered all around him.

And then, at last, he thrust into her and shattered too.

CHAPTER FOURTEEN

It was the early hours when Andrea woke up in the unfamiliar, all too decadently comfortable bed.

Seth was gone.

She sat up quickly, hugging her knees to her chest. Of course he was gone; what else had she expected? Because hadn't he said too many times that anything happening between them wasn't part of the agreement? Hadn't she agreed? Yet hadn't she gone ahead and slept with him anyway?

Tossing her head as if that could shake out the unwanted questions, Andrea slid to the edge of the bed and began to get up.

The sound of the door opening had her scurrying back under the safety of the covers.

'Suddenly shy?' Seth cocked an eyebrow at her as he entered the room carrying a large wooden tray.

The fact that he was wearing little more than a pair of charcoal joggers slung mouth-wateringly low around his hips really made her insides dip and spin in the most thrilling way.

'I thought you'd gone,' she stated before she could check herself.

He cast her an odd look.

'I thought maybe you'd decided it was another mistake,' she continued a little awkwardly. 'Not part of the agreement.'

At least he had the decency to look a little wry.

'It isn't at all in the agreement,' he conceded. 'Only I can't seem to regret one single second of what happened between us last night. Several times.'

She flushed, as she suspected he'd intended.

'As you can see, however—' he indicated the tray that was laden with two glasses of orange juice, bowls full of strawberries and melons and natural yoghurt '—I simply went for breakfast.'

Andrea glanced at the window.

'What time is it? It must be early.'

'Relatively. But I imagine Noah will be back here early enough, and I thought we should make the most of the few hours left.'

He paused, as if about to say more, but decided against it.

'That sounds...nice.' She lowered the sheet tentatively. 'And the breakfast?'

'I thought it might be nice to eat together.' His lips twitched. 'Call me crazy.'

Screwing up her courage, Andrea allowed the sheet to drop as she reached for her night top and briefs, and she forced herself not to rush to pull them on. This time Seth didn't comment, for which she was grateful. Perhaps his usual conquests weren't quite so bashful; but, whilst she might not have body image issues, she was acutely aware that she wasn't his usual brand of whippet-thin bedfellow.

'I don't make it a habit to prepare breakfast for women I sleep with.'

She jumped so easily, he could read her.

'Just the select few, then.' It wasn't easy to paste a nonchalant smile on her lips, but she managed it all the same. 'I'm honoured.'

He gave a low growl.

'You should be. You're the only one.'

This time, there was no concealing her reaction. She spun round to face him.

'The only one? I must say, I find that hard to believe.'

'That, I'm afraid, is your choice.' He shrugged. 'But that doesn't make it any the less true.'

She wanted to pretend she didn't care. That it didn't matter to her one way or the other.

'You haven't prepared breakfast for anyone else but me?' She was sceptical. 'Ever?'

'Not breakfast in bed, no,' he confirmed. 'Certainly not my bed. And not like this. Though, sometimes when I was heading out for an early work shift when Noah was a baby, my sister would creep down to the kitchen and I might make her scrambled eggs or a goat's cheese omelette.'

'I think I like her style.' Andrea grinned, as she dipped a forkful of juicy melon into her yoghurt, and this time it was a genuine one. 'Not that I'm not enjoying this offering, because I am.'

'You would have liked her style.' Seth nodded, before looking unexpectedly serious. 'You would have liked *her*. And she would definitely have liked you.'

Andrea rebuked herself for the way her heart lurched.

'Why do you say that?' she asked as casually as she could.

'Because you are the kind of woman she was always trying to push me towards. Stacey always hated the women I dated, and she made no bones about that fact.'

'You liked them, though,' she couldn't help pointing out.

'I was attracted to them physically, not mentally,' Seth countered with a momentary expression that suggested he was as surprised at his admission as she was. 'I can't say I *liked* them, precisely.'

Even as she was about to ask why he'd dated them if he didn't like them, she bit her lip. The answer was obvious, wasn't it?

'Sex.'

After the night they'd just shared, she could hardly complain.

'It wasn't just the sex,' he refuted, almost thoughtfully.

She was almost afraid to ask, afraid that he would shoot her down and tell her that it wasn't any of her business. And it wasn't. So she'd enjoyed one glorious night with him; it didn't now make them a couple. That wasn't Seth's way, and it wasn't what she wanted either. No matter how her heart pounded.

Still she found herself holding her breath.

'Then what?'

He hesitated.

'I don't know,' he ground out, though she could see that he was lying. 'Maybe because I don't think any woman has done anything to deserve being stuck with the real me.'

'The real you?' she prompted.

Seth didn't know whether it was the stillness of the hour or the night he'd just shared with Andrea that had him reaching inside himself for words he'd never dared voice aloud before.

'It's uglier than you think.'

She blinked at him.

'Ah, yes. And remind me—is that the ugliness of the brother who took in his sister when she was pregnant and alone, or the ugliness of a brother who fought for custody of his young nephew when the worst thing that could ever happen to a child happened? Or perhaps it's the ugliness of the surgeon who dedicates himself to saving his patients' lives every single day.'

'You think you know me, but you don't.' He laughed, but there was no humour in it, and he could feel its razor-sharp edges in his chest. He wanted to stop—why ruin the night they'd had?—but he couldn't. It was as if this long-buried truth had somehow been uncovered and now wanted a voice.

It was *demanding* a voice.

Because he wanted something else too. Last night had been like the wake-up call he hadn't known he'd needed. Not long ago he'd been living a life he'd thought was enough. Now, in the space of a couple of months, he had a ready-made family. A child and a woman.

Noah and Andrea.

Neither of whom he could ever imagine having wanted back then but now couldn't imagine living without.

How the hell had that happened?

But somehow, against all the odds, it had. Yet, if he wanted Andrea to want him, then she deserved to know the real him. Everything about him.

But would that scare her away? A part of him didn't want to take the risk. He wished he could be a better man, a different man—the kind of man that would be worthy of a woman like Andrea—but he wasn't.

Still, if he could give nothing else, then he could at least give her the truth.

'You deserve better than me,' he muttered. If she agreed, then he'd have his answer.

'You're going to have to explain that to me.' She breathed softly.

He was barely aware of crossing the floor to close the distance between them. Then, without

knowing what he was doing, Seth found himself
reaching out and sliding his hand against the side
of her neck to cup it, as if compelled by some desperate need.

Her pulse beat wildly against his palm, as if they
were connected by some invisible thread.

'Set me right,' she whispered, and he didn't miss
the tremble in her voice, as though she felt the same
thread. 'But you'd better make it good, because I
think it's you who doesn't know yourself as well
as you think you do.'

Perhaps it was the words, or maybe it was the
way she was looking at him, but Seth felt himself
fold then crumble.

'The truth is that I was never really a good
brother even before I found out that Stacey was
pregnant,' he began. 'My father was never the best
role model—an egocentric man, a compulsive cheat
and a distant father. He drove my mother to an early
grave with his selfish ways. And I was becoming
more and more like him every day.'

'I find that hard to believe,' she countered. She
looked at him as though he was so much better than
he knew he was.

'Did I tell you that, when he discovered Stacey
was pregnant, he called her a whore and told her
she ought to *deal* with her situation?'

Andrea shook her head, as he'd known she
would.

'So she came to me for support. And I didn't offer it immediately.'

He hated how the words sounded, almost as much as he hated the way this incredible woman was looking at him now. As if she simply didn't believe him, because she expected more.

'You took her in, did you not?' Andrea challenged softly. 'You told me that you gave Stacey a home whilst she was pregnant, and then both her and Noah a home for the first eighteen months or so of his life.'

'And then I paid her off. Just like I was ready to pay you off last night.'

And his lovely Andrea simply looked at him head-on.

'How did you pay your sister off?'

Guilt and grief chased through him. If he could have avoided answering, he would have.

'I found it tough the year or so the two of them lived with me,' he admitted, though it was an effort to force each word out. 'I knew she wanted company but, instead of going home when I could, I happily took on extra rounds, or studies, or surgeries. I deliberately worked longer hours, happy to have an excuse not to have to return home.'

'Perhaps.' Andrea shrugged. 'But you were still a new surgeon, learning your craft and building your career.' She shook her head. 'I imagine you would have worked long hours, whether your sister was back home or not. You're career-driven and—newsflash—surgeons don't make it if they don't work obscene hours, Seth. You certainly aren't the only surgeon to dedicate themselves to their craft like that even if—unlike you—not all surgeons have the talent that they need to accompany that hard work.'

'You're seeing what you want to see.' Was that really his voice? He didn't even recognise it. 'I could have given her more—my time, my care— as her brother, as well as Noah's uncle.'

'Are you forgetting that I've seen the photos of you with them both?' She shook her head at him. 'When we were looking for those photos Stacey had uploaded for you both, I saw the trips you went on together, the holidays you took them on. You made her laugh and—'

'Guilt,' he cut in, the word tasting acrid in his mouth. 'For not being around more. For not doing more.'

'Then you need to make up your mind, Seth. Did you avoid spending time with your sister? Or did you only spend time with her out of guilt? Because, hearing what you're telling me now, I suspect that the real guilt came from your fear that you're too much like your father.'

'I am like that man!' His voice was getting louder and he fought to control it, so unlike his usual composed self. 'I don't want to be. I've spent years creating rules for myself to keep me from being like him.'

'Rules?' Her brows knitted together instantly.

'You mean like never dating your colleagues? Like not breaching the parameters of the agreement we had?'

'Rules!' he threw back at her angrily, though his frustration was more with himself than with her. 'Yet there I was, doing all the same things as he would do. I threw money at the problem, just like he always used to. Paying her to leave my penthouse and take her infant son with her.'

'I thought Stacey asked for the deposit,' Andrea said gently.

He hated that she still refused to see him for what he was.

'She did ask for a deposit,' he heard himself saying. 'She said she wanted somewhere of her own. And maybe she did. But I didn't even ask her to stay. I was only too happy to throw more money at her and help her out of the door. I never intended us to drift so far apart, but then again I never did anything to stop it from happening.'

'You were—what?—thirty-two, thirty-three? An eligible bachelor who was focussed on your career as a surgeon. Yet you took your sister and her baby in for over a year. No one could really blame you for preferring the idea of having your home to yourself. I can't imagine you ever said anything to her about not wanting her there.'

'Perhaps not.' He raked his hand through his hair. 'But Stacey wasn't a fool; she must have known a part of me resented it.'

'Just as a part of me resented missing out on my childhood to care for my mother, perhaps?' she suggested. 'We're human, Seth, we aren't without our flaws. We aren't supposed to be. But it doesn't stop us from loving them.'

His chest ached with the desire to see himself through her eyes, even for a moment. To be the kind of man that she was describing. But he knew it wasn't who he really was.

His thumb caressed the line of her jaw and, as her eyelids momentarily shuttered closed, he had to battle the urge to bend down and kiss her. To pour out everything he felt—which wasn't love, it couldn't possibly be, but felt as close as his broken, damaged self could ever get to it.

'You always see the good in people,' he rasped. 'But you're wrong about me. I'm not a good man, but I want to be. I can be. With your help.'

For the longest time, she held his gaze. Then, without warning, she wrenched her head away.

'You don't need my help. I'm not wrong about you, Seth. Because, trust me, I know what *not a good man* looks like. Spoiler alert—it's nothing like you!'

He couldn't have said what it was about her tone that snared him but there was a bleak expression in her eyes that he'd never seen before. When she jerked her head, making it clear that she regretted the outburst, he found himself balling his fists.

As the word 'love' bounced frenetically around

his head once again, the idea of anybody hurting this incredible, unique woman slammed though him with an intensity that shook him to his core.

'Who was he, Andrea? What did he do to you?'

Andrea tossed her head.

How could she even begin to answer that? She cursed herself for even bringing up her worthless ex. Perhaps it was the shock of Seth's unexpected confession that had reminded her that she had secrets of her own, prodding her to share with him. As if there was an explanation for why she should suddenly feel the urge to open up to this man and make herself vulnerable in a way she'd never been inclined to with anyone in the past.

Not even her mother knew the full details of her past.

Because you care for him, that voice whispered in her brain. Just as it had last night. Just as it had been doing for some time, even though she'd pretended not to hear it. Andrea steeled herself.

'This isn't about me,' she dodged. 'This is about you not feeling like the *real* you. Why are you telling me all of this?'

His penetrating gaze warned her that he knew what she was doing, and she found herself holding her breath until he gave an almost imperceptible nod.

'Because last night, when I went to drop Noah off at your brother's, he asked me if we were going to get married.'

Her heart stumbled, regained its footing and then began to gallop.

'You told him that it wasn't like that between us?' she asked. 'That I might not be in his life much longer?'

Seth paused, but when he spoke it wasn't an answer, rather a startled realisation.

'I told him that we'd talk about it when he came home today. And that was what I planned to say. But...'

He stopped, raking his hand through his hair again. She realised she'd never seen him look so at odds with himself before.

'But?' Her voice was little more than a breath, yet it fizzed with anticipation.

How could she be so desperate to know what he meant to say yet so terrified to hear it?

'But then last night happened...and I realise that I love you.' His voice cracked, as though he could hardly believe it. As though he was grappling with the reality of what he'd just said.

Andrea wasn't sure how long they both stood there—a lifetime perhaps, maybe two—but, the longer she watched him, his eyes snaring hers, the clearer his expression became, the calmer. As if, now the shock was over, he was seeing things for the first time.

And then he repeated, more firmly this time, 'I love you, Andrea.'

As if he truly meant it.

Shock, and something far more potent, shot through her limbs, rooting her to the spot. A jumble of emotions tumbled through her.

With a jolt, she realised it was exactly how she felt too. All those *things* she'd been feeling these past couple of months suddenly made sense— thrilling, terrifying sense. She didn't just *care for* Seth. She loved him.

She *loved* him.

She'd thought she wasn't capable of love any more—not that kind, anyway. That losing her baby had robbed her of that capacity. Now she realised that wasn't true at all.

But she had to know Seth meant it. That it was *real*.

'You...love me?' She could hear the wonder in her voice but that didn't matter.

This was a moment she'd never thought would happen. Not for her. She was more than happy to drink in every single, extraordinary moment of it.

'I love you,' he repeated quietly. 'I want a future with you. A family.'

This time her heart screeched to a painful halt right there in her chest.

'A...family,' she echoed, not quite sure how she'd managed to speak.

Her tongue felt too big for her mouth, her skin too tight for her body.

How was she even still able to breathe?

Seth, by contrast, was continuing as though nothing was amiss.

'Noah also asked that, if we were going to have any babies, we have a baby sister for him, not a brother, because Billy could teach him how to be a good big brother to a sister.'

Slowly, so slowly, her heart began to thump again. It did so quietly at first, but got louder and stronger until it was hammering in her ears, deafening her.

'He asked you for siblings?'

'He did. And it made me realise that I want it all with you, Andrea.'

'No...' she whispered, but her throat was so dry and so constricted that she wasn't surprised he didn't hear her.

'I want a marriage, a family, a future,' Seth continued, his eyes shining with something she'd never seen in him before.

It should have made her heart sing. Instead, it made it plummet. And that glorious sensation inside her that had begun to blossom and grow instead started to wither and die—right in front of her eyes.

Family.

The sound echoed in her head, taunting her. Slamming her from the inside, as though it wanted to burst its way out of her body and rain down her shame for all to see. Her deficient body with its deformed womb.

The irony of ironies.

Family was the one thing she couldn't give him.

'You don't want a family,' she countered in a voice that was so taut that she kept waiting for it to fracture. 'You don't even want second dates.'

'I didn't,' he agreed. 'Until Noah came along. Until you came along. You both made me realise what I've been hiding from all these years, with my rules and my lines in the sand. You brought me back to life, Andrea. You made my heart beat again in a way I don't think it has done since my grandmother died.'

'No,' she managed, wondering if that strangled voice was really hers. 'You don't mean that. You don't love me.'

Yet all she could think was that he was right there. So close that she could reach out to touch him. But she couldn't move. Her eyes locked defiantly with his and she wasn't sure she'd ever seen him look so fierce, so passionate.

'I do love you,' he confirmed simply. 'And you can fight it, but I know you feel the same way.'

And she did. There was no denying it. But neither was there any denying that she couldn't promise him all the things he'd told her he wanted.

Family.

The word was like a noose around her neck, killing her.

'No,' she choked out, hating the very feel of the word in her mouth.

'Yes,' Seth countered. 'Everything we've shared these last few months shows it.

She wanted so, so much to believe him—perhaps she wanted it too much. Something unfurled in her belly but she couldn't put a name to it.

'You're confusing sex with love. Which makes you an even bigger fool than I am.'

'As hot as the sex may be between us, I am not foolish or inexperienced enough to confuse it with love,' he rasped, and she could have sworn she felt the words move over her skin. 'And perhaps I should have said it sooner, but I didn't realise it before. Or, if I did, then I didn't allow myself to believe it.'

'Then think again.' She shook with the pressure of the emotions. 'Because, whatever you're feeling, it isn't love.'

'It's love,' he repeated quietly.

'I didn't intend to do any of this.' She shook her head miserably.

He could never know how much it was killing her not to tell him she loved him too. But the woman he thought he loved didn't exist. She was too damaged, too imperfect—too incapable of giving Seth what he wanted. He just didn't know it.

But she did. Which meant that she was going to have to make the hardest decision for both of them.

'I don't know what you feel, or why you're saying this, Seth.' She mustered up every inch of strength she had. 'But I don't love you, and I certainly don't want a family with you. In fact, I think the best thing all round would be for me to leave, as we discussed last night.'

Then, before he could say anything to make her already fragile resolve splinter and break, Andrea rose from her seat and strode out through the bedroom door.

And out of the life of the only man she realised she had ever loved.

CHAPTER FIFTEEN

'OKAY, WE'LL FILL the cavity with physiological saline and then we can go ahead and close up,' Seth directed coolly, professionally. Giving no one else on the team any clue of the storm that had been raging around his head since Andrea had walked away from him.

He'd told himself it was a good thing. He'd told himself just how right he'd been to do it then and there, before anyone became invested. He'd shown her the real him and she'd turned away. Just as he'd feared she would.

But the hard part had been having to admit it out loud to his nephew. Andrea had barely been gone two nights when Noah had demanded to know where she was. He'd tried to explain. He'd taken his time, sat Noah down and assured the little boy he'd answer any questions that Noah might want to ask him.

Even so, he'd shocked himself at just how difficult it had been to find the words. As though his tongue hadn't wanted to speak them because his brain hadn't yet accepted that she wasn't coming back.

It was ironic—laughably so, really—that the only woman with whom he could ever, *ever* have imagined spending the rest of his life couldn't imagine spending her life with him.

It wasn't a situation in which he could have ever imagined himself before.

And, now that he'd had time to think, he realised how foolish it was to believe anyone could love him. Foolish to believe he was capable of being a family man. Foolish to believe that he deserved more.

But there was still a surgery to do. Still a patient to help. It was the first time they'd been scheduled onto a surgery together all week. Ever since the conversation that had resulted in Andrea walking out of his penthouse—and out of Noah's and his lives.

It didn't matter how many times he'd reminded himself that her walking away was the best—the only—course of action. He'd still spent the past seven days trying in vain to quell the sickening tumult that had tossed through him at the most unexpected moments.

He still fought the sensation in his chest that pulled so very, painfully taut that if it pulled any tighter then it would have nowhere else to go and would suddenly, violently, implode.

And he still acted, as he always did, as though there was nothing in his head at all but the surgery and the patient on that table in front of him.

As Andrea passed him the equipment he needed with her usual impressive instinct, he silently congratulated himself on the fact that neither of them had allowed their personal turmoil to adversely affect the surgery at all.

He wouldn't have expected them to. If anything, it had made him sharper and more focussed—grateful to have something tangible that he could solve as he'd spent the last five hours performing a resection of the spinal tumour, slowly and meticulously removing all final signs of the mass whilst ensuring he didn't damage the patient's spine.

The last part had been particularly painstaking. He'd cut away at the interloper little by little as it moved up across the anterior epidural space, whilst trying to keep far away from the anterior spinal artery—it was always such a delicate balance between not damaging the spine yet trying to cut away as much of the tumour as they possibly could.

Seth had been quietly confident about the operation. Constant monitoring of brain activity during the operation had suggested that signals in the patient had improved. Stimulation on the left side of her scalp had produced some very good results, and even though her left side was weaker there had still been improvements.

The more of the tumour they'd managed to resect, the more neurological activity had been evident in the legs. With any luck the patient should wake up with minimal to no deficit.

'You want to use a non-absorbable silk suture to enclose the dura in a watertight fashion using a running locking suture,' he advised Andrea.

And he told himself that it wasn't a sense of loss that was making him avoid looking into those violet-blue eyes.

'Watertight closure will ensure there is no spinal fluid leaking,' she agreed, her head bent so close to his that the faintest hint of her favourite vanilla shower gel wafted towards him.

Under the operating microscope, he concentrated on tying off the distal end.

'Good,' Seth managed curtly. 'Now we place some ties on top, and some haemostatic agents into the cavity. Okay, now what?'

'Irrigate the wound with saline?' Andrea suggested, and he knew it was only him who heard that tiniest hint of a tremor in her voice. 'Re-approximate the muscle layer, then close up the fascia.'

'Right.'

All in all, he told himself, it had been a good afternoon. Never mind the jumble inside him that made him feel turned inside out.

It had been a good afternoon, he repeated silently to himself, because he needed it to be a good afternoon.

'Congratulations on your baby.'

Andrea was proud of how composed and how at ease she sounded. Even if deep down she felt as though she was being ripped apart at the seams.

This past week had been a fresh hell. But, if she could find the courage to walk away from Seth and

Noah when the only thing she'd really wanted to do was to stay right there with them for ever, then she could certainly gather the strength to congratulate her ex-husband and his girlfriend who had just stepped through the doors in front of her, barring her way. Giving her no passage unless she pushed past them whilst they took their time manoeuvring their baby seat through it.

And Andrea refused to do that. She simply would not give them that power over her. Instead, she would show them that she was a bigger person than the two of them combined could ever be.

She might have known they'd have a way of making her feel small again. Or that Josh would. The new mum looked so entranced with her baby that she barely seemed to notice Andrea, the love in her eyes utterly pure and unfettered.

Andrea's heart twisted anew with the pain of what she would never be able to experience for herself.

'Have you ever seen a more beautiful baby?' The new mother sighed, besotted.

She clearly had no idea who Andrea was, and somehow that made it easier for Andrea to bear. How many times had she seen new mothers so cocooned in their magical bubbles that they were convinced that the rest of the entire world must surely be able to share in their sense of wonder? with no malice intended in their comments.

The girl seemed so naïve and innocent that Andrea was suddenly struck by how similar they were. The girl might as well have been her, a few years ago. Was that how Josh's so-called charm worked? He just chose the most gullible and gentle of females?

Her eyes slid to her ex-husband, the smirk on his face as he threw his arm around the young woman's shoulders almost making her feel sick.

That could have been her. Despite all her pain, she thanked goodness it wasn't. New baby aside, she actually felt a rush of utter sympathy for the girl. She had no idea what she'd let herself in for with a man like Josh.

'And a boy too!' He grinned triumphantly. 'You did so well, babe.'

Andrea hated herself for allowing the aimed barb to hit its target.

In Josh's wildest fantasies, he could never even be a fraction of the man that Seth Mulder was. *That* was a man worthy of love, worthy of happiness. Worthy of a family.

And a family was the one thing she couldn't give him. Losing her baby had been the most painful experience of her life. She'd spent so long in a black hole, wishing she could stay there and never come out. If it hadn't been for her mother needing her, or seeing patients face death every day, then she wasn't sure if she would have ever come out.

But she couldn't go through that pain again. Not even for Seth. Not even for Noah.

Andrea fixed her eyes on the steel doors in front of her and willed them to move the car seat faster.

'Well, congratulations again,' she managed. 'Anyway, I have work to get to, so...'

'Yeah, good job you've got something, eh, Andi?' Josh shot back, his grin overtly gloating as he used the nickname she'd always hated. 'Nice for old spinsters to have a little job to occupy their time.'

Then, before Andrea could catch her breath, he swept his puzzled new girlfriend away, practically pasting her to the wall as he pushed past. For several long moments, she leaned against the cold plaster—not sure whether her suddenly unsteady legs could hold her upright on their own. Finally, not knowing where it came from, she found the strength to push herself off and woodenly move through the still-open door.

Right into the furiously scowling Seth.

'What,' he began quietly, precisely, 'Was that?'

Her mind scrambled. He couldn't have heard, could he? But he was asking her what that had been about... Could she brazen it out?

'Oh, that!' She tried to wave her hand airily but snatched it down as soon as she saw the tremor in it. Hopefully, he wouldn't have heard the quiver in her voice. 'I was just congratulating a set of new parents.'

'You were being verbally mauled by that... excuse of a man,' Seth ground out, his hand sliding to her elbow as he began to smoothly steer her away.

She hated the way that the heat from his body seemed to sweep over her, warming up her icy body again and making her ache to lean into him. To take advantage of the support he was silently offering her.

She wasn't sure how she stopped herself from doing so. Instead, she forced herself to move forward, one stiff step at a time, and tried to ease her ramrod-straight back into something vaguely less uncomfortable.

'How much did you hear?' she managed to rasp out.

'All of it.' His tone was grim. 'Why didn't you tell me?'

The question wound its way through her and she was terribly afraid she would crumple right there in front of him, even as she offered a shrug of feigned nonchalance.

'It isn't something I particularly want to revisit.'

Was she ready to face up to how much a failure it made her feel, rightly or wrongly, knowing that her body hadn't been able to carry her own baby to term?

'Anyway, I have an emergency surgery to prepare for.'

But he was still ushering her the opposite way down the long, pristine corridors in the direction of his office. And she was still letting him.

'The surgery was cancelled,' he told her.

'Cancelled?' She frowned, not sure she believed him. 'Are you trying to stop me from going into surgery?'

His face pulled into something inscrutable.

'The heli-med called in,' he told her softly as he opened the door to his office and eased her gently inside. 'The patient didn't make it.'

Andrea stared at him.

The patient had died, and she'd assumed Seth's actions had been about her. What kind of a person—of a future doctor—did that make her?

The patient hadn't made it. Just like her precious baby. All of a sudden, the enormity of it hit her and she felt her legs buckle. Vaguely, she was aware of a cabinet digging uncomfortably into her back as she slid to the floor, but the stinging was nothing compared to the pain in her chest as it cleaved open.

She had no idea how long she sat there, sobbing, but when she came back to herself Seth was sitting on the floor right beside, his arms wrapped tightly around her.

'You told me the other week that you know what *not a good man* looks like. You meant him, didn't you?'

Somehow, Andrea ignored the deafening pounding of her heart. 'Yes,' she managed, barely even recognising her own voice.

'You lost a baby?' he pressed as gently and as kindly as he could.

As if he truly cared.

Still, Andrea couldn't bring herself to answer immediately. The silence seemed to swirl around the room, growing thicker with every passing moment.

'You don't have to carry this burden alone.' He lifted his arms around her. 'I'm here. You can share it with me.'

The silence grew more taut.

'Tell me again how you aren't a good man,' she murmured shakily as she watched the fierce protectiveness in his eyes.

Shame and grief sloshed around inside her. And something else, too.

Relief.

Because, even if the truth wouldn't change the fact that she couldn't be with Seth, or give him the family he wanted, she knew it was time to talk. Time to share the load she hadn't wanted to burden her mother with.

If she couldn't admit it to Seth, the man she loved—whom she had probably loved from that first day and had loved even more when she'd realised what he'd sacrificed to take on his nephew—then she would never be able to admit it to anyone.

Because, for her, no one else but he would ever count. Even though it wouldn't change anything, at least giving him the truth would mean he could understand.

Drawing a breath, she summoned every ounce of courage she had.

'Josh wasn't just my boyfriend…he was my husband.' Her temples throbbed with pressure, but she kept her hands tightly pressed against her sides. 'We were married just over a year, but together a few years longer than that.'

Seth squeezed her shoulder gently. Not talking, just listening.

'The day he actually left me,' she continued in a stilted voice, 'I was in hospital and the doctor had just told me that there wasn't a heartbeat. I'd had a miscarriage at eleven weeks.'

'He left you just after you'd lost your baby?' Seth rasped furiously, unable to contain himself.

She squeezed her eyes shut at the memory, but that didn't keep the pain out. A familiar band pulled tight around her chest. That sense of loss that she'd tried to put behind her had never quite gone away. Yet there was something almost…heartening about the expression on Seth's face.

'No decent human being would ever do that.' His voice vibrated with disgust.

She shrugged, as though it hadn't once scraped away inside her. As though it didn't still have the power to leave her with that yawning, gaping hollowness.

'Perhaps. But he isn't the first man to ever do that to his wife. He won't be the last.'

'Why?' Seth demanded. 'Why would you even be with a man like that? Why would you marry him?'

It was a question she'd demanded of herself a

hundred times over. She supposed this was the really shameful part of her confession.

'I was young; naïve, really,' she ventured, hating how weak that sounded. 'I was eight when my father died, and I was so busy caring for my mother that I kind of missed out on normal stuff. I had a few dates, but the minute they found out about my family situation, and the fact that I wasn't your usual carefree, responsibility-free single girl, they ran a mile. I suppose I was just grateful that he showed any interest in me.'

'So was he your first boyfriend and he took advantage?'

How pathetic that must sound to a man like Seth Mulder. But then, that was who he was, wasn't it?

'Looking back, I can see that our relationship wasn't a good one, though I didn't realise it at the time since I had nothing to compare it to. He was just after someone biddable and quiet who he could control,' Andrea forced herself to admit.

'Quite a man,' Seth said scornfully and getting up slowly, ostensibly to retrieve a box of tissues for her.

She couldn't help wondering if it was his way of putting some space between them.

'I later learned he had a bit of a gambling habit, and the fact that I saved money and spent so much time with my mother instead of going out meant that he had a cushion to fall back on when he lost. Which he did rather a lot.'

'Yet presumably you *loved* this man at some point?'

The blood roared in her ears.

'I thought I did once. Now I realise I was just seduced by his flattery. He knew how to turn on the charm, but if I could turn back time I would never be so gullible or foolish.'

'Don't ever take on the blame for someone else's failings.' Seth growled. 'He was the one who treated you abhorrently. You are not the one at fault.'

'I know that now,' she managed. She knew it logically, anyway. 'I never really understood what love was supposed to look like.'

It was odd how much easier it was becoming to share her story with Seth now that she'd started. As if she had nothing to lose by telling him about her hateful, sordid past. She had to keep reminding herself that it wouldn't change anything between the two of them, but it felt strangely freeing finally to be able to face up to her life.

'I can't imagine how deeply his betrayal must have run. How badly he must have hurt you,' Seth ground out, as though the words were bitter in his mouth. 'How much he still hurts you now.'

'He doesn't hurt me now,' she said suddenly, fiercely. 'The situation hurt me, but *he* can't hurt me, because he no longer has that power over me. He doesn't have my love, and he never really did. The whole time we were divorcing—which, to be fair was relatively straightforward, given that we had no children or property to split between us—I kept waiting for the pain to hit. But all my hurt was centred around the baby that I'd lost. And, yes, I felt isolated—I didn't want to admit what had happened to anyone. But, as far as thinking about Josh went, there was just a slowly building sense of relief to finally be getting free of him.'

Seth scrutinised her with a gaze that was so intense she wasn't sure how she didn't dissolve beneath it.

'That's good.' He gritted his teeth. 'Healthy, even.'

Andrea jerkily shook her head.

'Not that healthy. You were right last week when you said I was scared,' Her temples throbbed, but she forced herself to continue. 'When you told me you loved me, I wanted to say it back. I wanted to show you. But I couldn't because I was too scared of my feelings. And I was also ashamed.'

'Ashamed?'

'You said you wanted children, Seth, that Noah wanted siblings. I was too ashamed that my body had failed me, and I couldn't stand the idea that it might do so again.'

'Say that again?' There was no mistaking the incredulity in his tone.

'What if I can't ever have children, Seth?' The words crashed out of her like an avalanche, weighty, unstoppable and suffocating. 'What if I can't give

Noah siblings? What if I can never be…enough of a woman for you?'

Neither of them moved even a millimetre. Had she stopped breathing? She couldn't be sure. But, however much her brain flailed for words, none came.

So instead there was silence, and she didn't think anything could ever fill it.

CHAPTER SIXTEEN

A WHOLE LIFETIME might have passed but they still hadn't moved.

'You think you aren't enough of a woman for me?' Seth demanded at last, as odd things twisted and pulled inside his gut.

Was this what it had all been about? Was this why she'd run away? She'd been trying to spare him—spare herself—what she felt was the inevitable pain of him leaving her later if she couldn't give him the family he deserved.

'So, in your mind, I said I love you just because I think you'd be perfect for carrying my babies?'

'That can't happen.' Her breath juddered out.

'You think you can't have children?' he demanded slowly as Andrea swallowed hard. 'One miscarriage doesn't mean you can't have children.'

'It wasn't just the miscarriage,' she managed, each strangled word coming out after the next. 'I have a septate uterus—severely so. Corrective surgery would be a long shot, and the doctors told me that my chances of carrying a baby to term are less than fifty percent. I can't go through that again. I can't lose another baby…'

She stopped abruptly, shaking her head.

In that moment, if he could have taken her pain away from her, he would have done.

'Even if that's the case, I don't need you to carry my child for me to feel the way about you that I do.'

He could tell by her expression that she didn't believe him—her eyes shifting between despair to hardness then back again. Or that she wouldn't allow herself to believe him.

Seth silently cursed her ex-husband for the way he had treated his beautiful Andrea. And she was *his*—just as he was hers. Even if she was too scared to admit it right now.

'I don't need your pity, Seth,' she choked out. 'I told you the other day that I have enough going on in my life right now without additional complications.'

'You were scared,' he countered tersely. Was that really what she thought of him? 'You still are. Only now I understand why.'

She was so close he could smell that soft, faint cocoa-butter scent that had become so achingly familiar to him. His body ached simply to reach out—to reach for her. But it would be yet another mistake—and hadn't they already accumulated a litany of them?

'You pity me,' she ground out, forcing herself to step back from him. 'That isn't the same thing. I'm a means to an end for you.'

It sounded jagged and dangerous, and it lacerated him with every syllable.

'You're comparing me to your contemptible ex. Who, let's face it, is the epitome of an oxygen thief.'

And, though he hadn't intended it as a joke, she

snorted gently with laughter. The sound took the heat straight out of him. He would far rather spend a lifetime making this strong, intelligent, beautiful woman laugh than cry.

He'd moved away from her, not wanting to crowd her or suffocate her, but now he edged closer again, trying to show how sincere his words were.

'What happened to you must have been horrific; I won't presume to know,' he began. 'But it doesn't diminish you as a woman, Andrea. Nothing could. You're unique and incredible, and the only woman I've ever wanted to be worthy of.'

'What are you talking about?' Andrea shook her head desperately. 'Of course you're worthy of me. More than worthy. It's me who can't promise you the family you want.'

A hundred things pounded through his brain but he didn't voice a single one of them, and soon the air swirled around them, thick and heavy with the things they were struggling to say.

He had to make her understand.

Suddenly he found himself cupping her face in his hands. Moreover, she was letting him.

'A few months ago I would have said that *family* was the last thing I ever wanted,' he confessed slowly. 'Then you and Noah came along and I realised what it was to share my life with people who matter to me. You helped me to remember what it was like for my sister and I to be a family with our grandmother before she died.'

An expression of pure pain skittered over Andrea's face.

'And now you've remembered what it's like to have a family, you want one of your own,' she managed jerkily.

He had no idea how to chase it away. He just knew he wanted to do so more than anything else.

'You're missing the point,' he rasped. 'You have become my family, Andrea. You and Noah. You two are enough—more than I ever thought I would get. The truth is that I don't know how to be the man *you* deserve.'

Andrea gazed at him for a long moment before shaking her head in confusion. Then, abruptly, she lifted her arms to place her palms over the back of his hands. But, instead of peeling them away as he'd thought she was going to do, she simply left them there, warm and almost comforting.

'So you don't want a family?' Her voice sounded strangled.

'I want you, Andrea. I love *you*. And I love Noah.'

'I love Noah too.' She smiled automatically, in spite of everything else.

'The three of us are already a family—or could be. And that's perfect enough for me. But if we want more then we can do that any way we want to—by birth, by adoption, whatever. It won't make those children any less ours. We won't love them any less, and we could offer them a life that they need.'

'Seth...'

He slid his thumbs along her jawline, repeating himself as if to ensure she'd really, truly heard him.

'As long as you and I are together, we can make our family any way we choose to.'

'I don't... What if...?' She tailed off, her voice that little too high, her eyes that little too bright.

'It's you that made the family for Noah and me,' he told her ferociously. 'We love you. *I* love you. I think I have done from the moment I met you, though I never let myself consider it. And, when Noah appeared, and I finally had an excuse to let my guard down with you, you slotted straight into our lives as though there was a cut-out there made perfectly for you. You made us whole.'

'You could have any woman. One who could give you a real family.'

'You and Noah are my real family. It has always been you, Andrea. There has never been anyone else for me but you. I couldn't imagine sharing my life with any other woman. I never thought I would want this.'

He tilted her head up, knowing from that look in her eyes that she wanted so desperately to believe him.

'I love you, Andrea,' he told her again with all the certainty he felt coursing through every inch of him.

And he knew she was finally hearing him when her body started to tremble with the weight of his stare. Because this was it. This was where she either believed him enough, and loved him back enough to stop being scared, or she didn't. He didn't know how he could bear it if it was to be the latter.

Andrea stared intently into his eyes, and if felt as though he was stripping her bare. Yet then, somehow, building her up anew with his words.

She loved him—she was in no doubt about that. It had been coursing through her for weeks now, for months. But it felt too much to believe that he, Seth Mulder, could love her back, even when he'd told her.

Except he did. He'd said so again. She could read it in every sweep of his eyes and in every line of his body. And this time she believed him.

She'd known Seth the surgeon far, far longer than she'd known Seth the man, and never, not once, had he lied. He was tough, exacting and incredibly focussed. But he was also fair. And honest.

He was nothing like her ex whatsoever. To pretend otherwise would only do Seth and herself a disservice.

The simple truth was that she was scared, and that was why she was fighting against the very thing she wanted most. All the while telling herself that being strong and resisting love was the brave thing to do.

It wasn't.

It was time she learned to make the truly brave

decisions. And, as Seth edged another inch closer to her, something fresh lurched through her.

Hope.

Reaching out, she took hold of his hand, forcing her eyes up to his.

'I do love you, Seth Mulder.'

More than she'd ever known possible.

This man and his nephew were the family she'd never thought she'd have. Or had been afraid to have. Whatever the reason, the result had been the same when her fears meant she'd almost lost them.

'I'll never walk away from you again,' she managed.

She didn't know which of them moved first but suddenly his mouth was on hers and her body was moulding itself to him. And the last vestiges of that dark hollowness within her began to fracture and crack apart as new light started to spill out.

Andrea poured everything into that kiss. All the fears she had, all the doubts and finally all the promises that she wasn't yet sure she could voice but that she wanted to make to this incredible man all the same.

Finally, when Seth lifted her up against his deliciously hard body and she wrapped her legs around his waist as he carried her to his desk, they made a new set of vows and rules to each other—over and over again.

Rubrics of love and commitment that Andrea knew in her bursting heart would last for ever.

EPILOGUE

THEY BECAME MR and Mrs Mulder in a gorgeous private ceremony a year later, with a proud Noah in attendance. Their daughter was born a year after that, crashing into the world with a lungful of air that made her big brother grin with delight. A baby brother followed, with the same quiet certainty as his father, two years after that.

'I'm glad, Mrs Mulder,' Seth told her, with an indulgent smile at his contented little brood, 'That you broke though all my foolish barriers on love, marriage and family. Without you, I would never have known how it feels to be made whole.'

'That's because,' she whispered, taking her husband's arm and slipping it around her waist as she lifted her head to kiss him, 'Some rules were made to be broken.'

* * * * *

**Highland Fling With
Her Best Friend**
Becky Wicks

MILLS & BOON

Born in the UK, **Becky Wicks** has suffered interminable wanderlust from an early age. She's lived and worked all over the world, from London to Dubai, Sydney, Bali, New York City and Amsterdam. She's written for the likes of *GQ*, *Hello!*, *Fabulous* and *Time Out*, a host of YA romance, plus three travel memoirs—*Burqalicious*, *Balilicious* and *Latinalicious* (HarperCollins Australia). Now she blends travel with romance for Harlequin and loves every minute! Tweet her @bex_wicks and subscribe at beckywicks.com.

Visit the Author Profile page at
millsandboon.com.au.

Dear Reader,

I love a good best-friends-to-lovers romance. Maybe that's because I had a good guy friend once who I thought might one day become something more. It was scary and exciting, feeling those feelings bubbling up.

Sadly time and geography came between us, but I often wonder what might have happened if I had pursued it.

I may have snuck some old personal fears and feelings into this one, which makes Sadie and Owen's story one of my favourites yet. I hope you enjoy it. And if you have a friend you haven't declared your true feelings for, I hope you someday summon the courage to tell them! What do you have to lose?

Love,

Becky

DEDICATION

For the one who got away.
You know who you are.

CHAPTER ONE

Just an hour and a half from Glasgow, the Isle of Bute is a gorgeous island in the Firth of Clyde, where the hips and haws and the hum of the bees are all that interrupts the stillness...'

A CLATTER FROM the kitchen made Sadie look up from her laptop. Her good friend of a decade, Owen Penner, was bent over with his nose in her fridge, looking for something she'd probably forgotten to buy at the supermarket.

She carried on reading the guidebook, grateful it was a Saturday morning and they had nowhere else to be.

'It says here it's largely ignored by travellers to Scotland, who arguably miss its abundance of Scottish Isle beauty. Do you know how quiet it's going to be there, Owen, compared to Chapel Hill...or Boston? Are you sure you're ready for it?'

'Where's the orange juice?' He was distracted.

'There isn't any.'

'There's always orange juice at your place.'

Sadie tutted. 'Callum bought that, remember? Not me. Owen, it doesn't sound like you're very excited to be taking this position in literally two weeks' time...'

'Of course I'm serious.' Owen's tone changed abruptly as he closed the fridge and marched to her dramatically like a military soldier. 'Checking in with full attention, Commander Mills.' He saluted, sliding his six-foot frame back into the dining chair beside her.

Sadie pulled her newly styled honey-toned waves tighter into their ponytail, biting back a smile as his cologne hit her nostrils, plus that unmistakeable Owen smell—the personalised scent she'd missed the whole time he'd been gone in America, studying the intricacies of functional neurology and adding it to his repertoire. He might be one of London's top neurologists, and undoubtedly had one of the biggest brains she'd ever known, but Owen was still a man. Therefore he sometimes found it tough to multitask.

She'd never admit it, least of all to him, but if you looked beyond the chiselled cheekbones and sculpted nose, and the wicked gleaming brown eyes that drove his female conquests crazy, he was still kind of an adorable kid in a buff adult's body.

His biceps told her he'd spent a lot of his time

in Boston working out at an expensive gym with the rest of the fit American colleagues she'd seen on his social media, and now that it was coming on for spring, he probably knew how good he looked in a new green shirt that she'd never seen before.

She'd complimented him on it. Men these days didn't get enough compliments, which she'd read wasn't good for their mental health—an area of huge importance and interest to her since…well, since her brother's death. So she'd been making an effort to change that lately.

Not that it had changed anything with Callum.

It hit her with a jolt of pride that the sound of her ex's name on her lips just now, and the thought of him leaving the flat with her beloved Larry the cactus, wasn't still causing rafts of anger and humiliation and fear to bowl her over—not like it had done before. Thankfully Owen had returned home after his year away just days after the break-up, which had helped things immensely. But…*ugh*. Four years wasted.

Four years of planning a life with Callum Mc-Farley, all for him to tell her, *'It's just not working out. I don't feel a connection any more,'* right before she was due to leave for her coveted placement at Rothesay Recovery.

The high-end facility developed treatment plans to directly address each emotional, physical and psychological issue of its patients. She'd been all set to take a six-month placement in the role of occupational health consultant there, amongst the world's most exclusive clientele, all of whom were paying an absolute fortune to stay at Rothesay. After the break-up, though, she'd almost backed out.

The facility was so remote. She'd had a feeling all that silence would wreck her head, and she wanted to be her very best self for her patients. If it hadn't been for Owen suddenly announcing he wanted to go too, she would have cancelled.

'So, show me more testimonials,' Owen said now, his coffee steaming up his glasses.

She slid the laptop over to him and watched as he used his T-shirt to wipe the lenses before he leaned closer to read the testimonials from satisfied patients against a backdrop of the towering, castle-like mansion that housed the exclusive Rothesay Recovery.

She still couldn't quite believe they were *both* going to be working there. Together. Before he'd left to boost his career in the US, he'd worked at St Thomas's Hospital, while she'd been consulting at various places around London as usual. They'd actually never worked in the same facility before. And heading to this craggy, windswept part of Scotland's west coast would be a world away from his former plan to take a well-earned break from work altogether in Thailand.

'Southeast Asia will still be there later,' he'd told her, when she'd asked him why he'd give that up to go to Scotland with her.

But hadn't he said that nothing had ever worked him harder than the American health system?

'It's not the kind of island you had in mind when you showed me that resort on Kho Samui,' she said, testing him further now, studying the hilly background to the text alongside him. This page detailed the comprehensive treatments offered in this safe haven for high-profile, high-net-worth individuals who were struggling with various physical and mental health issues.

'It sounds like you don't actually want me to go,' he said, feigning a sorrowful look. 'You don't have to worry, Sadie, I'm committed.'

'That'll be a first.' She couldn't help a sly eye-roll—her way of teasing him, of course, no malicious harm meant.

Owen perched his glasses back onto his nose slowly and played with his phone for a second. For some reason the look that crossed his face at her words sent a spiky shard of ice through her heart.

'I'm teasing you,' she reassured him quickly.

He merely shrugged, and she felt worse.

Now that she thought about it, this notorious playboy who was her best friend in this entire city—OK, maybe in the entire world—hadn't mentioned being with anyone in a while. If he'd met anyone in America, he hadn't said so.

But seriously… Did she need to bring up the stream of women he usually enjoyed hovering around him like dogs in heat? She'd given up trying to meet his girlfriends over the years because they never lasted more than five minutes. He didn't do relationships—which was his prerogative, she reminded herself. Not everyone was like her. Serial monogamy was *her* trademark.

Sadie watched his handsome profile as he clicked through the website. Then he asked her what she was smiling at.

'You're so paranoid,' she said, nudging him, flushing.

She'd been thinking about how he had arms like a superhero now and wondering—with the strangest twinge of jealousy—how many women must have swooned over his British accent in America.

But she had also been thinking how proud she was to call one of London's most highly rated neurologists her friend. Owen might be a player in his personal life, but he was a hero in his profession. He'd saved more lives than he'd admit—humble as he was, at least when it came to his career.

While conventional neurology was designed

to spot diseases and pathology, often it couldn't properly diagnose a problem unless it was already advanced. Owen had come back from Boston one of the most qualified doctors in his profession. He was now equipped to advise and treat people searching for treatments alternative to what traditional neurology might offer them. He could identify which areas of the brain were compromised and figure out how to fix them, and do it all with the same effervescent charm that had always made countless people fall in love with him.

She was probably the only woman in their circle of friends he'd never hit on.

Gosh, it was ten whole years ago now since they'd met at Imperial College, she thought, accepting his offer of a cup of coffee and watching his tall frame as he slunk across the kitchen in his socks to get it for her. He'd accidentally flicked a pen in her direction back then, and had got blue ink all over her white jeans. She'd yelled at him. He'd apologised, bought her lunch, talked her ear off, and made her laugh—and also wonder how it was they'd never spoken to each other before that. They'd been four years into their seven-year course, after all. But then, she'd been a bit of a loner for a long time, grieving for Chris, her brother.

She straightened her back, seeing Owen glancing at her sideways, probably trying to read her mind. He often looked at her the way he was doing now, when she was quiet.

Owen had been instrumental in urging her out of her shell again after they'd become friends aged twenty-two, but even now, ten years later, she still felt like a shadow of the person she'd been before Chris had died.

'Like I said, it's going to be very quiet there,' she reminded him now, pushing thoughts of the past away with a mental broomstick and motioning to the screen before he could ask what was on her mind.

Scotland was exactly what she needed, for many reasons.

'Maybe some quiet will be good for me,' Owen replied with a shrug, but he was still looking at her with interest.

Owen didn't know much about Chris—not all the details anyway. Certainly not the fact that her brother had taken his own life. When the topic of his recent death had come up not long after they'd met she'd let him think it was an accident. Her grief had been all-consuming then, even four years after the event, and talking about it with Owen had been the last thing she'd wanted.

But he'd swept into her life and eased the suffering almost instantly. In fact, Owen Penner was still the friend she called when jokes and light-heartedness were required.

So her brother had loaded up on booze and steered his motorbike into a quarry right before she was due to start her course at Imperial College... So her parents had got a sad, quiet divorce while she was burying herself in her studies... It didn't mean she had to burden other people with her past, or have her issues picked apart and analysed.

She should've been a better sister—yes. She should've noticed sooner that her fun-loving, free-spirited brother had started showing signs of depleting mental health. She should have noticed her own parents slipping further and further apart after his death. But she hadn't seen any of it.

Sometimes she thought that maybe her career choice was an inevitable product of her trying to assuage the guilt she felt over Chris's death. Psychiatry hadn't felt like a great fit—she'd wanted to study something more diverse—but assessing patients' mental health was vital in her consultancy practice now, and she saw a part of herself—and Chris—in every patient.

'Will I need a kilt?' Owen asked now, breaking into her thoughts.

She snorted, imagining it suddenly. He'd look hot in a kilt. Really hot.

Why was she suddenly thinking things like this about Owen?

Because you missed him, she reminded herself, *and you appreciate him, that's all*.

She'd been three seconds away from withdrawing her application for the occupational health consultant placement at Rothesay Recovery the night Owen had offered to apply there too—they'd still had a placement of the same length for a neurologist open at the time.

'Why don't I go with you?'

He'd said it so matter-of-factly, right there and then over the takeaway he'd bought her, as if he didn't even have to think about it.

'Unless you really don't want me jumping in on your dream role?'

'Why would I mind?' she'd replied, quickly. It hadn't even crossed her mind to mind—only that he might not actually mean it.

God, she'd missed him when he'd left for America. Things hadn't been quite the same without him around.

'We've never been anywhere together outside of London, really, have we?' she said now, sipping her coffee, studying the three-day growth darkening his jawline.

He looked good with a bit of a beard, and a hint of his thirty-two years in the one or two flecks of grey she knew he hated. Owen was, without a doubt, the most physically attractive man she'd ever met. Callum—slimmer, shorter, never quite as successful, though not through lack of trying—had been intimidated by their friendship sometimes.

Make that the whole time, she thought now, remembering one afternoon out on the river in Richmond, when Callum had accused Owen of being in love with her. She and Owen had been having another one of their 'accent competitions', in which they competed to see who could do the best accents from around the world. Callum had called it stupid. Owen had rolled his eyes in her direction and whispered something in a very bad Mancunian accent and Callum had just exploded at both of them. Totally ruined the mood.

Owen had hooked up with some girl from Malaysia that very night in a pub. While she'd been in another corner, saying whatever she could to placate Callum on the subject of what he called her 'blatant flirting' with Owen.

That particular hook-up had been Owen's way of proving to Callum he in no way wanted *her* as another notch on his bedpost. She knew that much. But when he'd ended things, less than a week later, Owen had also been showing everyone—yet again—that he definitely wasn't the relationship type. He was there for all the fun, but Owen Penner just didn't fall in love. He didn't commit to anyone. It wasn't *him*. And that was fine by her. She knew where she stood with Owen and that was all that mattered.

Owen's eyes were still narrowed, as if he was

trying to remember somewhere they'd been together that wasn't London. Of course *she* remembered everywhere they'd ever been together. Just
as their relationship had never gone beyond the
friend zone, their friendship had never gone beyond Zone Five.

They talked on about the clients they might
meet, and the fishing they might do in the lake
on the Rothesay estate, and as the hours passed,
as they always did so easily in his company, she
allowed a little bubble of excitement to ripple
through her nerves.

'You've never been fishing in your life, Owen!'

'Well, *you've* never hiked up anything higher
than Primrose Hill, Sadie.'

He pulled his *Shrek* face at her then, which
made his chin curl up into his neck while he bit
on his lip, and she sniggered into her cup, thinking, as she always did, that even when he tried
to look ugly he couldn't.

She and Owen had fun wherever they went.
Why should Scotland be any different? Mind
you…they might have more alone time together
there, she and Owen. Would their friendship be
tested? she wondered suddenly, studying his
slender fingers on the laptop keys. Didn't remote living test people?

What about all those wilderness programmes
on the telly, about people forced apart by difficult circumstances. She would never do anything

to put her friendship with Owen at risk—*ever*.
God knew she'd already lost enough important
people in her life. To lose him too would be un-
acceptable.

CHAPTER TWO

OWEN SHRUGGED FURTHER into his jacket and scarf as the seagulls dived and darted at the front of the ferry from Wemyss Bay to Rothesay, the main town on the Isle of Bute. For a moment he imagined himself on a sunny beach in Thailand, cocktail in hand, the shadows of swaying palms playing across his shirtless chest, and wondered if he'd made a huge mistake.

But one look at Sadie huddled into her own scarf reminded him that he'd rather be in cold and rainy Scotland with her than lounging in Thai sunbeams with anyone else. They always had fun.

Besides, it wasn't *actually* raining…yet. It probably would soon enough, despite the current spring vibes. Scotland wasn't exactly re-nowned for its excellent climate and it was cold even now, in late March. But it was beautiful, and Sadie was beautiful, and everything was working out just fine.

He caught himself. What was he doing, thinking things like *Sadie is beautiful*?

Of course she was beautiful—that was an undisputed, undeniable fact, as pointless to observe as *Scotland is Scottish*.

'Look how gorgeous it is,' Sadie enthused with a slight squeal, looking around from behind her oversized sunglasses.

The smart Victorian buildings lining the seafront in Rothesay were bursting into view now, pretty as the postcard his mother had used to keep on the fridge. The water was as blue as it was in Thailand. He could even see trees that looked suspiciously like palms.

'It's exactly how I imagined,' she said. 'I can't believe we're actually here, Owen. I thought you might at least be *thinking* about changing your mind.'

Owen chewed on his cheek and stared at a strand of honey-brown hair blowing free from her ponytail around her face. He'd thought about it, yes, but his heart would never have let him. The thought of his hard-working, loyal and recently heartbroken friend of ten years missing out on an opportunity like this because of an idiot like Callum made his blood boil. The only choice had been to come with her.

'I had to see the home of whisky and haggis for myself,' he said. 'Otherwise you'd just try to show me on your phone, and we both know you take terrible photos.'

Sadie smiled and told him she was serious, and grateful. Then she looked at her feet, and sniffed self-consciously, as if she didn't know how to handle a man who actually stuck to his word.

So Callum was finally out of the picture. Good riddance. Of course it was only a matter of time before she gave that giant heart of hers away to someone else. She always seemed to be in a long-term thing with someone…almost as if she was afraid to be alone. The opposite of himself, he thought. She didn't exactly *need* a man, either, as far as he was concerned.

Sadie was one of the highest-rated UK-based consultants in occupational medicine. A client had sent 'thank-you' flowers to her door just this morning, right before she'd handed her keys over to the new renter and they caught the train to Glasgow. Proud wasn't the word for what he felt about her. She was winning at life on her own.

Sadie Mills knew how to reach people and make a legitimate, positive difference to their lives, just like he did. He wasn't going to blow his own trumpet, but he knew, professionally, that they were going to do good things where they were going.

They met their driver at the ferry port. A man called Caleb, who helped with their bags. Sadie had somehow packed the world into a sky-blue suitcase almost twice the size of his.

It suddenly occurred to him how remote they were actually going to be, living in a part of the nineteenth-century mansion that housed Rothesay Recovery, treating up to twelve live-in patients. They'd be joining fifteen other specialists who would cater to their wealthy clients' unique needs. The other specialists and staff would be on site, living and working alongside them, but on his days off he planned to explore the forests, take naked dips in idyllic lakes and embark on scenic walks through the Lowlands and Highlands by way of a few whisky distilleries. Alone.

It wasn't as if there would be any options in the hook-up department all the way out here. And Sadie was more fun than any of them had ever turned out to be, anyway.

He'd kind of missed her in America. He'd gone to her place the second after he'd ditched his bags at home, and she'd looked at him through her hair all night, eyeing up his new muscles even when she was sniffling over Callum dumping her.

His colleagues in Boston had liked the gym and he'd grown to like it too. Going there had turned out to be a better use of his time than chatting up women—none of them had been Sadie. He'd started to anticipate their weekly Sunday video calls. He'd even turned down a few dates to stay at home and talk to Sadie—

especially after she'd hinted that she might be leaving for Rothesay right after he returned. That hadn't sat well with him. He'd been looking forward to spending time with his best friend after being away for so long.

And now here he was. Along for the ride.

A shiver of anticipation tickled his spine as they slid into the back seat of the taxi. This was it. No backing out now. The six-month stint wasn't going to be the holiday he'd planned, for sure. He knew enough about private live-in residencies to know they involved some of the toughest work out there, but he was ready for the challenge…and so was Sadie.

It was a short three-mile drive to Rothesay Recovery.

'Working at Rothesay Recovery, huh?' the driver said. 'I heard a rumour that that actor's in there now. You know the one whose son died in that movie stunt?'

'Conall McCaskill?'

Sadie threw Owen a look that made him direct his smirk out of the window—she was clearly starstruck.

'That's the one.'

She pushed her sunglasses up onto her head and squeezed his knee. Owen cleared his throat, noting her hand on his jeans, her newly trimmed, polish-free manicure. They hadn't been told who the residents were yet. He'd assumed they'd have to sign NDAs when they arrived.

'So sad…what happened,' Caleb muttered, shaking his head. 'I heard he turned to the bottle pretty bad. You pair might have your work cut out with that one.'

Owen listened as Caleb made grand assumptions about the A-list Scottish actor, noting the sunlight in Sadie's hair. *You pair.* Did this guy Caleb think they were a couple? Lots of people did, but it had never happened. Not in this life anyway.

It *could* have happened. At least, he had tried once. He could be back on that dance floor in his mind in seconds if he wanted, but he tried not to think about it too much because… Well, what was the point?

He'd been young and drunk when she'd put him in his place, not long after they'd met. They'd been dancing in that cheesy club, Sylvester's, and she'd kept looking at him strangely, as if she was thinking something wicked. But the second he'd leaned in to act on it she'd sped from the dance floor like a meteor. Neither of them had ever mentioned it again.

It would have ruined their friendship, so it was probably better that nothing had happened. He would have messed it up anyway, if they'd got together. Much as he would now, probably. Getting into something serious was not on his radar—not with anyone, and especially not with a friend like her.

He found his jaw was clicking now, as he pictured that day on the boat in Richmond when Callum had outright accused him of being in love with Sadie. They'd only been having a laugh, like they always did, doing some silly accents or something. He'd laughed off the accusation, just as Sadie had. But that night in the pub he'd overheard them arguing. Sadie had said it over and over again.

'Owen is just a friend! That's all he will ever be, trust me.'

At the time he'd wondered why it had stung so much. It was the truth, after all. But it sounded like something his mother might have encouraged people to think—the woman who'd birthed him and then regretted it. In Josephine Penner's eyes the Penner men were useless, and her rage over his dad's incessant philandering had sealed his own fate, he supposed. He was never going to get himself into anything he couldn't get out of… There would be no wedding bells, no babies, no mortgages and trips to IKEA. No, thanks—not for him. All that couples' stuff only wound up in misery for everyone involved.

Maybe it was best he'd been shut down long ago by Sadie. Now they were purely friends—simple, no complications. Just the way he liked it.

'I've read about that hotel.'

Sadie cut into his thoughts. He realised he'd been staring at her face again, while she'd been looking at a spooky hotel outside. The Scottish sunlight made the blush on her cheekbones even pinker. She rolled down the window. The air smelled sweet and fresh, rolling in over her familiar perfume.

The Glenburn Hotel looked eerily empty.

'Looks like the perfect setting for a ghost story,' he said aloud.

Caleb bobbed his ginger head from behind the wheel. 'Aye, you're not wrong, lad. Plenty of ghosts around here—especially where you're going.'

'Stop it!' Sadie gasped. 'There are no ghosts where we're going... Are there?'

'There's talk of a Lady in White,' the driver replied.

Owen nudged her gently, grinning at the look on her pretty face. 'You don't believe in ghosts, do you?'

'Stop it,' she said again, and nudged him back harder, which prompted an attack of poking fingers on each other and laughter between them.

Sadie cleared her throat as Owen pushed her hand away from his ribcage one last time, registering as he did so just how hard his heart was bucking in his chest. Caleb was rolling his eyes, mouthing the word 'flirts'. But it certainly wasn't flirting. He and Sadie didn't *do* flirting. At least he would never do it. He knew how she viewed him. How could he forget?

He took in the trees and the wildflowers through the car windows as they drove, and found himself thinking, as he often did when it was quiet, about all the things he'd never told Sadie. Or anyone.

Like how, as a kid, he'd got to know the wobble of his mum's chin and what it meant—usually that she was about to spend some time sobbing behind the bolted bathroom door. The meltdowns often came right after his dad had left for some sudden meeting or appointment that they all knew had nothing to do with the business his parents had built together from the ground up.

If it hadn't for him coming along, maybe his mum never would have married his dad and ruined her life. If she hadn't tied herself to the man so irrevocably, in so many ways, maybe she wouldn't have felt obliged to stick around and endure all the lies and belittling put-downs and bitterness. Either way, he'd learned over the years exactly when to leave someone—*before* things had even the remotest chance of becoming serious.

Sometimes he got confused about Sadie— because he was a guy, he supposed, and because she was a beautiful, smart, thoughtful and successful woman, who had to all intents and purposes come to trust him. They'd come to rely on each other through the years. Neither of them was particularly family-orientated—at least she barely ever mentioned her divorced parents, and her brother had died in a motorbike accident the summer before she'd started university. She didn't ever talk about it. He didn't ask.

Sadie was independent, like him. Ambitious, like him. He respected her. Needed her, actually. Her kindness, her insights, her ability to cheer him up without ever being mean. Every other woman came and went. He would never risk losing Sadie's friendship—not for anything. She was irrefutably the best thing in his life.

'Here we are!'

Caleb was steering the taxi up to some giant arched iron gates. He jumped out of the car to press a button and within seconds they were rolling up the long, sweeping driveway. Sadie made that excited squealing noise again and gripped Owen's arm, and he tried to ignore a sudden lightning bolt that seemed to strike him at her touch. The same one he'd started to feel back in Boston, seeing his screen light up with her face...

'Look at that water feature! Ooh, check out that glasshouse—that must be the Victorian fernery... I can't believe these turrets... It looks just like a castle...'

Her being so excited was infectious. Owen smiled to himself. Thailand felt further away than ever, but this was definitely going to be interesting. The house was huge. All fishtail slated turrets and leaded crests, and bay windows with balustraded parapets.

A black-haired lad with a side parting met them in the grand entrance hall. He wore a smart white uniform and his badge read *Fergal: Welcome Host*. Owen watched the way Sadie looked the man up and down, then found himself catching her arm as another guy in the same white uniform wheeled their cases away across the chequered black and white floor. She shot him a look of surprise when he put his hand on her elbow, and he swiftly removed it, wondering why he'd felt the sudden need to have every ounce of her attention.

Stepping into professional mode, Owen made sure he looked suitably impressed as they were given a tour. It wasn't difficult to be impressed.

'The house dates back to about 1844, and the grounds extend to roughly three acres, including our therapeutic Victorian glass-covered fernery,' Fergal said, proudly. 'Our residents like that. In fact, they're all in there now, because it's potting hour. You can see the bay from your suites, I believe, and the golf course. But the best rooms are kept for our paying guests, of course.'

'Of course,' Owen echoed. He cocked an eyebrow at Sadie behind Fergal's back and mouthed

Potting hour? incredulously. She frowned at him, as if to say, *'Behave!'* But her lips twitched.

'Your rooms are on the second floor in the right-hand wing,' Fergal explained in his thick Glasgow accent as he led them up a grandiose staircase.

This time it was Sadie's turn to arch an eyebrow. She mouthed the word *Wing?* at him, while pulling a face, and he laughed, then turned it into a cough. Luckily their 'welcome host' was too wrapped up in impressing them to notice.

'I'll show you your rooms later, but first Dr Calhoun would like to meet with you.'

On the landing, Fergal swung open a huge wooden door and ushered them both inside the room onto thick olive-green carpet. Owen felt the tingling heat from Sadie's shoulder creep along his arm and excite his senses as they found themselves standing side by side before Senior Clinical Co-ordinator and CEO, Dr Christine Calhoun. In a setting like this, it felt like coming face to face with the Lady of the Manor.

'Welcome, Dr Penner, Dr Mills.' Dr Calhoun stood and smiled from behind a huge oakwood desk.

Her white teeth gleamed between thin lips as Owen shook the fifty-something doctor's hand.

'We feel lucky to have you both here,' she said in a distinctive Glaswegian accent, glancing between him and Sadie with interest, as if sizing them up in person.

Was she wondering if they were a couple too?

'Let's get to business, shall we? There are a few things you should know now you're here, that we couldn't discuss on the phone.'

'Is this about Conall McCaskill?' Sadie asked, folding her arms in her smart suit jacket. She was almost as tall as Calhoun in her heels.

Dr Calhoun shot her a slightly guarded look as she motioned them to sit. Quickly she produced the expected non-disclosure agreement forms from a creaking drawer, and placed them down in front of them.

'We can't keep a whole lot secret around here—not even with the blacked-out windows on our transport,' she informed them wearily. 'Mr McCaskill is on the premises, yes, you have heard correctly—along with quite an interesting intake. In fact, we're relying on you to help us make the breakthrough Maeve… Mrs Mc-Caskill…is hoping for from him. So far he's refused to speak with anyone, or even acknowledge his own PTSD. The team is excited about your credentials—both of you.'

Sadie turned to Owen, a look of steely determination flashing in her eyes. It fired him up on the spot, as if she'd shot liquid adrenaline into his veins. Then she crossed her legs and turned back to Calhoun, all business.

'You'd better fill us in, Doctor,' she said.

CHAPTER THREE

'MR MCCASKILL?' SADIE tapped her nails on the open door, two steps ahead of Owen.

Conall McCaskill was sitting in silence in a leather armchair by the floor-to-ceiling windows of his immaculate modern suite. Maybe it was his grief, or the leaf-brown V-neck sweater and dark army style trousers he wore, but he looked older in person than she'd imagined somehow.

Behind him the bathroom door was ajar, revealing a giant Bird of Paradise plant in a terracotta pot and a French rolltop bath with claw feet. It was luxury compared to their own rooms. Not that hers was bad. She just hadn't slept well, thanks to an old pipe, somewhere she hadn't been able to locate, that just wouldn't stop banging.

Owen pulled two chairs up, one either side of Conall McCaskill's and fixed a smile to his freshly shaven face. 'How are you today, sir?'

Charm personified.

Sadie took the other seat and smirked, remembering catching him taking a selfie earlier, on the

staircase. She'd done the same just moments earlier. Their uniforms were vastly different from
what they were used to. Nothing like their regular white coats. In her case it was a fitted cream
skirt and a sleek white shirt emblazoned with the
gold-embroidered *RR* logo. Owen wore a smart
white dress shirt and cream dress trousers that
hugged his bum just right...

What? She caught herself. Why was she thinking about Owen's bum right now?

There was something about him, she realised
suddenly. Something she'd missed while he'd
been in America. She couldn't put her finger
on it... *And neither should you want to*, she reminded herself. She was simply glad to have him
back, and for the chance for them to work together for the first time. Their friendship was
going to make them a great team.

Still, he did have an incredibly cute backside...

'We're doing the rounds...introducing our-
selves. We're the new recruits. I'm Owen Penner,
and this is Sadie Mills.'

Silence. Conall McCaskill still had his gaze
fixed on the statue of the mermaid guarding
the fountain outside the window. Sadie crossed
her legs and adjusted her watch, reining in her
thoughts of Owen's...physical attributes.

She'd dealt with this kind of thing before.
PTSD developed differently in everyone. But
never in her dreams had she imagined she'd see

it in the hero of her favourite childhood action movie *Surrender*.

If she'd known Conall McCaskill was on the residents' list before this she would have re-watched that movie. Or maybe that would have made this situation more difficult, she thought, studying his famous sloping nose and square jaw.

She and Owen could have watched it together, she supposed, her with her feet up on his lap, the comfy way they'd watched movies together since their Imperial College days. Well, apart from that time when Callum had caught them and instructed Owen crossly to keep to his own side of the sofa.

Owen started explaining what their roles would be. He was to discover what might be exacerbating Conall McCaskill's problems and help develop a strategy for calming any overactive areas of the brain. She was to help him regain his purpose in life, so to speak, by helping him with daily life skills and hopefully getting him back to peak performance in society—maybe even in another movie.

It was going to be a challenge. But then, it sounded as if the first psychologist he'd been to hadn't known what to make of his situation at all. Dr Calhoun told them he'd been sent there by someone from the film company's insurance provider. The notes stated that Mr McCaskill was dressed nicely and was well-groomed for his appointments, when in fact, according to Maeve, his wife, he hadn't showered in days and had gone in wearing the same jeans and stained sweater he'd been wearing for a week.

It was Maeve—famous in her own right—who'd insisted he see someone 'professional'. Hence Rothesay Recovery, and them.

The sullen-looking A-list film star looked like a completely different man from the accredited actor she'd grown up watching on screen. And, just as they'd been warned, he didn't seem too warm about the idea of them being there.

'I don't want any help.'

Conall McCaskill's gruff Scottish bark shocked her. This was not the confident, kick-ass, muscled gym addict she'd seen on her TV. He was only in his mid-sixties, but his son's tragic death had clearly aged him in many ways.

'We know you've been through a terrible tragedy—' she started.

'Well, you should—it was all over the Internet. Didn't even take them an hour to get the photos out there after they took Scott's body away.'

Sadie drew a breath. A breeze from the open window ruffled the actor's grey-streaked hair.

'It was a stunt that went wrong,' Owen stated next.

He was looking at the notes, which wasn't entirely necessary—they'd both read all about it when it had happened. Six months later it was still cropping up from time to time on the news—the stunt co-ordinator's legal trial was ongoing.

Scott McCaskill, Conall's thirty-two-year-old son, a movie stuntman, had been filling in for his father in a chase scene when the brakes had failed on the car he was driving. The poor guy had collided with a tree and the tree had won. A fake explosion had turned into a real one, which had probably finished him off, although no one really knew. Conall had seen it happen.

'We understand you haven't really had a chance to deal with it all,' Sadie said now, crossing her legs in his direction and noting, just for a millisecond, the actor's liquid blue eyes flash over her knees in the sheer pink tights. 'It must have been difficult to escape and get some privacy…'

'Why do you think they put me in here?' he snapped.

More silence.

Owen stood up and crossed to the window.

Sadie found she was holding her breath again.

Another long pause.

'I remember when I first watched you in *Surrender*,' Owen said.

He crossed his arms in his crisp white shirt, studying the mermaid statue, while Sadie wondered exactly how many hours he'd put into the gym to get biceps like that. How had he even found time for the numerous dates he must have been on while he was in Boston? He still hadn't talked to her about them.

'I knew you were a real hero, even back then.'

'DC Shawn was my *character*—i.e. not me,' snapped Conall.

'Yes. But around the same time you did that commercial to save the dogs in Vietnam. Right after that my friend's mother had to drive her to the cinema to put a bid on a cardboard cut-out of your character. There was a queue there already. Everybody wanted you—the *real* you, the Puppy Ambassador—in their living room.'

'Not any more.'

'Nothing's changed out there,' Owen assured him, and Sadie blinked.

That had been her mum who'd done that for her. She must have told Owen and forgotten. She barely spoke about her family to anyone. It hurt too much to think about how good things had been before Chris died. But the Puppy Ambassador—how could she have forgotten that?

She shuffled closer to Conall McCaskill on her seat, shooting Owen a look. 'I remember donating my pocket money to the cause,' she said. 'If my dad could see me now, he'd tell me to remind you how you made me want to get a dog. Of course we weren't allowed one—not even after my brother begged for one...'

She trailed off, straightening up on the seat. Conall McCaskill was frowning, as if waiting for her to finish. Even worse, Owen was looking at her sympathetically, which rattled her defences instantly. This was not the time or place. Why had she brought up her brother? Conall McCaskill was making her nervous.

'I wasn't allowed to watch *Surrender* unless I'd tidied my room first,' she said quickly, raking a hand through her loose hair. 'That's power, sir. No one else could get me to do that—'

'She's right about that,' Owen interrupted. 'She's the messiest person I've ever met.'

Sadie's mouth fell open. If they'd been anywhere else she would have play-punched him. But to her surprise Conall McCaskill's face softened. Only slightly, but there was an undeniable shift in his mood.

Damn, Owen was good. Buttering up a celeb's ego was probably the only place to start with any kind of treatment, and Owen had realised that immediately. Just the tiniest crack would do to loosen him up—then they could slip into his psyche and start with the real work. And trust Owen to lighten the mood, like he always did.

She'd address his comment about her messiness later, she decided, as Owen continued talking about his friend transporting the DC Shawn cut-out home in her mum's car, how his cardboard head had stuck out through the back window for the whole ride.

Maybe she'd let her standards slip a little since

the break-up with Callum. Owen had certainly done her washing up a few times, while she'd been sniffling into a pot of ice-cream on the sofa, feeling sorry for herself. Once, he'd even made her bed for her. She'd stood there, bleary-eyed, watching him from the doorway, while he'd propped up her childhood teddy bear and talked about making her comfy, thinking how even Callum had never made the bed. He'd always waited for her to do it.

'What's the deal with you two anyway?' Conall McCaskill asked now, turning his head back to her.

She realised she'd been looking at Owen in the sunlight, noticing again how good he looked in his uniform. It would have been so different here if he hadn't come too.

'What do you mean?' Owen asked evasively.

'You know what I mean. Are they sending couples here now? I know they've had a few singles who thought it was too remote. They wound up leaving the island.'

'We're not a couple,' she said quickly, as her heart lurched in her chest. 'We're simply colleagues and friends who've known each other a long time.'

Conall McCaskill scanned her from her chin up to her hair, his familiar close-set blue eyes roving her face as if he was looking for a reason to mistrust her. Owen was frowning, seemingly memorising the mermaid's scales in the garden.

She quickly changed the subject to the actor's treatment plan, explaining her planned series of daily hand-eye co-ordination exercises in addition to a strict dietary regime, which often helped PTSD patients more than it had been previously thought, according to some new research Owen had studied and implemented in the States.

'Colleagues and friends, huh?' mumbled Conall McCaskill, halfway through retying his shoelaces, as if that was better than addressing the difficulties she was observing in his ability to do so without cursing.

'That's correct.' Sadie stood up, allowing him the dignity of continuing without them looking, wondering why his scrutiny had unnerved her. Maybe she was just starstruck. This man was a Hollywood icon. She could think of several people who'd lose their minds if she told them she was caring for this megastar on his road to recovery.

Owen turned. 'We're here for *you*, sir,' he added, although it was Sadie he was looking at now.

In a flash she remembered the look in his eyes that had set her defences on fire before, the sympathy in his gaze after she'd mentioned her brother. If he was here because he felt sorry for her in any way...because of her brother, or Callum, or anything...

No. Surely not. Not Owen. Owen did things for Owen. Always.

Except when he's taking care of me... Then he's the least selfish person I know. Women have come and gone in his life, but he's always been there for me.

Sadie pushed the strange new revelation from her head before it could develop into questions pertaining to their strictly platonic relationship status. Meeting Conall McCaskill was getting to her, that was all.

Next on their rounds was Mr Vivek Kumar, a wealthy businessman who sat wringing his hands, his eyes all over the place.

'I can still hear the sound of the ice cracking under my head,' Mr Kumar explained, making Sadie's heart hurt for the man.

He'd slipped on some icy steps on a business trip to Colorado last winter and hurt his head. He had experienced difficulties in speaking and co-ordination ever since.

Sadie felt Owen's eyes on her the whole time she was assessing his ability to follow instructions, walking in various directions around the room. Every time he turned left instead of right her heart sank further, but Owen was making furious notes, and she knew he was devising a plan of his own that they'd incorporate into a healing schedule.

Again, the thrill of working with him to help a patient through a traumatic brain injury gave her a boost—although unfortunately so did remembering the way he'd put his arm around her shoulders this morning. Just for a second, by way of saying hello on the landing. It had sent a bolt of electric heat through her loins that had taken her quite by surprise. He'd ruffled her hair awkwardly afterwards, as if to turn his affection into something he might also show a puppy dog, and she'd blushed all the way to breakfast.

'How did you sleep last night?'

Owen had caught her up on their way into the fernery for potting hour.

'Why?' she asked him, noting that the patient they'd just assessed, forty-eight-year-old Portia DeMagio, was pressing a hand to her forehead ahead of them in the humid domed glasshouse.

Sadie frowned. She'd suggested Portia stay inside, as she'd mentioned feeling a little unwell, but Portia had insisted on getting some air.

The slight, smartly dressed sexologist, who lived in Edinburgh with her film director husband, was here to get to the bottom of her cluster headaches, which had been diagnosed as 'episodic'. Her illness was characterised by periods of weeks or months of attacks, alternated with pain-free periods. With surgical intervention ruled out already, Sadie was adjusting Portia's existing programme for coping with and hopefully reducing the ferocity of her debilitating headaches.

It really was a diverse list of live-in residents, but only two were here for potting hour. The others were attending a yoga class—with the exception of Conall McCaskill, who'd refused to join in with anything today.

'I just wondered if you'd heard anything in the night,' Owen said now, keeping his eyes on Vivek Kumar, who was settling his large, round, portly self into a seat at the glass table set amongst the ferns and flowers.

'Now that you mention it, there was something banging all night. A door or a pipe or something,' she said.

She noted how Mr Kumar was struggling with sitting too far away from the table, and then too close to Portia for his comfort. They'd concluded by now that his spatial awareness was very much impaired. Sadie helped him with his chair, and luckily Portia just smiled.

'I couldn't find where the noise was coming from.'

'I heard that too.'

Owen scratched his chin thoughtfully. His room was right next to hers, so she wasn't surprised.

'I thought maybe there was a window open in your room.'

'*My* room? Why would I leave a window open?'

'That's what I thought.' He leaned into her and lowered his voice, grinning. His mouth tickled her ear. 'Maybe it was the ghost.'

'Stop it,' she hissed.

Parminder, a trainee care assistant, looked up from her distribution of shovels and tiny plastic pots of shrubs, which were to be re-planted in peace and quiet.

'Stop what?' she asked, raising her perfect neat brows as they approached.

And Sadie had already caught her looking a little too long and hard at Owen—which annoyed her more than she wanted it to. It was up to Owen what he did and with whom—why should she care? Just because he had possibly come here for her, and not just for 'the challenge', like he'd said, it didn't mean he owed her his full attention all the time. It was probably only a matter of time before he noticed Parminder's crush, if he hadn't already.

Why am I so annoyed by something that hasn't even happened?

'I was saying we think there's a ghost in our wing,' Owen told Parminder.

Vivek rolled his sleepy hooded eyes. 'There's no such thing as ghosts.'

'Exactly,' Sadie replied, taking the heavy iron

seat next to Owen's and picking up a small shovel. 'Owen was just messing around.'

She waggled the shovel in his direction, laughing despite her strange mood when he pretended to swipe it from her hand.

Parminder cleared her throat...flicked her gaze between them nervously. 'I saw something in the garden my first night here,' she said, sounding a little embarrassed.

Owen put the shovel down and shot Sadie a sideways glance.

'At first I thought it was one of the residents, but it was after-hours, and they always lock the doors at night.'

'It was probably the caretaker,' Sadie said, nudging Owen's foot under the table.

'In a long white dress?'

Sadie swallowed—just as a bird landed on the glass dome above her and made her jump. Ghosts weren't real, but still... The thought of encountering anything paranormal here turned her stomach inside out.

'Lots of people wear long white dresses,' she said casually, digging her shovel into a mini plant pot in an attempt to calm her pulse. 'Even Owen here wore one once. Remember that Halloween party at Imperial? When you went as a corpse bride?'

Owen sniggered. Vivek and Parminder looked at them with interest, giving them the same kind of look that Conall McCaskill had given them earlier.

'You guys went to college together?' Parminder asked curiously.

Sadie nodded, chin raised, wondering why she suddenly felt more territorial over Owen than a guard dog on duty.

She was just about to regale them with another funny story about Owen when Portia DeMagio clutched her head again, dropped her shovel to the floor, and promptly fell face-forward into her plant pot.

'Oh, my God! What…? What…?'

Vivek was on his feet before anyone could move, but Owen urged him back into his seat while Sadie and Parminder gently lifted Portia from the soil and readjusted her in the chair. Her mouth was wide open.

'She's out cold.' Owen frowned, coming forward and checking her eyes while Sadie wiped the mud from her cheeks.

If only Portia had listened to her earlier and stayed in the main house when her symptoms had started.

'She told me she can usually tell when an attack this bad is about to happen,' she whispered at Owen.

'She shouldn't be blacking out on the meds she's taking,' he replied.

Parminder was on her radio. In less than a

minute someone was rushing down the path towards them with oxygen. Portia was already blinking, coming to on her own, even as they slipped the oxygen mask over her face. She was most apologetic for fainting, but Owen wasn't having any of it.

'We're rescheduling our next one-to-one, Portia,' he told her sternly as Sadie noted a fresh and telling sheen of perspiration on the woman's forehead. 'We need to get you off those meds. They're clearly not working.'

'Nothing's worked so far. That's why my husband sent me here,' she managed through her mask.

Sadie watched the woman grasp Owen's hand and squeeze it with a strength that defied her size and current situation. She'd mentioned her husband 'sending' her here to her too, in an earlier session.

'"We both will,' Owen replied. 'That's why we're here.'

Sadie stood back with Vivek and Parminder as Owen helped Portia all the way up the gravel path, past the mermaid, till they were out of sight. The poor woman spouted far too many apologies the whole way, and Sadie wondered how she'd been coping with events like this so far. Embarrassing, humiliating, debilitating...

Did her husband think this was his last resort? Sending her to this place? How many times had he scraped Portia off floors and carpets while fearing for his beautiful wife's life?

Cluster headaches weren't life-threatening, but another sufferer had once described them to her as *'Like your brain is being attacked by an angry elf with a machete'*. She wanted to help Portia. She *would* help. She and Owen would work together to make sure of it.

She would also have to work on not noticing Owen's impressive physique as much, she decided. How dare he come back from Boston looking hotter than ever...distracting her like this? Thoughts like that needed to be nipped in the bud pronto, before he caught her and started thinking she *liked* him, or something!

As if.

CHAPTER FOUR

BY THE END of the second week Owen had got pretty comfortable with a fishing line in his spare time, but he still felt as if Conall McCaskill was the one who was getting away. No matter how hard he tried to get him to talk in their sessions, the depressed actor used only grunts by way of conversation, and insisted on staring right past him for the most part, officiously offering to tell him the time, as if they needed confirmation that he didn't want to give them any more of his.

It was almost as infuriating as his new attraction to Sadie.

Maybe it was working with her…watching her in action around the patients. The way she'd been with Portia since the incident in the fernery was nothing short of dedicated. She'd sat with her every evening since, when she was reading and journaling in her room, making sure she wasn't alone long enough for another headache to creep up unannounced—which it hadn't, thankfully.

Maybe it was having her close again after so

long away from her...or the fact he hadn't had sex in a while...but he'd had a dream about her last night. The kind of dream that would not stop playing on his mind.

Owen cast his line over the side of the little boat while Rothesay Recovery loomed large in the sweeping estate beyond. Only his, Sadie's and Conall's fishing lines were disturbing the ripples of the blue lake. Of course Sadie had to be looking cute as hell in her uniform of a white shirt with a cream jacket and matching fitted skirt—her body was as fine as her brain.

Yes, focus on her brain, he reminded himself in annoyance, frowning into the lake. Her body was off-limits. Unlike the way it had been in that dream. Even thinking about it was torture.

But then, he'd rather think about *anything* other than his father right now. And the way he had casually announced his new engagement at the end of their recent phone call—as if it was more of an afterthought than a big deal.

Owen felt his jaw lock again. It *was* a big deal. *Jay Penner strikes again.* The ink was barely dry on his latest divorce papers. What would this Michaela woman be? His fourth wife? Fifth? He was losing track.

'So, have you done much fishing before?'

Sadie's voice broke into his thoughts. She was trying to make small talk with Conall from the other side of the boat they'd managed to coerce him onto.

'A few times with my co-star on *Ascension 2*,' was McCaskill's simple, bored response.

Owen fought not to intervene. His role this morning was to observe the actor's mood and motor skills in activities like this, now he'd put him on a new anti-inflammatory diet. Conall hadn't had an alcoholic drink in over a month, but Owen suspected his previous diet hadn't helped his PTSD.

Post-traumatic stress was a wicked beast. Sometimes he saw hints of it in his mother— caused by none other than his father, of course. Although she hadn't exactly distanced herself from him, or done anything to try and help her situation. The woman was the very definition of a martyr.

Jay Penner had walked out on the two of them when Owen was eleven, in favour of some woman he'd met on a first-class flight back from Hong Kong—Edwina. Every new relationship and marriage since then had merely put another knife through her wounds.

It didn't help that neither would step down from the business they'd built together. On the surface, everything was about Leap—the ground-breaking web design platform for which they were co-founder and CEO jointly. Under-neath… Who knew? His mother seemed to prefer being tortured rather than admit her own stubbornness and pride, and her unadulterated loathing of his father was a mask for a damaging kind of undying love for the man...bordering on the masochistic, in fact.

'Catching any sea monsters over there, Owen?' Sadie called, eliciting another grunt from Conall as she tossed her own line over the side with a yell a lot like a noisy tennis player might emit.

'Not so many,' he replied, momentarily forgetting his annoyance as he noticed her new sunglasses. They suited her. Then again, Sadie looked good in everything.

When he'd mentioned to his dad that he was here in Scotland on a placement with her, he'd heard a low murmur of approval in the back of his throat—Jay Penner's way of ranking a woman highly in the looks department. Dad must have seen photos of them together on his social media over the years, although Owen had managed to keep him away from her in person—more out of embarrassment than anything else.

Owen listened to Sadie and Conall making awkward, stunted small talk while his father crept in and out of his thoughts. The guy could push his buttons, for sure—it was a lost battle for him not to get wound up over the way he treated marriages like throwaway takeout containers.

His mum would probably call any time now, he thought, checking his phone. She'd tell him the same thing she always did: *'Don't you dare do anything to ruin anyone like your father ruined me!'*

She loved to impose her self-righteous opinions on him. The things he'd heard from her over the years still made him cringe. How the Penners—his grandfather and great-grandfather included—were notorious for having too much money and not enough morals...how she'd thought she'd be the one to make his dad into a one-woman guy...how stupid that had been because no one ever would.

His mother was *still* paying for her mistakes... still regretting getting in too deep. Regretting getting serious with his father, walking down the aisle and making babies with him.

Sadie's squeal drew his attention back to her. Her line had bounced back and hooked into her hair. Biting back a smile, he put his line down and crossed the boat to help. He wasn't great at fishing, but she was worse.

'What are you like?' he whispered as his fingers found the hook amongst her thick honey hair and untangled it gently.

'Thank you. I can do it,' she muttered suddenly, catching his fingers just as they went back in to smooth her hair down.

He tried to discern what the new scent was lingering in his nostrils. He sniffed again—lavender. The oil was in every female's room at

Rothesay. He'd seen the diffusers in a session with Portia.

Embarrassment flashed in Sadie's eyes as she glanced from him to a smirking Conall and he retracted his hand—*why had he done that?*

'I don't think the fish need to worry with you around,' Owen said, clearing his throat.

'Very funny,' she replied, trying and failing to hide her face behind her hair. Her cheeks were flaming ruby-red in the sunlight.

What the hell was that?

Conall was grinning at them. 'Did I ever tell you how I met my wife?' he asked suddenly.

'No, you didn't,' Sadie replied, flustered, before Owen could say a word. She shuffled back to the side of the boat and resumed her hopeless fishing.

'She was a production assistant on one of my movies. Cutest girl around for miles...wicked sense of humour.'

Conall's eyes found Owen's as he said it, as if they were sharing some kind of moment.

'Maeve was the only one on set who treated me like a human being and not some star who needed special attention. I appreciated that.'

Owen wound out his line. He didn't need to ask why Conall was mentioning his wife here and now. Clearly he was insinuating he and Sadie had some kind of husband-and-wife-type interaction going on—which wasn't entirely untrue, he supposed. They weren't having sex, for a start. Didn't marriage kill that kind of thing?

Wild passion withered. Attraction always faded.

He frowned at the water, remembering how his mother had verbally bashed his 'useless' father even while they were still together...even at the cost of making things deeply uncomfortable for him and any unsuspecting school friend he'd happened to invite to the dinner table.

'I can't believe Maeve sent me here,' Conall said gruffly. 'Of all people...'

'She wants you to get better,' Sadie told him gently.

'She's grieving herself. I told her she should come here too.'

She wasn't drinking herself into a heap every night, Owen wanted to say.

But instead he chose to listen while Sadie asked him more about his early encounters with Maeve. He knew she was dying to know. And they both knew Conall McCaskill's anhedonia—an inability to express any kind of pleasure—must have been making his wife's life a misery.

Maeve McCaskill had given up 'the biz' years ago, to launch a successful line of luxury cooking items and cook-books, promoted largely on her YouTube channel. She was a big hit on all social media, apparently, always cooking, and talking about how to use this particular air fryer or that tin for a batch of muffins—not that he paid much attention to things like that.

Unlike Sadie.

Sadie even had one of her aprons.

She'd always looked ridiculously cute in the pink frilly fifties-style thing—like a sexy housewife or something. One time, when they'd both had too much of her girly gin and elderberry mix, she'd danced around her kitchen while she was wearing it, and he'd had to stop himself taking the husband-and-wife game too far by hoisting her up onto the counter.

Owen cursed himself. Now he was imagining what sex with Sadie would be like up against the kitchen counter. It wasn't as if he'd *never* imagined it—even before the dream. He was a guy, after all. She'd just never go there with him—obviously. And he wouldn't initiate it. She'd accuse him of wanting to make her another notch on his bedpost, which he'd never do with someone like her.

If his mother ever met Sadie—which he'd been trying to avoid—she'd only take him aside and remind him of all the things he shouldn't do. Tell him not to ruin her. She might even tell Sadie what she loved to tell anyone else who'd listen—how his father and pretty much all the Penner men were useless. The shame and embarrassment he felt just thinking of her hearing all that caused a fire in his blood. He knew Sadie's approval of him was imperative.

She was professionally perfect to all who encountered her, but behind the scenes she was special—to him, at least—because she made no pretence about who she really was. Not like some of those girls who'd approached him in Boston...the ones he'd wound up going to the gym to avoid...

'Isn't that right, Owen?'

'Huh?' Owen turned. Sadie was scanning his face quizzically.

'I was saying to Mr McCaskill that he should invite his wife here for the annual gala that was coming up. You know...the event they've put up all the posters for?'

Owen vaguely recalled seeing some posters about the place.

'He doesn't think she'd want to come,' she continued.

'Why wouldn't she want to come?' Owen asked, catching Sadie's look. She was letting him know she was fishing for information as much as for the perch that were hiding somewhere in the water below them all.

It was interesting, seeing her studying this troubled man. Every half-smile, every grunt and sigh, was a piece of the actor's story, unscripted. He was telling her how she could help him without even realising it himself.

'Is it that you think she wouldn't want to come? Or do you just not want her to see you in this place?' Sadie asked him carefully. 'There's nothing to be ashamed of, you know. Everyone needs help sometimes.'

Silence.

Tension filled the cool morning air as Conall's face grew tight and sullen. His eyes darkened as he clenched a fist at his side. 'You know nothing about what we've been through,' he growled at them. 'Get me off this boat.'

'Mr Mc—'

Without a beat Owen stepped between Conall and Sadie. The look in the guy's eyes was not unlike the look on his character DC Shawn's face, right before he launched a hand grenade at an approaching battleship.

'Sir, if you'd just—'

'I said, *get me off this boat!*'

McCaskill's lips grew pursed and small, and his eyes went black as a thunderstorm. One look at his dilated pupils told Owen it was obvious their fishing trip was over. They'd pushed him too far.

Owen could almost feel Sadie's disappointment through the light squeeze of her fingers around his wrist.

'OK, we're going back,' he said quickly, reading her signal. 'Sadie, do you want to steer or shall I?'

* * *

Half an hour later they'd deposited Conall on the small wooden jetty with Parminder and were back on the boat on the lake—just the two of them. With two hours before their next appointments, Owen had offered to show Sadie a few fishing skills, despite her insisting he had none himself.

She was very quiet, though. Obviously she was still thinking about Conall…or maybe even that weird moment between them earlier…

No, surely not. Sadie had probably forgotten that already.

'He's been off the booze for a while, but the anhedonia is still going strong,' she was saying, with her rod dangled over the side, the sunlight still playing in her hair.

'I know that,' he said, rolling his eyes.

'It's not something *you've* ever had a problem with,' she responded.

Her eyes were twinkling now, but Owen bristled. 'Depends what kind of expression of pleasure we're talking about,' he replied, tossing his own line over the boat a little harder than he'd intended.

Sadie studied his face, eyes narrowed. 'What did I say?'

'You assume too much about me, Sadie Mills,' he answered.

She scoffed. 'I don't assume anything. You're a pleasure-seeker.'

'And what's so wrong with that?'

Sadie opened her mouth to reply, but closed it again, as if she regretted it already, and he bit back the words he was about to say as well. It wasn't worth it.

Or maybe it was. Too many people already assumed he was just like his father, and maybe they were right. At least, they *used* to be right, he corrected himself. When was the last time he'd been with a woman? He couldn't even remember now. His heart hadn't been in it for ages. He'd been too busy missing Sadie from afar.

'If you mean I seek out the good things in life—like spending time with *you*, like being here, trying to make a difference to these people's lives—then, yeah, I'm a pleasure-seeker. But if you mean I just sleep around…'

'But…you do. Don't you?'

'Not any more, if you must know.'

'I'm sorry.' Sadie flung her line out and frowned defensively at the water.

Great. Now he felt like an idiot for making a big deal out of her teasing him—but she might as well have lashed his nerve-endings with a million little whips. Maybe she still saw him the same way she had when they were in their twenties, but he *had* changed. It wasn't that he wanted to settle down, specifically, but he was definitely a lot more discerning about who he gave his time and attention to.

She didn't know that, though, looking at him here, where she'd stuck him years ago, in the friend zone. She didn't know how much he'd missed her. Maybe he hadn't realised the extent of it himself till he'd come home, he realised suddenly.

The silky strands of Sadie's hair blew out on the breeze and tickled his cheek, and he felt the oddest sense of being out of his depth, even with the shoreline right ahead of him.

'I'm sorry,' she said again, softer now. 'Owen, what's really bothering you? You've been weird all morning.'

'My dad's just winding me up,' he said quickly.

No point dissecting these feelings right now... or ever.

'Why?'

'He's getting married. Again.'

Owen was about to elaborate when his phone rang again. His mother.

Sadie's eyes burned into his back the whole time he was talking. As predicted, his mother was furious, but he knew the wobble of her voice by now, and all the things she wasn't saying underneath her irritation. She was heartbroken all over again.

'He'll chew this woman up and spit her out like he did to me—like he did to Edwina, and

Abigail. He's like a kid with a shiny new toy. I hope you never treat anyone like that, Owen…'

'Mum, you know what he's like. What do you want me to say?'

Sadie steered the boat back to the jetty after he'd ended the call. They both knew their fishing trip was over for a second time.

'Do you want to talk about it?' she asked, as he tied the boat's ropes to a post on the jetty.

The morning sun showed no sign of disappearing behind the famous Scottish rain clouds, but that conversation had sapped every inch of his own sparkle.

'I don't think there's much to talk about,' he told her tightly. 'He's always been this way. Done with one woman—on to the next. Maybe it runs in the family, huh?'

He said the last part rhetorically, under his breath, but she heard and caught at his arm.

'Owen, I really didn't mean what I said before. I don't know why I even said it. I haven't heard you talk about anyone in a while now. Was there no one in America…?'

Her voice faltered slightly as she asked the question. It caught him off-guard. Was that a twinge of discomfort at having to ask him such a thing?

'No,' he replied, searching her face.

Something strangely alien hovered between them as she held his gaze, then looked away.

'I know I've never met him, but I'm sure you're nothing like your dad,' she said quickly. 'Is your mum OK?'

'She'll be fine…she's used to it,' he replied, pulling his arm back.

His heart drummed incessantly as he headed up the gravel path.

Sadie followed him. 'How many wives has your dad had, exactly, Owen? You've never actually said.'

'Too many,' he replied, realising that till now he'd been too embarrassed even to talk about it with her.

He exhaled deeply, curling his fists into his pockets for a moment. He shouldn't be venting to Sadie like this…but she'd been unnerving him lately, and the boat had been small, and she'd heard his mother's words just now, even though she hadn't been on speakerphone. Humiliation was encroaching upon his cool, and it was not a nice feeling.

'I don't know why, but it's like Mum's still in love with him. Can you believe that?'

He expected her to laugh—the thought was insane, after all—but Sadie's eyes narrowed as she studied him. Then she shrugged. 'I don't know… I guess being in love is powerful, right?'

'Being in love is a waste of time,' he shot back.

He expected her to roll her eyes, the way she

usually did when it came to his opinions on anything regarding romance, but this time she didn't.

'You just don't want anyone to know how wonderful you really are,' she said on a sigh, sending his heart crashing into his ribs. 'I see that, Owen. And love is not a waste of time. Maybe you've just never let yourself feel it.'

'Oh? And you have?' Her nonchalance was infuriating. 'What about Callum? You guys never had anything in common—nothing at all, Sadie. Did you ever even love him for real, or were you just looking for a comfort blanket?'

The hurtful words were out before he'd had time to think. He stepped towards her, cursing himself. 'Sadie, damn it. I'm sorry…'

'Whatever. I haven't got time for this.' Sadie slipped from his reach, put her hands in the air and marched on past him, up towards the house.

Owen let her go, oscillating between annoyance, helplessness and confusion. She'd launched a truth bomb at him out of nowhere and he'd reacted by pushing her away—which was the last thing he really wanted.

What was going on between them lately? Maybe he should give her space, he decided. His father's news was getting to him more than he knew.

CHAPTER FIVE

'So, SPILL IT. What's the deal with you and Owen? You're practically giving off sparks.'

Portia DeMagio was looking down her nose at Sadie over her glasses, and she hoped she'd manage to convey non-comprehension, even as her pulse spiked at the sexologist's keen observation.

'Just now...before he left the room—you should have seen the way he looked at you. But you're ignoring him. Outside of these sessions, I mean. What did he do?'

'This session is about you, not me,' Sadie reminded her, with a smile she was sure hadn't made it to her eyes.

What look had he given her?

'Now, walk me through this week's journal entries,' she told Portia. 'I see you've been noting what you've been eating and drinking before the headaches start?'

'Yes. Owen's plan is already making a noticeable difference. His lovely face always helps, too. Am I right?' Portia shot her a sideways smile and kept her hands on top of the journal, tapping her fingers on the closed book. 'Come on! I see something's going on between you two.'

'We're not going there,' Sadie replied quickly, trying and failing to take the journal from the stubborn woman.

'Don't be offended. Reading people is my job.' Portia informed her, who was looking radiant in a red shirt and black trousers.

'It's *my* job to focus on you,' Sadie told her patient gently, and finally managed to extract the journal from her hands.

Together they went over her entries for the week, and discussed how Owen's cold laser therapy and new electrical muscle stimulation programme, combined with a plant-based diet, was already helping to reduce the severity of her headaches. Sadie was showing her how to stretch out any tight muscles that might be contributing to her headaches, and advising hot yoga, which Portia was insisting Sadie join in with.

There were regular yoga sessions here at Rothesay Recovery. Maybe they *all* needed some time out in a Zen space, Sadie thought. Her mind would not stop slipping back to that stupid heated encounter by the lake a week ago.

She was still fuming at the way Owen had spoken to her about Callum, saying what he'd obviously been dying to say since the break-up. The person she'd considered her closest ally had accused her of keeping a comfort blanket as a boyfriend!

You're only annoyed because he's right, the voice in her head kept telling her.

'Are you sure you're not going to give me at least a snippet?' Portia wheedled, looking up from her journal. 'If you won't tell me what he's done, start at the start. How did you meet?'

'At college.'

'Have you ever kissed?'

Sadie snorted, feeling her cheeks flame at the question. 'Absolutely not.'

'But you've thought about it. I can tell.'

Sadie sat back in her swivel chair and sighed. Thoughts of kissing Owen raced like poisoned arrows through her brain, faster than she could stop them. But it was no good thinking stuff like this...she'd stopped doing that years ago, after that ill-fated night at Sylvester's.

'You *have*—there's no point denying it!' Portia looked delighted. 'Heck, honey, even *I* have. He's a catch.'

Realising she wasn't going to let it go, and also maybe feeling a little comforted by Portia's profession, Sadie found herself wanting to tell her. What was the harm?

'Actually...there was one time we might have come close...'

They'd not long met. Her group of friends had made plans to hit a cheesy dance club called

Sylvester's, and she'd invited Owen along, too. She could still remember the adrenaline, walking into the club with its throbbing music and flickering neon lights, and seeing his handsome face light up, as if he'd been waiting just for her. She'd contemplated that maybe, just maybe, they might take their burgeoning friendship to the next level that night. They'd been dancing around some kind of strange attraction for a couple of months by then, at least.

But, being her, she'd been so nervous about the prospect, and the huge potential for rejection and/or heartbreak, that she'd lost count of exactly how many cocktails she'd poured down her neck. After getting hideously hammered she'd run off to be sick—and woken up the next morning with a severe hangover and even more severe memory loss.

She was glad that she hadn't done anything stupid. It wasn't as if she'd ever had a one-night stand, and she certainly shouldn't have started that night—with Owen, of all people! She'd simply had a momentary lapse of judgement and forgotten he was entirely unsuitable boyfriend material.

Also, she must have been a total idiot when she was drunk, because he'd done a disappearing act for several weeks after that.

A vague recollection of running from the dance floor had sneaked up on her from time to time, and another one of crawling into a taxi alone. She'd been so utterly embarrassed about the whole night that she'd never mentioned it again. Neither had Owen. In fact, the next time she'd seen him after that, she'd simply said sorry. And he'd said the same back. And, while she had never been entirely sure what *he* was sorry for, she'd decided it was far less humiliating to forget about it and stay friends.

'So, you admit you were attracted to him once upon a time?' Portia was twirling one of her artfully designed earrings around her finger, fascinated.

Sadie snapped back to the present. This wasn't very professional, she realised, but then, nobody here much cared for the regular way of doing things, and opening up to her patients often paid dividends when they did the same to her. If only Conall McCaskill would crack just a little more...

'At one time, yes, I suppose I felt some attraction,' she admitted. 'But we were young. It's different now.'

'You're good friends, aren't you?' Portia mused.

'Yes. Exactly. *Friends*.'

'We should always be friends with our lovers.'

'Maybe if we're living in a romcom...sure. Now, can we talk about *you*, please? How did you meet your husband?'

Portia's expression darkened. *Uh-oh.* Sadie

had a feeling the husband was still in this woman's bad books, for sending her here.

'We were indeed friends before we were lovers,' she said wistfully, after a moment. 'We had sex as an experiment—can you believe that? To see if we had chemistry. I dared him, thinking he'd turn me down. Don't ever assume a man will turn down sex, even if he *is* just your friend.'

She huffed a laugh as Sadie opened the journal and swivelled her chair closer, trying not to think about having sex with Owen. Although now she was, and her throat had turned into the Sahara Desert. Having his big new-muscled arms locked around her would feel like the ultimate definition of protection, and there was nothing that turned her on more than a guy who could make her feel safe.

'And now you're married,' she said, fanning out her hair and pressing a hand briefly to her hot neck.

'And now he's sent me here,' Portia replied acidly.

'Because he loves you.'

'He does love me...' She sighed, softening slightly, as if she was finally coming to terms with the fact that it might have pained her husband to send her here as much as it had hurt her. 'You know, it's funny. When I'm angry with him I want to have sex with him even more. This is the longest we've ever been apart...and celibate.'

Sadie bit back a laugh. She couldn't imagine experiencing that amount of passion. She'd certainly never had angry sex with anyone, and probably never would. Sex for her was always nice...kind of standard, she supposed. Never particularly passionate or exciting, just something you did in a relationship once or twice a month.

How embarrassing it was that she'd dared to accuse Owen of never letting himself feel real love.

She was used to blocking out the fact that she'd always chosen safety and security over real, burning passion, thanks to losing both after losing Chris. But wouldn't it be nice...wouldn't it be everything...to feel safe as well as sexy, and wanted, and in love. *Really* in love.

Portia was watching her closely. 'When Stan and I fight, we can go at it four, five, even six times a night,' she said. 'Get yourself a man who you can fight with, Dr Mills. Do you and Owen ever fight?'

Sadie cleared her throat. 'Um...not really,' she said, turning back to the journal, her mind spinning.

She and Owen had never had a disagreement at all before coming here. But she did feel that spark between them, if she was totally honest.

She'd felt it when she opened the door to him after he'd come back from America. He'd pulled her in tight and breathed in her hair on the doorstep, as if the smell of her shampoo was giving him life, and she'd cried in his arms, half over Callum, half in relief at having Owen home and all to herself.

She'd felt it on the lake, when he'd pulled that fish hook out of her hair tenderly, almost lovingly, just like a boyfriend would.

Things had been changing between them ever since he'd come back from America—it was pointless to deny it. But knowing what she knew about him now—how affected he'd been by his parents his whole life—his resistance to relationships made a lot more sense.

He would never give her what she needed.

All the more reason not to let these new feelings marinate, she decided resolutely.

Hours later, alone in her room, Sadie turned another page of her novel and failed, yet again, to take in what was happening in the story.

Owen hadn't come back yet. She'd been listening out for the familiar creak of his door, the sound of the key turning that always told her when he was back in his room. But it was already ten-thirty p.m., and still no sign of him.

Ugh. Maybe he was avoiding her after their altercation by the lake.

Putting her book down, she stared out of the window. Was he really still angry with her for the pleasure-seeker comment? It was clearly her fault they'd argued, but he'd pushed her buttons too.

'Sadie?'

A quiet knock on her door made her leap from the bed so fast she almost tripped over her shoes. Owen's mouth was right up against the door outside—she could see his shadow underneath.

'Are you awake?' he whispered.

Opening the door, she forced herself to look sleepier than she was, having been lying awake, wondering where he was. Seeing him in jeans and his familiar burgundy hoodie sent a warm wave rippling through her, but she crossed her arms over her dress and cardigan to refrain from hugging him.

'Awake,' she confirmed. 'What's up?'

'Are we still in a fight?' he asked, cocking an eyebrow.

She bit back a smile. 'No.'

'Good, because that was boring. I have something to show you.'

Owen took her hand and led her down the corridor, whispering that she'd have to tiptoe so as not to disturb the other staff on their floor. She knew Parminder was in one of the rooms near theirs.

In less than five minutes he was flicking the lights on in the library on the ground floor.

Sadie blinked. The fire in the marble fireplace with its raised slate hearth was crackling. The

gardens, which flooded the place with sunlight
during the day, were opal-black outside the tall,
narrow windows. Without the daytime backdrop,
the floor-to-ceiling bookshelves made her feel
as if she was back in the seventeenth century.

Owen led her to a soft green couch, motioned
for her to sit, and picked up a remote control.
Sadie gasped in delight as a huge white screen
appeared from the ceiling and a projector high
above her head shone the opening titles of Conall
McCaskill's movie *Surrender* straight into her
eyeline.

'How did you…?'

'I got Fergal to pull a few strings,' he said,
and shot her a wink. 'Told him I needed a peace
offering.'

He dropped to the couch beside her and
reached for a bag he'd obviously left there earlier. So this was what he'd been doing so late…
setting this up!

Producing two wine glasses and a bottle of her
favourite Chardonnay, he proceeded to apologise.

She interrupted him. 'Let's forget about it.'

'Deal,' he said with a relieved sigh, pressing
'play' on the movie and scooting to the other
end of the couch. She swallowed back a strange
disappointment at the distance between them,
and studied the lines of his handsome profile in
the low light. DC Shawn flashed onto the giant
screen. It was the famous scene where the char-

acter reeled off a list of curses in French, and it sent Owen's expression to new levels of amusement.

'Check Conall out—he looks so young. You know, I got those tests back tonight... Did I tell you I think his depression is linked to reduced activity in the left frontal lobe? Do you think he still knows any French? We should test him... add some language-related exercises into his programme.'

Sadie couldn't talk about Conall McCaskill's linguistic abilities right now. Reaching for the remote, she paused the movie. Crossing her legs towards Owen on the couch, she studied his face.

'You were right, Owen. What you said about Callum.'

Owen sucked in a breath through his nose and shook his head. Suddenly her heartbeat was loud in her ears.

'Sadie, it's none of my business.'

His face was deadly serious in the firelight, and she gripped her wine glass harder, so as not to lean across and wipe away the tiny black smear of what was probably coal dust across his left cheek.

'I made it your business when I cried on you over him,' she said tightly. 'I came to you because we always have fun. Because I knew my tears wouldn't last long with you around.'

Why was her heart doing that weird fluttery thing again?

'But you were right, Owen. He didn't exactly set my heart on fire. And I'm going to make better choices from now on.'

'Well, don't look to me as a role model,' he shot back, but his eyes narrowed as he searched hers, as if he was wrestling with a need to eject some further self-deprecation. She knew he always cracked jokes when he was nervous.

Owen took their glasses away and scooted a little closer. He reached for her with his big, familiar warm hands and held hers lightly, turning her wrists this way and that contemplatively as he spoke.

'I know I push people away when they get too close. But I'm not... I don't want to...'

'What *do* you want, Owen?'

Sadie felt her breath catch. She forced herself to meet his eyes, even though suddenly it felt like a loaded question that involved her and caused the blood to throb in her veins. What exactly was she wanting him to say, here?

'What I want is...' Owen faltered and went quiet, still turning her hands over in his.

The fire spat and hissed. A cat screeched somewhere outside. The moment felt eternal. A memory flickered to the forefront of her brain and fizzled out before she could catch it. Was it the memory of a moment when they'd been like this before? Close... On a precipice...

She found herself leaning into him slowly, studying the slight stubble across his jawline, then looking back up to his eyes. The gap between their faces grew smaller and smaller. For just a second she honestly thought they were going to...

Owen closed his eyes an inch from her face and dashed both hands through his hair. The moment evaporated. *Poof.* Gone.

'What I really want is popcorn,' he announced, unfurling himself from the cushions with the speed of a cheetah and making for the door. 'I left it in my room. I'll be right back.'

Sadie pressed her palms to her eyes. Her cheeks felt clammy and her toes were numb from sitting cross-legged, frozen in place, waiting... waiting...waiting for what?

Oh. My. God.

What the heck had just happened? Had they almost *kissed*?

Making a steeple of her still-warm fingers, she closed her eyes and caught her breath. That had been a lucky escape. He could have kissed her right then, and she could've kissed him back, and that would've ruined everything! Owen was the only stable thing in her life. Rocking this boat they were on was out of the question. Just because he'd done something nice for her…like a boyfriend would.

You must be out of your mind.

She raked her hands through her hair. Portia had got to her, she reminded herself. He might have been about to bop her on the nose or something equally playful. He would *never* try and kiss her. If Owen felt anything remotely romantic towards her it would have happened years ago, and nothing ever *had* happened. She'd never have let it—not with his reputation.

But, then again, she'd never seen him look at her like that before.

And he hadn't actually been with a woman in ages, if what he'd said about America was true. It was almost as if he'd come back from Boston a different person.

Maybe…

No. She hugged her knees to her chest against the cushions. Owen was off-limits. He'd never give her the commitment, the wedding, the children… He hated all that stuff. All the stuff she wanted. And even if he did decide to want it, who was to say he wouldn't change his mind? Then she'd lose her best friend for ever.

Will you just calm down?

Fanning herself and soothing her hammering heart with long, deep breaths, she settled into a corner of the couch and did not move—even when he returned with the popcorn and joined her in their silent agreement to act as if nothing had happened.

CHAPTER SIX

'WHAT AN ABSOLUTE BUTE,' Owen quipped, sweeping his arm out over the windswept ocean.

Sadie smirked and huddled further into her coat, which she'd already mumbled about not being quite warm enough. The beach at Ettrick Bay stretched a mile ahead of them, and if he tried hard enough he could *still* picture Thailand.

He went to take his coat off, then paused. Would it be too weird to offer Sadie his jacket after what had happened a few nights ago? The thing they still hadn't talked about.

'Oui, s'il vous plaît, j'aimerais votre veste,' she said now in French, which she was pretty good at.

They'd been encouraging Conall McCaskill to remember his French all morning. Sadie's mouth twitched with another smirk below another pair of oversized sunglasses as she held her hand out expectantly.

Shuffling out of his jacket, he settled on handing it over, rather than attempting to do the gentlemanly thing and draping it over her shoulders. For a moment, as she slid her arms into the well-worn leather sleeves and was instantly swamped, the tension that had been there all morning, and for the last few days, lifted.

'Do you think he's making any progress?' she asked him, nodding towards Conall McCaskill. He was squatting on the sand, looking content for maybe the first time ever, tearing bits of bread from a loaf to feed a flock of birds.

'I think so. I think he secretly loves saying lines from *Surrender* in French,' he replied. 'Especially the curse words.'

Thanks to his success in identifying the decreased activity in the actor's left frontal lobe as an antagonist for his ongoing depression, Owen had assigned him a number of rehabilitation exercises to target that area of the brain specifically. Unfortunately, frontal lobe damage often affected an individual's motivation to participate in goal-directed behaviours, like rehabilitation itself, so they hadn't told Conall what they were doing, specifically.

They were being sneaky, but successfully remembering parts of his old screenplay in French whilst casually taking in the sights seemed to be cheering him up.

To their shock, Conall strode over to a dog-walker, who'd stopped to stare in disbelief. He even crouched down to pose for a photo with her huge brown Labrador. Sadie chuckled and shot Owen a look—and *boom!* He was straight back on that couch the other night, closer than close, seconds away from kissing her, and forcing himself not to.

'You talk to him more than I do,' he said to her, clearing his throat, focusing on Conall. 'At least you seem to be getting to him with whatever it is you talk about in your sessions. He only agrees on outings if you come along too.'

'He mentioned his son to me yesterday, actually,' she said, hugging his jacket around her more tightly. 'It was the first time he's brought him up.'

'What did he say?'

'He didn't say much about the accident,' she said, thoughtfully. 'He just talked about the first time Scott said he wanted to be a stuntman. Somehow the kid got up on the roof in a Superman cape and tried to fly off it. He was only five years old. Wound up in hospital with a broken arm.'

'Ouch.' Owen sucked in a breath. 'Who could've predicted his stunts would actually kill him all these years later?'

Sadie looked at him sideways. 'Conall's lost a part of his soul, Owen. Everything is meaningless to him now, which is why he's so angry and cold. I saw myself in him the whole time he was speaking, because it was how *I* felt after Chris died.'

Her chin wobbled slightly, and then she bowed her head. Suddenly Sadie had that look his mum had always used to have when she was trying to stop another tidal wave of emotion from sweeping her away. A stone formed in his stomach.

'Did you talk about Chris to Conall?' he asked now, remembering she hardly ever talked about her brother—not to anyone.

She nodded, biting down on her lip.

'You can talk to me about him if you ever need to,' he heard himself say, reaching for her hand amongst the folds of his jacket.

Why had he never said that before?

'Thank you,' she whispered, squeezing his fingers only slightly before dropping them. 'But this isn't about me.'

They stood together, watching their patient, and he wrestled with the questions he'd never felt permitted to ask her before.

'What happened that made you never want to talk about it?' he ventured eventually, deciding now was as good a time as any. 'If you want to tell me now, I mean. No pressure.'

'Nothing,' she said quickly. 'People die, Owen, and it's horrible, and gut-wrenching, and a million things you can't describe. But that's just a part of it. After that there's nothing. That's the worst. When you can't even think of a reason to breathe.'

Sadie wrapped her arms around herself again and a chill seized his bones, rooting him to the spot. Death's shadow hadn't fallen on him yet. At least, it hadn't taken anyone close to him. He'd always assumed he'd deal with it just fine. Everyone died, like she said, but it was a part of life; it shouldn't necessarily stop you living yours.

But something about her face had him holding his breath. He'd just put up walls...so as not to feel anything. Maybe that was why he'd never pressed Sadie on the details of her brother's death. Deep down he couldn't face what was coming for him. One day that pain would become his, with his mum, even his dad, for all his sins. And, sure, things weren't perfect, but he wasn't ready for *that*. Not by a long shot.

'It took me a long time to get myself out of that and deal with both my parents...'

'They divorced right after he died, didn't they?'

'Not right after. It was more like a slow unravelling. It eventually happened during my first year at Imperial—before we'd even met.'

'But it's not like you never speak to them,' he said.

He'd heard her on the phone with them, separately, a few times.

'I speak to them. But it's never about anything

real. They don't talk about Chris…or what was wrong with him. Seventeen-year-old guys don't just decide to die unless there's something really wrong, Owen. He was my younger brother and we were close. I should've noticed it sooner. My parents…' She trailed off, closing her mouth firmly.

'He *killed* himself?'

Owen's heart was skidding under his shirt. How had he never known this? He'd always assumed it had been a terrible accident.

'He said he couldn't "do life" any more,' Sadie said. 'I found the note. He stuck it on the inside of his bedroom door, right before he took his motorbike out. I think he fell in with the wrong crowd…drugs, maybe. He'd started getting moody and secretive…but before that he was the happiest, most laid-back kid you'd ever met.'

'Holy hell…'

Pulling himself together, Owen took her shoulders gently, forcing her to face him, tilting her chin up.

What the hell? I should've known this sooner.
But she'd never said any of this before.

'I'm so sorry you went through all that, but surely you don't blame yourself in any way, do you, Sadie? Your parents don't blame you for what happened?'

'I don't want to think about it, Owen,' she said, avoiding his eyes. 'Your friendship means so much to me. You help me more than you know, even when we don't talk about all that stuff.'

Owen flinched inside at the way she emphasised the word friendship—like a reminder to him not to get too close.

'You wouldn't be you if that "stuff" hadn't happened,' he said. 'And for the record you can *always* talk to me—about whatever you like.'

He almost added something like *That's what friends are for*, but he refrained. He wasn't much of a friend if he hadn't even known all this till now. He'd been too wrapped up in his own family sagas to notice she'd had one of her own—something way, way worse.

'I'm so sorry I never knew about any of this,' he said.

'Why would you? I never told you.'

Dropping his hands from her shoulders, he wrestled with a sudden urge to pull her closer, but he knew nothing would suffice in this moment.

The wind whipped up her hair and the seagulls swooped around them and he couldn't get her words out of his head. How could he not have known? And what else had he totally missed about Sadie? If she blamed herself in any way for not seeing suicide speeding up on her brother—or, worse, if her parents blamed her for not being an attentive enough sister... Well, that was a hell of a lot more than he knew what to do with right now. It needed some serious processing.

'Did you want to kiss me the other night?' she asked him suddenly, out of nowhere.

What?

Sadie was scanning his eyes. He was still reeling from the news about her brother's suicide and now she was bringing this up?

'Because you *have* to be thinking about it, too. It was a bit of a weird moment between us, right? On the couch…before you went to get the popcorn?'

Owen's stomach tied itself into one huge knot as he grappled with how to answer. Her gaze was loaded. He'd assumed they'd both decided to forget it, but here they were. She'd clearly been thinking about it as much as he had.

Before he could stop himself he launched into an award-winning American accent. 'You're pretty as a picture, but you're the last person I'd want to kiss, Sadie Mills.'

Sadie just nodded thoughtfully and was silent for longer than was comfortable. Then she said a very quiet 'Good…' and he kicked himself as she pulled out her phone, signalling the end of their discussion.

Great job, Owen. Way to ruin a serious conversation.

'Hey, you two. *J'ai besoin d'une tasse de café!*'

Conall McCaskill was done with feeding the

birds and was strolling purposefully towards them, shouting something about coffee?

'Sure, we'll swing by the tearoom,' Sadie chirped, and then she said it again in French, stepping away from Owen and motioning them all down the beach.

Owen's jaw ticked as he followed after them, watching her in his jacket.

You're the last person I'd want to kiss, Sadie Mills...

Why the hell had he said that—and in such a stupid way, too? Right after she'd dropped the bombshell about her brother.

Sadie knew him. She knew he used humour whenever he felt cornered, or when he wanted to distance himself from something...or someone. He'd said she could always talk to him, and then he'd shown her she actually couldn't.

Idiot.

In the quaint, aquatic-themed white and blue tearoom, Conall wore sunglasses—which, of course, meant more people recognised him than ever. Word was already out that he was staying in the small town, but when Sadie asked if he'd rather leave and go back to Rothesay he was firm in his decision.

'Non, merci.'

Outings like this were imperative when it came to Sadie monitoring his progress in society.

And Owen took this new attitude as a sign that the actor was feeling better about being around people than before—thanks to the confidence boost whenever a forgotten word or phrase came back to him, and of course Sadie's constant efforts to coax his grief out into the open, instead of smothering it with rage and alcohol.

His thoughts kept slipping from analysing Conall's movements to Sadie. What she must have gone through, losing her brother to suicide. She'd learned her skills from her own experience as much as from her studies—what to do and what *not* to do when a person's grief overcame them in her presence. He'd pretty much made a habit out of making life a joke around her since they'd met, so it was no wonder she hadn't ever opened up to him properly about the things that actually mattered to her.

But then on his end there had always been an underlying fear of letting her get too close, he supposed. Just in case those feelings ever came back.

Showing his true emotions had brought him nothing but disdain from his mother while he was growing up, and he wasn't very good at showing them now. Not that getting yelled at for being a sniffling and 'useless' person when he was eleven was an excuse any more. That had been years ago!

'Is it OK to get a photo?' A young mother approached, wanting a selfie with Conall.

'No charge for you,' Conall told her, sliding out of his chair and causing the rest of the people in the café to turn and stare.

Owen moved his chair to make more room, and both his arm and knee made contact with Sadie's. She shot him a sideways glance and immediately the tension was back.

Undeniable.

It practically filled the busy bustling tearoom. She shifted her chair around too, so they weren't touching, and Owen found his foot tapping impatiently under the table. Was it going to be weird between them now?

'We'll have to go if this continues,' she told him, bobbing her head towards the photo session.

For a second he thought she meant if this weirdness between them continued, and he was about to agree. But…

'I know this was his idea,' she went on'. 'But we're not supposed to be encouraging people to—'

'I know when you two are talking about me,' Conall interrupted, as the woman moved off with her daughter. 'I decide what I do with my fans, and when.'

Their surly star was back, grumpy as ever.

Conall slipped on his jacket while someone

else sneaked a photo of him from behind. 'But you're right—we should get going.'

Owen went to hand Sadie his jacket again. It was still pretty chilly outside. But this time she refused.

They spent the ride back in their private car in silence. Both Sadie and Conall stared out of the window from the back seat, seemingly lost in thought. Owen ground his teeth in the passenger seat.

It *was* awkward now. Even if Conall hadn't been in the car it would have been awkward. Confusion spun into irritation. Did she honestly think he would have kissed her that night?

OK, yes, maybe he'd been thinking about it, in another momentary lapse of judgement, but he'd never actually *do* it. That would just be messy. Sadie needed someone who could give her all the things he couldn't offer anyone right now—maybe not ever. Who could blame her after what she'd been through?

He was just contemplating how he could continue to be there for her as a friend, and thinking how much that actually sucked, when Sadie's phone chirped loudly in her pocket. Her face fell as she answered the call.

'What is it?' he asked, instincts primed.

'It's Portia,' she told him, one hand over the phone. 'Driver, please hurry—we need to get back!'

CHAPTER SEVEN

THEY FOUND PORTIA flat on her back in the yoga studio. Dr Calhoun was on her knees, one hand on Portia's clammy forehead, trying to force the poor woman to keep the oxygen flowing. The harrowing howls coming from Portia vibrated in Sadie's ears.

'It started with the usual tingle and escalated faster than usual,' Dr Calhoun explained as Sadie and Owen knelt at her side.

'You were doing so well on the new programme,' Sadie said to Portia as Owen took over with the oxygen. 'It's just a setback. It has made a difference, I promise.'

'I know, but I could feel this coming on when I woke up.' She winced. 'Ooh, I miss Stan… I need my husband.'

'We'll call him soon,' she promised.

The other in-patients were hovering outside the studio, dressed in their activewear. They'd been midway through a blissful yoga-nidra class, apparently, when Portia's cluster headache had caught up with her.

'You can leave me with Owen and Sadie,' Portia managed to tell Dr Calhoun, clutching Owen's wrist as he tried to adjust her mask. 'They know what to do.'

Portia drew a few more sharp consecutive breaths from the apparatus as Dr Calhoun closed the door after her, but her eyes were streaming like waterfalls and Sadie could only imagine the searing red-hot agony she must be experiencing around her skull.

Suicide headaches. That was what they called them.

The name usually sent her mind in a thousand directions, but today she pushed all thoughts of Chris away. It had been bad enough seeing Owen looking at her with pity just now, after what she'd told him. Ever since he'd been looking at her differently, and it made her deeply uncomfortable—especially as she'd brought up their almost-kiss, too.

Well, she couldn't have ignored the giant elephant in the room much longer, even if *he'd* wanted to.

She helped him now, getting Portia to her knees instead of lying on her back.

'Deep breaths from your belly, not your mouth, remember,' he told her. 'Concentrate. Distract your mind. It can only focus on one thing at a time…'

Sadie held Portia's hand, wishing that were true, while Portia did everything Owen asked and had probably instructed her to do before, in case this ever happened.

The yoga studio was small, white and bright. Various ferns in crocheted hanging baskets made living drapes over the floor-to-ceiling windows, and six purple yoga mats sat ominously empty nearby on the hardwood floor. Not a place for this much pain, Sadie observed grimly.

'That's right…in and out…deep and deeper,' Owen instructed—right before Portia emitted another yowl that tore Sadie's heart into shreds.

She squeezed Portia's hand tighter and reminded her that this would pass. Even though the cruel attack seemed to last for ever.

'I ate a bacon sandwich,' Portia told them eventually, squeezing her eyes shut as if it hurt to speak.

Owen's brow crinkled in confusion.

'It's the only thing I ate that was different,' the woman explained after a moment, courageously swallowing back another stab of pain.

'She's been keeping a journal,' Sadie explained.

'Oh, yes,' Owen replied, without meeting her eyes. 'So it's nitrates…the nitrates in bacon that's one of the triggers. Good to know.'

'It's always the things I love most that cause this,' Portia said next, still wincing although the deep breaths and oxygen finally seemed to be helping somewhat. 'It used to happen after I had sex with my husband. I'm sure he thought I was possessed. He refused to make love to me for months—can you believe it?'

'Well, if sex caused you this much pain, I can,' Sadie replied thoughtfully, imagining for a moment being possessed, her legs locked around some equally wicked demon lover, begging for more. Owen's face flashed onto the image and she swallowed it away.

What?

'We'll get your sex-life back on track, don't worry,' Owen announced.

'Promises, promises,' Portia responded. Her headache was seemingly abating with every breath. 'It's not every day someone like you tells me something like that, Dr Penner.'

'Good to see you've got your sense of humour back,' Sadie interjected, helping her sit up as a stab of something like jealousy surprised her.

The forty-eight-year-old woman was decidedly less pale now, and it hadn't escaped Sadie's attention that she was very attractive for her age. Hmm… Maybe telling Portia about her and Owen's past had ignited Portia's imagination. Maybe she was conjuring up all sorts of thoughts about

Owen in the confines of her room, Sadie thought. She was missing her husband, after all.

Irritation tingled around her nerves as Owen waggled his eyebrows in her direction. He was clearly humouring Portia she was their patient after all.

When Portia announced that she was feeling much better they helped her out of the studio together, supporting her on each side, and took her back to her suite. Sadie stood outside the bathroom while Portia changed out of her yoga clothes, and felt Owen lasering her back with his eyes.

Every time he addressed her about anything at all, she regretted asking if he'd wanted to kiss her. But if she hadn't it would have made things even *more* awkward. He must be thinking about it too—how could he not be?

Asking him about it had been a good way of trying to distract him from asking any more questions about Chris or her estranged family, she supposed. That topic always brought up way too many emotions. More than she had the time or energy to deal with—especially with patients around.

Conall McCaskill was in her head *and* in her heart already. All that pain in his eyes… All she'd seen in the way he'd wrung his hands on his lap when he'd talked about Scott in their last session… It had touched her, and dragged her through Chris's death all over again. It was to be expected, always. It was part of her job. But this time Owen had seen it.

She had no place for vulnerability. It would only set her back on this path she'd forged for herself since all that.

They closed the door on Portia's suite, leaving her to rest, and walked down the photo-lined corridor. Sunlight streamed in through the windows onto Owen's face as they made small talk about how Portia's diet would need even closer monitoring, with the help of Saskia, the resident nutritionist.

Sadie had one foot on the stairs when Owen took her arm and pulled her back up to the landing. Her heart skyrocketed right up to the turrets as he searched her eyes.

'Sadie, how are you?'

'What? I'm fine…'

'I've been thinking about what you told me earlier…about Chris.'

Oh, God.

He paused, and something about his hand on the sleeve of her jumper made sweat break out on the back of her neck.

'Listen, if you ever need to—'

'I don't. I told you,' she said quickly, hating the look of sympathy on his face. Fresh annoyance at herself made her cheeks sting as she removed herself from his concerned grip. 'I shouldn't have told you the details. You didn't need to know.'

Owen stepped back from her, looking slightly wounded. 'I'm just sorry I never asked you about it before.' He lowered his voice, his obvious concern for her making his eyes crease. 'He committed *suicide*, Sadie…that's a little different from dying in a motorcycle accident. You do know that's what I thought happened, all this time?'

'Why wouldn't you have thought that?' she said staunchly. 'I didn't elaborate on the details.'

'I know—but why not?'

Sadie shrugged, wishing her stomach would stop tangling itself into that giant knot. This was exactly what she didn't want to happen. Her best friend looking at her as if she needed to be swaddled in cotton wool, or as if she had some problem he now had to fix, like everyone else in here. It was bad enough that she hadn't seen it coming with Chris. The last thing she wanted was for Owen to start poking around.

'It happened a long time ago, Owen. I'm fine,' she said stiffly, adjusting her wristwatch.

'But you're not, are you? And Conall's getting to you, bringing it all up whenever he talks about losing Scott…'

'It's my job, Owen. And I'll deal with it like I always do. Without your help.'

Owen straightened his shoulders and blew air from his nose, and she knew she wouldn't escape this confrontation. She'd told him something deeply personal and made it his business—like she always seemed to do with Owen lately, despite trying not to.

'I have to go to my next appointment,' she said, hurrying on down the stairs ahead of him.

'Of course you do,' he muttered behind her.

Great—now she'd offended him. And she knew that was grossly unfair. But it was better than feeling torn by his lips being too close again, his eyes being too probing again.

What was she meant to do with all this? It was bad enough that she was even having these weird new feelings for her friend. And he felt the same, she could tell. When he'd said he'd never kiss her this morning…that had been a *blatant* lie. He always did one of those stupid accents whenever he felt put on the spot.

But Owen Penner never wanted more than a good time, and she was not about to let him make *her* his next good time—not for anything.

Sadie continued with her appointments and somehow managed to eat her dinner in the little courtyard outside without Owen interrupting her, like he usually did. As the sun set that evening she still hadn't seen him again.

Good, she thought. For both of them.

She needed to stop treating him like one of her 'comfort blankets' just because there was no one else around who knew her. She'd already decided there would be no more comfort blankets, and here she was, spilling all her issues out to Owen!

That would get her nothing apart from his quick rejection—like he rejected anyone who got too close to him.

Something woke her at three a.m. Sadie shot up in bed, fresh from a fitful dream about Chris calling out to her from somewhere she couldn't reach. Awful!

Pulling on her white embroidered robe and slippers, she made her way downstairs. Sleep would be impossible now, so she might as well make a cup of tea and get some fresh air.

The spring night was unusually mild and welcoming outside. Sadie found herself strolling by the fernery, breathing in the sweet scent of the jasmine trees that lined its entrance, recalling bits of her dream. Just talking about her parents and Chris so briefly to Owen had brought everything back. No wonder it was creeping into her dreams.

Everything was haunting her now—the fact that she hadn't seen just how much Chris had needed help. The fact that guilt had kept her away from home for so long…long enough that she hadn't even known her parents were getting a divorce until after it had happened. She'd been the worst sister and the worst daughter.

Her stomach knotted again as she sat by the

silent mermaid fountain, thinking of Owen, too. He'd looked so hurt that she'd never told him the truth about her brother. All this time she'd let him believe what had happened to him was an accident. All this time. And now he probably thought she didn't trust him with anything serious. That all they had were their laughs, their jokes, their good times.

But it was getting harder not to trust him with *more*...she realised. He was always there for her. He would always be there for her.

As a *friend*, she reminded herself, as soon as her heart started its involuntary fluttering again. All this wandering outside the lines had to stop.

Being in love is a waste of time.

He'd said it himself, the day his mum had called. It wasn't something he was looking for right now—maybe ever. He'd probably stay single till he reached his fifties and wanted companionship—and if he did, so what? Why should that be *her* problem? Why was she even still *thinking* about all this? Their friendship was too good to risk for anything!

With a sigh at the moon, she decided that maybe it was time to go back inside.

Nearing her room, she heard a whisper in the corridor that made her start. She tiptoed to the end of a towering oak bookcase and peered around a row of old encyclopaedic volumes to see someone standing outside Owen's door.

A barefooted Owen was propped up in the doorway on one muscled arm, his broad naked chest on full display, and wearing a pair of comfy checked pyjama bottoms. Pressing her back to the wall and huddling into her robe, she tried to make out what was going on, but she couldn't hear a thing...except soft laughter between a man and a woman.

At four a.m.?

Hunched in the shadow of the bookcase, Sadie tried her best to slow the sudden pounding of her suspicious heart. Eventually Owen closed his door, with one last soft, telling chuckle. His visitor walked straight past her, oblivious, and Sadie dared a peek just as whoever it was unlocked a nearby door and slipped inside.

Even from the back, the woman's long, black satiny hair and dark exotic grace was a giveaway.

Sadie stood there, fuming in the darkness.

Parminder.

Owen was meeting Parminder in the middle of the night.

CHAPTER EIGHT

OWEN CARVED INTO a slice of the chicken on his plate, tracking the busy dining room for Sadie. She hadn't stepped foot in here at the usual time for the last five days, and he had a feeling she was afraid he'd probe her about her past again. As if he'd dare!

If she'd wanted to talk about the grief and the guilt she still carried around she would have told him the full story before now, but obviously she didn't trust him with the serious stuff. He was the joker. The stand-in comfort blanket till she found someone more suitable to handle her heart. The *pleasure-seeker*.

'Penny for your thoughts!'

A voice broke into his depressing internal monologue.

'What?'

'You look like you're thinking about something very serious. And you're murdering your peas.'

Parminder slid in next to him, and he realised

he'd turned his green peas into tiny explosions, smashed on his plate. He also noticed she'd undone the top three buttons of her shirt, revealing just a hint of cleavage—for his benefit, no doubt.

Parminder had been finding new reasons to talk to him for days—ever since she'd knocked on his door in the middle of the night several days ago in a skimpy nightdress, claiming to be scared after seeing a ghost. It was in his best interests to be polite to her right now, but he'd have preferred to eat in peace or with Sadie.

Where was she, anyway? Avoiding his probing was one thing, taking it to extremes by missing the famous Rothesay Recovery Sunday lunch was not like her at all.

Parminder started telling him about Conall McCaskill's latest spat with a doctor. 'He was only doing a regular check-up, but Mr McCaskill almost got violent. Apparently he only wants to deal with you and Dr Mills going forward.'

Owen frowned at his potatoes. Conall's recent setback was the talk of Rothesay this morning, and it was very disheartening to say the least. He still wouldn't talk about Scott's accident with him, but all healing was a work in progress, after all.

'Might be time to help redirect that anger into something more aggressive than potting plants… like woodwork, or bag punching…' Parminder was still offering advice on Conall, and he forced himself to pay attention.

'Maybe he could learn to play the bagpipes,' he offered. 'Those guys always look like their lungs are about to burst. Could be a good way to tire him out. I'll talk to Sadie about it.'

Speak of the devil.

In walked Sadie—finally. His back tensed all over again as their eyes met.

'Would you mind?' he asked Parminder quickly, and reluctantly she shuffled over and made room for Sadie next to him at the table.

'I knew you wouldn't miss the roast lunch,' he said as Sadie slid into the seat, eyeing him cautiously. Her potatoes were drowning in gravy, as usual. 'Is there chicken under there somewhere too?' he joked, trying to lift the immediate tension between them.

'I like gravy,' she said simply, reaching across him for the pepper.

He caught her arm softly and leaned closer, away from Parminder's hearing. 'Are you OK? You've been...noticeably absent.'

'I've been busy,' she replied curtly, removing her arm and shifting her eyes to Parminder. 'I'm sure you have been too.'

He frowned at her. She knew his schedule the same way he knew hers. She hadn't been *that* busy.

'What were you two talking about just now?' Sadie asked casually.

The way she'd pulled her hair back tight and buttoned her blouse three times higher than Parminder's, right to her throat, made her look like a strict headmistress.

'Parminder and I were discussing how Mr McCaskill should play the bagpipes,' he said, thinking how hot she looked, all prim and proper. 'Maybe we can add it to his rehab regimen, to help him get some anger out.'

Sadie huffed a laugh. 'Just because he's Scottish it doesn't mean he automatically wants to know how to play the bagpipes, Owen. Besides, bagpipes make people angry.'

He chuckled. 'You have a point. But I've come here to Scotland. I want bagpipes.'

A smile teetered on her lips, but it vanished as Parminder cut in enthusiastically.

'Maybe *you* should learn, Owen?' She tossed her veil of long black hair over her shoulder and almost knocked a spoon off the table, too. 'We'll get you a kilt too. I bet you'd look good in one.'

'Now, that I wouldn't mind,' he mused, imagining it for a moment. 'I've heard the fresh Scottish air feels damn fine blowing in under a kilt...'

Sadie stood up again quickly, taking her plate with her. 'I've left my book upstairs. I'll eat in my room.'

Parminder stopped her giggling abruptly and scraped her chair back, looking at Sadie in horror. 'You're not going upstairs on your own, are you?'

Sadie paused. 'What do you mean?'

'Well, aren't you scared you might see the ghost?'

'I don't believe in ghosts.'

'Parminder's eyes grew wide and beseeching. With a lowered voice she said, 'I saw it...*her*. The other night. Ask Owen. I saw the Lady in White.'

Owen pulled a face. How was he supposed to know what she'd seen? He'd been fast asleep till she'd pounded on his door. 'All I know is that you were scared enough by something to wake me at some ungodly hour,' he said.

Slowly, Sadie lowered herself into the chair again, turning to Parminder. 'You saw the Lady in White?'

Parminder bobbed her head, her eyes darting around the room. 'I got up for a wee and I saw her walking in the garden...all around the fernery and the fountain. But she could be anywhere, right? I haven't been anywhere on my own in this place all week.'

Sadie just stared at her plate. A small smile crept over her face before she picked up her cutlery and resumed eating without a word.

'I know you don't believe me,' Parminder continued, glancing vexedly at her.

'I believe you saw *something*,' Sadie said carefully.

Her eyes flashed to his, and for just a second he saw the old Sadie...the Sadie he'd missed since things had started getting weird. Maybe things *could* go back to normal between them, he thought, wondering all of a sudden what her secret was.

Later that afternoon, Sadie caught him just as he was about to start his regular session with Conall McCaskill.

'Apparently he's asked for both of us today,' she said, smoothing down her shirt and skirt as they took the corridor towards the actor's suite.

'Parminder told me he only wants to deal with us from now on,' he admitted.

Sadie stopped abruptly, arms folded. She had that look on her face, as if she was about to own up to something.

'About Parminder... You know, I've been so annoyed with you for hooking up with a staff member. I thought you were sleeping with her.'

'Why did you think that?' he asked, mimicking her stance while he processed this new information.

So was that why she'd been so cold with him recently? It wasn't just because he'd overstepped some mark and dredged up deep-rooted insecurities she hated to admit to, even to him... it was because she'd deemed him an unprofessional playboy and didn't want to be associated with his behaviour.

Neither was good.

Unless...she'd been *jealous*?

He studied her intently as she spoke, running the possibilities around in his head, noting with some element of concern that he rather enjoyed the thought that she'd been jealous.

'I saw her the other night, after she'd knocked on your door. I was already awake, and coming back to my room. I think it was me she saw down by the fernery, Owen. I was wearing my white robe!'

'The ghost of Sadie walks the grounds at night, tricking the staff?' He smirked.

Sadie pretended to thump him. 'Don't tell her. Then I'd have to admit I saw her that night at your door but didn't say anything, and she'll think I'm weird.'

'You *are* weird,' he confirmed, and she pulled a face at him that made him laugh. 'You didn't tell *me* what you saw, though. That's not like you. Usually I'd get an earful about something like that. Were you jealous?'

'Well, obviously this place is not haunted,' she said thoughtfully, without answering his question. 'Even though there are still those weird banging noises at night. Have you heard them lately?'

'No, but at least now you know it's not *me* who's been doing the banging,' he replied, watching her fiddle with her shirtsleeve buttons, seeing the way she was biting on her lip, the fresh blush of colour on her cheeks. 'For the record, Parminder's crush is all one-sided,' he told her seriously.

'Well, that's good to know,' she replied, talking to the floor. 'Because it wouldn't be very professional to start something up while we're... while you're here.'

'Noted,' he said with a salute, refusing to mention her fumbled Freudian slip as she led the way into Conall McCaskill's suite.

That look. He'd know it a mile off. Women always had that lips pursed, eyes narrowed look when they were jealous. God, if only he could act on his sudden burning urge to grab her, throw her over his shoulder and carry her up to his room. And then throw her on his bed and show her just what her jealousy did to him.

Luckily the A-lister was in a better mood today, but they still had to discuss his recent violent outburst with the other doctor.

'He mentioned Maeve...how I'm upsetting her because I refuse to subject her to this ridiculous gala event, but what did he expect?' he huffed, stretching out on the couch like a cat. 'What if I don't want to attend myself? Did anyone even consider that? It's not like I can be "switched on" all the time. I told you—I decide when I see my fans.'

Owen caught Sadie's look and shut his mouth. OK, so the guy had a giant ego, but it wasn't entirely a bad thing—at least he was getting some of his confidence back, largely thanks to their speech and language sessions that were bringing up things he actually enjoyed remembering and forcing his depression aside in small bursts.

But Conall's wife had been on the phone several times asking for him, and the stubborn man was refusing to speak to her a lot of the time. He blamed her for sending him here, for assuming he needed special help. His pride had taken a kick—that was the real issue here.

'It's not about subjecting anyone to your fans…it's not a public event,' Sadie informed him softly. 'They do it every year. It started as an fundraising event to entertain Rothesay's supporters, and now every year it marks another year since the recovery unit became what it is now: a successful space for healing.'

Owen heard Sadie's voice, laced with empathy.

'It's supposed to be a chance to include people's spouses,' she continued. 'Perhaps Maeve would like to feel more involved with your healing process, seeing as she's still going through her own. It won't help that process if you feel like someone is shutting you out.'

Owen braced himself for another verbal tirade, but Conall just fiddled with the buttons on his stylish tweed jacket and scowled at the ceiling.

'I suppose you would know that,' he said eventually.

He went on to explain how it was the processing of his grief that had caused his violent outburst, something Sadie had encouraged with her sessions, although he regretted lashing out at the doctor the way he had.

Owen prepared his upcoming questions for the actor's weekly analysis, wondering exactly how much Sadie had divulged to him about her own loss. Just by relating to Conall she'd got more out of him than anyone. But she'd never thought to burden *him* with the truth before.

That was still bothering him like a mosquito… the fact that she didn't trust him with anything serious. But then, it wasn't as if he'd ever given her reason to. She'd always had boyfriends for that. He wasn't settling down…he wasn't cut out for being anyone's rock. Never had he given anyone any indication that he'd stick around for more than a few weeks, and Sadie knew all that. But…

But just now she'd pretty much confirmed a case of the green-eyed Loch Ness monster. That look on her face!

He shook himself, pulling his attention back from dangerous territory. Sadie was not someone he could afford to go there with—not for anything. They'd never had to rely on one another solely for attention before—that was all this was. Even though he'd missed her like hell in America, and was still figuring out what that meant, exactly.

'I asked for you both today because I know I need to talk about the accident itself, and I don't want to say it twice,' Conall was saying now, wringing his hands on the couch. 'I know I've been a little bit of a…well, a *lot* of a grump. But I just miss my boy so much…'

His voice wobbled suddenly. Sadie reached out to place a gentle hand on his.

'I see it every time I close my eyes,' said Conall. 'There isn't a day that goes by when I don't blame myself…'

'It was not your fault,' Owen said, standing up in a primal urge not to upset *anyone* in the room any further.

'But I could have prevented it. If only I'd been watching more closely. It was *my* damn movie set!'

'That doesn't mean anything. It was an accident. Both Dr Mills and I know that—everyone knows that.'

Sadie was silent for a moment, tapping her nails on the arm of her chair, and he wondered again, now he'd learned about Chris's suicide, why she'd chosen a career that must dredge up so many bad memories. And this must feel very close to home for her: Conall McCaskill playing the blame game with himself.

Conall wore the look of a gladiator about to

step into an arena with a tiger. Owen half expected him to shut down again and refuse their help entirely, but then Sadie let out a sigh from somewhere deep in her soul.

'The hardest thing is finding a place to start. I know that,' she said into the silence. 'Deep inside, you feel like if you start thinking about it you won't be able stop. But somewhere in between, Conall, there is a place where you can learn to live with it. You have to trust that you will get there.'

Owen felt a lump in his throat like a golf ball. And then, just like that, the stoic, moody, grieving Conall McCaskill broke into a thousand pieces. Their favourite actor literally *surrendered* in a way no one would ever have expected. It was like opening a valve...everything came rushing out.

It was nine a.m.

Scott was late.

Conall yelled at him for holding up the shoot.

The props department said everything was OK.

Usually Scott would check things himself too... go for a test run. But they were on the clock, time was ticking...

Conall was annoyed with his son for wasting everyone's time.

And then the car sped out of control, and that

*stupid altercation was his last communication
with Scott...*

Maybe it was witnessing someone so strong
expressing his emotions in a way he himself
had never quite been able to. Maybe it was the
look on Sadie's face. But to his shock, as Conall
wiped a hand across his eyes, Owen found he
was fighting back a kind of tidal wave of emotion the likes of which he'd never felt before.

Some time later he found himself at the end of
the dock, looking over the lake, his eyes on the
bobbing fishing boat. Conall's emotional out-
pouring was still playing on his mind, and his
mother would no doubt add to it shortly.

Three missed calls from her, he noted, shoving
his phone back into his pocket. He should give
her the benefit of the doubt—but then she only
ever bombarded him with calls like this when his
dad had done something to offend her.

'Thinking of going fishing again?'

Sadie had found him. He made room for her
on the wooden jetty beside him.

'Conall has called Maeve and asked her to
come to the gala.'

'Good,' he replied as she sat down and drew
her knees up.

She'd changed into jeans and a short green
linen jacket, and he could smell lavender again.

He swallowed back the now familiar pang he felt at her closeness.

'You left that session as soon as you could,' she said. 'Is he getting to you, too?'

Owen grunted. He'd made an excuse to leave without accepting the cup of tea and signed autograph Conall had offered them, and it hadn't all been to do with his next appointment with Vivek Kumar, nor the missed calls on his phone.

'Seeing someone like that, so famous, being so vulnerable... I don't know,' he admitted, tossing a stick out into the water. 'I guess it got to me, yeah. I was more worried about it all affecting *you*, though,' he added quickly. 'After what you've told me lately.'

Sadie's lips twitched. 'That's sweet,' she replied simply, then leaned back on her elbows, as if she were taking in the sky. 'But why do you think I chose this career, Owen? Hearing people work through their grief gives me strength, even after all this time.'

'You're saying helping them helps you, too, in some way?'

She nodded. 'You don't need to worry about me...really.'

Owen thought he would probably always worry about her now, but he understood about her work.

'Do I need to worry about *you*?' she asked him

after a moment, sitting back up and touching a hand to his arm.

He felt himself tense and dragged a hand through his hair.

'I know you try to keep your emotions out of things, Owen, and that's just how you are, but...'

'You're right.' He bristled at her blunt observation. 'Maybe I've never got my dad's voice out of my head, telling me Penner men don't cry. Stuff like that stays with you, Sadie.'

'Your dad said what?' Sadie's jaw dropped.

He massaged the back of his neck. Why had he just told her that?

Sadie pressed a warm hand to his arm, as if rooting him to the dock, and he wrestled with what to say now that she was waiting for an explanation of some kind. He'd never told anyone about the day that had probably shaped him more than he'd ever admitted. He couldn't avoid it now, though. The words were spilling out of him before he could think to shut up.

He'd been eleven years old, almost deafened by the row going on in the kitchen. His mother had been yelling at his dad.

'Penner men are useless—all of you. Useless! Your father was the same, and your grandfather too. I don't know why I thought you'd be any different, Jay...

That was when he'd realised his dad had crossed some unthinkable line and his mother was approaching the end of her tether. He'd been sniffling on the stairs, scared the world was crumbling down around him, when his dad had marched right up to him and boomed, *'Penner men don't cry!'*

It had shocked him to the core. But he'd never cried after that. Not a tear...not a trickle of emotion. Not even after his dad had packed his bags and gone to live with his newest fling. His mum had done enough crying for both of them, anyway, and the last thing he'd wanted was to be useless to her.

Owen paused in his monologue, realising Sadie was staring at him, mouth agape.

'Wow...' she breathed. 'Things are even clearer to me now.'

He felt his eyebrows knit together. 'What do you mean?'

Adrenaline flared in his veins as Sadie's eyes glowed with unexpected affection. Somehow the look on her face riled him up all the more, and he wished he could read her mind. She was probably analysing him...putting him into some box. A guy with daddy issues—*great.*

'It was ages ago. Like I said, I was only eleven,' he reminded her stiffly.

'Like you said, stuff like that stays with you,' she replied, turning him to face her.

She pressed one warm palm to his cheek and stroked her thumb softly to the corner of his mouth. His throat tightened as the lips he knew so well but had never actually tasted hovered tantalisingly close. So close that her breath tickled his nose.

An entire drum kit was going off in his chest now.

For a second longing surged through him, and he braced himself...

Her kiss landed on his forehead, right above his brow. 'You are a special kind of person, Owen,' she said.

Special? Great.

Owen dropped her hand, curling his fists into his sides as her warm smile stretched against his skin. A friendly kiss on the forehead. A compliment on how 'special' he was.

God, Owen, you're an idiot. What else did you expect, anyway?

He pulled away, blew out his cheeks and avoided her eyes, even as heat coursed in his veins. That had been weird.

Resting back on his elbows on the dock, he trained his stare on the water, running over his holiday allowance in his head, feeling his stomach revolt at the pity in her eyes. Humiliation, confusion, the urge to run all made a knot in his insides.

'I have a phone call to make,' he said tightly. The words came out a little more coldly than he'd intended.

Sadie frowned at him. 'What did I do?'

'Nothing,' he said. 'I do have a call to make. And I don't need you to psychoanalyse me.'

'It's a little late for that.' She smirked, getting to her feet.

Owen grunted, not giving her the satisfaction of any acknowledgement. He wanted to confide in her and run from her all at the same time. What the hell was that all about?

As she headed for the house without him, he forced himself to stay put.

CHAPTER NINE

VIVEK KUMAR LOOKED more melancholy than usual when Sadie met him in the music room on the day of the gala. He was staring unseeingly at the piano keys. She closed the door behind her, and crept across the plush red carpet, concerned at his expression. He rested his arms across his portly stomach, then unfolded them, and then folded them again on the piano, frowning at the keys as if he didn't know what to do with them.

'You don't have to do this now,' she said kindly, gesturing to the sheet music on the stand. 'If you're having trouble remembering.'

Vivek was a gifted pianist—at least, he had been before the traumatic head injury that had left a scar inside as large as the one that was displayed on his shaved head, down his neck and across his right shoulder.

He exhaled long and deep through his nose, without looking at her. 'No. I want to,' he said, putting his hands to the keys.

He paused, as if trying to force open some

database in his head that he didn't have the password for. Sadie held her breath, staring out through the floor-length windows at the billowing white marquee now dominating the grounds, ready for this afternoon's event. It seemed like people had been talking about it for weeks but she couldn't seem to get excited about it.

Traumatic brain injuries disturbed the delicate chemistry of the brain so its neurons couldn't function normally. Huge changes to Vivek's thinking and behaviour were still taking everyone by surprise—not least him. Sometimes he remembered how to play. Sometimes he didn't. Owen had told him it might take weeks or even months for his brain to resolve the kind of chemical imbalances that could occur with a TBI.

Owen...

She found herself training her eyes on him as he stepped from the marquee and held up a hand to her from the other side of the window. In seconds he was entering the room.

Sadie let free the breath she was holding, then drew in another one. She couldn't help but note that he looked very handsome in his uniform. More so than usual. He'd caught the sun on his face over the past week or so, often fishing alone after his shifts. Now, halfway into May, it was unusually sunny for Scotland at this time of year.

'Are you going to play for us?' he asked Vivek,

closing the door behind him and putting a folder down on a plush velvet chair.

Sadie felt their shoulders brush momentarily as he moved to her side behind the piano stool, and she tried not to feel the now-familiar sensation of unease at his closeness.

He regretted telling her about his dad the other day—she could tell. As if she could possibly be repulsed by seeing the real, vulnerable Owen behind the tough-guy facade.

The doctor in her was intrigued. His parents' harsh words back then had most definitely left their mark. And his mother was *still* in his ear about his dad. What she'd overheard on the fishing boat, back when they'd first heard about his dad's new engagement, was making more and more sense now.

What was it she'd said? Something like, '*I hope you never treat anyone like this.*' Almost accusingly. Almost as if she expected him to turn out just like his dad.

Owen just put up a wall whenever she'd tried to talk more about it to him, and that was understandable, she supposed. She knew there was nothing worse than people probing her about *her* parents. But the thought of anyone making him feel less than adequate about anything was infuriating. He was one of the kindest people she knew...and if they hadn't been best friends, and if the example of his parents hadn't made him dread the thought of ever being in a relationship himself, she might just consider…

She caught herself.

Nope. There were no 'ifs' with Owen. His friendship was all she needed.

Wasn't it?

'I wanted to play for my wife later.' Vivek cut into her thoughts. 'She's bringing my niece, Ashanti. I wanted it to be a surprise for them,' he said despondently.

Owen put a comforting hand to his shoulder. 'You've already made so much progress, Vivek! We haven't been working on your gaze stabilisation and eye-tracking exercises for long and you already say you're not feeling dizzy or off-balance any more, right? That's a real mark of success. We can't force these things. It's possible the piano may come back to you…give it time.'

Owen shot her a look that said maybe it would, maybe it wouldn't. People were only just beginning to understand the severity of concussion—people who had been injured decades ago were only just starting to see why they'd been thinking or acting a certain way for so long. So many brain injuries went undiagnosed…but so many were diagnosed properly, thanks to doctors like Owen.

He was kind of an amazing person…

The thought caught her off guard, especially

as it came with a sense of longing to be in his vicinity always…to be cared for by him.

'Sorry I'm late, by the way,' he said now. 'Maeve McCaskill has just arrived. There's a bit of a crowd in the marquee already.'

'Ooh, really? She's here?'

Sadie cleared her throat. That might have come out a little too enthusiastically.

Owen's mouth twitched. 'You're not going to ask her to sign your apron, are you?'

'I would if I'd known to bring it with me,' she admitted.

'My wife has all her stuff,' announced Vivek, turning from the piano as if a light had come on in his mind. 'She's always leafing through this one cook-book…'

'Ah, so you remember that.' Owen grinned. 'Do any specific dishes come to mind?'

Vivek's smile faded. He shook his head, which told them he did not without him saying another word.

Sadie assisted Owen with Vivek's memory-strengthening exercises, sometimes watching the crowds gathering outside the window for the gala. It was their last session of the day, and once they were done it would be time to put her best dress on, as well as her best foot forward, for the event everyone had been looking forward to for weeks.

Just a few hours later she was chatting with

Portia and her husband Stan—who was just as fabulous as Portia. Their chemistry was undeniable...

And then Owen approached, with the McCaskills on either side of him, as if he'd been appointed as some kind of celebrity security guard. Sadie tried to keep her squeal confined to her throat as none other than Maeve McCaskill held her hand out.

'I've been looking forward to meeting you,' Maeve said warmly, taking her aside so they could talk in private.

She was the epitome of breezy sophistication. But through her admiration, it hit Sadie...what this woman—a mother—had gone through, and how she'd come out the other side. She felt a rush of empathy that almost brought tears to her eyes.

'I'm so glad you could make it,' she said, sincerely. 'And I'm so very sorry for your loss.'

'I wanted to thank you personally for everything you and Dr Penner have done for my husband,' Maeve replied coolly. 'Conall talks about you very highly.'

'He's come a long way,' Sadie said, noting the jolt in her stomach at hearing the words 'you and Dr Penner'.

Owen was looking at her from where the band was setting up, now. He was dressed in a designer jacket and chinos, holding an orange juice, watching her.

She'd expected another smirk from him over her being starstruck, but he seemed to be appreciating her ocean-green summer dress and her smart hip-length jacket and silver sandals. It was one of her favourite outfits, but she'd never felt so self-conscious under his gaze before.

Ever since he'd opened up to her about his parents she'd found herself thinking even more about that almost-kiss. Their relationship felt more honest now...deeper. She'd even considered lately that perhaps she'd pushed him away all these years by refusing to talk about her own family, and he'd responded by doing the same. Now that they were talking about things—serious things—it was clear they had far more in common than she'd ever realised before.

She *was* psychoanalysing him, in her head. But only because he'd become a hundred times more interesting to her.

And sexy.

How had she failed to notice how sexy he was?

Maybe it had taken coming here to the Western Scottish Highlands, far away from everyone who knew them, for her to see how she'd been blocking out her attraction to him ever since that night in Sylvester's. Because of course nothing had ever happened between them...or would *ever* happen. They'd both kicked down that bridge and set fire to it. Which was good.

Except he looked so damn gorgeous right now,

and she couldn't deny she'd been as jealous as hell over Parminder. God, what would it be like to kiss those lips after all this time...?

Suddenly it occurred to her that Maeve McCaskill was still talking to her...and she was zoning out, thinking about Owen again.

The afternoon stretched into sunset. There were games on the lawn, activities in the fernery, a banquet feast complete with a suckling pig, and now this—an organised boat ride around the lake, led by Owen himself.

He looked like the sexiest of sailors at the helm. He'd loosened his shirt at the neck, and his hair in the breeze was cutely dishevelled. Sadie waved off a bee that was buzzing around her face and took in the scene around her from her seat on the wooden boat. For one glorious afternoon Rothesay Recovery had felt more like a country retreat than a luxury medical facility. She couldn't help a huge surge of pride for her patients over everything they'd achieved so far.

Portia nudged her suddenly, waving off the same bee with her other hand. 'Owen looks like he needs some help up there,' she said, winking at her before burrowing her face lovingly in her husband's shoulder.

They seemed so in love, Sadie mused, remembering how Portia had said they were friends first. Friends who'd had sex as an experiment.

Interesting... I would actually love to try that

with Owen. I wonder if he'd go for it... Why does he have to look so hot right now?

'How long have you been with Owen?' Maeve asked, catching her off-guard. 'I was just thinking how good you two look together. Conall never told me you were—'

'Oh, no, we're not a couple,' Sadie cut in, fixing her eyes on Ashanti, Vivek Kumar's seven-year-old niece, who was asking Owen if she could steer the boat.

Had these women read her mind? But Owen *was* looking at her with interest. He'd probably overheard what Maeve had said. Sadie felt her face flush, and was just about to change the subject when a cry from the front of the boat rendered everyone silent.

'It stung me!'

The little girl was on her feet now, flapping her hands about. A ruckus ensued. Poor Vivek looked dumbstruck as his wife scrambled to reach the child and pull her down to sit on the bench, almost toppling overboard. Then Owen stopped the boat in the middle of the lake just as Sadie launched forward to help. The jerk sent her flying, but Owen caught her in his arms and righted her before she'd even had a chance to catch her breath.

'Thank you,' she gasped, gripping his forearms, stunned for a moment.

Poor Ashanti was shrieking in agony, and the boat was bobbing vigorously now.

'Everyone stay calm,' came Owen's authoritative voice. 'It's just a bee sting.'

Just as he said that, however, the little girl seemed to droop and fold like a piece of paper, straight into Sadie's arms.

'She's passed out!' she cried, horrified, sliding to the floor with her.

Owen made a shield around them with his body and his arms.

'Is she allergic to bee stings?' she heard him ask the Kumars.

'I don't know...' came the reply.

'Sure seems like she is,' someone else responded.

Vivek's eyes grew wide as saucers, but then the girl seemed to regain consciousness, and sucked in a breath as if her life depended on it. She panted a little, her cheeks paling further, and in the middle of the chaos Sadie heard Conall McCaskill step in and offer to take the helm.

With concern, Sadie registered the distance to the jetty. There was no doubt about it—the girl was in the early stages of anaphylactic shock and there was nothing they could do without a shot of epinephrine—which no one had. She and Owen were the only medical staff on the boat.

Owen had called the emergency services already, and was radioing Rothesay Recovery. Everyone was flapping about in a panic now, as she cradled the semi-conscious girl in her arms. Conall McCaskill clambered to the front seat and started steering the boat back the way they'd come. They'd travelled pretty far out from the shore on the huge lake.

Sadie felt Owen's steady hand on her shoulder. 'We've got this,' he whispered to her, causing her ear to tingle. 'She's going to be OK.'

Sadie met Owen's piercing eyes. The fact that he was here gave her comfort, in spite of the situation. She trusted him, and so did everyone else. He had this under control.

Just then a judder from the engine sent them both flailing into each other again. Ashanti gasped as the sound of the motor sputtered into nothing. McCaskill tried to get it going again, tugging with all his might, but he failed and another panicked ruckus broke out amongst the passengers.

Owen was peeling off his shirt.

'What are you doing?' she asked, but Owen already had one foot on the side and in seconds was in the water, gripping the boat from the outside.

'Pass her over to me—we don't have much time,' he said.

'Is he insane?' someone muttered behind her.

But Sadie lowered the young girl into his arms and quickly tore her dress over her head before sliding into the lake too, causing Vivek to gasp and avert his eyes, and Portia to clap her hands approvingly.

Together, she and Owen kept Ashanti's head out of the water as they swam back towards the jetty, every stroke feeling as if they were carving through ice, despite the earlier warmth of the day. The little girl's eyes and lips were swollen, as if the bee had injected its venom straight into her face. Sadie was sure her own face must be blue, and already she could barely feel her fingers and toes, but nothing mattered except getting this girl to safety. Untreated anaphylaxis could lead to death within half an hour.

Parminder met them on the jetty, her bright patterned floral sundress a beacon to swim for. They were all shivering wildly, but Owen made a quick job of lifting the girl to the dock, where Parminder wrapped a blanket around her. Fergal handed Sadie a towel to cover herself—but not before making a full body-swipe with his eyes over her bra and knickers.

An ambulance's siren was already adding its own soundtrack to the air and Owen had started CPR. The scene was surreal, and she was sure the cold would have buckled her knees if she hadn't already been on them on the jetty beside him.

They could have died in that freezing cold lake... A life lived with Owen that ended without so much as a kiss...

Why are you thinking about this now? You're clearly in shock.

Just as two paramedics tore down the path through the garden with a stretcher Ashanti spluttered back to consciousness again, and complained of being cold and dizzy. A rush of relief brought tears to Sadie's eyes as Owen wrapped both of his big arms around her shivering body. She leaned into him, letting the paramedics take over with the epinephrine. Their praise for their quick thinking and heroic action washed over her—all she could think, as she huddled into Owen, was it might have been too late for Ashanti.

It had almost been too late.

'She's going to be OK,' Owen told her, as if he was reading her mind.

His eyes were flooded with concern for her and she wondered if her lips were blue. She let him help her to her feet as the ambulance sped away.

'They'll have to keep her in overnight, in case the symptoms recur, but she's fine—you guys made sure of that,' Parminder said.

Sadie realised people were watching them, standing locked together wrapped in towels and blankets. She pulled away from Owen just as a noise behind them made them all spin around. Sadie blinked. There in the distance was the boat, Conall McCaskill at the helm standing tall, steering towards them at speed, like the action hero he'd once been. Everyone on it was cheering.

'How did you get it to go again?' Sadie said when he pulled up at the jetty, windswept but delighted to learn that Ashanti was fine. He was wearing a look of determination on his handsome face that Sadie hadn't seen since the night they'd re-watched his movie, *Surrender*.

'You don't spend years on movie sets without learning a few things,' he said simply, helping his wife back on to safe, solid ground. A glimmer of pride in his eyes twinkled its way through his tough exterior. Even more so when Maeve flung both arms around him and kissed his cheek, as if she knew she was finally getting her husband back.

'We should go and get changed,' Owen said to her, as someone handed them their clothes from the boat.

Vivek's frantic wife was ushered away by Fergal, to follow the ambulance to the hospital.

The adrenaline was wearing off now, and Sadie was starting to shiver even more. Owen's arm slid around her waist again, and this time she didn't shake him off. She needed him and he knew it.

Her heart thumped wildly, both at what had just happened and his closeness, and their dripping wetness left a watery trail all the way back to the house.

CHAPTER TEN

SADIE STUMBLED HALFWAY up the staircase. Owen
caught her, pulling her soaking frame against
his bare chest.

'Careful,' he said.

'I'm so cold.' She shivered, as if he might be
in doubt. 'How are you not freezing?'

'Adrenaline?'

He met her eyes for a second as she drew long,
jagged breaths, and then held her close to steady
her as they made their way up the rest of the
stairs, trying to ignore the way her skin against
his was igniting every cell in his body.

The house was eerily quiet everywhere. Most
people were still out in the grounds, enjoying
the gala. Hopefully that poor little girl would be
OK—at least the paramedics had assured them
she would be.

He helped Sadie unlock her door and realised
her legs were wobbling like a newborn foal's.
She'd pulled a towel around her tightly down on
the jetty, although Fergal had got a good look

before that. In any other situation, seeing some guy's eyes roving her body like that, he would have launched himself at them.

Now, in her room she dropped the towel to the floor and sank onto the bed in exhaustion. Then she gasped, her eyes full of horror. 'Oh, God, sorry!' Grabbing the towel up again, she pulled it back around her and he had to laugh.

'I've seen it all before,' he told her quickly, hoping she hadn't noticed the effect she was having on him, sitting there half naked in her knickers and bra. Her cheeks were flushed, but at least she was getting some colour back.

Sadie stood and crossed to the mirror while he lingered in the doorway. 'No, you haven't,' she replied after a pause. 'Seen all of me before…have you?' She looked wary now, as if she was racking her brains for something she'd forgotten. 'Seeing me in a bikini doesn't count,' she followed. 'Bikinis aren't generally this see-through.'

He bit back another chuckle, picturing the polka dot bikini she'd tottered around in on Hampton Heath that time he'd joined her and Callum and a bunch of other friends for a picnic. London had been so hot that day. Not as hot as Sadie, though. Callum had been watching Owen the whole time that day, as if he was daring him to look at Sadie so he could accuse him of wanting to hit on her or something.

It wasn't the time to tease her now, and definitely not the time to mention the way her nipples were probably the cutest little things he'd ever seen, pushing out against the lace of her wet bra. He should probably get out of here, he thought. But something rooted him to the spot even as she crossed to the bathroom in the towel.

'Need me to help?' he heard himself say, and then he caught himself. 'I mean…in case you fall again or something. I can wait.'

'I'm fine.'

Sadie paused with one hand on the bathroom door and he found himself looking at her feet, then tracing her legs with his eyes from her painted toenails to the rim of the towel, inches above her pale knees.

'I can probably shower on my own,' she added slowly, over her shoulder.

'You probably can. But do you want to?'

The words were out before he could even register he'd said them out loud. He pulled his eyes away, but not before catching a look on her face that he didn't recognise. She wasn't laughing, but she didn't look offended by his silly quip either. Not so long ago she would have rolled her eyes and told him to stop joking around, but now…

Now he was incredibly turned on, and Sadie had probably noticed.

'What are you implying?' she asked him.

He sucked in a breath, imagining his lips tracing the flesh across her shoulder blades under a steaming gush of water, his hands on slippery tiles, then on her bottom, finally tasting her...

His feet wouldn't move. He started willing his erection to comply with his wishes and not the wishes that would get him in trouble. This was the moment he was supposed to say nothing and walk away.

Just walk away, Owen. Go back to your room, go and get showered alone, and stop being an idiot, thinking things like this about Sadie.

'Owen, are you OK?'

She was looking at him in concern now, maybe reading his silence as distress on his part over what had just happened with Ashanti... And why did she have to look so gorgeous right now?

'What you just did...that was...' Sadie abandoned the bathroom door and walked back towards him, clutching the towel around her. 'That was amazing. I'm really proud of you, you know? That child lived to see another day because of what you did.'

'You did it too,' he said, looking straight into her eyes as her words lit him up and set his heart racing all over again. Genuine praise from Sadie, he realised, was something he lived for. 'Although you couldn't wait to rip your dress off in front of Conall McCaskill.'

She bit her lip and smirked, and instinctively he closed the gap between them and kicked the door shut behind him. An almost indecipherable moan escaped her mouth as she placed a palm against his bare chest, over his heart.

Her breath was a whisper across his mouth, inches from his lips. 'You're right. It's all about Conall McCaskill,' she said.

They were silent for a moment that felt too long—as something should have been said or done. She seemed to be testing the drumming of his heartbeat in her presence, and he was clearly failing to prove that he saw this half naked woman, beautiful inside and out, as just his friend and colleague.

'Conall thinks you are a hero too,' she told him quietly, clearly choosing to ignore the way he'd just shut himself in her room, and they way his chest was throbbing under her touch. 'I bet you never thought you'd see the day.'

'To be honest, I'm not really thinking about that right now,' he managed.

Sadie didn't move her hand. His heart was a riot, giving him away as much as the bulge in his boxers. Swallowing, he let his mind play out a hundred ways this could go.

Her hand on his torso felt hot as fire, and he knew without a doubt that she was waiting for him to do something now. To kiss her. One kiss. Just to see. Just to see if whatever this was, was real. And definitely not a 'friendly' kiss on the forehead this time. She wanted more. When a woman got that look in her eyes in front of him he was usually ready to give them more.

Her lips hovered close as she studied his gaze, then his mouth, as if she was tracing a prospective pattern. One kiss and he'd have to have another. He knew it. And another, and another.

'This is…' He stopped and let loose the tortured growl that had been building in his throat.

Sadie stepped away instantly. 'You're right,' she said quickly, flustered, turning her back. 'You're right. It's the adrenaline. I don't know what I was…'

'Get in the shower,' he heard himself say, flinging the bedroom door back open. This was messing with his head. If he didn't leave now he really would ruin everything. She'd regret it too—she was just caught up in the moment, like he was. 'I'll see you downstairs,' he said.

They'd have to talk about this later—there was no way they could avoid it. But right now it was better for both of them if he left and cooled down.

It took everything in his body and soul to turn away from her and go back to his room alone.

Sadie kicked herself internally more than once as she showered the events of the day and the lake water off her body. If only she could shower away the embarrassment and humiliation… What had she been thinking, practically asking him to kiss her…? Well, with her eyes and actions, at least…

He'd been joking when he'd suggested showering with her. Of course it had been a joke—to lighten the tension, probably. That was so Owen. Maybe it had just been his awkward way of making light of the fact he'd seen her in wet, see-through underwear.

She'd been trying to forget all the awkwardness, but the more they opened up and talked, and worked closely like this, the harder it was to ignore her feelings for her friend.

You have to, she reprimanded herself in the mirror. *Even if Owen Penner is no longer a notch on the bedpost kind of person, he is still your* friend!

She pressed her head to the shower tiles and let out a groan. This was all too confusing.

Her throat turned to sandpaper as she remembered the look in his eyes, right before he'd left her room…

The whole time she was drying her hair, a voice in her head was screaming. *If he really doesn't like you like that, Sadie, why did he shut the door to your room like that? Why did he look so tortured? And why was his heart freaking out under your hand?*

They had a problem. That much was obvious right now. Clearly they were both re-evaluating a few things. But what if she did get the whole package from her best friend and then he realised his mistake and snatched it back? Better not to even go there. God, no... The pain, on top of everything she'd already been through, would finish her off.

She sighed to herself, putting the final touches to her make-up, puckering her lips...imagining Owen's on hers. If she kissed him once she'd want more—she was just that kind of person. So for many, many, *many* reasons she simply couldn't do it, she reminded herself. Ever.

With that decided, she psyched herself up to see him downstairs, reciting a couple of positive affirmations at her reflection in the mirror whilst simultaneously admiring her breasts in the low-cut aubergine-coloured wrap-around dress. It was sophisticated enough for no one to question her professionalism, yet sexy—no one could deny it. At least she had that.

Was she dressing for Owen to find her sexy now?

No, of course you're not—don't be ridiculous.

Outside on the lawn, Owen was the first person she laid eyes on. He was chatting to the CEO, Dr Calhoun, and some of the other staff.

Vivek took her aside and thanked her profusely. Ashanti had made a full recovery already. His wife was on her way back from the hospital, having left the girl to sleep. Sadie told him she was glad, and then made small talk for about an hour with the guests…grazing from the buffet, purposefully avoiding Owen.

He was probably doing the same thing—although every time their eyes met across the lawn goosebumps broke out on her arms. A certain kind of ache, and a longing such as she'd never experienced before was threatening to snatch away all her common sense.

Some time later, the saxophonist on the marquee's stage was doing a fine job of remastering a classic, and she was so absorbed, standing next to Portia, that she was startled when Owen tapped her on the shoulder.

'Good party,' he said.

She crossed her arms. Her feet were already itching to move away. His cologne was too seductive—it made her mentally revisit the way he'd looked earlier, half naked in her bedroom.

'It's OK,' she replied, feeling Portia's eyes on them.

She walked towards the buffet table and busied her hands picking out an olive. Owen did the same, watching her every move, the picture of sophistication in his blue designer suit—an outfit she'd seen him wear on dates. A lot of dates. With different women, none of whom were around any more, she reminded herself.

'Are we good?' he asked, after a moment.

'I don't know what you mean,' she lied, popping the olive into her mouth and vaguely registering Vivek taking to the stage, and talking to the pianist.

'I think you do,' he said, causing a ball of nerves to lodge in her throat. 'Listen, Sadie, we need to talk about—'

He was cut off suddenly by the sound of the piano. They both spun around to face the stage. A beautiful piece of music she recognised was spilling from the instrument under Vivek's hands. His wife, now back from the hospital, was gaping at him from the sidelines in awe, wiping tears from her eyes. Conall McCaskill gave an enthusiastic whoop, and Sadie couldn't help the huge smile that broke out on her face.

'He's remembered how to play,' she whispered to Owen with pride, momentarily forgetting the tension between them.

'Come on!'

Owen grabbed her hand. Before she knew it they were on the dance floor, and Vivek's talents had extended into a slow but moving rendition of *Can't Help Falling in Love*.

They weren't the only ones dancing, so it shouldn't have felt strange at all, but the second Owen's hands landed on her hips the room fell away. She closed her eyes, testing her senses, praying for them all to switch from red alert back to their normal state around him. It was impossible. He pulled her closer, hip to hip, and as they swayed together every inch of her felt magnetised...especially when he lowered his lips to her ear.

'Did you want to kiss me up there in your bedroom before?' he asked her.

She drew a breath, pressed her cheek to his shoulder as her mind whirred. How the tables had turned! Hadn't she said the exact same thing to him after that night in the library? He'd brushed her off then, but the thought of doing the same to him now didn't sit right.

'I think I did, actually,' she admitted after a moment. 'But I know that was stupid. Thrill of the moment kind of thing...after what happened...'

'Whatever it was, I shouldn't have just walked away,' he replied.

'You did the right thing.'

'I bet you want to run right off this dance floor again,' he said, and she felt his smile stretch out like warm honey against the crown of her head.

'Again?' she replied, confused. But he'd caught her chin with one hand, gripped her hand with the other, and she forgot what she'd been going to say.

The way he was looking at her... He wanted her, she could tell. No question. Her blood fizzed like champagne in her veins.

'I don't know what this is, but we can't keep dancing around it, can we?' he said now.

Sadie swallowed. 'We should do exactly that—

just keep dancing around it,' she forced herself to say.

Not, *between it, over it*. Not *into it*. But every cell in her body was alive now, as if some new lifeforce had been summoned from the depths of her being, not to be switched off or drowned out. Talking about it was a bad idea. It would only lead to her admitting something she wasn't ready to admit—to him, or to herself. That she had a huge and ever-growing crush on her best friend.

This was bad. Very bad. It could never happen.

'You know what? I'm really tired,' she said, disentangling herself from his arms. Maybe if she excused herself, she could sleep this insanity off.

'No, you're not tired,' he countered, taking her hand again and holding it tightly. 'You just don't want to talk about it.'

'You're right—and I didn't think you wanted to, either,' she said, noting how goosebumps were travelling up her arm, the way his gaze bored into hers.

'We have to.'

Somewhere in the background rapturous applause for Vivek filled the air.

Owen lowered his voice again. 'We *have* to. Sadie, because we both know something's going on here, I can't even think straight around you any more. Something happened when I got back from Boston…'

'Nothing happened, Owen, and nothing *will* ever happen,' she snapped, begging her eyes not to give her raging desire away.

No one had ever looked at her as Owen was looking at her now. Enraged, confounded… consumed by the kind of longing she'd never known he was capable of expressing. Owen never wanted to talk about anything serious, and the fact that he did now, about *them*, fired her up and sent the fear of God rushing through her all at once.

'Fine. Go,' he said coldly, releasing her and turning his back to her.

Shocked, she almost relented. But why open Pandora's box now when it had always been just fine closed?

Quickly, while the crowd was distracted by Vivek taking a bow, she turned on her heel and left before she could make a huge mistake.

CHAPTER ELEVEN

OWEN PACED HIS BEDROOM, dragging both hands through his hair. Midnight had come and gone. He'd helped clear up after the gala—anything to keep Sadie's words from haunting his thoughts.

'Nothing happened, Owen, and nothing will ever happen.'

Weren't women supposed to be the ones who wanted to talk things though? Clear the air and all that? *Never go to bed feeling angry*—wasn't that what they said?

He ripped off his shirt and tossed it to the floor, flopping back on the bed in just his suit trousers, cursing at the ceiling. Admittedly his pride had taken a blow. Sadie Mills had abandoned him on a dance floor for a second time, and this time he'd walked right into it.

But they'd come so close to making out more times than he could count already. She was telling herself not to, just as he was, and he got it. Of course he got it.

There was no point in them hooking up. It

would only end in disaster, and more awkwardness than he cared to invite into this precious platonic thing they'd cultivated over the years. But he'd tried to do the right thing: get this blatant attraction between them out in the open so they could at least discuss it and move on, one way or another. He hadn't laughed it off or run away. He'd been trying to give her what he owed her. A chance to get their friendship back on track.

And all she'd done in response was close herself off completely. Was she trying to kill him slowly? It sucked, being the one given the brush-off, he realised with dismay. Maybe this was karma. That was what his mother would say, anyway.

Owen sat up straight. *Screw this.* He wouldn't sleep unless he saw her and cleared the air. This would only drag on into his dreams, into tomorrow. He'd just go and knock on her door, he decided, and demand they talk about it. She would not dismiss him.

Forgetting his shirt, or maybe just not caring enough to bother putting it back on, he felt a brute determination lead him to yank his door open. He was going to march straight to her room. To hell with the time—so what if she was sleeping? This had to end now.

No sooner had he stormed to her room and raised his hand to the door than the wooden panels disappeared in front of him and he almost fell through the doorway.

'What the…?'

'Owen!' Sadie gasped right in front of him. 'I was just coming to…'

'Talk?' he finished, failing to hide the way his eyes had fallen straight to her exposed cleavage in her nightdress.

She bit her lip, shifted on her feet. 'I told you… I don't want to talk about it.'

And before he could even gather his thoughts or protest, she launched herself at him like a rocket.

Her lips were on his now, her hands were in his hair, and she was kissing him as if her life depended on it. They staggered backwards against the banister in the hallway, fraught with passion. He hooked an arm around her waist, aware of the hard wood against his back, her leg around his middle, one hand on her backside.

Then a door creaked somewhere in the corridor. A voice came… 'Hello? Do you know what time it is?'

Who was that? he thought.

Who cares?

Owen pushed Sadie back into her room. Her mouth was red-hot, lips still parted, begging for more of his attention. She didn't want to talk, and neither did he now, as he let his tongue delve into her mouth deeply, then let it linger as they slowed their pace inside the closed room, but only for a moment. Then they crashed together against the dresser, making her hairbrush clatter to the floor.

Lips still locked together, he lifted her nightdress swiftly over her head, lifting her hair with it. The soft, sensual strands floated back down around their faces as his hands stroked her back and hips...new parts of Sadie he'd never thought he'd feel.

He wanted more. He could hardly wait.

Her bare breasts were bouncing in front of him now, teasing him as she started to unbutton his trousers. He shuffled out of them, bent to lock his mouth onto a pert pink nipple, standing up and ready for him. He circled his tongue around it and she arched into him, before staggering backwards again towards the bed, pulling him with her and muffling a cry of pleasure behind her hand before deciding it was pointless.

With a groan that was equally loud and equally telling of his intentions, he released her nipple, placed a hand behind her head, and arched over her on the bed, studying her face for the first time in this new situation. She was utterly breathtaking. A new version of his friend. Hot, messy, begging for him without saying a word.

He should back off. *So what if she started it?* came the voice in his head. But he couldn't stop now—not of his own volition.

He lowered his bulk onto one forearm and pressed a palm to the front of her knickers—the only thing left between their otherwise naked flesh. He was throbbing for her everywhere.

'Are you sure this what you want?' he asked.

'What do you think?' she gasped, reaching for him again.

As their tongues entwined around each other's he could barely think straight. Had she planned this? Or had she left her room to come and find him on a snap decision, like he had?

Who cares?

She moaned again, softer this time, as he slid his fingers down, circling her navel before going further into the fine, silken hair, stretching out the fabric of her knickers till she scrambled halfway out of them, leaving him to free her of the rest. She responded, exploring him with her hands, fingers, mouth, until they both knew they weren't going to stop.

'I know I have something, Owen…just wait…'

He ran his eyes over her in appreciation as she reached for her purse on the nightstand and scrambled around for a condom. She was everything he'd imagined, maybe even better. He urged her on to her back again when she had the foil packet clenched in her hand. He brushed his fingers lightly, tauntingly, over her mound and she gripped his shoulders hard, in a way he knew would leave circular half-moons in his flesh from

her nails. Her eyes shone with new wickedness
and a determination that sent an inferno through
his blood as she locked on to his gaze.

Suddenly he wanted to possess her completely.
He wanted to bind Sadie to him in every single
way possible, regardless of the consequences.
Maybe she was thinking the same thing. The
way she rolled him over and took him in her
mouth was nothing short of exquisite, as if she
was trying to show him she was the best thing
he'd never had.

'You are amazing, Sadie...'

'Shh...don't speak.'

Fine. There were no words anyway. God, he
wanted her. If having her lips locked around his
shaft was anything to go by, the act of sex itself
was going to be something he would have to try
very hard to make last for as long as possible.

That was not going to be easy.

Sadie's fingers pulsed hot and urgent against
his hardness as they rolled on the condom together. He lifted his head, fighting the urge to
ask again if this was what she really wanted.
She wasn't backing off. Sadie was doing anything but that. He'd never seen her like this, so
determined, so... *So not like Sadie.* He'd never
imagined she could be so forceful, or that she
could possibly want him. Would she regret this
afterwards? Why were they doing this? It was
wrong... It would not end well...

'Owen, make love to me.'

How could he refuse?

He positioned himself over her. Sadie was wet and ready for him, and she drew a sharp breath as he slid into her. He took it slowly, went inch by inch, in awe of every second as he went deeper... This was insane! His mind reeled, then went blank. All he felt was bliss, comfort, connection...

She wrapped her legs around him and held him still, clamping her teeth for a moment into his shoulder. Instinctively, he knew she wasn't asking him to stop. He stayed inside her a moment without moving, placing delicate butterfly kisses on her mouth, relishing the way she caressed his face with her fingers, stroked his hair. Their passion built again slowly, gradually, until Sadie was bucking under him, faster and faster, making sounds that made him want to spill into her with every thrust.

What followed was an exercise in mutual pleasure and gymnastics and still no words... They were just exploring and discovering and appreciating every inch of each other. The birds started tweeting outside the windows. The sun threatened to spoil the night and the way she moved in the shadows.

On the edge of her third or fourth climax, Sadie enveloped him with both her arms and her legs. He tried to pull out, to shift position—

why end this now? He wanted to prove he was the best she'd ever had too. He could make this last even longer...he had to. The sun was coming up. One-night stands had time limits. Sadie wasn't going to do this again and neither was he.

'Come for me,' she urged, her legs around his waist, gripping him even tighter, begging him not to withdraw.

This time he saw how tired she was, realised how sore she'd be once they released each other and...and what? Went about their friendship as if none of this had ever happened? What could possibly come after this for them? This was a one-night thing only. Wasn't that why they'd made it last all night?

With one final thrust he pressed his hot mouth to hers and heard a husky primal sound echo around the room. He realised it was coming from both of them, and they were coming together yet again.

The contractions made them judder and shudder and gasp, till he rolled from under her, breathless, floating back to reality as if he'd just been lifted up somewhere else and then thrown cruelly back down to earth. That had been like nothing he'd ever experienced—with anyone. That had been something raw and untamed and totally unprecedented. Mind-blowing. He almost didn't know what to think. He had too many thoughts.

He pressed his back to the sheets, finally allowing the softness of the mattress to lull him. His eyes closed. Exhaustion was an understatement. Sadie's fingers curled into his and he heard her emit a laugh of shock, or wonder, maybe both. He wanted to laugh too, suddenly. This was crazy. And reckless. Even now, when he was spent and sticky and tangled in her bedsheets, all he wanted was to hear her say she wanted to do it all over again.

Sadie's breathing slowed and he sensed her succumbing to sleep. As he let himself do the same, common sense crept in and started whispering at him.

What the hell did you just do that for?

Already the moment when he'd been free to touch her and cross any line he wanted was galloping from the present into the past, where it was morphing and twisting into something else. He could feel it already. Tomorrow there wouldn't be kisses and cuddling—not even if he wanted it more than anything. There would only be regret.

He turned away from her, so he wouldn't drape an arm around her sleeping frame and hold her tight for what was left of the night. He wasn't the kind of man Sadie needed in the long run and he never would be. She knew that. She'd just forgotten momentarily, that was all, and he'd gone along with it. If he carried on like this, disrespecting their friendship for the sake of sex, he'd lose her altogether!

Stupid.

Tomorrow he'd make sure they were cool— if that was even possible after he'd given in to her so fast… And he'd definitely make sure she knew that nothing like this would ever happen again.

CHAPTER TWELVE

SADIE SHUFFLED ON her feet in warrior pose, feeling too hot in the glaring sun that was streaming through the roof of the fernery. The yoga instructor had organised another hot session amongst the plants, and while she was glad of a little Zen, admittedly she was a little sore from last night. She could barely remember the last time she'd had so much sex in one night.

'And…let's move into our planks, everyone.'

Sadie followed the instructions, keeping an eye on her patients. She was pleased with Portia's progress. Despite her initial setback, the yoga was helping to strengthen the appropriate muscles around her head, neck, and shoulders. Relaxing facial exercises meant her episodic headaches were now fewer, with far more space between.

As for Vivek's hand-eye co-ordination—he seemed to be a different person after remembering his piano ballads the night of the gala.

The mood around the place was light. It was just Sadie's heart that felt heavy, as if it had suddenly taken on way too much. She kept getting flashbacks of the way she'd pounced on Owen in her bedroom doorway, the way he'd responded, and how it had escalated way beyond what she'd initially intended.

She also had a feeling Parminder knew. She was loitering outside now, on duty in case anything went wrong, but she kept giving her the eye. Parminder had heard them going into her room last night...she was sure of it. *Ugh*, she'd lost all control of her mind!

'And let's meet in our downward dog,' came the next instruction, leading to Vivek's disgruntled groan.

Sadie bit back a smile. 'You can do it,' she encouraged him.

OK, so he'd been happier *before* his therapeutic stretching session in the humid fernery, but soon he'd be Zen again. More Zen than her, anyway.

Her heart gave a little bunny hop as another flashback came for her—Owen's face hovering above hers, the light behind him outlining his strong muscled arms and chest, their perspiration adding to her wetness as they slid and sparked together.

A trickle of sweat dripped from her forehead to her mat. The memories were as persistent as a team of fruit flies around a glass of Pinot Noir. She could recall every single detail of the four times they'd taken each other in rapid succession, stopping only once for Owen to fetch more condoms as discreetly as he could from his own room.

Sadie shifted position on her yoga mat... closed her eyes. Each time her body took on a new shape she was thrown back to her naked gymnastics with Owen. She'd initiated it, yes but she hadn't exactly meant to. She'd been going to apologise for shutting him out. She knew he hated that, maybe as much as she did. She'd been on her way to talk about their obvious attraction, to get it out in the open, maybe even try and laugh about her crush in the hope that it would disappear, but she'd wound up doing none of that.

Just seeing him in her doorway, just as she'd flung open the door, shirtless, looking both furious and full of intent, she had felt something wild overcome her.

There was something to be said for not being the quiet, shy, serious one, for once. And maybe Portia had got her thinking about experimentation, but she'd been uncharacteristically spontaneous last night. The way Owen had always been. The way she herself had never been.

And it had felt amazing!

Even if she really should *not* have gone there with her best friend.

Portia had been right about a man never turning down sex...but she hadn't exactly given him much choice in the matter, pouncing on him like a jungle cat.

Ugh. Now what?

They'd already had an awkward 'good morning,' after waking up together. And maybe she'd made it more awkward by whispering, 'Thank you for last night' before he'd left her room. But she'd been nervous. They'd crossed some line last night and she didn't want to stick around to hear how he regretted it already. Or worse…that he'd enjoyed it and wanted to do it again.

That could never happen. This was Owen! Even once was one too many times.

'Sadie?'

Her heart pole-vaulted right up into her throat at his voice behind her. She sprang from her yoga mat as the instructor put a finger to her lips to shush him.

Owen grimaced. 'Sorry,' he whispered to the room, getting down on his haunches beside her.

Portia grinned at them from a cat cow position even as his familiar cologne made a knot of Sadie's stomach and sent her back to the way he'd tasted when she'd taken him in her mouth. God, he'd been so hard for her. Such a thrill…

Such a stupid, idiotic thrill to have acted on once, let alone multiple times!

'Ashanti's back from the hospital and has something she wants to give you before she goes,' he whispered. 'She's already said her goodbyes to Vivek, before this session—do you think you can duck out for five minutes?'

Sadie watched his mouth move but didn't hear a word he said. Every nerve-ending was alight again, just from seeing him. She wanted to reach for him suddenly, to reconnect, to feel some sense of reassurance that he hadn't forgotten what had happened, even though she herself had literally just decided to try and forget it and how different it had been from anything she'd experienced before.

'Sorry, what do you want?' she asked him when they were outside.

She gulped the cool air like a goldfish, hiding behind her hair, making a thing of rolling up her mat. Her hands were shaking.

He studied her, a crooked smile on his face. 'Ashanti? She wants to see you before she goes.'

'Oh, yes. Right.' Sadie met his eyes finally. For just a second she felt calm. Then the butterflies started up again.

'Are you OK?' he asked her, searching her face.

He was looking at her too intensely, so she looked at her nails instead. 'Why wouldn't I be?'

He urged her around to the side of the fernery, out of sight and earshot. Then he lowered his voice. 'Last night was… I wasn't exactly expecting that, Sadie…'

'It shouldn't have happened,' she blurted.

Owen straightened up. 'I know.'

What?

OK, she hadn't anticipated he'd agree so quickly. But they were best friends, for God's sake—it really *shouldn't* have happened.

'Sadie, I don't want to ruin what we have… or you.'

'Or me?' She frowned, letting his words sink in.

Was he insinuating he'd break her heart when he moved on—like he always did, at lightning speed? Was one night with her enough to restore his inner playboy?

'Don't worry, I know exactly what last night was about,' she told him, crossing her arms around herself, suddenly feeling smaller. 'We're both tired, and single, and far away from home. It won't go any further.'

'Maybe we just had to…you know…get it out of the way?' he followed up, cocking one eyebrow at her.

Sadie gave an insouciant shrug, but inside his words were scalding her and pouring ice-cold water on her at the same time. She was definitely the one to blame. Her annoyance was only with herself, over starting something that to all intents and purposes was probably the most idiotic thing she'd ever done.

Well done, Sadie.

'It was great sex, though,' he said now, searching her face.

'It was,' she agreed distractedly, swallowing back a sudden urge to blurt out what she'd been thinking all morning.

That it had felt like more than sex—to her anyway. That there had been a couple of moments last night when the pleasure of the physical act had been secondary to the closeness, to the soul connection. That had been something else she'd never felt before. As if she were so crazily intertwined with Owen on every single level.

It was probably all one-sided, though. *He* probably hadn't felt anything like what she had, making love to her. He was Owen, after all. Not only had he had way more sex than her, with more people, but he always kept his emotions out of everything. Why should sex with her be any different?

The gardener walked past and did a double-take. Sadie took a step backwards, realising she'd been standing less than inch from the tips of Owen's shoes.

'Well, now it's out of the way,' she joked, going in to punch his arm lightly for good measure. 'I guess we can go back to being friends?'

'I guess so,' he replied, but his eyes seemed to be making a data log of her innermost thoughts.

She straightened her shoulders, even as her

heart bucked and flapped behind her Lycra yoga top. It went haywire as Owen swept her hair gently behind her ear and examined what she knew was his stubble rash on her neck.

A look of dismay and regret crossed his face. 'I'm so sorry,' he growled.

'Don't be,' she told him quickly.

A little scrape or two from Owen's facial hair was not a promise. Right now it felt more like a scar. When would she be able to get *out* of here?

'I don't want things to get complicated…' he said, carefully.

'Mmm…' she replied to his lips, wondering why on earth she was still picturing him naked in her bed and feeling her core throb all over again. It was almost as if her body was completely unwilling to listen to her brain.

Very Important Friendship plus Sex equals Inevitable Disaster.

Catching her eye, he held her gaze and she found her heart thudding wildly as they played a game of who would look away first. What had they gone and done?

She followed him to Reception, where Ashanti was waiting with a bouquet of flowers for them. Sadie accepted the sweet gift and noticed every movement Owen made as he instructed the girl to always carry an epi-pen and told her that bees weren't exactly bad, just bad for *her*. He was good with children, she registered absently. She'd never really seen him with any before.

He kept catching her eye, sending more flashbacks to her frazzled brain. Last night had been so surreal… Had that really been them? Had *they* really done that? Had they really agreed all that hot, sweaty, passionate, frantic, soul-shifting sex was never going to happen again?

Of course it can't happen again. That was what you call a one-night stand, Sadie, and it was fun, but now it's done, so get over it.

Maeve wandered through to Reception with Conall just as Ashanti and Vivek's wife were leaving. She caught Sadie's arm and leaned in, dropped a kiss to her cheek, then reached for Owen's hand.

'Before I go, Sadie, Owen, I want you to know I feel like he's a different man because of you.' She nodded Conall's way and he simply shrugged and sniffed, as if it was no big deal. They all knew it was.

'We'll have some pre-exit evaluations this week,' Owen said. 'All going well, we should have him home with you by next weekend.'

Maeve lowered her voice, drawing them both closer. 'I'm planning a little something in honour of our son. We never had a tribute or a memorial service because Conall couldn't…well, you know. Anyway, I know it would mean a lot to

Conall if you were both there. If you could get away? We're in a wee hamlet not far from Loch Ness on the Great Glen Way. If you haven't seen much of Scotland I know Conall would be happy to show you. I dare say he'll be taking some more time off work…'

'Thank you,' Sadie said quickly, wondering how on earth she could refuse such an offer. Their home would be a mansion—the real celebrity deal! She couldn't help the excited look she threw Owen, but he frowned.

'We'll have to see what the schedule is like,' he said—to *her*.

'Of course.' Maeve smiled, squeezing both of their hands.

Sadie chewed on her cheeks, forcing a smile in return. Owen was being realistic. They were busy. A new patient was arriving in less than a week. But already she was panicking that he'd only said that as an excuse not to be around her, and now she'd have to go to the McCaskills' alone, without her best friend there to laugh at her over how starstruck she'd inevitably be the *entire* time.

That would be no fun, she realised. Owen made everything more fun. Including sex, now… apparently. Which was annoying. Sure, they'd acted like insatiable teenagers most of the night, but that didn't mean laughter hadn't sneaked in occasionally—like the first time she'd seen the hugeness of his shaft and he'd asked her, with a gleam in his eye, 'What did you expect?' She'd told him she'd never thought about it. He'd told her she was lying.

Soon it was just her and Owen standing in Reception.

'I should…um… I should get back to my class,' she said, thrusting the flowers at him. 'Put those in water, will you?'

'Yes, ma'am.'

She hurried back to the fernery, forcing herself not to look back in case he was staring at her bum in her leggings, or in case he wasn't. She didn't know any more which would offend her the most…

Yoga wasn't easy. There was definitely no Zen involved on her part, although her patients seemed totally blissed out. She couldn't get last night or her earlier conversation with Owen out of her head. They'd agreed it was a mistake, and that it wouldn't happen again, more or less, which should have been totally fine. It had been great sex. Undisputedly the best of her life—not that she'd tell him that. Why feed his ego?

Owen Penner was everything she'd always steered clear of. Unable to commit, allergic to love, renowned for distancing himself entirely from anything that no longer matched his needs or challenged his emotions. So wrong for her, in so many ways. Why think about it at all?

Forget about it. It was just a bit of sex between friends. It probably happens all the time. Stop making it into such a big deal!

By the time another night came around Sadie was practically chomping at the bit to go and knock on Owen's door again. She buried her head in her pillow, smelling his now far too familiar scent on her sheets, resisting the urge.

What if she suggested something crazy…like friends with benefits? That way she'd be in full control. She'd know it was just for fun, and she wouldn't be in danger of getting in too deep with someone entirely unsuitable.

Argh! Sadie yanked the covers over her head. What was she even thinking about this for? She wasn't going to be like the other girls he'd brought into his bed and then gone cold on. That wasn't in her plan—no, thanks. No more heart-break for her. She'd gone through enough after Chris's death…

Owen wouldn't get close enough again to come even halfway towards 'ruining' her—not if she had any say in it. She'd be his friend, he'd be hers…he'd make her laugh, she'd make him laugh—that was what they did. She couldn't lose that. She loved it, needed it—she'd come to rely on it.

Getting their friendship back on track was all that mattered. Tomorrow she'd wash him off her sheets, she decided, and she'd wash that night right out of her brain too.

CHAPTER THIRTEEN

OWEN LOOKED UP as Sadie entered the room and apologised for running late. His instincts were on red alert the second he saw her face—even more so when she whispered that she'd just had to deal with a family emergency.

She took a seat and switched to professional Sadie mode in front of their new patient, a fifty-four-year-old lady from Dundee called Amanda Bond, who'd brought her Siamese cat with her as a therapy animal following a nasty fall down an airport escalator that had affected her in a multitude of unpleasant ways—not least giving her a fear of staircases.

Amanda excused herself to fetch the cat's food before the session, and he took Sadie aside.

'What's going on?' He frowned, realising his hand on her arm was the closest he'd been to her in over a week. Since their night of...whatever they were calling it.

She retracted her arm quickly and adjusted

her hair, as if his touch was acid, and told him, 'Nothing of concern.'

She was lying.

'So fill me in,' she said, picking up Amanda's file.

He bit hard on his cheeks, willing himself to stay on topic. So she didn't want to talk to him about it here—fair enough. But she barely spoke to her mum and dad, so whatever the 'emergency' was, it must be something pretty serious.

Maybe she wouldn't want to talk about it anywhere, he realised as she introduced herself officially to their new client—she was Sadie, after all. She was doing her best to go back to normal, like he was, but they both knew things were very far from it.

Every joke between them had fallen kind of flat lately, and as for the serious stuff—well, that had all been swept under the nearest Scottish carpet. Still, they both had a job to do.

'Her last neurologist put her through a four-hour test designed to make her face her weaknesses, then came to the conclusion she was faking the results because she scored too poorly in the memory part,' he told her.

'She said my scores were lower than a patient with dementia,' Amanda cut in, coming back into the room and placing a bowl of food down for the cat. 'I was just telling Dr Penner that I was prescribed Ritalin, anti-depressants and sleep meds. Not all at once, but… I knew none of that would heal me. I went to a cranial sacral therapist next, which helped with the brain fog, but I still wasn't *me*. I didn't know what needed when it came to therapy, apart from Sonny.'

Their patient crouched down to her cat and stroked its soft cream-coloured back. 'I just knew I needed something else. It was a year—a whole year—before someone suggested I come here.'

Sadie turned her gaze to him. Owen could feel it. He could literally sense her looking at him—a gift he'd honed since that night, when he'd tuned in to her and tasted parts of her he was starting to forget already. Which was probably a good thing, he reminded himself.

Focus.

'So here you are,' he said, standing up and crossing to the window, where the gardener was scrubbing something off the stones around the mermaid fountain. Rain was coming…hovering. Probably waiting till they set off later for the McCaskills'.

He turned to look at their patient. 'And you've been extremely patient this morning throughout yet another examination, Mrs Bond. We've concluded that most of your issues are coming from your eyes.'

'I suspected that all along. No one would believe me,' Amanda said incredulously.

He was about to reply but Sadie cut in.

'Dr Penner knows a lot about these things… it's almost like an instinct now, right?'

'Well, we still need to run more tests, of course,' he replied, turning back as his heart surged with pride.

Sadie nodded. 'Of course. But all those other doctors were likely ignoring your concerns about your eyes because they weren't specifically trained in what to look for when related to traumatic brain injuries and concussions. Not like Owen… Dr Penner is.'

She caught his eye and he wondered for the thousandth time why compliments from Sadie made him feel this way. They triggered something in him that made him feel accomplished on a level no one else could reach. It had been the same in the bedroom, he thought reluctantly. More than just proving what he could do with his tongue. It had become an almost instant need for her to want him, to be pleased with him as a whole, mind, body *and* tongue.

'Millions of brain injury survivors are basically disregarded by the medical community and written off as having mental health issues when it's all about the physical. We'll work together on a treatment plan,' Sadie explained. 'You're in the best hands here. For now, just settle in and enjoy some relaxation—it's all part of the process, right?'

Amanda beamed—the first time Owen had

seen her look genuinely excited to be here. 'I hear the yoga classes are great.'

'If you don't mind the heat,' said Sadie. 'Did Dr Penner explain how we'll be away for the next few days?'

'I did,' he replied. 'Dr Calhoun is scheduled to oversee everything.'

Sadie tapped a pen to her knee and caught his eyes again. She was probably as apprehensive about this time off as he was. They could hardly back out of taking up Maeve and Conall McCaskill on their offer to attend Scott's memorial, so rather than spending the time off for himself as he'd planned—hiking in the Highlands, clearing his head—he'd now have to spend it in a mansion with a famous film star and his social media star of a wife…and Sadie.

'I bet Sonny here will like this place while we help get you better,' Sadie was saying now, bending to stroke the cat.

He'd bet she'd love a cat, now her ex was out of the picture. Callum had had allergies—how lame. What kind of grown man was allergic to a little cat?

He caught himself. What was his problem, hating Sadie's ex even more than before?

Because you want her in every single way you had her that night, and you know you never will again, while he had her for years.

Talk about the longest week ever. He'd been

going to bed at night after satisfying himself in the shower first, just to numb the urge to bang down her door again. His back had burned from her scratch marks the whole of the next day, and the love bite she'd given him on his thigh had been bigger than the patch of stubble rash on her neck. Both had faded now. The last reminder that they'd done anything at all...gone.

God, she was already hard to get over. He'd made her come over and over and over and he'd been exhausted, but completely unable to stop. She was the first woman who'd ever been able to exhaust him to the core, and still he wanted more...

More than sex? It had crossed his mind briefly. She was different. She touched him...parts of him no one else had even got close to reaching.

But no. Why even go there? Relationships ended in misery for the most part, and their friendship was not going to end up like his parents' marriage. No way. It was far too good to watch it crumble into misery and hatred.

Maybe this time away as friends and colleagues would help them get things back to normal, he thought, with a glimmer of hope that lasted just five seconds before morphing into dread.

It would take more than a faded love bite to make him forget that night!

* * *

As predicted, it was raining. Owen watched the clouds swallow every other boat in their wake as the ferry bobbed towards Wemyss Bay. On the train across to Glasgow, where they were due to be met by the McCaskills' driver, Sadie was quiet, huddled into another colourful jumper, scrolling on her phone while the evening turned greyer, then blacker, outside the windows. They were alone in the carriage and eventually he couldn't stand the silence.

He tapped the glass front of her phone till she turned it face down on her lap. 'So?' he said.

'So, what?'

'The call with your family earlier on. Everything OK?'

She gave a long, exaggerated sigh and shrugged. 'My mother's in hospital.'

His heart jolted. 'Is that not…concerning you?'

'It's nothing too serious. She's having metatarsal foot surgery. It's just… I offered to go there, and she told me not to.' She held up her phone and showed him the text from her mother.

Owen felt his brow crease—it seemed the woman really was blaming her daughter for something to do with Chris's death. He'd been so sure—that Sadie had just been feeling guilty all this time because she had no one to reassure her otherwise. But here was proof, he supposed.

'Call her,' he said now, anger flaring up on her behalf.

He didn't know the full story, but if she'd offered to go to her mother and been asked to stay away...well, maybe there was more to it.

'I have. She said she has some things to discuss with someone first, and she'll call me back later. She's already decided she doesn't want me there.'

'Don't be ridiculous. It'll be something else—you'll see.'

He reached for her fingers impulsively and she let him hold her hand on her lap. A voice in his head said that he was being a comfort blanket... or a stand-in boyfriend till the next one came along. But to hell with it. That was what friends did.

He forced himself not to say anything that might sound like he was slamming her parents. He didn't know them, and they had their own set of problems after what had happened with her brother, but it sounded a lot as if they had no idea how the whole thing had affected Sadie all these years.

'You know,' he said, tracing a thumb over her knuckles, 'I really hope you don't think that just because we...' Damn, why couldn't he get his words out? 'I hope you know I'm not going to stop being there for you if you need me. I will never stop caring about you.'

A thousand questions flared in the grey of her irises when she looked at him. 'I know,' she replied after a second, before resting her head softly on his shoulder. 'That means a lot to me, Owen. I know you mean those things when you say them. You're a good friend.'

He toyed with how the word 'friend' felt now, coming from her lips. It was all they'd promised to be for each other, all he could offer her...only he'd never given anyone the kind of emotional support he now found himself offering Sadie. Weirdly, he was wanting to offer it more, even after sleeping with her, which was kind of new.

'Did you hear anything else about your dad's wedding?' she asked now, her head bumping on his shoulder with the train's motion.

'He wants me to go. I said I wouldn't,' he replied, prickling at the thought of it.

The invitation had come via email just a few days ago. He'd declined and had yet to respond to his father's follow-up email, asking him to reconsider. Of course his dad wanted his successful son in attendance, even if their relationship was far from perfect. The rest of their extended family weren't so bad—it would be nice to catch up with them, at least. If it wasn't for...well, *everything* else, he might consider it.

'Your mum doesn't want you to go, right?'

He frowned into the top of Sadie's head. How

did she know that? 'I don't do everything she asks me to—' he started, already on the defence.

'You love her,' she interrupted. 'You want to do right by her. That's who you are, Owen, and there's nothing wrong with that. But do you *want* to go?'

She lifted her head to study him and he avoided her eyes, shrugged towards the window. They were supposed to be talking about *her* parents, not his. Just being around his father made him feel like a treacherous son to his mother, yes, but also as if he should have called him out on his lecherous, cruel behaviour years ago, instead of bottling it up inside, letting the effects of it mark his own relationships, or lack thereof. He wasn't an idiot—he knew he probably looked at relationships through a warped lens, or at least a different one from Sadie, because of his parents. But he couldn't exactly unsee what he'd seen, or undo what he'd experienced.

'If you want to go, I'll go with you,' she offered now. 'Maybe if you take a friend with you it'll be easier…'

'No,' he said. 'Thanks, but no.'

Just the thought of it was like dunking his head in an icebox. His mum might not want to be there herself, but that didn't mean she wouldn't be calling everyone else for the gossip. He'd be forced to be a part of that tornado and its wreckage, and so would Sadie if she went with him.

Friend or not, she'd also get an earful about the Penner men's playboy ways, how his dad's weddings were now an annual event, how she should watch out in case she was next in line to need a divorce lawyer...blah-blah. All the usual jokes that weren't really jokes. It made him loathe the very notion of marriage and weddings in general... No, thank you. Hell, no.

'I heard your mum on the phone that day, out on the boat,' Sadie said now. 'She's in your ear all the time, Owen, dragging you into things. Doesn't that drive you crazy?'

He stared at her, then dropped her hand, embarrassment making him twitchy.

'Maybe you need to talk to both of them,' she continued. 'You're not a kid any more. They can't keep—'

'We were talking about you calling *your* mother,' he interjected.

Sadie bristled and tutted and took her hand back, slinking back in her seat. 'At least your family involves you, Owen, even if it is too much sometimes.'

He simmered next to her. How had this escalated so fast into another altercation? It was not what he'd intended, but she knew exactly how to rattle his cage—and he hers, apparently.

'Look, I'm sorry,' he offered. 'But I don't need to go to my dad's wedding, and neither do you.'

'Fine,' she huffed. 'I get it. You can be there

for me, but I'm not allowed to be there for you. No one gets close to Owen, huh?'

'I told you not to psychoanalyse me.'

She threw her hands in the air, then picked up her phone again, glowering into the screen. 'I wouldn't dream of it.'

Shame took hold of him instantly. He was hurting people with own stupid attempts at self-preservation. He was hurting Sadie now, by pushing her away again when he'd promised not to! She deserved more.

He ground his teeth at the window. 'No one gets as close as you've got,' he told her reflection suddenly. It was the truth. 'But you have your own issues, Sadie, you don't need to take on any of mine.'

His voice was so low and quiet it was practically a growl, but her head snapped up from her phone. 'I thought that was what friends were for—' she tried.

But this time he couldn't keep his mouth shut. 'Stop it, Sadie. This is verging on insanity now. We can't go back to being *friend*s.'

'What do you mean?'

She looked dubious now, and even more hurt than before. He caught the back of her head and drew her closer, tangling his hand in the hair at the back of her neck.

'You know what I mean,' he said, even as her own hands found the lapels of his jacket.

He wanted to kiss her, to lower his mouth and take hers and show her what his tongue and everything else could do.

She groaned. 'I do know what you mean,' she said, almost regretfully. 'I can't stop thinking about it.'

'Well, that makes two of us.' He drew a deep breath, forced himself to release her. 'But you know I can't give you what you want, Sadie, don't you?'

She clenched his jacket, and unclenched it, and he almost expected her to untangle herself and agree with him. Surely she knew that. This was a warning. He was letting her off the hook right here and now. She knew what she had to do.

'What is it you think I want, exactly?' she asked instead.

'Someone who can give you more than I can.'

'That's such an *Owen* thing to say.'

'But I'm right. I know you, Sadie.'

They'd been inching closer with every word. Her knees were pressed to his now.

'Maybe you do...maybe you don't,' she said, her eyes glimmering with challenge. 'I'm learning some new things about myself lately.'

What?

'I don't want to ruin what we've got already but...maybe we should try being friends with benefits?' she whispered. Then she snorted a laugh and buried her face in his jacket. 'I can't believe I just said that to you. Is that crazy?'

'Yes,' he told her, even as he stiffened in arousal. That was the hottest, most unexpected thing that had ever come from her lips. He released her quickly, balling his fist. 'Don't you think we've made things weird enough already?'

'You're right,' she said with a quiet moan, long and lingering, deep in her throat. 'We probably shouldn't…'

The train rattled on, the rain slammed the windows, and for what felt like for ever he sat there, millimetres apart from her, in what felt like a battle with his own personal angel and demon.

Torture.

Do not go down this road, the angel in his head warned him.

Just do it. She knows it's just a bit of fun…she suggested it herself, said the devil.

He couldn't help it. Hot fire took over as his mouth found hers and in seconds she was straddling him on the seat, kissing him passionately in return, picking up right where they'd left off before.

Even if they hadn't been sitting in an empty train carriage, he didn't think they'd have stopped kissing. Except a train with all manner of filth and grime on its seats was no place to take things further. Besides, anyone could walk in on them.

Regretfully, he pulled back and she sighed in agreement, sliding off his lap.

On the platform at Glasgow he was still wrapping his head around what had just happened when Sadie clutched his hand and pulled him towards a guy with a sign bearing their names.

Halfway there she stopped and pressed her mouth to his, standing high on her tiptoes. He promptly dropped their luggage.

'Are you ready for this?' She grinned. A wicked gleam took over her eyes again.

Who was this woman?

Owen didn't know what 'this' was, exactly, but in that exact second he decided he was done with caring.

CHAPTER FOURTEEN

SADIE GAZED UP at the remains of the crumbled tower, imagining being out there in the middle of Loch Ness in the heavy winds that had taken down this castle's walls in 1715. Their tour of Urquhart Castle had gone ahead despite the rain, and she cuddled into Owen's arm under the umbrella, feeling bad that she wished the tour would be over, so they could get back to the warmth of a quaint pub and a hot chocolate.

She yawned.

Owen nudged her. 'Why are you so tired?'

'Very funny,' she whispered back.

He knew damn well why she was so tired. They'd kept each other busy till four a.m., and then the McCaskill housekeeper had knocked on the door at seven, urging them to get up for their tour.

Conall didn't have time to take them out again today—he was preparing for the memorial service to be held tonight at their home. But yesterday he'd driven them into the majestic Highlands, where the scenery changed dramatically at every turn, and where the pancake-flat terrain of the Lowlands was transformed into glistening lochs, forest-filled glens and craggy mountains.

Scotland was home to some of the most alluring scenery she'd ever seen. She'd almost forgotten it had once been a battleground for some fiercely territorial Highland clans... All she knew was that she and Owen were now embroiled in something so utterly fabulous that put all that gorgeous scenery to shame.

Sure, it was all spectacular, but she could just have easily admired the contours of his abs all day in bed instead of these mountains. She wanted it all before they were forced to get back to the real world, where they'd inevitably have to stop, and where he'd move on at some point, like he always did. Had he really changed? She still couldn't be sure... But last night. *Oh, God.*

She swallowed back the lump in her throat that warned her how tough he would be to get over. She'd just have to deal with it. She *would* deal with it—this was the new her! The new Sadie, who could be just as emotionally detached as him, and love every second of it.

Every time she'd felt Owen's eyes on her yesterday she'd had to resist the urge to touch him. They hadn't let on to the McCaskills that anything was out of the ordinary, although maybe word would get back to them from the housekeeper that her bed hadn't been slept in, she mused, once more zoning out of the tour.

She smiled to herself, tightening her arm on his, as the tour guide pointed to another crumbling wall and explained something about the nobles who'd partied there when it had been the Great Hall.

Talking of great... *What. A. Night.* Last night had possibly been better than the last one they'd spent together. Behind the closed doors of Owen's room in the McCaskill mansion she'd lost count of how many times they'd had sex. Once in the marble-clad shower, twice on the shag pile rug by the fire, twice this morning in the bed...

In that moment when she'd suggested a 'friends with benefits' arrangement she'd been trying to channel Portia, like before. It had felt so freeing, letting herself give in to her desires, knowing she was in full control.

There was also the small issue of her trying to forget the fact that her mother didn't want her in attendance at the hospital and wanted to discuss it with someone else. Whoever that someone else was... Was her mother in a relationship now?

She felt shame flood through her. Was she maybe using Owen a little bit? As a distraction?

The rain blew in on her cheeks and she turned to Owen, who moved the umbrella further to her side to protect her. Maybe she'd thrown herself at him on the train to stop the usual doubts and guilt over her brother from creeping in again. Every time she felt ignored or unwanted she did have a tendency to turn to the closest person for attention. She was probably doing it now, she thought, sniffing into the drizzle.

How many messages had she left her mum and dad so far? Three for her mum, offering to go and visit, and even one for her dad this morning. She'd had nothing in response except a short text message from her mother, saying she'd call later.

It was tearing her up, the way they never reached out to her. She and Chris had been so close. With only a year separating them, she'd sometimes felt they were more like twins. How could she not have known he was thinking about ending his life? He'd always confided in her about everything. Her parents obviously still wondered about that, too. She'd found the suicide note straight away, after all. It had been as if she'd known exactly where to look… It was all too horrid to think about, let alone talk about.

'What's that?'

Owen interrupted her thoughts by pointing at something in the lake.

'Is that the monster?'

She followed his finger, squinting through the rain, just as he nudged her again and laughed. 'My bad—it's another tour boat,' he said. 'You don't honestly think there's a monster down there, do you?'

Sadie shrugged. 'Anything could be down there,' she replied, just as a huge gust of wind snatched the umbrella from Owen's hand and sent it bouncing down the path towards a rocky cliff-edge.

'No! That's Maeve McCaskill's brolly,' she heard herself cry in horror.

Maeve had given it to her this morning—ahead of the forecast for rain. Before she quite knew what she was doing, Sadie was running headfirst after it into the rain, the abandoned tour group far behind her.

'Come back, that's Maeve's umbrella!'

The silly thing bounced and tumbled, a bright red blur against the stony grey castle. It seemed to enjoy leaping from her grasp the second it was within her reach. To her utter horror, it toppled towards a savage clifftop in a dramatic display of somersaults, and just as she took one more step forward, an image of Chris hurtled into her mind from nowhere.

Stop!

'Sadie, what are you doing? Leave it! It's just an umbrella!'

Owen was pulling her backwards against the wind, into him. She felt the breath leave her body in hot, short gasps as he urged her back onto the path with him, still holding her as she spun her head in all directions.

'He was just here, Owen,' she heard herself say through her tears. 'Clear as day.'

'Who?'

'Chris! I heard his voice.'

'No, you didn't—that was me.'

'I heard him!'

Owen's eyes had turned to narrow slits. He was drenched now—they both were. She sniffed in embarrassment, realising several of the other tourists were watching them. Quickly he led her away from all the eyes, hurrying her down the path past the group towards their tour boat, where it was dry. As posters of Loch Ness and the monster closed in on her he sat her down by a heater.

She barely noticed the other people staring as they started boarding and shuffling past. All she could see was Chris. Her brother. That was the clearest image she'd had of him in years. She could have sworn her late brother had just stopped her plunging off a cliff face—the way he had on his motorbike.

'I feel sick,' she told Owen, who bundled her closer and rocked her.

He said nothing as the engine started and they chugged away from the castle.

'You think I'm insane, but I heard him. I heard my brother,' she insisted, halfway back.

Owen still hadn't spoken. He'd just let her cry. Now he sighed hotly into the top of her head.

'You've just been thinking about him, Sadie, because of all this stuff with your parents…your mum going to hospital…and the memorial service later. It's making you think about him more. You need to talk to them—tell them about all this guilt you carry around with you. I bet they don't even know.'

She buried her head into his shoulder. Maybe he was right.

'Don't ever scare me like that again,' he ordered.

'I'm sorry.'

'You were willing to risk dying over Maeve McCaskill's umbrella? I mean, I know you're a fan, but…'

'Owen.' She turned to him and couldn't help but release a fresh batch of tears as they stung her eyes. 'I was starting to forget him. I was starting to forget what he looked and sounded like till just now. I miss him. I miss him so much.'

'I know you do.'

Owen looked awkward now, as if he didn't know what to do with her, but he held her as she sobbed into him on the boat.

By the time they were in the car, on their way back to the McCaskills' she felt utterly traumatised…but mostly by her own outburst. She hadn't been able to hold it in in front of Owen, whereas usually she'd have kept all that entirely bottled up with a lid on, where it belonged.

Back in her room, she undressed and stepped into the steaming hot shower. She waited for Owen to get in with her. He didn't. In fact, when she exited the bathroom in a towel he'd gone. Back to his own room, probably, to get ready for the service.

She kicked herself.

This friends with benefits thing was meant to be fun, and here she was letting herself get all emotional over her parents and Chris in front of him—what an idiot. He didn't need her laying all that on him. He had his own family dramas going on, what with his dad's wedding—which of course he'd be attending if it wasn't for his mother, always in his ear about what a screw-up the man was.

No wonder Owen kept his emotions at bay, after them *both* telling him that crying was a terrible thing. No wonder he felt awkward and had physically left the room just now, after she'd let Niagara Falls out of her eyeballs.

Well, she'd save him from any more of that.

He was happy to be fun summer fling material while she was enjoying being single and spontaneous for the first time in...*ever*. He wasn't here to console a crying wreck, and she wasn't about to let him think she was after another comfort blanket. From now on there would be no more tears, only fun!

Going for the black satin jumpsuit on its

hanger—something she'd been saving without really knowing what she'd wear it for—she wondered absently whether Owen would be wearing a kilt tonight, like all the other men at the service. Did men really wear nothing underneath their kilts?

Yes, focus on that Sadie. That's right. Just one more distraction is perfect—far better than actually facing your problems.

Her reflection seemed to mock her even as she dried her hair poker-straight and applied scarlet lipstick. OK, fine. Maybe hearing Chris's voice earlier, imaginary or not, was yet another sign that she had to initiate a certain kind of talk with her parents when they next opened the door for her to do so, as Owen kept saying she should. Chris would want that.

She should bring the guilt and shame that she and maybe even they still felt out into the open so they could say their pieces and all move on. What would she tell a patient if they told her the biggest block to moving on from something was their own fear?

The Mills family really had to talk this time, she decided, hands on hips in front of the mirror. Not like they usually did, about their cats, and what they were cooking for their respective Sunday dinners, and how the wisteria was blooming early. They had to talk about Chris.

CHAPTER FIFTEEN

MAEVE MCCASKILL LOOKED as solemn as Sadie had ever seen her tonight—which was only to be expected. The ten-foot glass dining table was laid out with her caterer's finest—for once, Maeve hadn't cooked anything herself. Sadie had offered to help in any way she could, and was dutifully helping to distribute little booklets with Scott McCaskill's face and birthdate on them.

She was standing in the doorway on the top step to the house, surrounded by perfectly pruned conifers, welcoming the drove of guests, when Owen came to her side in a green and blue tartan kilt, complete with plaid and knee-high black socks.

She had to do a double take. He quite possibly looked hotter than she had ever seen him look.

'You're giving me serious *Outlander* vibes. You'd better get lost before I ravish you,' she whispered, and he chuckled into his blazer and scarf, taking a pile of booklets from her. 'Have you got a musket under there?' she added cheekily.

'No, I'm just pleased to see you. How are you feeling now?'

'Better,' she said, blinking and shifting uneasily. 'Sorry about before.'

She assumed she'd probably scared him off... made an idiot of herself.

Owen sniffed. 'Don't apologise to me,' he said, turning her throat as dry as paper.

He couldn't meet her eyes now. So he *did* find it uncomfortable, her turning to him with her tears.

'Did you talk to your mum yet?' he asked, his eyes on the driveway, where a girl in leathers had just rolled up on a red Vespa.

She was about to answer, but Conall McCaskill was approaching in a matching kilt. He thanked them both again for being there, and for handing out the booklets. Taking one in his big hands, he sighed at the photo of Scott, running a hand over his tuft of a grey beard.

'Aye, he'd have hated all this,' he said gruffly, handing it back and gesturing around at the guests, some mingling on the driveway, some behind them in the house, others out near the stables—the McCaskills had seven horses. She recognised quite a few of them. There were actors and directors...friends of Maeve's who'd guest-starred on her TV programme. In any other situation she would have been more than star struck, but the excitement was dimmed somewhat by the occasion.

'Did you have a good day today, at the Loch?' asked Conall, his eyes glinting between them. 'Quite a romantic place, that castle, wouldn't you say, lad?'

That famous knowing half-smile was directed at Owen and it threw her off-guard. She compressed her lips, forcing a polite nod.

'We had an interesting time,' Owen said carefully, as someone in the rose garden, where the ceremony was due to take place, fired up the bagpipes.

Conall excused himself, leaving Sadie cringing.

'Don't worry about it,' Owen told her over the sound of the pipes, probably reading her thoughts. 'If they know, they don't care.'

Sadie couldn't read him. Did he care if anyone knew? Maybe not. Since when did Owen Penner care who knew about his conquests? That was what she was, she supposed. And she'd walked right into it.

'Nice heels,' he said, and smirked, oblivious, his fingers teasing at the gold zipper along the pocket on her hip. 'And that is one sexy one-piece you're wearing.'

'Don't think I wore it for you,' she quipped, seizing back control of her flapping heart, which was starting to feel like a lost bird in her chest.

She wasn't about to start caring that she was just a conquest now—she'd started the whole thing! But this was quite confusing. How *was* she supposed to feel around him now?

Don't be stupid, it's just sex. Feel what he feels about it—nothing, she reminded herself, before her thoughts could take her down a dangerous path.

The ceremony was beautiful. Sadie held her candle close as some of the guests made their speeches in the rose garden. Balloons were launched, candles were floated out on the lily pond, all overlooked by three marble statues of muscled Scotsmen on horseback. She learned a thousand things about Scott, a man of many talents, while she kept her eyes on Conall and Maeve, bowing their heads at the front.

She couldn't help her heart bursting with empathy for Maeve, for how poised she looked when she was probably breaking inside. Her mother hadn't been so strong at Chris's funeral...

It felt like so long ago, but also as if it was yesterday...walking into his room and finding that note. She'd racked her brains for all the things he might have said, the hints at his state of mind she might have missed. How hadn't she even noticed he was suffering?

But then, if it *was* her brother who'd stopped her on that cliff today, and not some perfectly timed memory of him, like Owen said, maybe he'd forgiven her.

If only her parents could, too, she thought, glancing at her phone for a message from her mother, as if one might suddenly appear, like Chris had.

Later, she was talking with one of Scott's friends when she got the call she'd almost been expecting not to come. As nerves consumed her she saw Owen watching her leave the crowd and walk towards the stables. It was quiet there. It smelled like sweet hay and expensive hobbies.

'Hey, Mum, how are you feeling?'

Her mother sounded strangely cheery as she talked about the friendly, encouraging doctors she'd seen after the operation on her foot, and asked about Scotland.

Sadie told her nothing about the developments with Owen—they didn't talk about things like that—but she told her about the film and TV award in the McCaskills' pool room as she psyched herself up to segue into the subject of Chris, wondering how best to do it.

Should she mention she thought he might have saved her today? Or would that sound crazy coming from a medical professional?

She walked through the sweeping stable doors, murmuring at her mother's words, and ran her hands over a smooth leather saddle on a mount on the wooden slat wall. Then, just as she was about to come out and ask why on earth she hadn't wanted Sadie at the hospital with her for her operation, and whether it was because she blamed her in some way for what had happened to Chris, her mother took a deep breath.

Then she blurted something so unexpected Sadie landed flat against the stable wall in shock.

Owen found her several minutes later. He cut a handsome sixteenth-century figure in the stable doorway, where he was devoid of any telling modern landmarks or objects.

'I guessed you were finally talking to your mother,' he said, striding purposefully to where she sat on a wooden bench, tapping her heeled foot against a box of riding crops.

He sat beside her, sending a shock of cologne to her nostrils when she didn't answer. She almost didn't have the words.

'What happened, Sadie?'

'He wants to be there for her,' she said, refocusing on the news she'd just been blasted with out of nowhere.

Owen looked confused.

'My dad… I think he freaked out, hearing how Mum wouldn't be able to walk too well for a while. They've barely spoken in years. She said she didn't quite know how to tell me…she had to talk to him first…but they got to thinking about it and they've decided to give things another shot. He's at the hospital with her.'

She must have looked as perplexed as she felt. Owen folded his arms over his chest, nudged an elbow against hers.

'Well, that's good, isn't it?' he said. 'Maybe he's just realised he needs to start looking out for her again. Do you think they ever really fell out of love, after your brother…?'

'I don't know,' she said, staring at a stray bit of straw at her feet. 'It felt like it to me. But I just don't want him to get all involved with her again, and get into her head, and then decide it's not what he wants. She's been through enough. They both have.'

She looked at him sideways then, realising how maybe it wasn't just her parents' situation she was talking about now. Owen's jaw shifted this way and that, then he stood and pulled her with him, till her arms locked around his broad shoulders.

She toyed with the fabric of his plaid for a second, and then he said, 'Did you tell her how guilty you've felt all this time about what happened? Did you give her a chance to tell you that none of what happened to your brother was your fault?'

Sadie flinched in his arms. She'd meant to start that conversation, of course, but the news about her parents' reunion had kind of cancelled it out. It was obvious they didn't want her around, though, wasn't it? Neither had asked her to visit.

'I will talk to them both together—next time,' she said resolutely.

Maybe she had taken yet another coward's way out of confronting them and her guilt.

You'd rather hide in Owen.

Owen's dark eyes were laced with doubt. She still wanted to hide in him, but that wasn't going to solve anything.

'It's not like you're my boyfriend,' she snapped. 'You don't have to take on all my drama. I wish I'd never told you I heard Chris before either... we're supposed to be having fun.'

His eyes narrowed further and his nostrils flared. 'You're right.'

'I know I'm right!' she said, even as the little white lie came back to taunt her. She'd wanted to tell him about Chris—needed to, in that moment.

She tried to step back from his unnerving, disapproving stare, but he clasped her by the back of her neck, tangling his hand in her hair.

'Then let's have fun,' he said, against her lips.

Sadie gasped, letting him urge her back into an empty stall. He kicked the door shut behind them with one shiny shoe and kissed her with such ferocity and intensity her lips and chin burned with the most delicious heat. She was flat against the wall now, clutching the plaid across his shoulder, her tongue dancing with his, her heels buried in hay.

Somewhere beyond their stall a horse snorted softly. The smell of horses and him mingled in her nose till she was so turned on by the thrill of what they were doing, and where, she could hardly stand it. She had to have him.

Her hands lowered to his kilt. Owen moaned against her mouth as she found his hardness under the folds, throbbing for her. So he hadn't worn anything under it… God, this was the most erotic moment of her life.

She shimmied out of her jumpsuit, noting the way his eyes roved hungrily over her body as she stood naked in front of him. Stepping forward, she was about to help him off with his plaid and claw his shirt undone when something huge and hard that wasn't Owen sprang up between them and thwacked her on the head.

'Sadie!' Owen made a grab for her as she folded like a card to the floor and crumpled onto the hay.

What the…?

Pressing her hands to her forehead, she checked herself. No blood. Thank God.

Owen snatched up the pitchfork that must have been hiding in the hay and tossed it like a poisoned rod to the other side of the stall. She'd just got bopped by a pitchfork.

'Lucky it wasn't the spiky end that got me,'

she said, as embarrassment turned her cheeks as hot as flames.

Owen was beside her in the hay now, checking her head all over, his eyes wide and wild. 'Are you hurt?'

'No, just mortified.'

'Would you just stop trying to kill yourself today?' he said in exasperation, before grimacing at his choice of words. 'Sorry, that came out... that's not what I meant.' He lowered himself to his side, checking her face again.

'I'm OK,' she told him, rolling onto her back, catching her breath.

Draping a hand over her forehead, she wanted to laugh, for some reason, but Owen leaned over her on one strong forearm, his eyes searching hers in concern.

'Owen, I'm OK.'

The seriousness of his face made her reach for him. She needed him closer, almost as if she had to console him for getting hurt in front of him— twice! Her fingers found the buttons on his shirt, and soon the kilt was cast aside and they were lying flesh against flesh in the prickly hay. This time he was less ferocious, more tender. She gave soft, encouraging moans as his kisses left a tantalising trail along her collarbone and his fingers traced circles around her nipples, moving down to the softness of her inner thighs, exploring her in the faint beams of moonlight peeking in through the skylight.

Dust from the hay swirled up as they moved and gave him an almost heavenly glow. His intensity turned her skin to goosebumps. Usually she'd be embarrassed, laid out like some wanton object of desire, but she closed her eyes and revelled in the way he made her feel sexy...like a goddess!

She was so absorbed in his touch and how different his tongue felt sweeping hers that she almost missed him unwrapping the condom. He must have been keeping it in his sporran, in case the kilt had to come up—or off, as the case might be. She almost made another *Outlander* joke, but when her eyes flashed open Owen was positioning himself over her and the look in her eyes rendered her silent. They burned into hers, devouring her whole, until she felt as if she was drowning in their depths, completely lost.

There was only them. Only this moment.

Owen rocked deliciously inside her as the hay tickled and scratched her skin, and she found her hands cupping his face, stroking his hair. She never wanted to look away from his eyes. Sadie could have sworn that she was seeing right through to his heart. He was letting her see all the way to the core of the real Owen, and what she saw almost made her cry.

She ran her hands over his bare chest and abs,

memorising the coarse, rugged texture of the thick, dark hair around his navel, committing to memory the feeling of having him fully inside her, and what it meant.

She tightened her arms around him, burying her head in his neck, breathing him in. So this was the difference between lust and love...between screwing and creating something sacred. She had never made love to anyone like this—had he?

'Sadie, what are you doing to me?'

His voice was all desire, all awe and need, as he rolled her over on top of him, clasping her backside, begging her with his body and his hands to ride him. She obliged willingly, bringing him to the brink and then slowing down again as he moaned into her mouth and kissed her as she'd never been kissed before.

She couldn't possibly have ever felt closer to him...or anyone. He said her name over and over, and the sound of it coming from his lips while they were connected like this made her feel a thousand things at once—scared, confused, powerful, wanted, *home*.

It was like being on a completely different planet, just the two of them soaring through some heavenly space, and after he'd jolted and convulsed in deep satisfaction she felt a kind of bonding with him such as she'd never known, like two turning into one. He clasped her hand above her head, stayed inside her, working his fingers on her till she bit down hard on her own hand, trying to stop vocalising her orgasm—it was all she could do not to scream the stable down.

'My God, Owen…' Her words came out muffled and full of her aching for him. She was coming so hard her knees were shaking, clenched to his sides like a vice.

Tumbling off him she fell to the hay, breathless, waves of pleasure still shuddering through her. Owen folded around her, his arms and legs like a cage claiming a tiny creature he never wanted to release. She smiled like a cat, curling into the warm hook of his arched pelvis, allowing this new flood of mutual pleasure and bliss to reach her heart.

And then he said, 'You really know how to show a man the benefits of your friendship, Sadie.'

She froze. Owen nuzzled into her neck. The party outside had gone quiet…maybe everyone had gone. How long had they been here? Why did he have to say that after they'd done *that*?

Oh, God. His words were like a blow to her abdomen. She felt as if he'd lifted her soul clean from her body, then slammed it straight into a brick wall. She couldn't help it…water pooled in her eyes even as she squeezed them shut.

Owen's breathing slowed as they lay there

glued together, and Sadie was glad her back was pressed to his chest. This way he couldn't see the tears that were clouding her vision, choking her throat.

That hadn't been just sex, or fun between friends—not for her anyway. It had been even more intense than the first time they'd done it. Maybe she'd wanted to hide in him initially, forget the world for a moment, but that had been making love—real, proper, soul-propelling, top-level, out-of-the-blue love stuff—and she couldn't even find the strength to deny it.

What was she doing? This was her all over, she thought helplessly. She couldn't just enjoy sex for what it was—her whole body, mind and soul had to turn it into something more. And now she'd gone and ruined things with Owen.

Blinking her eyes free of tears, she buried herself in his arms, memorising what it felt like to be there, knowing it had to be the last time she allowed herself to do it. She wasn't built the same way he was—what was the point pretending to herself? She was *already* doing what she'd sworn she wouldn't do—she was getting attached.

CHAPTER SIXTEEN

'PENNY FOR YOUR THOUGHTS?'

Owen turned to Portia, who was looking the picture of health now—if a little windswept in her pink down jacket and jeans.

'I'm not really thinking much,' he said, casting his eyes back to the colony of seals lounging in the secluded bay.

They'd taken an afternoon trip to the west coast of the Isle of Bute, where Scalpsie Bay had drawn them in with its resident herd of grey seals, sunning themselves on the rocks just offshore. Sadie was further down, with Amanda Bond, who on this one occasion had been persuaded to leave her therapy cat Sonny at Rothesay.

'Beautiful view,' he commented, watching Sadie as she crouched on a rock, a foot away from a giant seal.

He was talking about her backside in her jeans, which he hadn't seen up close since the night of Scott's memorial in the stable, over a week ago now.

'How's your head today, Portia? I know you had one mild attack while we were away, but nothing since?'

'They're getting easier to handle, thanks to what you and Dr Mills have shown me,' she replied. Then she nudged him with her elbow, nodding towards Sadie. 'Speaking of Dr Mills...what is going on there? You haven't been the same since you got back from Conall and Maeve's.'

Man, this woman was astute. Or maybe he and Sadie were just too obvious. He raised his shoulders, stuck his hands in his pockets and motioned Portia to walk with him up the beach.

The clouds that streaked across the clear blue sky were turning golden at the edges in the afternoon light and the tide was out, for now. It was the best time to take what Dr Calhoun called a 'healing hike' in one of the island's top spots. The undulating green of the hills ahead was therapy in itself—not that it had worked on him. Not on this situation with Sadie.

'Things are complicated,' he heard himself say against his will.

It was funny, but he always felt compelled to open up to Portia on a personal level. Did Sadie feel the same, or was he just slipping up because their patient was a sexologist? She was definitely skilled at reading people.

'Complicated how? Usually it's people who insert complications where there really aren't any.'

He thought how best to respond. 'Well, we went from being friends to colleagues. Now we're...'

'Sleeping together. Is the sex good?'

Portia's grin took him by surprise. In fact, he was so struck by her bluntness he laughed. God, if she only knew the things Sadie could do with those full satin-soft lips...the way she could kiss. A surge of blood tore through his body and made him shuffle awkwardly in the sand.

'It's...well...'

'I knew it!' Portia clapped her hands in glee. 'So, how are you going to overcome these so-called "complications" together?'

'There is no "together".' Owen kicked up a stone, glancing towards Sadie again, who seemed deep in conversation with Amanda Bond. And then she caught his eye.

He had a flashback. Sadie lying down in the hay, her eyes searching his, taking him inside her slowly, intentionally. He could almost pinpoint the second it had stopped being a frivolous act of sexual gratification and turned into a level of lovemaking he'd never experienced. It had felt as if she'd let him in, admitted a trust in him that was not to be taken lightly.

The intensity of everything that had gone unsaid between them then had blown his mind—

even more than their first time, when he'd only felt a taste of it and then pretended it had all just been in his head. So he'd gone and cheapened it by saying something stupid, like he always did.

Either way, it didn't matter any more. She'd put a stop to it that same night. She'd practically run from the stable before he'd even got the kilt back on, citing the need to shower the dust off her. When he'd gone upstairs to her, the door had been locked. It had stayed locked until the next day, when she'd emerged with her bags and the driver had taken them back to the train station.

'She doesn't want to ruin our friendship,' he explained now, still holding Sadie's gaze. 'So there will be no more sex.'

'Rubbish,' Portia scoffed. 'She'll be back— mark my words, lad. You can't turn something like that off so easily once it's been turned on. So to speak! Besides, friends make the very best lovers. Trust me. I know.'

Owen dragged his eyes from Sadie's, wishing he hadn't been quite so open with a patient. It wasn't just unprofessional, it had dredged up that awkward conversation on the train back to Glasgow, when he'd asked why she was acting so weird. Sadie had told him she couldn't do 'this' any more. That 'this' was going to ruin their friendship after all, and she'd made a mistake. She valued having him in her life too much to make things complicated.

She'd done a complete one-eighty on what she'd initiated on the way there…as if one long weekend with him was all she'd needed for her 'wild woman sex fix' and that was that.

Was she turning into *him?*

If he wasn't so utterly confused he'd probably find it funny.

'She has a point though,' he admitted out loud, watching a speckled baby seal waddle out of the water and tip its head at them in interest. 'I would rather have her as a friend than not at all. She's a pretty special woman. And I'm not exactly her type, anyway.'

Portia smiled. 'You look exactly her type to me.'

Owen shook his head.

'Let me guess—she wants something serious, and you don't think you do?'

'I know I don't.' Owen inhaled the salty sea air as a flash flood struck his brain, sweeping up every argument he'd been subjected to between his parents over the years, all the family engagements they'd ruined with their petty war.

He hadn't told Sadie, but his mother had actually attended his dad's last wedding, at an idyllic winery near Bridport. She'd got drunk on rosé and taken Abigail—his father's last wife—behind a tractor, where she'd proceeded to remind her to hire a cleaner ASAP, because her new husband sure as heck wasn't going to do anything around the house. That had been just one item on her long list of things to expect or *not* to expect from a Penner man.

They'd been out there at least half an hour. Abigail had wound up in tears. His dad had had his mother escorted out of the winery.

'*They used to be so in love...you wouldn't have been able to stand that either,*' someone at the wedding had whispered to him, all while his parents were yelling obscenities at each other in the car park.

He'd stood there in the chaos thinking, *If this is what falling in love amounts to, forget about it.*

'I just can't give Sa... Dr Mills what she deserves,' he told Portia. 'She knows that. Anyway, let's talk about you, shall we? How's the journalling going?'

Portia smirked. She wanted to dig but he wasn't going to let her. Why tell one person about his inability to be in a relationship of any kind? It wasn't as if he was proud of it. But then again... his friendship with Sadie had always come first. Sadie had always been the one person he could count on, the one who wouldn't judge or mock or scorn him for anything. He'd gone to her for light relief from all the others...all the women who'd wanted more than he'd cared to offer.

Sadie had always been there for him.

Had he been a total idiot, denying himself a chance with her all this time? he mused to himself. Maybe he'd always wanted her underneath it all. Even before going to America.

But she'd only told him things because he was there—she'd pretty much said so. *'It's not like you're my boyfriend...you don't have to take on all my drama.'*

His phone rang. *Mum.* Speaking of drama...

Signalling to Portia to meet him further up the beach, he took the call, feeling Sadie's eyes on him again.

'Owen, your dad says you're not going to the wedding. I wanted to say thank you—you know your support means a lot to me. That man is unfathomably selfish sometimes...'

He bristled, stopping on the sand as she ranted about how hurt she was at not even getting an invitation—as if she could have expected one after last time! Usually he'd zone out, like he'd been doing for years... Only Sadie was still lasering him with her stare from afar, as if she knew he was letting his mother go on and on and on— like last time she'd overheard something like this conversation between them on the boat.

Fury made his blood run hotter even in the cool wind. Sadie was right. He could never totally zone out from this. This feud between his parents was the centre of his world, the reason for everything he'd put himself through over the years.

'Mum—enough,' he snapped, halting her mid-sentence. 'I love you, but this is toxic. Maybe I'll go to the wedding, maybe I won't, but that's *my* decision to make, not yours. I know you're still in love with him. Did you ever consider that's why you're really angry with him?'

Silence.

Then, to his utter shock, his mother started ranting even more. She was livid, practically possessed with her righteous rage. How dared he suggest that? How could he even think she'd still have feelings for someone so hostile and weak? Blah-blah-blah...

He sank to the sand on his haunches, tossed a pebble at the shoreline while she went on and on, and on some more. Why had he thought she'd take his opinions on board?

'That's your mother, isn't it? Give me the phone.'

Owen spun around. Sadie was behind him suddenly, towering over him, hand outstretched, hair flailing in the wind.

'Give me it,' she said again, just as his mother reiterated—loudly—how he was so selfish, just like his father.

He knew they could both hear it.

Amused, he stood and handed Sadie the phone, expecting her to hang up on his behalf. Instead, he watched in shock as she pressed it to her ear.

'Josephine? This is Sadie,' she announced, with an authority he rarely heard, but which turned him on instantly. 'Sadie. Yes, that's right. Owen's best friend. And do you know *why* he's my best friend? Because Owen is the least self-ish, most sensitive, most caring man I have ever met. And, with all due respect, he doesn't need you or anyone else to keep telling him otherwise. Now, if you'll excuse us, we have work to do.'

Now she was hanging up, as angrily as anyone could on a smartphone, prodding one finger heavily at the screen in an exaggerated swipe.

She handed it back to him, then crossed her arms. 'You're welcome,' she said as he slid it slowly into his pocket.

'You're my hero,' he said, and smirked, resisting the urge to tell her how aroused he was by her in this moment. She shot him a flicker of a smile, which somehow didn't feel exactly as if it came from her heart. 'I mean it,' he said, but she rolled her eyes.

He followed Sadie's lead, heading back to the slope they'd walked down to reach the bay, thinking how he didn't know whether to be horrified or impressed by what had just happened. He'd bet no one had ever dared confront his mother like that before...no one except him, barely three minutes before Sadie!

Their driver was waiting at the top of the slope, but Sadie stopped just ahead of him, as Amanda let out a sorrowful groan. Their exit was blocked. Since their arrival a couple of workmen in yellow jackets had taken it upon themselves to repaint some lines on the slope. A glaring orange barrier at the bottom told them it was now a no-go zone. *Great.*

Owen strode ahead, waving at the guys. 'We need to get back up!'

'Take the stairs! Just walk around to the right,' came the reply.

'I can't take the stairs.'

Amanda was gripping Sadie's arm now, and Sadie was doing her best to console her. Amanda still had a deathly fear of staircases, thanks to her accident at the airport. Already her face had turned pale, the seals behind them on the rocks forgotten.

Owen tried again. 'Please, if we can just squeeze past you, mate?'

'No can do, lad. There's wet paint everywhere—sorry.' The man went back to his pot of white paint, but not before Owen caught sight of his name badge: *Peter Forry-Stewart.*

He did a double-take. His godmother was a Forry-Stewart. He vaguely remembered she had some connection to Glasgow, though the two women hadn't spoken in years, to his knowledge…not since he was little. Why, he didn't know.

'Your mother wouldn't be Aisling Forry-Stewart, by chance, would she?' he asked.

Peter looked up in surprise. 'Yes, that's her.'

Owen had to go—poor Amanda was less than happy behind him, and he could hear Sadie soothing her as best she could—but he took a business card from the man, for Aisling Forry-Stewart's Beauty & Botanics shop here on Rothesay, and told Peter he'd pay her a visit for old times' sake. Peter looked touched, but still wouldn't let them use the slope.

At the staircase, Amanda had gone from being slightly pale to apparition-white, and not even Portia's light good-natured banter and jokes would calm her. She sank down to the stony bottom step and at Sadie's instruction took long, deep gulps of sea air.

'I can't do it… I can't do it,' she mumbled.

Amanda was about to have a panic attack, which would be a setback no one had anticipated—least of all today. Owen had already had her on the tilt table this morning, where he'd utilised electric stimulation to calm her startle reflex, but now here she was, startled and shaken by the prospect of climbing some stairs.

She kept putting her palms over her eyes. Taking her hands gently, he crouched in front of her. 'You don't have to climb the stairs if you really don't want to,' he said, catching Sadie's wary glance.

'The tide's coming in pretty fast, though,' Sadie observed. 'There's only one way I can see of solving this situation, Dr Penner.'

She was right.

Owen pulled up his sleeves, not missing the way Portia and Sadie exchanged appreciative glances at his muscular arms in the sunlight. 'Do I have your permission to carry you, Mrs Bond?' he asked.

He felt Sadie watching him the whole way up the stairs, with Amanda Bond's arms looped gratefully around his neck and a crowd of onlookers cheering.

Hero, Sadie mouthed at him, as he helped their patient into the car. He offered a mock salute over the roof, and for a moment it felt as if things were almost normal between them. Being her hero wasn't exactly why he'd done it, but if that was what she thought, he'd take it.

He was quiet on the journey back to Rothesay, thinking how it hadn't exactly been a heroic move risking his friendship with Sadie for sex. He shouldn't have gone there. He might feel as if he wanted more than her friendship sometimes, but he had to remember what was more important. Her confronting his mother like that on his behalf—that had been crazy! It meant more than he could ever express. And she'd done it not because he'd needed her to, but because she *cared* enough to do it.

There weren't many people in his life who cared that much about him—not when he flitted between lovers with barely a thought as to how it might affect them. If he ever did anything to stop Sadie caring about him he'd never forgive himself.

She'd given him a ticket out—freedom, singledom, the chance to move on unjudged, no questions asked. She'd given him what he always wanted after a few weeks of hot sex with someone new.

Yet here was the problem.

The thought of never making love to her again made his heart physically ache for her closeness, as well as a certain kind of fire start to rage in his belly... All the things he'd missed out on till now, going from one fling to the next, never investing, never allowing himself to get close enough to anyone to really *care* in case...in case he ever had to experience the kind of grief that came from losing someone he cared about, the kind of grief he'd watched consume his mother.

He'd picked up so many pieces over the years he was staggering under the weight of them all. His parents, with or without their acknowledgment of doing so, had rendered him so jaded about love that he'd openly rejected it, time after time, told himself he didn't want it for himself. He'd literally made himself believe he wasn't good enough to be anyone's boyfriend or husband. But he wasn't his father. He'd never let the love of his life turn sour and self-destruct.

He'd never wanted anyone as much as Sadie—

never even thought it was possible. Maybe he *should* ask her to his father's wedding, he mused. A date out in the real world, somewhere he could show her off proudly to his family—a chance for her *and* them to see that he'd changed. She'd know she was special to him if he asked her to the wedding. He'd never let anyone meet his family before.

CHAPTER SEVENTEEN

ON THE DOCK beside the lake Sadie sipped her coffee and swiped her tired eyes, trying to wake herself up. She'd barely slept. The banging in the walls was back, and this time it was louder than ever. Knocking on Owen's door had proved fruitless. He'd probably slept through it.

Thinking about it now, though, that was probably for the best. What good would have come from going to his room, to his bed, when she'd put a stop to that kind of thing ten whole days ago, on the train back from the McCaskills'?

Rejection was not something she handled well. There was no way she was about to admit she might be falling for him—not when he'd warned her he couldn't give her what she needed and she'd gone and ignored that warning anyway. They hadn't so much as touched each other since and she'd spent her nights alone, telling herself not to waste so much time thinking about something that was over. Finished. Done.

Her dad's name flashed up on her phone

screen, interrupting her thoughts, which were about Owen, as usual. Bringing her knees to her chest, she gathered her strength. He was probably calling to say how he and her mum didn't need her at the hospital, even after she'd offered—*again*.

Picking up the call and casting her eyes to the grey-skyed horizon across the water, she let him talk about the weather, and then asked after her mum and told him again how happy she was that they were giving things another go.

Her father seemed to stall.

'Yes, about that... Sorry I haven't called before. Your mother and I have been busy...and I know how busy you are, especially now you're in Scotland.'

Sadie's heart was pounding in her chest now, the way it always did when she sensed another excuse coming. This was why she'd been stalling on talking about Chris, avoiding calling them as much as she probably should. She couldn't stand to hear the fresh sadness in their voices over something she might've been able to prevent.

'I didn't want to bother you with coming to the hospital—you have enough of all that, what with your day job...'

'If you guys don't want me around you only have to say. It's nothing new,' she cut in, tossing a stone into the water—hard.

Ugh. She had to address this head-on—not

dance around it like she'd been doing. Again. Enough was enough, and she was way too tired to care anyway.

'I feel guilty enough, Dad, about what happened to Chris,' she said now. 'I don't need your fabrication...'

'What?'

Something in her father's voice made her swallow back her next words.

'Sadie, I was just going to suggest we all meet, the three of us, somewhere nice...when your mother's in recovery.'

'Oh.'

'We haven't really had any proper family time in a long while. We realise we've both made a few mistakes there. But I can't believe you're telling me you feel guilty about Chris. What happened was no one's fault—least of all yours!'

Sadie blinked at the lake. This wasn't at all what she'd been expecting and she cringed. Her father must think her a raving loon. She listened with an increasingly reddening face as her dad recounted with regret how consumed he'd been by his own grief for Chris, how her mother had shut him out and he her because of it—how they'd never intended her to get caught in the middle or blame herself.

The floodgates had been well and truly opened. They wanted her around...they wanted to talk about Chris together and remember all the things that had made him special. They hadn't meant her to feel this way for so long—just as Owen had said—they'd just thought *she* didn't want to talk about it.

Her dad even suggested she bring someone with her to their family reunion, if she wanted to. 'Maybe that nice man your mother says you're in Scotland with?'

Of course she told him no, that she'd come alone, because she and Owen were just friends.

By the time they hung up, all she wanted to do was go to her parents. This was a chance to make up for lost time, without the threat of self-inflicted guilt hovering above them all like a storm cloud. A thousand memories were ploughing through her mind now—all the times she'd possibly mistaken their wariness to interrupt her or bother her for a lack of caring. She'd seen everything through the perspective of her own guilt when she needn't have done anything of the sort.

Despite her total exhaustion, Sadie found a new spring in her step as she made her way to the morning's peaceful potting session. She was excited to tell Owen what had just happened. He'd roll his eyes, tell her he'd known all along she had nothing to worry about, she knew it. He'd do all the things a good friend would do.

She just needed to stop wanting to sleep with him more than she ever had before, she thought, grimacing at her shoes as she crossed the dewy lawn. Or wondering what it might be like for him to meet her parents. They'd love him. He always made things more interesting.

There was nothing like sexual abstinence to make the heart grow fonder, she thought with a sigh, tossing her coffee cup into the trash on her way into the fernery.

Parminder called Sadie over the second she stepped foot inside the heat-soaked Victorian glasshouse. 'Did you see this?' she asked excitedly, waving what looked like the local newspaper in the air above her head.

Intrigued, Sadie took the paper—then felt her eyes bulge.

Someone at the bay had witnessed their little escapade with the stairs the other day and had sent a photo in. Apparently Owen's actions had started a small quest amongst the locals to determine who the 'hero' was who'd carried the 'sick woman' up the stairs, and now Owen's bulging biceps were a prominent feature on page two.

'Oh, he's going to love this,' she said, smiling to herself at the photo.

Those arms around her had felt so right…like a barrier against the world.

Maybe it wouldn't be such a stupid idea—fessing up to her feelings. Anything that consumed her thoughts like this was worth fighting for, wasn't it?

She took a seat at the round table under the indoor palms. Was he missing her at night too and just didn't know how to say it? She had been the one to end things after all—and rather abruptly at that. What if she just owned up to the fact that she'd been too afraid to like him? *Really* like him. Maybe even love him. In case he ever changed his mind.

Either he felt the same, and they could try and make a go of things, or he didn't. In which case she'd do her very best to keep him as her closest friend. It would be hard. Probably impossible. But if she didn't at least talk to him, take a risk, she'd never know what might've been.

'Going to love what?'

Owen had walked in behind them with Vivek and Portia, ready for this, their last activity. Both were being discharged that afternoon. Sadie groaned internally at how handsome he looked today in his uniform as he pulled out a chair for Portia.

'You're famous,' Parminder said, beaming.

She took the paper from Sadie's hands and placed it on the table so they could all see it. Owen's face was unreadable, but Sadie knew he was secretly loving the acclaim.

'You're the hero of Rothesay now,' Parminder teased him as he took a seat.

The fernery was hot today. The sun was streaming through the roof and windows and

Sadie hoped she didn't look as tired as she felt as she fanned her face.

'Is that where you went last night?' Parminder asked Owen. 'Off with one of your new admirers? I saw you coming back late again... What was it? Two a.m.? I couldn't sleep, as usual.'

Sadie balked. *What?*

'I don't have any new admirers,' he answered coyly, swiping a pot from the centre of the table and handing a packet of seeds to Portia.

Something in his voice sent a red flag waving in Sadie's mind. He couldn't even look at her now. He was hiding something.

Oh, my God.

He hadn't been asleep when she'd knocked. He hadn't even been there!

A wave of nausea swept through her belly and lodged in her throat. There she'd been, just seconds ago, fantasising that maybe...just maybe... she could change him. That he might just want to try and be boyfriend material for her. *Idiot.*

Owen's eyes penetrated hers across the table the whole time they were potting plants, but she couldn't look at him. She'd told him she valued his friendship too much to risk ruining it, and that was true... But now she burned for the other parts of him.

The Owen who comforted her and protected her and gave her the best advice out of all her friends. The Owen who could make her laugh and minutes later make her tremble in awe and wonder at all his previously hidden talents. She physically ached for him, especially now she was picturing him with someone else. *Already.*

Suddenly the shock of Parminder's revelation twisted into fury. Sadie bit hard on her cheeks and tongue, then rammed a seed so hard into a plant pot her finger shot through the bottom of it. He was seeing someone else. *Already.*

Portia's brow was furrowed as she looked in her direction. 'Are you OK, Dr Mills?'

This was no good. Sadie pushed her chair back. 'I just remembered I have some paperwork to attend to. Dr Penner will finish up with you. Please excuse me.'

She couldn't be near him a moment longer. All she could see in her mind's jealous eye was him cosied up with some woman in the town— some admirer he'd turned to the second she'd put a stop to their 'benefits'.

Hurrying back to the house, she busied herself with discharge paperwork she could easily have done after the session, despite her shaky hands. This was always going to happen. He was always going to move on. She knew that. This was Owen! This was what he did.

Let him go, she told herself.

But her bottom lip and her chin insisted on wobbling, and her tears blurred the paperwork. Folding her head onto her arms on the desk, she sobbed as she hadn't sobbed since that day on the loch after she'd thought she'd heard Chris. Deep, soul-crushing, lung-busting, body-shaking sobs.

This was the moment she'd feared most—the reason she'd been off and on with this arrangement since the start. She was crying over Owen.

God, she'd been a total idiot, falling for the most notorious player she'd ever known, giving him all of herself, knowing deep down she was putting her stupid soft heart in the firing line. She'd fallen harder than she'd even thought, without ever meaning to, and he hadn't even been able to wait five minutes to hook up with someone else!

One cry, she told herself as she sniffed behind the closed study door. *One cry and then you're done. He will never know this happened. You will not waste your tears on him!*

Sadie hoped she was managing to appear unfazed when, a few hours later, Owen took her aside on the front steps.

'It's pretty sad to see them go, isn't it?' he said to her. The driver was here to take Portia and Vivek to the train station with their bags, and they were bidding them a warm farewell with promises of follow-up video calls over the next few weeks.

Just as she was about to descend the steps in her floral shirt and capris, a lipstick-wearing, radiant-looking Portia took Sadie aside. 'I want updates on *you*,' she said, pursing her lips, then glancing sideways at Owen. 'Don't think we're not all rooting for you.'

Even Vivek seemed to be holding back a smile as he looked her way from where he was shaking hands with Owen. Were they all talking about them? she wondered, deciding it was better not to think about it.

'You've helped us more than you know,' Portia said, her kind eyes twinkling. 'I hope you do something nice for yourself where that one is concerned.'

'Owen and I are most definitely just colleagues,' Sadie reminded her, and not for the first time. Although now the words bore a certain heaviness after all the what-ifs and maybes of the past few weeks.

They said their final goodbyes, which was indeed quite emotional for Sadie after all this time of getting to know her patients. She was going to miss Portia's little insights, as invasive as they sometimes were.

Sadie was all set to get back to work on Amanda's new schedule when Owen cornered her in the hallway.

'Sadie?'

His hand on her wrist made all the blood rush to her head and she froze, instantly picturing his hands on someone else.

Quickly, she pulled her hand back. 'I'm pretty busy, Owen…'

'I just wanted to tell you I've decided to go to Dad's wedding,' he said, dashing a hand through his hair.

'Good for you,' she responded, a little more coldly than she'd planned.

He didn't seem to notice.

'I was thinking maybe…' Owen trailed off, shaking his head.

He folded his arms across his chest and stepped aside for Fergal, who was pulling the luggage trolley back towards them from the doorway. Was it her imagination, or did Owen look sheepish? She straightened her back. Of course he probably felt bad for sleeping with someone else so soon, but that was his prerogative, she supposed. He could do what he liked.

'What's wrong?' he asked her now, and she realised she was scowling deeply at the space between his eyes, digging her nails into her palms, imagining him in his tux at the wedding, looking dreamy as hell…checking all the women out, no doubt.

'Nothing's wrong. I told you—I'm busy,' she said, feigning a smile she knew probably hadn't made it to her eyes. 'What were you thinking?'

He looked at her long and hard, as if something heavy was percolating in his brain. She braced herself to hear who he was taking to the wedding—because it sure as heck wasn't going to be her now he'd moved on.

'Forget about it,' he said eventually.

Great. As if she would.

If only her heart wasn't going a million miles an hour. Maybe he wasn't taking anyone at all. Why should she care? Especially now, when there was nothing between them but some vague and twisted form of friendship—what was left of it, that was. It had only ever been going to end this way, with her a mess and him absolutely fine.

'You're angry at me for something,' he accused her now. 'Out with it.'

'Don't be ridiculous,' she shot back.

He huffed a laugh. 'So we're right back here, are we?'

She pulled her eyes away from his challenging stare. That time he'd accused of her being jealous—of Parminder of all people—she'd laughed him off. He knew when she was jealous! He probably knew she was now. But if she voiced her concerns about whoever he was meeting at night, he'd ask her what right she had to question him when *she'd* called things off. Besides, he hadn't made any promises to her. He wasn't exactly in the habit of making promises to anyone—that was why she'd called it off!

Unless... He does look pretty angry. Did you just jump the gun? This is all such a mess!

Owen was still simmering at her. The hallway closed in even further. Even the fountain outside seemed to fall silent.

'You don't want to talk to me?' he asked.

Before she could get her head straight and form a sentence, he threw his hands in the air.

'You know what? If you still don't want to talk to me about anything real, Sadie, maybe we should think about ending *everything* between us—including this so-called friendship.'

His words left her cold. She was still grappling for speech when he brushed straight past her and stormed up the stairs.

CHAPTER EIGHTEEN

SADIE SQUINTED AT the map app on her phone and took a left, as instructed. For all the time she'd been at Rothesay Recovery, she hadn't exactly spent much time in the town itself, but she needed to post a card to her mother, and it only felt right to do it herself on this Saturday morning instead of handing it to someone at Rothesay.

She'd also seen Owen leave a few minutes before her...

The birds in the trees seemed to be judging her as she took the path towards the row of shops, along the harbour. 'Stop it, birds. It's not like I'm following him,' she said, and tutted at them.

Well, she wasn't. Not really. That would be silly.

OK, fine, she was kind of following him. To see where he'd gone... To see if she was right and he *was* with some new lady friend. Only she'd stopped to check the map and the next thing she knew he'd disappeared. And now she was just feeling silly—and guilty.

The hungry seagulls swirled overhead, squawking into her thoughts and only momentarily blocking the vision of Owen's face...how angry he'd looked yesterday. He'd accused her of not wanting to talk about anything real! But it was *too* real, knowing he'd moved on so fast. How was she supposed to talk about that?

No one had ever made her feel so heartsick, so angry, so entirely impassioned and...scared. She wanted him...wanted nothing more than to tell him how she felt, which was jealous as hell. But what if...?

What if...?

What if he *did* feel the same, and they got together, and then he changed his mind?

That was the real reason she'd said nothing when he'd challenged her. The real reason she'd tried so hard not to fall for him in the first place.

She sighed long and hard, staring at the mountains ahead. As usual, she'd cut off her own nose to spite her face and that was why she'd followed him. To find him and tell him once and for all how she felt. Madly, jealously, in love with him?

This was what Portia had been talking about, she thought, stopping to rest her arms against the high brick wall around the harbour. Three white boats bobbed in the gentle breeze, while behind them the tops of the rolling hills were swallowed by clouds. It seemed fitting for her clouded brain.

She'd found someone who fulfilled every part of her. None of the other men in her life had come close to making her feel like Owen did, which was exactly why she'd felt safe with them. None of them had ever had the capacity to break her the way losing Chris had broken her.

The way losing Owen would break her.

She snapped a photo of a speckled brown bird that had flown onto the wall beside her. A cute young couple had stopped a few feet away and were kissing over their coffee cups.

Callum was back in her head now...their last goodbye and how it had ended. There hadn't even been a row. She'd been stunned by his announcement, and reduced to tears by the sudden rejection—not a thing she'd ever handled well—but she hadn't been broken.

It hadn't been a powerful love with him, she supposed. Not the kind of love he deserved or *she* deserved. Definitely not the kind she'd tasted with Owen. This was something real... And maybe it was time to trust herself to deal with it and not be so scared by the thought of something else ending that she hadn't even let it begin!

The bird flew away and came to a new perching position on one of the boats. Frowning at the water, and hugging her jacket around herself more tightly, she wondered why on earth she'd let it go this far—pushing away the only person in the whole world she could stand to be around twenty-four-seven. Maybe even pushing him unwittingly towards someone else.

She pressed on, away from the harbour towards the post office, nodding to a passing dog-walker with a German Shepherd. There was still no sign of Owen, but as she rounded the corner something caught her eye. A small shop with a green-and-white-striped frontage: Beauty & Botanics. Something about the name was familiar, but what?

Oh, yes. Owen had a business card from there. She'd seen it sticking out of his back pocket, that day he'd carried Amanda up the stairs. She hadn't thought anything of it at the time, but... Oh, God. Was he with someone else right now?

Someone who worked in this shop?

Owen hadn't exactly meant to burden this woman with the details of his current situation when he'd taken it upon himself to pay her a visit, but he was grateful for someone unbiased to listen. It felt like a long time since he'd spoken to anyone outside of Rothesay Recovery, or anyone who didn't know Sadie, for that matter.

He stood up from one of the two plush green velvet seats by the shop window to accept the cup of mint tea Aisling handed him. This was his second visit. The first, of course, had been the other night, when he'd somehow got so caught in the catch-up and conversation with his god-mother that he'd lost all track of time.

'So, tell me, where did we leave off?' she said now, swiping her long grey-blonde hair over one shoulder and lighting a candle.

The smell of lemongrass mingled with the posh soaps and other products dotted amongst the plants. It was as Zen as the fernery in here—like a five-star version

Aisling was a wisp of a woman, the same slender build as his mother. The two had gone to school together and drifted apart after his mum's divorce.

'Did you ask your friend Sadie to your dad's wedding?' she asked.

Owen glowered for a moment into his teacup and forgot his Zen. 'I started to…' He paused, remembering the look on her face, filled with all the accusations she'd been storing up unspoken, her eyes burning into him like red-hot pokers. 'I think she thinks I've moved on from her, but she's too stubborn to ask because *she* ended things and she doesn't want to look jealous. I know her, Aisling. I know her better than she knows herself.'

Aisling nodded slowly, thoughtfully. 'If you know she's jealous, and it's eating you both up, the question is, Owen Penner, what are you going to do about it?'

Owen sat back down, stirred his teabag around by the string. It wasn't as if he hadn't been thinking about that ever since. All of it—everything they'd done over the last few weeks. The times when he'd dissolved into her, let her claim him fully. He'd never done that with anyone—never even dared to let someone that close.

Now he knew he was capable of it, he wanted to do it again and again. But she didn't trust him. Of course she didn't trust him. He hadn't fought for her when he'd had the chance. He'd backed off, as she'd asked. He shouldn't have done that—shouldn't for one second have let her think he was putting her in the same 'been there, done that' category as the other women she'd seen him get bored with.

He'd been trying to be respectful, to keep their friendship alive. But what a joke. He didn't want her at his dad's wedding as his friend—he wanted to show her off and kiss her and dance with her, knowing she wouldn't run from the dance floor this time…knowing she'd stay in his arms where she belonged.

'I want to be with Sadie,' he heard himself say now. 'She doesn't trust me not to hurt her, and I didn't trust myself not to either—not for a long time. But I know I'd never do that…not any more.' He put his cup down on the little dresser by the door. 'I couldn't. I love her, Aisling. I really do. And you have no idea how weird it is to hear myself say that out loud.'

He wrung his hands together on his knees. It felt as if a lead iron weight had been lifted from his shoulders, just knowing he could actually say something like that and mean it.

'She doesn't think I can give her what she needs, and I don't blame her after all this time, but it's different with her.'

Aisling was smiling. 'If she's the one, everything will feel different. You know, your mother tore herself apart over your father. I saw the way that love destroyed her. That was a different kind of love, Owen. It put me off the whole notion of being with someone for a long time…maybe that's why your mother and I drifted apart.'

She cocked an eyebrow, studying him intently as she stroked a finger over a row of fancy-looking lotion bottles. Owen was floored. His own mother had lost her friend because of her issues with his dad? It was just like Sadie said: he'd been preparing himself for the worst in relationships his whole life—never getting into one, telling himself he didn't want one! Choosing to believe love was a waste of time…

But deep down he'd probably always just been waiting for Sadie.

Owen almost laughed as the shock set in. There would never be a time he wouldn't want to laugh with Sadie, make love to her, fight with her! He could live in that cycle his whole life and never get bored.

'I was about to tell her once…how much I liked her,' he said now. 'I almost kissed her. We were twenty-two—can you believe that? She ran off the dance floor before I had the chance. I told myself I was glad, because I would've ruined a good friendship—you don't get drunk and kiss your friends! I hooked up with someone else to get her off my mind, and the next thing I knew I was stuck in the friend zone permanently.'

'You wanted to kiss me that night in the club?'

Sadie's voice behind him sent his stomach plunging to the floor. She'd appeared in the doorway like a ghost, in jeans and a cashmere sweater. Owen got to his feet, stunned. How long had she been there?

He cleared his throat, dashed a hand to his hair. How much had she heard?

'I did,' he admitted. 'Actually, since the moment I flicked ink at you…on purpose.'

'Owen!'

She put her hands over her face, but he took them in his in a second, and Aisling crept into the back of the shop, to give them privacy.

'I can't believe this,' Sadie whispered, swiping at her eyes.

He pulled her closer, scooping her face towards his, close enough to taste her lips again. But she was talking.

'I came to try and find you...to tell you I'm an idiot, that I miss my best friend and I don't want to lose him. But I miss the man who loves me the way you do *more*. I want both, Owen.'

Owen's heart was a riot as he scanned her eyes. 'I want to be both of those things for you,' he said, without looking away.

He knew now, with no trace of uncertainty that he'd do anything for her and go anywhere with her.

'Maybe I was too scared to admit I liked you back then,' Sadie said now, turning his hands in hers. 'Maybe I got stupidly drunk that night, trying to feel brave enough to kiss you first. But I was so drunk that I ran away and threw up. And then...'

She paused, biting on her lip, and he might have laughed, if it hadn't been for the giant lump blocking his throat.

'Owen, we would never be here now if we hadn't been best friends first.'

'Trust me... I know,' he managed, bringing her hand up to kiss her fingers.

Outside, someone reconsidered entering the

shop and he swept her away from the doorway, under a line of hanging baskets. He heard Aisling shuffling boxes somewhere in the back room.

'Who *is* that?' Sadie asked now.

'My godmother.'

Sadie's eyes widened, and then she frowned as if she was putting the pieces of a puzzle together.

'I love you,' he whispered, circling her waist, taking her by the hips. She always had fitted against him just perfectly. 'I'm in love with you, Sadie Mills, and it's all your fault for making me miss you so very badly while I was away in America.'

Her eyes clouded over, misty with tears. He attempted to dry them, but it didn't work.

'I thought love was a waste of time...' she said after a moment.

Her voice was broken, but she was looking at him as she'd never looked at him before, and it made his heart expand to the size of a football.

'Not our kind of love,' he said.

He was surprised at the words now falling so effortlessly from his mouth. She was right. If they hadn't been such good friends first, things never would have reached this point of trust... of no going back.

'We will never end. I won't let us. Never. I'm tying you up in chains...'

'To your bed, I hope?' she teased.

'If that's what you'd prefer.'

Owen lowered his lips to hers for a second time, open-mouthed. Her tongue was hungry, but soft, like velvet treacle sliding seductively across his, and he responded to her sensuous kisses again and again. Her hands were in his hair now, her fingers caressing the back of his neck, and as he kept on kissing her and kissing her he felt the fire in his veins, the spark of the start of something he knew he would never let die out. He would burn for her until the day he died.

Four months later

Sadie caught Owen's eyes across the garden and he winked at her. He looked amusingly animated, talking with a cousin, and almost as handsome in his tux as he had been in that kilt. But unfortunately there were no hay-strewn barns at the unique waterfront location his dad's new wife had chosen for the wedding.

Nevertheless, the yacht club in Cornwall was a stunning yellow-brick venue, to the right of a half-moon sandy bay. She could not wait to get back to their historic hotel, to lie under the cool sheets with Owen. But that would come later... as would she, many times, if this morning's session was anything to go by.

'Are you glad you let me ask you to come here,

finally?' he teased, when he found her moments later, looping his arms around her from behind.

'Oh, absolutely.'

She leaned back against his chest and closed her eyes, smiling at how his being like this with her, doing 'boyfriend' things, made her feel. She felt like a goddess around him, and he wouldn't stop telling her how good she looked in her dress. And out of it.

'I was just wondering if your mother was going to show up,' she said.

Owen smiled into the top of her head. He'd told her about his father's last wedding, how his mother had been escorted out of the venue, but things were different now. For a start, she wasn't at this one.

'Even if she was here, I have a feeling she'd be OK,' he told her. 'She's been making a concerted effort to be happy for him lately. And me, too.'

He dropped a kiss to her head and she turned in his arms. Sadie knew her words to his mother had hit home. Apparently, she'd been quite impressed with her, and had been asking after them as a couple ever since. While Sadie hadn't actually met her yet, it was only because she'd taken herself on a therapeutic trip to Borneo, to relax around orangutans—something she'd always wanted to do.

'She finally admitted she'd never fallen out

of love him—can you believe that?' Owen said. 'They actually spoke like civilised beings. My dad apologised…he even asked her here. She said the orangutans were more civilised than the Penner men, but at least she smiled when she said it.'

'Well, if you need me to talk to anyone here, I have a few *nice* things I can say about the Penner men,' she told Owen now, pulling him closer by the lapels of his jacket and pressing her lips to his.

He smiled under her kiss, which sent a wave of tingles through her belly to her lacy underwear. She would never get enough of this feeling. Her best friend and her boyfriend, all in one unbelievable package.

Of course people here were talking. They'd never seen Owen with a girlfriend before. He'd warned her in advance what people might say. But it wasn't as if that fazed her—not any more. They both knew what they'd built together was unshakable.

It had been strange at first, leaving Scotland and heading back to their normal lives. Only, now 'normal' was so much better. Owen had pretty much moved into her place. They were taking some time out from work to plan their next adventure—potentially spending some time in Thailand, as Owen had planned before—and then a couple's work placement in a medical team on a cruise ship in the Caribbean. Everything was exciting. Anything felt possible.

'I want your best friend benefits to myself... should we get out of here?' he whispered now, as the band started up next to the dance floor.

She frowned up at him. 'You're not even going to ask me to dance?'

'That depends. Will you stay on the dance floor or will you run away?'

'Very funny.'

Surrounded by wedding guests and in front of his rather shocked-looking father, Sadie kissed him in the confetti swirls and made a point to explain—again—how she was sober this time, and was not about to dash away and be sick.

He laughed, of course, sweeping her up in his arms and spinning her around until she told him that, OK, she might be sick after all.

Ugh! To think he'd felt the same back then! And neither of them had followed up on it!

Not that she would have been ready... It had taken all these years for her to be ready for Owen, she thought, letting the music carry her mind elsewhere. It had taken all this time for him to be ready for her, too.

Her parents loved him, of course. They'd all gone away for a weekend, to the Lake District, where they'd laughed and cried and talked openly about Chris. It had felt so freeing, after all this time, not to carry guilt or shame, just to remember her brother as the amazing guy she'd grown up with.

She had to admit it had been nice to see her mother laughing and snuggling against her father again, too. Even nicer that she'd been able to do the same with Owen, knowing she could laugh or cry and he'd be there, like he always was.

She'd never said *I love you* so many times, and she still felt the buzz and the butterflies. Just waking up in his arms was enough to make her start every day with the kind of joy she'd thought belonged only to children's television presenters. It was, as Parminder had joked when she'd video called them last week, *'Quite disgusting to witness.'*

Parminder had thought they might both like to know that they'd finally located the source of the banging in the walls at Rothesay. It was not a horrible haunting, as some people had loved to imagine, but rather a family of squirrels!

Secretly Sadie was glad she hadn't known that before—not because she enjoyed the thought of ghosts, but because seeing Owen with Parminder that night had woken something up in her...some dormant attraction to her best friend and the jealousy that had forced her to address what she really wanted in a partner.

'*Now* can we get out of here?'

Owen's whisper in her ear sent a shiver through her shoulder blades and she realised she'd zoned out on the dance floor, her head on his shoulder, moving to a slow song. A lazy smile crept over her face. This was her best friend, through and through—impatient, keen to move on to the next good thing. Only this time, and every single time going forward, she was going *with* him.

* * * * *

MEDICAL

Pulse-racing passion

Available Next Month

All titles available in Larger Print

Tempted By The Rebel Surgeon JC Harroway
Breaking The Single Mum's Rules JC Harroway

....

Finding Their Forever Family Caroline Anderson
Redeeming Her Hot-Shot Vet Juliette Hyland

....

Brought Together By A Pup Sue MacKay
Winning The Neonatal Doc's Heart Amy Ruttan

Keep reading for an excerpt of a new title
from the Western Romance series,
THE LAWMAN'S SURPRISE by Catherine Mann

CHAPTER ONE

CHARLOTTE PACE WASN'T a morning person.

And pregnancy had made her double down on those feelings.

If only she could just lie under the covers and nurse the saltine crackers for another half hour until it was time for work. But the insistent knocking on her cabin door couldn't be ignored.

She swung her feet to the floor and gripped the edge of the mattress, willing her crackers and flat ginger ale to stay down. Fingers curled into the plush mattress topper and the flower-patterned quilt. Her doctor assured her the nausea would likely ease in her second trimester, but right now she didn't feel on the upswing to better. A deep breath later, Charlotte stood, thankful she didn't have to search for a robe since she'd fallen asleep in an overlong T-shirt and a pair of running shorts—drawstring loosened to accommodate her three-month baby belly.

Another round of knocking echoed through the two-bedroom cabin.

Too bad her teenage brother who lived with her couldn't be bothered to roll out of bed up in his loft room. His surly attitude grew worse by the day since he'd started living with her. She'd known becoming his guardian four months ago when their mother entered a psychiatric facility would be difficult. Her brother—Rory—had always been a handful. But she'd had no idea how out of control he'd become.

She wanted to sit down with him, talk things out... But at the moment, that went on the list of things she just didn't have the time or energy for.

Fishing under the iron bed, she found her favorite gardening Crocs, the once-bright daisy pattern dulled long ago. Still, she associated them so strongly with gardens that she smiled just at the sight of them. Her soul sang when she had her hands buried in the earth. She'd majored in horticulture in college. Now, she was head landscaper at the Top Dog Dude Ranch, the Smoky Mountain Tennessee soil giving her the perfect canvas to create.

She'd left her previous—better-paying—job for the position at the Top Dog Dude Ranch to help her mom. The job came with a flexible schedule, a cabin and access to the ranch's meal plan—a bonus since even last year her mom was already struggling. That flexibility sure would be stretched to the max after the baby arrived.

Worry dumped acid on her already churning stomach.

Crocs in hand, Charlotte stood while her fluffy pup uncurled all twelve pounds of herself from the floral quilt. Covered in long white-and-black fur, Primrose was some kind of Maltese mix with expressive brown eyes.

"Rosie girl, do you think you could run over to Rory's room and scratch on his door until he wakes up?" Charlotte stuffed her feet in her shoes. "We shouldn't be the only ones up so early."

The dog tipped her head to the side, showcasing a thatch of fur tied with a pink ribbon. Primrose jumped from the mattress, to the bench at the foot of the bed, then to the floor, tail wagging in a fan of fur as she waited by Charlotte's feet.

Kneeling, she straightened Primrose's bow. "I know, girl, I love you, too." Standing, she left her bedroom and wove around the sofa, calling out, "Hold on. I'm coming."

And Primrose kept on trotting alongside her. Not surprising. She was the epitome of a Velcro dog. Thank goodness she could come to work with Charlotte or the pup would grow so anxious she would chew holes in couch cushions and pull the stuffing out.

Tiny dog nails clicked along the planked floor. Charlotte hadn't been able to resist painting the nails pink.

Like a little girl.

A lump lodged in her throat as she wondered about her own baby. Taking in a dog two months ago probably hadn't been the wisest move, given she'd just found out about the pregnancy. But when she'd gone to visit her mom, she'd discovered that her mother had a new roommate at the psychiatric center who had been despondent over losing her pet. Worse yet, her kids had dropped off the senior dog at the shelter.

Even knowing her life was already too busy, Charlotte had made a detour on her way home. Just to look at the pup. Simply to reassure the women that her dog was fine. Hoping the pet had already been scooped up by some wonderful family. Only to learn that at nine years old, little Primrose didn't stand much of a chance of finding a new forever home.

The second she'd seen Primrose sitting all soggy in her water bowl, Charlotte had been hooked. Even the name *Primrose* seemed like kismet for a horticulturist like her. Sure, she didn't need a dog. She was overwhelmed with her job, the pregnancy, caring for her brother and her mom.

But she wanted Primrose. Her heart was still broken from her failed relationship with her baby's father. Seeing Primrose made her smile for the first time since Sheriff Declan Winslow had walked out of her life a month prior, their breakup irreparable. She'd hoped having him called up for National Guard duty would give her heart the time and distance to heal.

She'd been wrong.

"Primrose, stay," she told the dog, unlocking the dead bolt and swinging the door wide.

Only to have her breath catch in her throat.

Her brother hadn't answered the door because he hadn't been in his bedroom. Rory was standing on the porch, shuffling his feet behind Moonlight Ridge's very own Sheriff Declan Winslow. Her baby daddy. Back in town, not that he'd bothered to tell her. Looking too tall, lean and handsome in his tan uniform, with his wide-brimmed hat held against his broad chest. His hair was trimmed even shorter, no doubt from his Guard time.

Her mind echoed with strains of their final fight. While she knew he was an honorable man, she'd gotten frustrated with the way he always held back a part of himself. Then he'd told her he wasn't the white-picket-fence, family-man type.

Words that still squeezed her heart.

And with her waistline expanding, she was fast running out of time to tell him that family man or not, he was going to become a father.

DECLAN WINSLOW HAD struggled to find a way to let Charlotte know he'd returned from National Guard duty. In all the half-baked plans he'd made, he sure hadn't expected it to look like this. Standing on her porch bringing her delinquent brother home.

A phone call would have been better, yet he'd procrastinated. Now, here he stood, struggling to maintain objectivity in the face of her rumpled appeal. Her blond hair was tousled, a long T-shirt grazing her curves.

Deep blue eyes studying him with wary suspicion.

He deserved that. He wasn't proud of the way he'd broken off their relationship, but he didn't regret it. He wasn't the man for her. Not by a long shot.

A little furball of a dog shot through the door. A stray? People dumped their animals at the ranch far too often. The Maltese mix ran circles around Charlotte's ankles, leaping back and forth over her Crocs, drawing Charlotte's attention away. Snapping the thread of tension. Declan drew in his first full breath since he'd laid eyes on her.

The scent of mountain air, of a spring morning, filled his lungs. Small-town Moonlight Ridge, Tennessee, was his home and he loved it. Although being sheriff now that the Top Dog Dude Ranch was expanding brought a host of complications to his job with so many tourists. At least the ranch honored the landscape and the values of the area.

Charlotte knelt to scoop up the dog, cuddling it close to her chest before meeting his gaze again. "What's wrong?" She angled toward her brother. "Rory? Is everyone okay?"

Declan gestured to the ranch guests beginning to trickle from their cabins to greet the day. "Do you mind if we step inside? We're, uh, garnering quite a bit of attention out here."

"Of course," she said nervously. "Thanks for noticing. The last thing I want is gossip in my workplace."

Nodding, he gestured to her brother, who carried his teenage attitude like an imaginary overstuffed book bag slouching his posture and slowing his steps. "After you, kiddo."

Rory shot him a scowl before his gaze slid away and he shouldered past. "I'm not a kid."

The teen was no doubt using defiance to cover up the fact that he was nervous. And he should be. Declan wanted to clap him on the back and reassure him, but he also knew it was time for this teen to meet tough love. He'd gone too far this time, way beyond just sneaking out in the middle of the night.

Declan followed the boy over the threshold and inside. The cabin looked much like others at the ranch, with log walls and a rustic decor. But the space carried the imprint of Charlotte as well, in the arrangements of dried flowers filling the air with hints of lavender and evergreen.

His eyes drifted to the white sofa with her pink floral throw blanket, a phantom image of the two of them sharing stories late into the night drifting into his mind.

A defeated sigh brought him back to the present.

Charlotte cradled the dog closer, fidgeting with the bow on the canine's head. "So clearly Rory snuck out again."

Again? "It was more than just slipping out." He steeled himself for what he would have to say next, hating that it would hurt her. "Rory was caught breaking into the Top Dog gift shop."

Her knees folded and Charlotte dropped to the sofa, floral throw pillows spilling away. "Rory, what were you thinking?"

The teen shrugged, staring at his untied high tops, laces covered in mud and speckles of paint. His lanky body radiated surliness. But Declan knew from experience that was likely a blanket to cover a more vulnerable emotion.

Charlotte's hands shook as she stroked the dog repeatedly, as if for comfort. "Oh, Rory. You've pulled pranks before. But breaking and entering? Potentially theft? This takes things to a whole other level. One that can ruin your future."

"It's no big deal," her brother said belligerently. "Everybody does stuff like that. It's just kid stuff."

Charlotte's mouth dropped open and she blinked fast, her eyes stunned, before she set her jaw in a firm line. "I thought you weren't a kid."

Growling, Rory pivoted away and stomped up the steps to his loft bedroom, slamming the door.

"Rory," she called out, standing. "Come back down here."

But the door stayed closed. The music started. Loudly. Dried flowers vibrated ever so slightly.

Sighing, Charlotte swayed, then reached behind to brace herself as she sat again. Worry creased her already weary face.

Declan understood her worry—and he shared it. Rory was a kid in crisis, teetering on the edge of no return. He needed an intervention.

Sooner rather than later.

Declan hooked his hat on an antler coat tree on the wall. "I would let him cool off for now. It'll give us a chance to talk."

"Um, thank you. For bringing him home." She stayed seated, holding the pup close like a comforting pillow against her stomach. "And I'm sorry you had to deal with him."

Declan sat in a fat leather chair across from her. Sitting beside her would be too risky. Too tempting to reach out and comfort her. He needed to embrace professional distance. "Rory didn't take anything." This time. "He and his friends—Truitt and Kai—were painting graffiti on a wall. The alarm went off in the shop, which alerted the police department. I was at the station, so I took the call. Rory and I both tried to call you, but it went straight to voice mail."

Declan hadn't dated Charlotte long, only a few months, but long enough to be a part of Rory's life. To get to know him, to see firsthand how he was struggling with the move, sneaking out at night and hanging with the wrong crowd. And Declan hated the feeling of failure right now, telling him that he should have seen this coming. Should have been able to prevent it. That he'd let the teen down by not staying in touch after the breakup.

She chewed her bottom lip. "I was worn out and had the ringer off. Lucky thing you were back in town," she said, with a tinge of accusation in her voice. "I realize this could have been worse."

Maybe he should have called to tell her that he was back, but it wasn't like they were a couple anymore. They hadn't spoken since he left town.

Until this morning, he hadn't thought about how that would have affected Rory too, feeling let down by another adult that waltzed out. "I know he's a good kid at heart, but I can't help him much longer if he doesn't find his way to a serious course correction soon."

"Understood." She pressed a hand to her forehead, her face turning even paler. "I'm not making excuses. I get that I need to do better."

"*Rory* needs to do better." He leaned forward, elbows on his knees. He hated that she was taking the burden of this all on herself. "You've done nothing wrong."

An awkward silence settled between them, here in this room where they'd spent evenings with her cuddled against him on the sofa, a fire in the fireplace, a bowl of popcorn—extra butter and a sprinkle of cayenne pepper—in her lap while they watched a movie.

She fidgeted with the dog's paw, her thumb stroking the pink polished nail. "I didn't know you'd gotten back."

"I returned about a week ago."

Surprise flickered across her face. And something else. Disappointment? Once again, he kicked himself for not figuring out a way to let her know he'd returned. Not that he expected to pick up where they'd left off. She'd asked for a break, a breather, and instead, he'd ended things completely.

He cleared his throat and pointed to the furry scrap. "New stray at the ranch?"

"No, I adopted her from the shelter. Her name's Primrose." Charlotte smoothed her fingers over the graying fur on the dog's muzzle. "She's nine. I was worried no one would take her."

Signature Charlotte move. A big heart for the strays in life, like him.

He was treading into dangerous territory here. Back to business. Declan sat straighter in his seat. "So, returning to the problem at hand with Rory."

"What happens now? Is there going to be a court date?" Her voice went higher, her fidgety hands landing on a pack of crackers on the end table, gripping, twitching. "Do I need to get a lawyer?"

"No lawyer needed. Rory got off lucky." He didn't know many people who would be as forgiving as the Top Dog owners had been. That small-town community spirit— looking out for a neighbor, giving people second chances— was a large part of what drew Declan to leave the big city and take the job here, even if it paid less. Some things in life went beyond any price tag. "Hollie and Jacob said they don't want to press charges. They asked me to reassure you they don't blame you and this will have no bearing on your job."

"Seriously?" Her blue eyes went wide, long lashes sweeping upward. "That simple?"

"Yes. And no." He waggled his hand. "Jacob wants Rory to do volunteer hours to show he's sorry."

"That's all? No time behind bars? No court-appointed community service?"

"More of an informal community service. Each kid has been assigned a different task—we figured less time together might be warranted. Truitt will be picking up trash and Kai will be painting over the damage in the shop. Rory will muck out stalls in the stables."

Her mouth twitched. "He would probably rather go to juvie."

A chill settled inside him. "Not if he ever toured the place. Trust me, this is a cake walk comparatively."

She reached out. "I didn't mean—"

"It's okay. I understand what you meant. You've been woken up fast to a difficult situation with no morning cup of coffee." He knew how she woke up slowly, needing two cups of java on her front porch to greet the day. There was still so much he remembered about her—and now that they were face-to-face, he realized he was doing a lousy job of making himself forget. Telling himself that he was getting over her had been a lot easier with distance between them.

"It was an...unexpected way to greet the day. I wouldn't have minded an extra half hour, that's for sure."

It struck him again how tired she looked, pale, holding on to her dog for dear life. Concern tugged at him. He wanted to ask how her mother was doing. If Charlotte was taking time for herself.

But that wasn't his business anymore. He pushed to his feet. "I haven't told Rory about the arrangement. I figured he needed to sweat for a while. I'll be in touch later today to make sure everything's all set with the O'Briens."

"Thank you again. I don't even want to think of how bad this could have been if you hadn't been the one to catch the call and smooth things over." She stood, swaying for a moment, before continuing, "I don't know what I would have done if I lost my job."

Unable to resist, he cupped her shoulder. A simple touch. Plenty of space between them. Her eyes held his, her gaze filled with so much worry it was all he could do not to haul her to his chest and reassure her again that all was well with the owners of the ranch. They were good, fair people.

Like Charlotte.

She deserved better than he had to offer. Better than him.

Backing a step away from her before he said or did something they would both regret, he swept his hat off the coatrack. "Try to get some sleep. You're looking pretty…" Pretty. Just pretty. "Looking pretty exhausted."

LET'S TALK ABOUT BOOKS!

JOIN THE CONVERSATION

MILLSANDBOON
AUSTRALIA

@MILLSANDBOONAUS

ESCAPE THE EVERY DAY AT
MILLSANDBOON.COM.AU